the
destruction
of the
books

TOR BOOKS BY MEL ODOM

The Rover
The Destruction of the Books
Hunters of the Dark Sea

the destruction of the books

mel odom

TOR®

A TOM DOHERTY ASSOCIATES BOOK
NEW YORK

THE DESTRUCTION OF THE BOOKS

Copyright © 2004 by Mel Odom

This book is printed on acid-free paper.

A Tor Book
Published by Tom Doherty Associates, LLC
175 Fifth Avenue
New York, NY 10010

www.tor.com

Tor® is a registered trademark of Tom Doherty Associates, LLC.

Library of Congress Cataloging-in-Publication Data

Odom, Mel.
    The destruction of the books / Mel Odom.—1st US ed.
        p. cm.
    "A Tom Doherty Associates Book."
    ISBN 0-765-30723-5 (alk.paper)
    EAN 978-0765-30723-1
  1. Libraries—Fiction. 2. Librarians—Fiction. 3. Apprentices—Fiction.
4. Books and reading—Fiction. I. Title.
    PS3565.D53D47 2004
    813'.54—dc22   2003027368

First Edition: July 2004

Printed in the United States of America

0   9   8   7   6   5   4   3   2   1

For my son, Chandler

Look, Littlefoot! Daddy built a world for your
imagination to play in!

Acknowledgments

As always, I couldn't have come this far without Brian Thomsen, my editor, who steered a straight course for me even when things were at their most confusing.

And I couldn't have explored the world of *The Rover* further without the generous patronage of Tom Doherty, a gracious man and a publishing legend.

Also, Ethan Ellenberg, my agent, who has always stood beside me in the fiercest conditions.

The Dread Rider

The horse's hooves thudded against the ground as the rider urged his mount along the trail. Forest spread out around him. Gray clouds steamed from the horse's nostrils and disappeared into the darkness of night.

From the last hill, he had seen the light of the old inn tucked away into the mountains where he had ridden to bring the prize that he carried. Delivering the package gave him no real satisfaction. As soon as he finished this task, another would be given.

He only hoped that the next task wasn't as bloodless as this one. He had learned to kill a long time ago, and his knowledge of enjoyment over such a thing had taken place in the instant after he'd claimed his first life.

The horse faltered beneath him. The hooves skittered out of beat against the hard-packed earth and bare stone showing where constant travel had worn everything else away.

The animal was dying.

The rider knew that and didn't care. He had killed three of his last five mounts, ridden them till they had died, then had walked the necessary miles to his next stop, where he was given a fresh horse.

In the beginning, he hadn't been alone. Twelve others had ridden with him.

Thirteen. The number was auspicious for a number of reasons, but the auguries of his kind had demanded that thirteen ride at the wizard's call. They never veered from their auguries, just as they never veered from a task once they had accepted it.

Now there were three of them left. Ten others had died in combat along the way, combating harsh terrain, fearsome creatures, and bandits and men who tried to kill them for the gold they carried, as well as the package they had been given to deliver.

Only one rider yet remained behind him. The other had fallen to a pack of bloodwolves miles back. The predators had taken the horse out from under the third rider, and they had left him there to sort out his own fate with the creatures.

There had been no thought of going back for their comrade. They only battled together while they were riding, while they were heading in the same direction to accomplish the task they had undertaken.

Maybe the other rider would arrive at the inn in the morning. Maybe he wouldn't. It didn't matter. All that truly mattered was the journey, as fast as they could go.

 Long minutes later, the horse coming loose beneath him, the rider arrived at the inn. The horse almost made it to the stable before its heart gave out.

Acquainted with the feeling, knowing that the horse was nothing more than falling dead meat, the rider pulled his right leg free of the stirrup, threw it over the horse, and leapt from the saddle. He landed on his two feet as the horse collapsed into a death sprawl ahead of him and to one side.

The other rider thundered to a halt just behind him and leapt from his mount as well.

Standing straight and tall, ignoring the amazed looks of the two men and the dwarf sitting outside the inn on the covered porch smoking and drinking tankards of ale, the rider adjusted the twin swords at his hips and started walking.

He was taller than most humans. Dressed as he was in the hooded cloak and all in black, he knew he was a frightful thing to behold and he took pride in that. Besides being a skilled rider, he was a deadly warrior. All who had heard of him, and most had, knew those things about him.

The humans and the dwarf on the covered porch gave him no acknowledgment and quickly broke eye contact.

Besides the height and the dress and the demeanor he carried, the rider knew his eyes marked him as well. While he was delivering, they glowed, identifying him for all to see.

He strode into the main hallway, swept the area with his gaze, and felt his companion slightly behind him and to the right so they could both fight if it came to that. He walked to the desk, where an old man and woman stood awaiting his arrival anxiously.

"Yes?" the man asked, smiling hopefully, as if the rider might take some relief or pleasure in that expression.

"I am here," the rider said.

The old man was taken aback. "I can see that. Do you need a room? Perhaps for you and your friend?"

"No." Irritation chafed at the rider. He didn't like talking, didn't like standing, didn't like having nothing to do after he had arrived.

"Rider."

A man's voice called his attention.

The rider swiveled his head toward the speaker and saw a human standing halfway down a staircase leading to the inn's second floor.

"It's me you're here to see," the human said. "I am Dannis."

The rider recognized that name. The humans, dwarves, elves, dwellers, and even goblins insisted on that kind of individuality. It was a strange concept to a rider. Riders simply knew each other. There was no need for names.

"Come on." Dannis waved him up the staircase.

The rider led the way, flanked by his companion. The human led them upstairs to a small, neat room bathed in lantern light.

The rider didn't care for the light. Mostly, he rode at night and his eyes didn't function as well in lighted areas.

Dannis was a compact man with long, hard years and a smooth-shaven face. Someone whom most would overlook, but the rider sensed the magic within the man. With his own kind, the rider knew that magic was an innate thing. But the humans took magic upon themselves, putting it on their bodies like a sickness.

"You have the package?" Dannis asked.

Without a word, the rider stripped the carryall from his shoulder and handed it over to the human. During the journey, all of the riders had sensed the magic within the package, but none of them had investigated it. That type of behavior wasn't part of their nature. He wasn't curious about it now.

Dannis opened the carryall with the air of a man doing something awe-inspiring. He took out a rectangle of paper that opened and opened and opened yet again.

The rider glanced at the markings on the surfaces of the open rectangle of paper and saw that some of the surfaces held images.

"Have you looked at this?" Dannis asked.

"No." During the course of his duties, the rider hadn't been asked to check on the state of the object. Some things that he carried were perishable. That was important to know.

"Do you know what it is?" Dannis seemed proud of his new possession.

"No."

"It's a *book*." The human smiled. "Not many of these left around these days."

The rider had heard of books. Once they had all been thought destroyed by Lord Kharrion, the being who had brought all the goblinkin hordes together and nearly taken over the world. During that long war, the riders had served with the Goblin Lord as well against him. Both sides had paid gold for their tasks, and those tasks—the rides hurtling across the landscapes—had given riders their reasons for living.

The rider waited.

The human seemed disappointed. "I don't suppose you'd be impressed."

The rider felt that was self-evident and didn't respond.

"A funny thing about this," the human said, unable to conceal his pride over the object, "it looks like a book, but it's a trap. A very clever trap, but a trap nonetheless."

That caught some of the rider's attention. He knew all about traps.

"And a most compelling trap for those for whom it is set." Dannis slid the book back into the carryall. "At the time we set up delivery here, we did not know where the trap's final destination would be. We have since learned the whereabouts of the person we are setting the trap for. I was told you might accept another assignment."

Excitement flared within the rider. "Yes."

Dannis handed the carryall back, adding a sack of gold that completed the balance for the task. "I need this taken to Hortugal. Do you know where that is? One of the goblinkin cities the South?"

"Yes," the rider said, and he didn't tell the human that riders knew where every place was.

"You don't have a problem with goblins, I take it."

"No," the rider replied. Goblinkin were just like bloodwolves. If they got in his way or interfered with him, he killed them. Just as he did with humans, dwarves, and elves.

"There is a wizard there. His name is Ertonomous Dron. Deliver this package to him and tell him to go to Kelloch's Harbor."

The rider considered that. Kelloch's Harbor was far to the north.

"The package can be delivered to Kelloch's Harbor," the rider pointed out.

"No," Dannis said. "That wouldn't do at all. I don't mean to offend, but you don't fit into the trap at all."

"All right."

"When can you leave?" the human asked.

"Now," the rider answered. And he spun on his heel and did.

13

1

Kelloch's Harbor

re *now!* What'd ye think ye're a-doin' with yerself?"
Startled by the booming voice that penetrated
even the raucous nightly crowing and lying of the sailors
and cargo handlers that filled the Broken Tiller, Juhg
looked up. His hands moved automatically to close the
journal he'd been working in. Just as rapidly, for he had
learned to be quick of hand if he wanted to eat or go un-
punished among the goblin slavers that had once owned
him, he shifted the handmade book beneath the plate that
still held half his dinner. The dim oil lanterns and tallow
candles that lit the tavern created long and deep shadows
that aided his efforts.

Raisho, a young sailor of *Windchaser*—the ship Juhg
currently sailed with—stood in front of the small table
Juhg had taken at the back of the tavern. Raisho was human, an inch or two over six feet, and broad of shoulder
from pulling oars and shifting cargo all of his life. At
twenty years, he was young for an adult among his kind,
and he still went smooth-shaven because he could not yet
command a full beard. A red leather band festooned with
osprey feathers held his unruly black hair back in a queue
that left his forehead bare and trailed a ponytail to the base

of his neck. The sun, wind, and weather had tanned his skin deep, supple warm ebony, save where it was marked with a seaman's indigo blue tattoos wishful of good luck. Lantern light glinted on the silver hoops he wore in both ears. His dark brown eyes sparkled with merriment at Juhg's reaction.

Although tall for a dweller, Juhg stood only a little more than half his friend's size. His fair hair and skin that still held the cherry glow of a new-found tan contrasted sharply. Raisho looked every inch a sailing man, while Juhg looked something like a miniature version of a merchant in the hand-tailored clothes that he took such care in. Except that no merchant was ever a dweller in the northern climes of the mainland.

Nor did any dweller know how to write. Fear trailed cat's claws across Juhg's shoulders. He swallowed hard.

Thankfully, no one in the loud tavern appeared to have noticed the young sailor's comments. The Broken Tiller lived up to its name as a place where men who fought the sea for a living gathered to spend their time in lazy circles of talking, drinking, and eating. Small and crowded by a low ceiling, the tavern had an earthen floor covered by crushed oyster shells that staved off most of the mud when the torrential rains that often wracked the coast came stealing in the light of day or the loneliness of night.

"You might warn someone when you were about to pounce on them," Juhg replied irritably.

Lowering his voice, Raisho said, "An' ye might want to give a thought that maybe ye ain't back on Greydawn Moors, or at the Vault, where dwellers read an' write an' such like it ain't nothin'."

Despite his embarrassment at being surprised, Juhg knew the young sailor was correct. Writing in the journal, even as compelling as the exercise had been and as active as his mind insisted on being, was a mistake. Juhg was a dweller, one of a race that had been enslaved by goblin slavers for centuries, even after the evil Lord Kharrion had been defeated by the combined remnants of armies made up of humans, elves, and dwarves.

The dwellers hadn't fought in those battles against Lord Kharrion and his goblin hordes. Dweller natures prevented them from massing for battle, as the gods had intended. The Old Ones had shaped dwellers to be survivors, and one of the greatest survival skills was cowardice. Still, the lack of effort for the dwellers' own freedom and lives had left rancorous feelings among the other peoples of the world.

"Were it not me," Raisho said, "an' were it a goblin what found ye a-scribblin' in that book, why, ye'd be drawn an' quartered an' thrown out into that muddy street what lies outside them doors."

"I know." Juhg took the book from under his plate and pocketed it in his worn gray traveling cloak.

He rolled the quill he'd been using back into the waterproof oilskin that he carried them in, keeping all the quills straight and orderly as his training dictated. He wasn't neat and orderly by nature; those skills had come from his training at the Great Library. Capping the inkwell he'd kept out of sight on the chair beside him, he put the small bottle into his pocket as well.

"Ye mind if I sit?" Raisho asked.

"I'm sorry. Please do." Juhg gestured to the other side of the table.

Raisho didn't find a chair immediately to hand. He glanced a little farther afield, then hooked a chair with a foot and yanked it over. He sat in the chair, taking care to shift the cutlass and long knife he wore at his hips. When he finished with his adjustments, both blades lay quick within reach.

"What are you doing here?" Juhg asked.

"Came to find ye."

"Why?"

"Wanted to share me good fortune with the one what was somewhat responsible fer it." Raisho rubbed his palms together. Calluses midwifed by long hours of handing ship's rigging and scraping barnacles rasped against each other.

Juhg raised his eyebrows. "*Our* good fortune, you mean?"

"Aye." Raisho nodded with good-natured reluctance. "Our good fortune, then."

Unable to keep either impatience or hope from his voice, Juhg finally gave up any attempt at feigning disinterest. After all, the purchases at the last port intended for sale here were primarily his suggestion based on independent reading he'd undertaken. "You sold our goods well?"

A broad white smile split Raisho's face. "Well enough, little bookworm. Well enough, indeed." The young sailor jingled a modest purse. The silvery tinkle of the coins inside sounded promising.

In spite of himself, Juhg's ears pricked and he began attempting to guess at their profits based on the clinks he heard. Much of those profits, he knew, depended on how well the Cheemantine blankets had brought in an unproven market.

"The blankets?" Juhg asked.

Raisho nodded. "Mighty cold up here, but people still have an eye fer fashion. As ye guessed."

Juhg smiled. Buying the blankets had been a gamble, and he felt satisfaction that the investment had paid off. Cheemantine blankets served to fight the chill of long winter nights, but each was uniquely made with patterns that were—reportedly, at least—not duplicated by the blanket makers. Even among the poor, hardscrabble environment of Kelloch's Harbor, Juhg had felt certain buyers would want individual things, items that others around them could not duplicate.

Raisho lifted a hand and drew the attention of a serving maid.

She was a young lass, dressed in a simple homespun gown, and quick to respond to the young sailor despite her tired eyes.

"Don't go around advertising your newfound wealth," Juhg cautioned. His innate dweller's nature to run and hide in the face of physical adversity rose to the surface. "Otherwise you'll lose that profit, and perhaps your very life, before you make it back to the ship."

Raisho grinned again. "Not without me bustin' a head or two, I won't."

"It could be that I would be with you. Kelloch's Harbor is not a safe place. This place is not a town built on trade. It's a waterhole filled with cutthroats and scoundrels." Juhg drummed his fingers on the leaning tabletop. Sometimes the young sailor chose to be very dense about inferred dialogue. Juhg felt uncomfortable with some direct conversations circumstances had forced him to have with his friend and fellow investor.

"Oh."

"And I cannot run nearly as fast as you can."

"I would stand an' fight at your side till the bitter end," Raisho promised. "I wouldn't leave ye there."

Juhg knew that Raisho meant what he said. *Unfortunately, it would only mean the doom of us both.* The dweller sighed, one of the acts that everyone accused dwellers of holding in common, a trait that all nondwellers lamented. Only dwellers, general opinion said, could issue such deeply piteous and heartfelt sighs.

The young sailor was an accomplished swordsman and practiced his chosen craft, in addition to his sailing, every chance he got. Upon occasion when events had forced Raisho to use his martial skills in *Windchaser*'s defense against pirates or goblin ships, Juhg had complimented the young sailor on his bravery. Raisho had always said that Juhg was the bravest person he had ever known: a dweller who had left—by choice—the sequestered safety of Greydawn Moors, a Librarian who had chosen to voyage back out into the rough-and-tumble world he'd barely escaped from.

The serving wench stood at Raisho's side and glanced at him demurely. "And what would you be after having, milord?"

"Milord!" Raisho laughed merrily and slapped his thigh.

The serving wench reddened at the young sailor's loud reaction. Others in the tavern turned to look, but found that no violence was in the offing and quickly grew bored enough to return to their cups and their conversations.

Juhg felt sorry for the serving girl. Raisho meant nothing by his outburst, but she did not know him and did not know that.

"Raisho," Juhg said. "Please be mindful of her time. The tavern is full and she is very busy." He didn't want an angry seaman ready to fight them over the attentions of the serving wench.

Juhg tried not to let the reaction bother him. Here on the mainland, away from the safety of Greydawn Moors, most humans didn't respect dwellers. Most humans thought of dwellers, if they thought of them at all, primarily as a cheap labor source or vermin. The goblins often referred to dwellers simply as *eaters,* and talked of them as charitably as they would of a locust invasion.

Dweller villages found outside the few cities and towns that dotted the coastlines fell hard to the goblin slavers. Once the goblins clapped every captured dweller into chains, the goblins burned the villages as though they were lice-infested nests. Even if a slave escaped, there was no home to return to.

"I'll have ale," Raisho told the serving wench. "Quickly now, an' plenty of it. I've got me a powerful thirst." He glanced at Juhg. "What will ye have?"

"Chulotzberry tea," Juhg said. "Please."

"Of course, milords." The serving wench ducked her head.

"Thank you," Juhg called after her. A human serving him still struck him as strange. At the Great Library, dwellers still handled the menial tasks. But many humans who came to the Vault of All Known Knowledge for answers to questions had treated him as an equal.

In fact, he was even on speaking terms with the Grandmagister's wizard friend Craugh. And Craugh, wizard of no little repute and an enigmatic history, claimed few as friends. His wizardly powers, town gossips said, sometimes increased the population of toads when someone irritated him past the point of tolerance.

"So what brings ye here?" Raisho asked, indicating the tavern with an expansive wave. "If ye'd wanted to be safe, ye'd have stayed aboard *Windchaser*."

"I wanted to feel firm land beneath my feet again," Juhg answered honestly.

Raisho shook his head sorrowfully. "I told ye afore ye left that the sea would be no place for ye, Juhg. 'Tis a hard life upon the salt, an' a lonely one at that, even in the best of circumstance. Ain't fittin' for a dweller because ye all are so much of family."

That was true of most dwellers, Juhg silently agreed. "I have no family." He had intended the statement only as one of fact, bereft of emotion. Instead, his words sounded bleak and harsh, even to his ears. His loss never stayed far from his heart.

Raisho stopped smiling and broke eye contact. "Ye're a good friend to me, Juhg. Don't ever feel like ye got no family, 'cause as long as I still breathe, ye'll have all the family I can give." He raised his eyes to Juhg with some embarrassment. Raisho wasn't a man who easily spoke of tender feelings.

"Thank you," Juhg said. "I wish I had something to offer in return."

"Ye do. I've sailed a lot of the Blood-Soaked Sea. Seen dozens of ports like the hog's wallow we're in now. I've seldom had the friendship the likes of the one I now have with ye." Raisho grinned and wiggled his brows. He lowered his voice to a hoarse whisper. "An' I've never had me one what could make me a rich man with tradin'."

Juhg laughed in spite of the tension of the moment, in spite of the mistake he'd very nearly made with the journal keeping he hadn't intended to be doing. He returned his attentions to his plate. Dwellers, after all, had earned their goblin nicknames.

The serving wench returned with the young sailor's ale and Juhg's glass of chulotzberry tea. Raisho curled a silver coin, much too much for the drinks, into the young woman's hand.

"Thank ye," he stated kindly, with a smile as generous as the tip. "I meant ye no harm. Honest I didn't."

She nodded and smiled, and Juhg guessed that she knew the nature of the coin pressed into her hand. "Let me know if you need anything further, milords." She backed away, then turned and fled.

"So?" Raisho asked expectantly.

"What?" Juhg asked, acting as though he didn't know what his friend referred to.

"Yer book. What was ye a-writin' in it?"

Juhg chewed the olive flatbread carefully as he surveyed the tavern. The Broken Tiller served mostly sailors and longshoremen who ferried the goods from the ships out in the harbor. Unfortunately, pirates mixed in with that clientele on a regular basis, though they never came into the harbor flying the black flag.

The tavern looked as though the initial builders cobbled it together from shipwrecks that chanced upon the craggy shores or the reef farther out in the harbor. Probably beginning as a single structure enclosing a great room and fashioned from the stern of a large merchant ship, the tavern now stretched out with four similar rooms, all cramped and close-quartered. Narrow doorways, not quite square, joined the rooms.

Similar architecture covered the broken hills that framed the port village, all of them at one time or another pieces of sailing ships or cobbled from crate timbers or masts. If he hadn't known that humans and a few dwarves plying blacksmiths' trade lived there, Juhg would have sworn the place was home to dwellers. Dwellers held fame as a people who made lives for themselves from the remnants of worldly goods left by others, though some insisted those goods were little more than trash and unwanted debris.

"I was writing my thoughts," Juhg answered obliquely, wishing that his friend would drop the matter.

"What thoughts, then?" Raisho gestured toward the heaped plate.

"Please," Juhg said, though his first impulse was to claim the food as his own. He was back on the mainland now, not in Greydawn Moors, where no dweller went without food after a full day's work. No dweller there claimed a stone for a pillow either. When he'd sailed aboard *Windchaser* from the Yondering Docks where the Blood-Soaked Sea lapped upon the shores of Greydawn Moors, Juhg had prepared himself to return to that hand-to-mouth existence. He was ashamed that such selfish thoughts of gluttony came back so easily.

"Yer thoughts," Raisho reminded as he helped himself to a corn cake.

He slathered the corn cake with creamed butter and golden orange fire-pear preserves.

"Mine," Juhg agreed. "How are the firepear preserves? I haven't tried them." He'd been afraid to because the strong smell had burned his nose.

"Ye won't like it. Too strong." Raisho helped himself to another corn cake, the next to last, and covered it with firepear preserves.

Unwilling to quietly watch his final corn cake be devoured in such a cavalier fashion by Raisho, who often exhibited a dwellerlike appetite by eating when there was no way he could possibly be hungry, Juhg claimed the remaining corn cake. He helped himself to preserves, scented the concoction again, and told himself that the firepears could not possibly be that hot. Biting into the cake, he found he had a mouthful of what felt like coals pumped to full heat by a blacksmith's bellows. Or maybe he had a mouthful of stinging brinebees. Hurriedly, he grabbed the glass of tea and drank deeply, seeking the soothing and healing balm of the chulotzberry.

"I warned ye," Raisho said.

Reluctantly, thinking that he might try cleaning the firepear preserves off to at least salvage the corn cake, Juhg realized the futility of the effort and shoved the morsel over to the young sailor.

Raisho smiled broadly as he accepted the surrender. "Thank ye kindly."

"Don't mention it," Juhg croaked, then drank more tea. He focused on the remnants of his meal, getting most of them slightly ahead of Raisho's questing fingers.

"The book."

Juhg regarded his friend. He had known Raisho for three years before signing ship's articles with *Windchaser* and Captain Attikus. Raisho usually didn't possess the tenacity of thought he now so plainly exhibited.

Keeping his voice pitched low, Juhg said, "I was making notes about this place."

"The port?"

"Yes. Kelloch's Harbor."

Raisho sorted through Juhg's plate and found a sizable chunk of prick-lemelon. He popped the green and red fruit into his mouth and relished the salty sweet rush of flavor.

"I could order you a plate," Juhg said. "We could pay from our profits."

Grinning, Raisho agreed. "We could. We could indeed. But I'm not that hungry." He took a baked potato in his fingers and upended the tuber to pour the honey-glazed seaweed into his mouth. He chewed and sighed with content.

Juhg marveled at the young sailor's capacity. Even Taurak Bleiyz, fictional dweller hero—*And wasn't that a redundancy?*—and champion whose own appetites were legendary, would have been shamed by Raisho's ability to consume.

"All this writin' ye're doin' here an' aboard *Windchaser*," Raisho said, "makes me wonder if 'n ye were truly ready to leave the Vault."

Glancing around quickly, Juhg made certain that no one had overheard the conversation. "Raisho, I beg you to watch your tongue. I swear, it fairly luffs in the breeze created by your breathing. No one here knows of that place, and it would be better to keep it that way."

Greydawn Moors existed on no known map. Old magic, ancient and powerful magic, had created the island where the Vault of All Known Knowledge had been hidden away since Lord Kharrion had begun gathering his goblin armies. Those magicks wielded by the human wizards had torn the island from the sea bottom. Dwarves, according to the histories, had shorn up the thick stone columns that held the island in place at the ocean's bottom. Elven warders had made the risen island fertile and loosed the great aquatic monsters that roamed freely in the Blood-Soaked Sea beneath the pall of continual gray fog kept in place by an ancient enchantment.

A sober expression fitted itself to Raisho's face. "I know. I know." He waved Juhg's warning away. "All this secrecy, it's just easy to ferget, ye know."

"No," Juhg said distinctly, "it's not."

"Aye. Perhaps it's not. Perhaps it's just me."

"And perhaps it's the ale," Juhg suggested.

"I was just of a mind to celebrate, is all." Raisho pushed his ale mug away, then folded his arms across his chest petulantly. "Wasn't exactly me fault ye weren't in the first tavern I went a-lookin' fer ye in."

"No," Juhg said agreeably. "I suppose it wasn't. And I suppose there were a half-dozen such establishments between that one and this one."

"I don't know," Raisho agreed guiltily. "I didn't count."

Juhg didn't want his friend to feel too badly. Raisho's mistake was less than if he'd drawn attention by writing in the journal. Juhg used his knife to nudge a flutterfish fillet toward the young sailor.

Raisho took the fillet in his fingers, tilted his head back, and dropped the food into his mouth. He chewed contentedly. "I thought ye knew all about Kelloch's Harbor from them—" He stopped himself before he said *books*.

Before leaving Greydawn Moors, Juhg had prepared for his journey by choosing the ship he would secure passage on. From there, based on his knowledge of Captain Attikus' normal trade routes, Juhg had assembled a book regarding conversations he'd had with sailors who had frequented the taverns along the Yondering Docks.

"The knowledge that I had," Juhg said, "was good enough to prepare a modest trade venture, but there is so much that was left out of my . . . sources."

"So ye're figurin' on remedyin' that? With yer own efforts?"

Juhg pondered that. He didn't have an actual reason for all of his writing. He just couldn't seem to help himself. Still, Raisho's supposition gave him at least an excuse for his efforts. "It seemed the thing to do. I can always send the . . . my work . . . back with another ship. Or with *Windchaser*."

Shaking his head, Raisho asked, "Have ye given any thought to the possibility that ye weren't through with yer work there? That maybe Grandmagister Lamplighter was right about yer callin' an' what ye was truly meant to be?"

Quietly contemplating another bite of pricklemelon, Juhg said nothing.

"I can see that ye have thought about all of that," Raisho said a moment later. "Ye miss all them . . . Well, ye know what I'm talking about."

Juhg did indeed. Raisho's deliberate nonuse of the word *books* resonated within him. The Vault of All Known Knowledge was the world's repository of literature, of nonfiction and fiction. When Lord Kharrion had led the goblins across the world to pillage and loot, they had deliberately destroyed books. Vast libraries, some that had existed in fact and some that existed only in legend, were lost.

Thousands of books remained within the Vault, though, and cataloguing them all had taken generations of dwellers in an attempt to put the collections to rights. Juhg missed the Great Library. All those years ago, the Builders had raised the structure so hurriedly that blueprints of the vast buildings and caverns did not exist. The wings and hallways and stairways meandered all across the mountaintop. The lower sections of the Library stood honeycombed from the Knucklebones Mountains up above the Ogre's Fingers. Some dweller historians continued to maintain that the

Builders had constructed part of the island from the body of a giant ogre Lord Kharrion had ensorcelled into his service.

Those events had taken place during the dark times known as the Cataclysm. Even now, after all those centuries had passed, the books gathered in the Vault of All Known Knowledge remained zealously guarded by the dweller Librarians, as well as the elves and the dwarves who lived there.

"I couldn't stay there," Juhg said.

"Grandmagister Lamplighter made a home fer ye," Raisho said. "As he made homes fer others over the years who he brought home from his travels. Ye could still be there. An' if 'n ye so chose, why, I'm sure the Grandmagister would welcome ye back with open arms."

Juhg knew that.

"Way I heard it," Raisho said in a softer voice, "ye were like to a son to him, ye were."

"I know," Juhg said. "But my family may still be out there." Then he corrected himself. "*Here.* They may still be *here.* I've got a mother and a father, two brothers and a sister that I know of."

"If 'n the goblin slavers the Grandmagister freed ye from didn't do fer 'em."

Juhg glanced at the young sailor.

Raisho's blue eyes held a stricken look. "Didn't mean no harm nor foul, Juhg. Just tryin' to put everythin' in perspective fer ye because I care about ye. Which is why I put in a good word with Cap'n Attikus fer ye."

"What do you mean?"

Embarrassment colored Raisho's face. "Nothin'. I meant nothin'. Just me mouth betrayin' me mind again."

"You meant something," Juhg said with a little force. During their three-year friendship, he'd never put too much pressure on the ties that bound them. "What did you mean?"

Raisho scowled. "Don't ye be botherin' the cap'n with it. Like as not, he won't be overly fond of either of us if ye go off askin' him about this. Better we should just keep it betwixt us."

"What word did you put in?"

Shrugging, Raisho answered, "Weren't much. Cap'n Attikus, he just wasn't too happy about takin' on a scribbler, is all."

A scribbler! Juhg couldn't believe it. Captain Attikus was one of the few ship's captains in all the world who knew Greydawn Moors laid across the forbidden expanse of the Blood-Soaked Sea. The captain knew why the island had to remain hidden. If the goblin ships discovered the existence of the Vault of All Known Knowledge, they would sail on Greydawn Moors and burn the island down to the waterline, showing no mercy to man or beast.

Librarians at the Vault held great respect from those who knew of them. Unfortunately, not many knew of them.

"A *scribbler*!" Juhg gasped in disbelief. Anger stirred within him. "The term is grossly offensive." Accepting it meant accepting an insult to the time and effort his teachers had put into him as well. He couldn't do that.

Raising his hands meekly, Raisho said, "Now, now. Don't go off an' get yer dander all riled up."

But Juhg couldn't stop himself. He had lived as a slave for fourteen years before Grandmagister Lamplighter had freed him and brought him back to Greydawn Moors. "Librarians offer so much more than merely readers and writers. They hold storehouses of knowledge, hold keys to information that many would consider to be magic, and ways of understanding that can give people access to worlds. Real worlds as well as made-up ones. Where would civilization be without biographies, volumes on agriculture, sailing, and construction? Where would the imagination be without the heroes in stories? Where would the heart be without passionate tales of love and loneliness and sacrifice?"

"Avast there, matey," Raisho said. "It's not me ye're in need of convincin'."

Juhg slumped back in the rickety wooden chair. He nearly tumbled off the worn cushion his height had forced him to use in order to reach his meal. "I thought the captain was an ally."

"The cap'n *is* an ally." Raisho scowled. "Ye'll find none truer than Cap'n Attikus an' the crew of *Windchaser*." He paused. "He just weren't very happy about takin' on someone so . . . so . . ."

"Short?" Juhg supplied with just a hint of sarcasm to point out his friend's poor attempt to excuse the sea captain.

"New to the sea," Raisho said.

"I am a skilled sailor," Juhg protested. "I learned my skills aboard *One-Eyed Peggie* when the Grandmagister returned from the mainland all those years ago."

"The cap'n didn't know that."

Juhg stopped for a moment. His advent to Greydawn Moors had been almost thirty years before. As a dweller, he was still young, not even of middle age before he hit his fiftieth birthday. But thirty years was most of a lifetime to a human. Few humans probably still lived who remembered the story, and humans rarely lived on Greydawn Moors.

"You're right," Juhg said.

"Cap'n Attikus," Raisho pointed out, "likes to run a tight ship."

Juhg knew that as well. During the past few weeks, Captain Attikus had impressed the dweller.

"Even with what I said," Raisho went on, "I doubt the cap'n would have taken ye on if 'n it hadn't been fer the Grandmagister talkin' to him."

"Wick . . ." Juhg caught himself using the Grandmagister's name with such familiar abandon and stopped at once. "The Grandmagister put in a good word for me?"

"Aye." Raisho nodded. "Several, in fact."

"I didn't know that."

"I don't think either the Grandmagister or the cap'n wanted much known about it. If 'n I hadn't been aboardship finishin' up some sail an' riggin' repairs, why, I wouldn'ta known it either."

Juhg pondered that. Grandmagister Lamplighter had acted loath to lose him from the Vault. *Was that an act? Was I really a mistake that he had made but couldn't admit to?* The questions pounded at Juhg's mind. During the nearly thirty years he had been at the Great Library and studied under the Grandmagister and the other First Level Librarians, he had never felt as if he belonged.

"Don't get all caught up in them names an' the circumstances of how ye came to be aboard *Windchaser,*" Raisho said. "Ye're aboard her, an' ye're doin' a powerful good job of mendin' sail an' keepin' the ship tidy. An' Cook? Why, Cook says he's never in all his days had a finer helper. Nor one who knew more recipes than him."

"That was a gracious compliment," Juhg acknowledged. *Not that Cook would ever bestow it upon me.*

"It were." Raisho nodded, obviously feeling the conversation was once more safely out of treacherous waters. But being Raisho, he couldn't leave it there. "What I was a-gettin' at was that maybe ye ain't as done with that part of yer life as ye thought ye was."

"I'm done," Juhg said decisively, but he felt the declaration was more for himself than Raisho. Still, his inner turmoil would subside somewhat if his friend made no further mention of the Library.

"The Grandmagister, why, he told Cap'n Attikus that ye was a natural to . . . to that trade. He seemed right sad to lose ye."

"And I was sad to lose him," Juhg admitted. "But my life is not there on that island. After everything I've been through, Raisho, after everything I've seen and everything I've read, I want a bigger world." He shook his head and lowered his voice in shame. "Librarians aren't supposed to want that. They're supposed to want books and tea and the occasional bowl of pipeweed."

"Mayhap," Raisho said, nodding.

"I can't do that." But he had wished that he could, pleaded with himself to be happy with a small life. He used the search for his missing family only as an excuse to leave, and guilt stung him over that. "Greydawn Moors is just too . . . too . . . small."

Raisho nodded for a moment and took up a chunk of pricklemelon. "Seems to me that the Grandmagister gets around a lot fer a dweller. Never heard of a Grandmagister afore him that left the island."

"Never," Juhg agreed. Grandmagister Edgewick Lamplighter had been like no other head of the Vault of All Known Knowledge who had ever gone before. Juhg didn't know the reason for all of Wick's adventures to the mainland, but he knew the reason for some of them.

When he had found Juhg, Grandmagister Lamplighter had been seeking the truth to the legend of the Jade Basilisk. Both of them had barely escaped from the Arena of a Thousand Blades only a half step ahead of death. If Cap'n Hallekk and the crew of *One-Eyed Peggie* hadn't been waiting along the coast, they would have never gotten free of the Darkling Lands and mad King Kuthbart.

Thinking of Grandmagister Lamplighter put a lump in Juhg's throat. Juhg had been taken from his parents at a young age when the goblin slavers had descended upon their village. He hadn't truly known them, other than to remember them. But he had gotten to know Grandmagister Lamplighter.

When Raisho said that Juhg was like the son that the Grandmagister had never had, Juhg knew that wasn't true. More accurately, Juhg was thought of as kindly as a favored nephew. The Grandmagister had several of those, as well as nieces, and he was a favorite uncle among his family.

Knowing that the Grandmagister thought so highly of him had made leaving the Great Library harder. Still, Juhg had loaded his pack on the night that he said he would, and had made his way down to the Yondering Docks in a borrowed wagon the following morning. When *Windchaser* slid out into the harbor under the pull of the breezes, Juhg had spotted the Grandmagister among the crowd that had turned out to see the ship off.

"Mayhap Grandmagister Lamplighter wasn't cut out to stay on the island neither," Raisho stated.

"If Grandmagister Lamplighter would have had his druthers," Juhg said with full confidence, "he would have been content to stay on the island, in the Vault, and visit Hralbomm's Wing on a regular basis."

Hralbomm's Wing was where the Librarians kept all the epic poems and works of fiction in the Great Library. The Grandmagister had admitted that in his youth, before his promotion to Second Level Librarian, he had spent far too much time among those stacks. But Juhg knew that the Grandmagister still spent considerable time among those books.

Juhg did not feel the same about the romances and lighthearted adventures captured between the covers of those books. He had lived the harsh lives of those who had suffered in those tales, and he did not like having to relive those experiences in any form. Heroes, in the real world, didn't often come along.

"All I'm sayin'," Raisho said in a quiet voice as he glanced over his shoulder, "is that mayhap ye keepin' yer hand in at writin' an' such ain't a bad thing."

"Unless I get caught at it and put to death for it, of course," Juhg reminded.

"Well, that's like not to happen, what with me keepin' a weather eye peeled on ye."

Juhg started to point out Raisho's engagement with making a profit when he'd fallen victim to the lure of the clean white pages of the journal. During the long days of the voyage across the Blood-Soaked Sea, especially after seeing some of the monsters that lived in the murky purple-red depths that he had not before seen, Juhg had crafted himself a book. He'd boiled rags for the paper himself down in the ship's galley, then cured and cut the paper. Making ink was an easy task.

And after that, he'd willingly filled page after page with drawings and narrative about the things he'd seen and done.

All of that was at the tip of his tongue when Herby entered the Broken Tiller with a concerned look on his young face and the flea-infested spider monkey riding across his shoulders. Juhg only hoped that some merchant or sailor or longshoreman who had just found his purse picked clean wasn't a step or two behind the pair.

mel odom

2

The Thief's Story

a pensive look pinched Herby's features. He was eleven years old, little more than a child by human standards. Unkempt dark hair stuck out all around his head. His brown eyes were set too close together and he had a pointed nose. Despite the length of time he'd spent at sea, his skin remained fair and always looked fresh-burned.

Most people passing him by on any street in a well-to-do city would have thought him nothing more than a beggar boy out trying to earn a few coins to escape another beating at the orphanage where he lived. The stained and worn breeches, cloak, and shirt he wore promoted that illusion. He went barefoot, not because he had no shoes—Juhg knew the boy did—but because climbing was easier with his feet unencumbered. The thick calluses on Herby's feet proved resistant to the cracked oyster shells that covered the tavern's earthen floor. Mud caked the boy's toes and spattered up his legs and breeches.

His spider monkey was a gaunt thing hardly as big as one of the cats that roamed *Windchaser*'s decks and holds as mousers. Charcoal gray fur covered the monk's skinny, lanky body, but left an oblong of white fur around his pink-ash flat face. One rear paw was white as well, but the other three were clad in dark fur. His tail darted back and forth across Herby's narrow shoulders.

Herby called his amiable companion Gust, but that had been shortened from the crew's appellation, "that dis*gust*in' monkey," when they complained to the captain about the beast. Gust also suited him because when a sailor got aggravated at him and started throwing things, the monk would be gone as quickly as loose canvas carried off by a gust of wind. There were other names the sailors called the monkey, but the captain would allow none of the names, no matter how hard Herby tried to get by with it. On occasion, Herby still called the monkey by the foul names the ship's crew had given the beast, but never within Captain Attikus' hearing.

"Boy," Raisho growled, scowling mightily. "What have ye done?"

Juhg knew that the bald bartender behind the scarred counter kept a covert eye on them.

"Nothin'," Herby shot back as if offended. He snuffled and wiped at his nose with a grimy hand. The spider monkey mimicked the gesture, snuffling even louder than the boy. "I ain't done nothin'."

"Cap'n Attikus," Raisho said, "might be somewhat soft in the head over ye, but I ain't, boy. Ye get caught stealin' so much as a pie here in this town, why, a hangman'll stretch yer neck fer ye. An' I'll let 'em."

"I ain't done nothin'," Herby repeated as Raisho continued to stare harshly.

32

On his shoulder, the spider monkey stood and shook his tiny fist at Raisho, raising his voice in furious chittering. Gust looked as though he was set to leap from Herby's shoulder and launch into a blistering attack on Raisho. Some of the tavern patrons deep in their cups laughed at the monk's screeching antics and called out encouragement to the creature.

Juhg sank back into the shadows with the tavern wall at his back. Going there to eat as a patron in spite of the fact that he was a dweller was one thing, but drawing extra attention could prove even more dangerous.

"I don't believe ye," Raisho declared.

Herby's lower lip stuck out petulantly. "Wasn't ye I come here to see, Raisho." He nodded toward Juhg. "'Twas the little dweller."

Little? Juhg thought, knowing he was almost the same height as the boy when he drew himself up. Curiosity scrambled through him. He remembered the teachings of Irnst Voggal, one of the great body language experts who had specialized in haggling and was the author of *Quivers and Gestures: The Secret Language of Successful Trade and Barter,* whom he had studied in the Vault before leaving Greydawn Moors. According to the passages and examples in that tome, Herby's widened eyes and careful focus were classic examples of a person wanting to close a deal.

"Ye'd best be a-watchin' yer mouth an' yer manners," Raisho warned.

Gust stood to his full height on Herby's shoulder. The monk clutched the boy's hair in his tiny fist and shook his other hand at Raisho as he yammered in full voice.

"Juhg," Herby said in a soft voice that carried no farther than the immediate table, "there's something I should tell ye, but this tavern, why, it ain't the place fer it. Not fer none of it if'n we want to live."

Juhg hesitated only for a moment. The natural curiosity of a dweller possessed him, but he lacked a lot of the caution that seemed consistently paired to that trait. He'd lost some of his fears while in servitude to the goblins. Waiting for his death every day in the mines or at the end of a barbed whip had worn that dread of death from his mind and flesh, given way to an acceptance that such a thing might occur at any time. Occasional trips with Grandmagister Lamplighter to the mainland had worn away other fears.

Raisho looked at Juhg.

Making his decision, propelled by his curiosity and Herby's earnestness, Juhg nodded. "We'll go outside." He produced a waterproof cloth and wrapped choice bits of food from his plate. As a dweller, he hated to see a meal go unfinished. Especially now that he was back on the mainland and less in control of his life than he had been in decades.

Eyeing his ale mug, Raisho made an obvious decision not to pursue the drink after being chastised. He pushed up from his chair, causing the spider monkey to lean back fearfully. One of the animal's forearms wrapped under Herby's chin and around his throat as he hid behind the boy's head.

"Disgustin' monk," Raisho snarled.

Tucking his pouch of food into his cloak, Juhg followed Herby back through the crowd. His mind chafed at the possibilities the boy's appearance represented. Although Captain Attikus liked the boy, Herby seldom brought good news to the crew.

And why would Herby come to me instead of Captain Attikus? Juhg wondered. Suspicion occurred to him because of his dweller nature, but pursuit of hidden meanings was his through his Librarian training.

The wind outside the Broken Tiller blew crisp and clean from the north. Chill mist rose from the Sea of Frozen Teeth out in the harbor, named so because four months out of the year icebergs drifted down constantly from the northern reaches during the spring when the Frozen Ocean thawed, and peppered Juhg's face and hands like the pecking of tiny birds' beaks. The breeze washed away the stink of pipeweed, stale ale, and food that clung to the dweller's clothing from the tavern. Already growing cold, he pulled his traveling cloak a little more tightly about his shoulders.

Fur ruffled by the wind, Gust quickly clambered beneath Herby's loose cloak. A moment later, the monk turned and thrust his face out, obviously curious. Light from the oil lantern mounted on the tavern wall beside the door behind Juhg turned the little beast's eyes the bright orange of Vendorian coins.

Rickety wooden stairs zigzagged twenty feet up the side of the rocky outcrop that held the tavern above the broken reefs that encircled the port area. The Broken Tiller perched near the water's edge. Only a narrow lip of rock, little more than an animal's run, jutted at the bottom of the twenty-foot drop. The tide exhumed the bedrock beneath the lip, hollowing away the loose soil and creating small caverns that echoed with the booming splash.

No level ground truly existed in Kelloch's Harbor. The town builders had hung, perched, jammed, and piled their businesses and homes in the crags and broken spaces between the twisted shards of the Razor Mountains. None of the larger cities or trade guilds dared follow a pirate ship into the port for fear of pirates attacking in the narrow confines of the harbor.

From a distance out at sea, the civilized places—and that, Juhg thought after seeing the place, required callous disregard of the term—pocked into Kelloch's Harbor looked like a collection of flotsam and jetsam that had washed up on the craggy beach from a flotilla of dead ships. The builders had used few fresh-cut timbers. When Juhg had arrived in the predawn hours that morning, the businesses and houses had been dark. Now lanterns ensconced in hurricane glass and flickering fireplaces devouring driftwood and firewood hauled from the other side of the mountains lit those places.

Like glimmerworms coiled in the empty sockets of a jumbled pile of skulls,

Juhg couldn't help thinking with a chill that cut more deeply than the howling winds. From time to time, he realized that having a good vocabulary and an imagination to match were detrimental to a feeling of security.

"All right, then," Raisho growled to Herby. "Let's have it. I don't fancy standin' around out here freezin' meself stupid."

Herby wiped at his runny nose and snuffled, echoed a moment later by the monk. "It's important, Raisho. Unbe*lief*able important."

Raisho hissed angrily between his teeth. Gray vapor spewed into the air before him, but the breeze ripped it away.

"It is cold out here," Juhg said in a reasonable voice before his friend could give vent to his temper. *And dangerous.* Juhg watched the shadows below them constantly, wondering when one of the regular denizens of Kelloch's Harbor would take it upon himself to come up and rob them at sword's point. Thankfully, the rickety stairs that swayed in the wind rendered such a venture dangerous for a would-be robber as well. And Raisho was big.

"It's a goblin ship," Herby said.

Lifting his head, feeling the old fear return to him in a blaze, Juhg gazed out into the harbor. He took an instinctive step back and bumped into the tavern wall behind him as he sought deeper shadow.

Twenty-seven ships, including *Windchaser,* lay at anchor in the deep water before the broken rock of the beach. Docks ran out over the water, built on pilings sunk deep into the rock and much of the harbor bottom.

A few small skiffs still plied the relatively calm waters, hauling cargo from the ships to the warehouse crews. Lower down, the tall, spiked hills that surrounded the harbor on three sides protected the ships from most of the wind.

The lanterns at either end of the cargo skiffs swung in the wind, casting constantly shifting ellipses of light over the dark bay. White curlers of foam, dulled by the lack of moonlight behind a mountain of dark clouds that promised more rain, rolled steadily to crash into the rough, broken rock of the beach. Carrying cargo both ways helped keep the light, flat-bottomed craft from capsizing in the turbulent water. Out beyond the shelter of the mountainous walls surrounding the port, the Sea of Frozen Teeth warred with itself, creating fierce waves thirty feet tall that smashed against the protective ring of the mountains.

Juhg recognized all of the ships. Humans crewed most of them, drawn always by their fascination with the sea. The Old Ones who had created the races of the world had given the humans mastery of the water-ways, of the rivers and great oceans that covered most of the world. Dwarves—whom the Old Ones had instilled the understanding of the earth, of smithing metals, and of gems—seldom crewed ships except for trade. A few of the dwarven ships served as pirates in the Blood-Soaked Sea, further guarding the secret of Greydawn Moors and the Vault of All Known Knowledge. Elven ships were scarcest of all, and each of them carried a tragic legacy of deceit and betrayal.

"I don't see a goblin ship out there," Juhg said.

"Nor do I," Raisho growled.

"It's not out there now," Herby said. "It's comin' in."

A chill, colder even than the frozen teeth the whirling wind brought, rushed and twisted through Juhg's guts. He hadn't seen a goblin in thirty years.

Raisho shrugged. "Even so, boy, ye needn't fear fer yerself so. Here in Kelloch's Harbor, why, they'll not be allowed to go clappin' honest sailors in irons." He glanced at Juhg. "Nor dwellers either, bookworm. So cease ye to be a-frettin' as ye are."

"I'm not fretting," Juhg said, knowing he covered his anxiety badly. *But I will be staying aboard* Windchaser *till the goblin ship is gone or we set sail.*

There was no need in taking chances. In fact, drawn to his journal as he was, Juhg would appreciate the chance to work in peace. Then again, days and probably weeks would pass before *Windchaser* again put in to port. He missed being on land. Even during the few travels he'd shared with Grandmagister Lamplighter, he'd never truly enjoyed sailing. Then his mind, freed from his fear now that he had a plan, focused on the other aspects of Herby's news. "The goblin ship isn't here now?"

"No." Herby shook his head.

The monk shook his head as well, then reached up and laid a hand against his young master's jaw. Gust cooed sympathetically.

"How do you know it's coming?" Juhg asked.

"Heard it, is all." Herby spat over the side of the landing, eliciting a stern curse from below.

A group of longshoremen swayed along the broken path that led down to the harbor. One of them raised a lantern. All of them wore cloaks, but the wind pressed the material against their bodies and revealed that none of them was a warrior. Their vicious threats against Herby stopped the instant the lantern settled on Raisho. Grumbling, the men lowered their lantern and moved along.

"Where did you hear about the goblin ship?" Juhg asked.

"Around." Herby shuffled his mud-encrusted feet.

Juhg didn't understand how the boy's feet withstood the biting wind or the seeping cold of the wooden landing. "Herby, if I need to, I'll go to Captain Attikus and ask him to get to the bottom of this."

"Ye'd rat me out after I brung this to yer attention as I did?" Herby frowned petulantly and crossed his thin arms over his skinny chest.

"Yes," Juhg replied.

Herby cursed offensively.

"No more of that," Raisho growled. "An' ye'll give us an answer right quick-like."

Blowing his breath out angrily, Herby said, "I was out back of a shop."

Juhg maintained his patience with effort. "What shop?"

"The cooper's."

"Which cooper?" Raisho asked.

"Ain't but one cooper." Herby grinned in delight at knowing more than either Juhg or Raisho.

"You were interested in watching barrels being made?" Juhg's tone plainly indicated the doubt he felt. Beside him, Raisho moved restively.

Frowning, Juhg said, "I heard the cooper doesn't just make barrels."

"Who gave you this tidbit of information?"

"A boy."

Juhg sighed. "What boy?"

"A boy I met on the docks."

"What business did you have with this boy?"

Herby raised his blade-thin shoulders and dropped them. "Just talk."

"About what?" Juhg asked.

"Thievin'," Raisho rumbled. "The kind of thing what's always on his crooked little mind."

"Thievin's not always bad," Herby argued.

Glancing around quickly, Juhg made sure no one stood nearby. However, the cold wind carried words a long distance. He heard fragments of conversations while standing on the landing. A lot of those came from skiff crews and even sailors aboard the ship. The harbor water carried voices and noises farther than the land did.

"Maybe," Juhg suggested, "we shouldn't talk so much about . . . about that . . . occupation."

"Thievin's not always bad," Herby insisted. Some of his petulance turned to challenge. "Why, them stories Juhg sometimes tells is all about thieves what steals fer their kings or fer the love of a lady. Where would Portablaine have been in *The Terror of Qulog's Tower* had he not been a thief?"

Surprised, Juhg knew that Herby's argument held weight. The ship's boy didn't usually harbor deep or serious thoughts.

"There was a lot of warriors what lost their heads an' such while tryin' to rescue the fair Princess Ellaquar from Qulog's flesh-eatin' trolls," Herby went on. "But Portablaine done for 'em. Bein' a thief, why, that is a callin' fer some."

Raisho took a step forward, towering over the boy with his girth. Even as humans went, Juhg knew, not many years separated the two. But those years were enough to ensure enmity.

"Well, then," Raisho stated, "I won't be surprised if'n yer puffed-up pride puts you in a troll's pot someday. Get yerself baked into a troll pie, ye will, the way ye're a-goin'. Maybe ye'll break the cap'n's heart when ye do, but I'll shed no tears over ye."

Herby leaned back over the landing railing.

Gust shoved his head out and shrilled loudly.

"I'll shed no tears," Raisho corrected, turning his baleful glare full upon the monk, "unless them trolls find themselves too particular to bake up that noisy fleabag with ye."

Gust withdrew meekly into the protection of Herby's cloak.

"The cooper," Juhg reminded. Thoughts of the goblin ship possibly pulling into the harbor at any moment bounced through his head.

Sliding away from Raisho, Herby turned his attention to Juhg. "The cooper's a fence. He trades in stolen goods. Takes 'em in, breaks 'em down, changes 'em, or just swaps 'em out fer other stolen goods or coins. Whatever as may come into his hands."

"What business did you have with such a person?" Juhg asked, fearing the answer.

Herby kept silent for a moment. Out in the harbor, men laughed and cursed and bemoaned the work they had before them the next day. Drunken sea shanties sailed between the tall mountain walls that enclosed Kelloch's Harbor.

"Been thievin' again," Raisho accused.

"The captain told you not to do that," Juhg remonstrated. The image of the young boy hanging from a gibbet in the harbor filled the dweller's mind. Books in the Vault of All Known Knowledge possessed pictures of such grim deaths. Tongues lolled from mouths set above broken necks and below bulging eyes. The sudden visual onslaught almost made Juhg sick.

As despicable as Herby could be in his personal grooming and his choice of trades, he was still one of the best audiences Juhg had found aboard *Windchaser*. The other sailors liked the tales that he couldn't help telling during the quiet hours of a voyage, but Herby hung on every word of every adventure Juhg could remember reading in Hralbomm's Wing.

Maybe some of the guilt is your own, Juhg told himself. *You filled the boy's head full of the foolishness from Hralbomm's Wing. Maybe you didn't put that calling in him, but those stories have given him an excuse to pursue his course.* If they lived to get out of Kelloch's Harbor, the dweller promised himself that he would tell no more such stories to the boy.

"I didn't steal nothin' from our crew," Herby said.

"Then who?" Raisho demanded.

In a quieter voice, Herby said, "I slipped through some of the taverns." He shrugged. "Had a bit of luck."

Raisho swore as he turned to Juhg. "This little gutter rat is gonna be the death of us. Ye know that, don't ye?"

"It's a skill," Herby protested. "A game. I'm just trainin' meself to be more'n what I am. Just like ye do with that blasted sword."

"An' what are ye a-doin' with yer ill-gotten gain from yer little game?" Raisho demanded.

Herby didn't answer. Juhg knew speculation aboard *Windchaser* held that the boy kept a treasure cache hidden on the ship. Several of the sailors had searched for it, but nothing ever came to light.

"The goblin ship," Juhg prompted.

Snuffling, shooting Raisho a look of dark condemnation, Herby looked back at Juhg. "The cooper said to another man in there that the goblin ship is comin' in tonight. At least sometime afore cock's crow."

"What man?"

Herby shrugged. "A cap'n. Or a quartermaster. Somebody what handles manifests an' cargoes an' such. Somebody what had business with the cooper."

"Was that man waiting for the goblin ship's arrival?"

"I don't think so. The cooper, his name's Muole, he was just talkin' about the goblin ship like it were somethin' new."

"Ain't new fer goblins to be a-tradin' this far north," Raisho commented. "Like as not, they trade with pirates what put into port here."

Men like we're supposed to be, Juhg thought. *Windchaser* enjoyed, if such a thing could be possible, the reputation of being a pirate ship. Not a formidable pirate ship, of course, because such a reputation often worked against a ship and her crew, made them more watched while they tried to spy on the mainland and carry news to Greydawn Moors while they traded for things the island dwellers wanted. It was better that they be mediocre pirates and excellent spies.

"Weren't because the ship's a goblin ship," Herby said. "The cooper talked of it because of its cargo." He smiled, and Juhg knew the boy enjoyed the secret he held.

"What cargo?" Raisho demanded impatiently. He lifted a huge hand in a threatening manner.

Gust retreated farther under Herby's cloak and made fearful clucking noises.

"Out with it, boy," Raisho snarled. "Ye tires me with yer endless prattle an' half-truths."

"A book," Herby stated quietly. "The goblin ship's supposed to have a book aboard her."

Listening to the answer, Juhg felt his world capsize and he thought he was going to throw up. *A book in the hands of goblins?*

"Impossible," Captain Attikus said in a calm voice. "This has to be gossip and twaddle and suchlike that surfaces in a port of liars and thieves. Can't be any truth in that story."

"I know," Juhg replied patiently, watching as good sense and pride struggled within Herby to keep still or argue with the captain over the information he'd brought forth. "And yet, Captain, what if Herby has the truth of it?"

Raisho snorted. "Herby an' the truth ain't ever been bunkmates."

"Ye big lummox!" Herby squalled, doubling up his fists and making as if to launch himself into a sudden attack on Raisho. Of course, in the captain's presence as he was, Herby knew he would be immediately protected from Raisho's wrath.

With a shrill cry of alarm, Gust hurled himself from Herby's shoulder. The monk landed on the captain's private desk in his personal quarters, where they had all gathered. Woodworking tools scattered and the oil lantern seated there almost overturned. Only Juhg's quick reflexes prevented the mishap as he caught the lamp and held it till the monk vacated the desk.

"Herby!" Captain Attikus warned sternly.

The boy stepped back but didn't give up his show of anger. He waved to Gust, who dove from the desktop and hid beneath the desk.

The captain shifted his gaze to the young sailor. "Raisho, that'll be just about enough out of you, too."

"Aye, Cap'n." Raisho scratched the back of his neck self-consciously. "I apologize, Cap'n, but the little guttersnipe just brings out the worst—"

"Belay that as well, sailor." Captain Attikus drew himself up to his full, impressive height. He stood taller than Raisho, but was built like a wolf, lean and hard. Gray touched his temples, constrasting sharply with his curly black hair. His face was long and lean, mapped by scars and wear from worry and weather. Even standing still, the captain never appeared truly at rest, always churning beneath the surface even as the sea did. He wore a long coat over his nightclothes and padded about in thick woolen slippers. "I'll have no man talking ill of another man in my crew."

"Aye, Cap'n," Raisho grumbled.

Captain Attikus pierced Juhg with a green-eyed stare. "Do you believe the lad's tale about the book, Librarian Juhg?"

Despite the fact that everyone aboard *Windchaser* knew that Juhg had willingly stepped down from his station at the Vault of All Known Knowledge, Captain Attikus insisted on addressing him by his title. The habit made the dweller uncomfortable. During his stay at the Vault of All Known Knowledge, he'd seldom felt he earned either his stay or his promotion to First Level Librarian, despite the hard work he'd done. Knowledge that the island was not his native home remained always in his mind.

Juhg felt the certain weight of the captain's gaze upon him. He framed his answer judiciously. "I believe Herby thinks he heard what he says he heard."

Irritably, the captain waved the answer away. "That wasn't what I was asking."

Juhg took a deep breath and released it. "Captain, the goblinkin aren't known for keeping books. While the goblinkin served Lord Kharrion, those creatures destroyed every book as quickly it was found."

"Aye." The captain nodded. "As I understand from tales of the Cataclysm as well." He folded his arms behind his back and paced the short length of his personal quarters.

Windchaser wasn't an accommodating ship when it came to personal space. She served primarily as a merchant ship, but one that held a fighting deck and plenty of hands aboard her to battle pirates or sea monsters, or take ships that might threaten Greydawn Moors by sailing too close and risking discovery.

"I believe Herby heard what he says he heard, too," Attikus stated.

Herby shot Raisho a snide look. Raisho chose to ignore the look. Captain Attikus pretended not to see either of them, though Juhg knew the captain seldom missed anything.

"But the question begs," the captain said. "What would a goblin ship be doing with a book?"

"I don't know," Juhg answered. "As you said, sir, it has to be gossip. Maybe the cooper was lying to a prospective customer."

"Possibly, Librarian Juhg. Possibly. You've been trained to think more on these weighty matters than I have."

Juhg cringed anew. He didn't want any of the responsibility for making a decision in whether to believe in the existence of the book; and he certainly didn't want *all* of that responsibility.

"A book in the hands of goblins might prove a frightful thing," the captain continued, looking straight at Juhg.

"Yes," Juhg reluctantly agreed.

"It might behoove us to see whether the book—and the goblin ship, for that matter—exist at all."

"Yes," Juhg said.

"I'd rather this not get around to the crew just yet."

"I understand." With part of *Windchaser*'s standing orders regarding protecting Greydawn Moors and the Great Library hidden there, Juhg knew that news of a goblin ship possibly in possession of a book would unnerve some of the older crew.

Looking at Raisho, Captain Attikus said, "Do I make myself clear?"

"Aye, Cap'n. Very clear."

Attikus shifted his fierce gaze to Herby. "That goes for all of you."

"Aye, Cap'n." Herby saluted smartly, and the monk stepped out from under the desk to carry out the same action.

Captain Attikus looked at the sailor and the young boy for another long moment, then muttered, "Hmph." He turned to Juhg. "Seeing as how I want discussion of this situation kept to a minimum, I'll need you to keep a weather eye peeled for these events, Librarian Juhg."

Juhg batted his eyes, hoping he hadn't understood what the captain had so eloquently stated without saying. "Captain, I'm afraid that I don't know—"

"I want you to look for that ship, Librarian Juhg," Captain Attikus stated.

"*Me,* Captain?"

"Aye. You know what a goblin ship looks like. You've probably had more frequent and closer experience with one than any of the men aboard *Windchaser.*"

Juhg knew that was true. He'd been captured, then shipped to the slave market in a goblin city, then shipped again to the goblin mine owner that purchased him. Juhg knew goblin sailing vessels; knew the stink of them, as well as the harsh life afforded aboard them.

"Begging the captain's pardon," Juhg said, "but sending a dweller in search of a goblin ship might not be the best course of action."

"But I think it is, Librarian Juhg. Of any man aboard this ship, I know that you'll be the one who works the hardest not to be seen by the goblins."

Juhg swallowed with effort. Getting caught again by goblins since departing Greydawn Moors became a possibility as soon as *Windchaser* entered the Blood-Soaked Sea. Nightmares sometimes still clamored in his sleep, forcing him to get up from his hammock and walk the deck until he felt safe again.

"I'll send Raisho with you," Captain Attikus went on. "Stay along the taverns fronting the harbor and you should be fine. Raisho can watch over you."

"Aye," Raisho said.

Juhg surveyed the young sailor and wondered if the captain knew just how much ale Raisho had consumed during the night. Raisho swayed ever so slightly as the ship rocked on the choppy harbor water. Captain Attikus usually wasn't one to miss a detail like that.

"Easy along, sailor," the captain told Raisho. "I'll have the Librarian back in one piece, or things aboard this ship will go hard on you."

"Aye, Cap'n," Raisho responded. "Juhg's me friend. I'll watch over him sharp-like."

Captain Attikus nodded. "See that you do, then. See that you do." He glanced at Juhg. "As for you, stay alive, Librarian Juhg, and let me know what you find out."

"I will, Captain," Juhg said, but a thousand arguments spun through his mind as to why he should not be the one to go.

3

A Dangerous Venture

Wrapped in his cloak against the continuing wind, Juhg scanned the harbor. Without moonslight and in the shadow of the tall mountain peaks surrounding the port, the search for the goblin ship remained daunting.

However, the chill air did serve to bring Raisho back to full alert, in spite of the ale he had consumed. He stood on the lee side of Juhg as they sat huddled on one of the low promontories facing the harbor water. The waves smashed constantly against the rocks at their feet, sending spray and mist up over them as the hollow booms and meaty smacks rolled around them. Men's voices, unhappy men and angry men, sounded all along the four piers that serviced the cargo skiffs. Block and tackles raised the cargo nets filled with crates, barrels, and cloth bags from the skiffs, then swung them over to the waiting shore crews working by lantern light on the piers.

The salt spray stung Juhg's eyes and caused small tears that froze on his cheeks. He wished he wore a beard as some dwellers did, but he had never cared for them. Grandmagister Lamplighter shared that grooming habit as well. But a beard would have offered a little more warmth.

Before leaving *Windchaser,* Juhg had added another layer to his clothing. He'd also retrieved a pair of woolen gloves that he hadn't felt he'd needed that evening. He felt a little warmer in the early morning than he had earlier. The drastic change in temperature after the sun set had surprised him.

Raisho had also dressed more warmly and appeared to be entirely comfortable in a long cloak that hung shapeless and drab from his broad shoulders.

They ate from the cloth bag of apples and cheeses Juhg had appropriated from the larder aboard *Windchaser.* Supper in the tavern had been shortly after the sun disappeared over the Sea of Frozen Teeth. Most of the night had passed since then. Juhg felt certain that cock's crow couldn't be far away.

Nearly all of the lighted windows in the establishments and homes that sat anchored in the craggy mountainside above the harbor lingered in darkness now. Only laborers and possibly thieves remained at work, and Juhg doubted there was much call or good working conditions for the latter. Few outside of the merchants and ships' captains in the harbor boasted anything worth stealing, and those had guards posted.

No armed guard patrolled the streets as in some cities Juhg had seen while in the company of Grandmagister Lamplighter, but the men in Kelloch's Harbor wouldn't have hesitated to take a man's life if that action suited their needs. In fact, Juhg kept expecting to see the corpse of a luckless victim wash up onto shore at any time.

Or maybe a dying man clinging to his last breath, the dweller thought unhappily. In the past, he had seen such things, but he had been gone from them for a long time. Greydawn Moors hadn't featured such dangers, or even fostered thought of them.

Except for the Yondering Docks, he amended silently. Wild men came to port there. The dwarven pirates aboard *One-Eyed Peggie* had shanghaied Grandmagister Lamplighter there to fill out their crew and set the Grandmagister upon the adventures that had changed his life all those years ago.

"Sails," Raisho called softly.

So tired he could barely keep his head up, Juhg stared out into the harbor. Beyond the sheltering circumference of the mountains, the sea raged. White-capped waves swirled high into the air. The spring thaw had been going on for more than a month, but great slabs of ice—some of them as large as trade ships—still meandered down from the north. An unfortunate encounter with an iceberg could sink a ship in heartbeats, possibly take down an entire crew before longboats could be put to sea. Icebergs had claimed ships in that fashion even in the daylight hours. A ship sailing at night took awfully big chances.

But when else would be a good time for a clandestine ship to enter the harbor? Juhg knew the timing couldn't be better. Even with the crews still laboring to shift the arriving and departing goods, no one would pay much attention to a newly arrived ship unless they were told to work the cargo.

"How many sails?" Juhg asked, searching through the tangled masts of the ships already at anchor in the harbor.

"Three." Raisho cautiously made his way up the rocky incline for a better view. "For'ard, aft, an' amidships."

Juhg followed his friend. He didn't want to be far from Raisho's protection, should things turn nasty in the night, but curiosity also pushed him. His need to know things had earned him Grandmagister Lamplighter's good graces on many occasions. Most Librarians tended just to accept facts, but Juhg had always tried to understand most of what he read and be able to correlate those ideas and facts to other things he already understood.

Grandmagister Lamplighter had rewarded attention to learning, not just reading and filing. Knowing the contents of the Vault of All Known Knowledge was one thing, the Grandmagister had contended, but being able to use those contents was the truest test of a Librarian. The Grandmagister did not tell all of his charges that. Not all of the Librarians were interested in that aspect of the knowledge they shepherded; most were content simply to organize and cross-reference the tomes they cared for.

"A three-master." Juhg caught hold of a rocky outcropping and hauled himself up the incline. Stones rattled loose beneath his boots and cascaded down the stony incline. Dweller feet and footwear didn't often go together. Dwellers, by nature, tended to go barefooted, and remained a cobbler's nightmare to fit because their feet tended to be so large and wide. Herby's penchant for going unshod had nothing on a true dweller. "If it's a three-master, Raisho, she could still be a merchanter. Goblins don't often use three-masters because they have to maintain too many crew."

"Aye, but if'n she's a slave ship," Raisho said, "she's a big one."

Goblins preferred small ships. Smaller crews meant less chance of two groups dividing from the original and fighting for control. Smaller cargo space meant that the area filled more quickly and required frequent trips back to spend the crew's ill-gotten gain.

Memory of long, hot hours spent belowdecks in the slaver ships pursued Juhg up the mountainside. He went on all fours, like a mouse hugging the ground while knowing it was in the hawk's eye. He felt that old fear of goblinkin almost overcome him, almost send him into hiding to leave Raisho to fend for himself, to spy alone.

Stop!

Juhg forced himself to breathe when his lungs threatened to seize up. He also made himself keep the young sailor's pace.

Only a few feet farther on, Raisho came to a halt. The young sailor remained within the embrace of shadows that fell along the south side of the northern mountain ridge. He kept one hand on his leather-wrapped cutlass hilt. He stared out to sea across the harbor.

"Do ye see it?" Raisho demanded.

Crouching on the incline, precariously balanced but trusting his dweller's innate surefootedness despite the boots he wore, Juhg followed the line of Raisho's pointing finger.

Out in the Sea of Frozen Teeth, a single ship fought the wind and the waves. Sails streamed from three masts, just as Raisho claimed. Her prow crashed through the tall waves that sent spray up over her bowsprit and rat-  lines.

"Do ye see it?" Raisho asked a little louder.

"Yes," Juhg said. "You don't have to shout."

"I didn't think ye heard me over the surf. It's powerful loud up here."

"Not as loud as you are. My eyes just aren't as good as yours."

"From all that scribblin' an' drawin'," Raisho agreed. "Tasks like that, why, I bet they're unforgivin' hard on a man's eyes. That's why ye can give me the sea an' a favorable wind any day over workin' at a job within walls."

The ship rolled over the unruly waves, bobbing like flotsam instead of cutting a straight course for the protection of the harbor. Lighted lanterns danced aboard the vessel, revealing the crew running about her decks to make certain they weren't about to crash into an iceberg or reef or another ship lost in the night. Once, the lanterns touched a large gleaming ice mass to starboard and the helm made the necessary corrections to pull away from the danger. The sails luffed a bit as the crew adjusted them, not pulled clean and tight as *Windchaser*'s crew kept them.

"Is she a goblin ship?" Juhg asked.

"Can't tell yet," Raisho called back. "But she's definitely a cog. See that round-bellied cut of her?"

Juhg took in the ship's design, memorizing her lines. In time, should he ever want to or should there ever be a cause for it, he knew he could draw the ship in his journal.

A cog was a small three-master. Used primarily along coastal waters and seldom straying out into the deep sea, cogs served as trading ships. A cog's wide-bodied build, like that of a duck, ensured the vessel could carry a lot of cargo for such a short keel length.

"Crew's not green," Raisho said. "They're workin' her sails, right enough, but they're sloppy."

"That doesn't mean it's a goblin ship."

"No. I've seen other ships' crews struggle so. But goblins, Juhg, they ain't ever come natural to the sea."

"Nor do dwarves," Juhg pointed out.

"No," Raisho agreed. "But she definitely ain't no elven ship. Ye can tell that straight enough. An elven ship, she's all grace an' power."

And cursed, Juhg thought unhappily. He shook his thoughts from that.

Rocking precariously, rolling hard to port as the prow cut the cold black sea under her, the ship caught the wind and sailed into the harbor. As the sea leveled inside the rocky breakwater that protected the port, the crew furled the sails. The distance made seeing the crew with any clarity impossible. In the middle of the harbor, the ship dropped anchor and glided to a halt.

"She's sittin' light in the water," Raisho commented. "See how she's driftin' an' fightin' her tether?"

Juhg studied the ship, noting that her masts and yardarms bobbed continuously. "Yes."

"Means she's carryin' little or no cargo."

That fact afforded a little relief. If the ship was a goblin vessel and she was a slaver, dweller slaves—and maybe a few others—would fill her hold. And why would any ship sail into Kelloch's Harbor without something to trade? A crew's provisions cost a lot. Repairs cost even more. If no countertrades were in the offing, the price demanded would be in gold.

"Wouldn't want to try an' get a night's sleep aboard her," Raisho said. "Way she's buckin' an' twistin' even out in them protected waters, why, a man in his hammock would swing all night an' have terrible nightmares of storms an' shipwrecks an' such."

Juhg waited patiently, hopeful that they would identify the ship in the next few minutes as just another merchanter. Dawn would come in a short while. Surely, then he and Raisho could return to *Windchaser* for the night's rest they'd missed.

"We need a glass to see her better," Raisho said a short time later. "Didn't think to ask the cap'n fer one."

Even if they'd possessed a spyglass—which, Juhg admitted in light of tonight's activities—would have earned that name, he doubted they could have seen the ship. As soon as the new arrival came to a rest among the other ships, most of the lanterns faded from sight. Shadows filled the decks.

"Can't see her clear enough from here," Raisho whispered.

"Neither can I," Juhg replied in a low voice, thinking they had done all that they could do. Captain Attikus would surely understand that.

"We're gonna have to get closer."

"No!" Juhg exclaimed.

Raisho sat with his back to the mountainside and looked at Juhg. The young sailor took a deep breath. "Not ye, bookworm. I'll do it. The cap'n, he's gonna want a full report of what's what. I ain't goin' back without one after him tellin' me to come all this way. Cap'n Attikus ain't a man to leave things half done. I ain't plannin' on bein' one neither."

"What are you going to do?"

Nodding toward the unknown ship and grinning wolfishly, Raisho said, "Go out there. Have meself a look an' see if'n I can tell whether that's a goblin ship or not."

"You could get killed," Juhg pointed out.

"Well," Raisho said, a white grin showing, "I plan not to."

With the lateness of the hour, several of the cargo skiffs bobbed at the ends of hawser ropes along the uneven shore. Iron mooring rings hammered into the stone held the lines in place. The crews that had manned the skiffs had left the light craft there for the next day. Some of the skiffs rubbed against the stone surfaces and each other, creating hollow *thuds* that provided part of the undercurrent of noise in the harbor. Throughout all of the noises, the sea lapping at the limestone foundation of the mountains remained constant.

Juhg stood flattened against the mountainside along the ledge that led to the docks. Water had worn the place smooth and straight for the most part, but chisels and hammers had shaped the rest. He stood on a section slick with the salt spray and seaweed the tide had brought in.

"This could be a bad mistake," Juhg whispered.

"Usually," Raisho said, "mistakes don't come any other way." He paused. "Except maybe . . . worse."

Juhg forced himself to swallow the lump at the back of his throat. He knew that Captain Attikus would chastise them for taking such a chance, but at the same time he knew that the captain would appreciate any news they brought about the ship.

If they got news and didn't end up in chains or dead.

Shadows from a nearby merchant ship covered the skiff area. In the darkness fostered between the moonless night and the black sea, Juhg knew their chances of being seen taking one of the small craft were slim. Most of the ship's crews had turned in, either drunk from a night spent in the taverns or worn-out from long hours laboring with the cargo and setting their ships to rights.

Raisho untied the line holding one of the skiffs. Pulling the rope, he tugged the skiff to the stone shelf where they stood. He gripped the skiff and guided it alongside. Water slapped the hull like hollow drumbeats. The lanterns at either end of the craft clanked at the ends of the short chains that held them to the posts.

"Wait," Juhg said.

Raisho looked over at him.

"You shouldn't go out there alone," Juhg whispered.

After a brief hesitation, Raisho said, "I have to admit, I don't fancy it none. In case there's trouble."

"You could get caught."

"Maybe I'll get seen, but catchin' me?" Raisho shook his head. "No, now, that's a whole 'nother tale to tell."

"What I mean," Juhg said, regretting his words but knowing he couldn't live with himself any other way, "is that I'm coming with you."

Raisho scowled. "That's not a good idea."

"Neither is going in the first place."

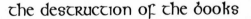

"I'm able to take care of meself, bookworm. Now, ye, on the other hand—" Raisho stopped, kind enough not to point out that Juhg lacked in the area of fighting prowess.

"Two are better than one." Juhg forced himself to step away from the shelter of the stone. He carefully crossed through the maze of lines before him, joining Raisho. Water lapped up over the edge and swirled around his ankles. Thankfully, the boots remained watertight, but the water was cold and penetrated the thick socks he wore. "You take too many risks. I won't do that. I'm more careful than you are."

A frown twisted Raisho's features. "I'd rather see ye out of harm's way."

Juhg looked at his friend. "And that's how I'd prefer to see you."

Grinning, shaking his head, Raisho said, "Well, then, ain't we a right an' fine pair?"

"If you go, you go with me," Juhg said, hoping his friend would back out. At the very least, Raisho would recognize the danger of taking him aboard. "We could wait on the shore and see who comes off that ship."

"An' if'n they don't come? Or if'n they don't come till daybreak, when maybe they can see us right back? When maybe they're rested up again?"

Juhg didn't have an answer for that.

Pulling the skiff hard against the stone shelf, Raisho said, "It's better this way, bookworm. I'd prefer facin' 'em while they're all tuckered out a mite from fightin' the sea." He patted the skiff. "I'll hold 'er. Ye just step aboard."

With definite reluctance, Juhg ignored the fearful clamoring inside him and stepped into the skiff. Short-legged as he was, he wasn't able to put his foot in the center of the craft and keep it balanced. The skiff threatened to slide away. Raisho cursed quietly but held on to the little boat.

Gingerly, Juhg moved to the center of the skiff, then to the prow. He had never liked small boats. Ships, at least, carried enough mass and solid footing to inspire a little confidence.

Raisho stepped aboard easily, hardly stirring the skiff. He took the bench seat in the bow and motioned Juhg farther toward the prow. "Light the lantern there. Then take up that pole an' shove us off."

"We're going to be seen." Juhg took out the tinderbox he carried.

"We don't light these lanterns, we're gonna get noticed somethin' fierce out there." Raisho started removing the oars from the oarlocks.

Realizing the logic in Raisho's words, Juhg bent to the task. He raised the slim tube of hurricane glass to expose the wick. The thick stink of cargiff oil stuffed his nostrils.

Juhg struck sparks with his flint and steel, then blew an ember to life on the wick. A yellow glow, much too cheery for anything like the clandestine work they were doing, at least to Juhg's way of thinking, sprang easily to life. He crossed the skiff with the lantern and lit the one aft.

"Fair enough," Raisho said, settling both oars into the water with slight splashes. "Now, ye just set yerself an' let's be about our business."

Nervously, Juhg took an oar from the prow and sat on his knees. He cast off the prow line, then paddled to bring the skiff around to face the open water. Once he'd turned the boat toward the middle of the harbor, Raisho gripped both oars and pulled. The skiff lurched forward with surprising speed, skating over the tops of the incoming waves.

Remaining on his knees and paddling, Juhg aided in guiding the skiff. With the skill that he had, Raisho could have done the job himself, but the forward oar made steering easier. Salt spray broke over the skiff's prow and coated Juhg, stinging his eyes and nostrils. Mercifully, the traveling cloak kept him dry enough. The lantern bobbed and waved overhead.

Voices carried farther and faster over water. Juhg had become aware of that at the Yondering Docks while learning the rudiments of sailing. Snatches of conversations reached the dweller's ears. Judging from most of what he heard, Kelloch's Harbor held a number of cutthroats and pirates tonight.

Or maybe they're just sailors, Juhg told himself. *Maybe all these tales of violence and robbery and sea monsters are balderdash.*

But he knew that wasn't true. The constant threat of pirates, murderers, sea monsters, and evil wizards kept Greydawn Moors hidden from the rest of the world. And the possibility of a book in goblin hands caused Juhg to reach inside himself for the courage he needed to take the trip with Raisho. That, and his friendship with the young sailor.

Surprisingly, none of the few scattered sailors standing watch on the ships around the harbor paid the skiff any mind. A few other cargo skiffs plied the waters, their lanterns waving as gaily as the one above Juhg's head.

The dweller watched the suspect ship's decks. Few shadows moved there, and only a few lanterns marked the ship's presence. He didn't understand that. A crew just coming into harbor usually stood at the ship's rails to see the other ships and what was available. When the captain released them from duty, except for a guard crew, they headed for the taverns.

" 'Ware there, bookworm," Raisho called softly.

In almost the same instant, Juhg spotted the soft lantern glow that sprouted up amidships. As he watched, goblin sailors climbed from belowdecks.

The goblins stood almost as tall as humans, provided the goblins didn't stand hunched over as they normally did. Almost as broad across the shoulders as dwarves, goblins tended toward skinny and fat, depending on how high up one was in whatever hierarchy one belonged to. The higher up in the hierarchy, where the spoils grew more plentiful, the fatter the goblin.

The lantern light ghosted over the goblin sailors, adding a glowing sheen to the splotchy skin that somewhat masked the horrid gray-green natural hue. Triangular heads held wide jaws and broad, flat skulls that tapered to narrow chins the same blunt shape as a leatherworker's punch. Spiky black hair covered the heads, matched by the spiky beards the males and the females wore, as well as the tufts of hair that jutted from the huge, wilted ears that framed the fierce features as forcefully as bookends.

 Goblin children possessed faces that nothing could love, not even goblin parents. As a general rule, goblinkin children were uglier than the mothers and fathers. The little creatures grew up hateful and jealous, and remained so. Only Lord Kharrion had ever talked the goblinkin hordes into setting aside traditional feuds and enmity long enough to become an army.

The goblins dressed as sailors, wearing breeches and shirts, but the creatures could never have passed for anything other than goblins. Swords and knives hung from waist sashes. The sailors spoke in goblinkin tongue: rapid clicks and whistles that made them sound like animals.

Juhg tried to make out the splinters of bone and beads woven into the goblins' whiskers. Tribes and clans marked members by the patterns and number of beads and bones used in beards. Generally, the bones came from humans, elves, and dwarves the creatures had fought and killed.

Or humans, elves, and dwarves the goblins caught unawares and murdered, Juhg amended. None of the bones were supposed to be those of dwellers. No goblinkin would ever admit to using a dweller's bones, and that possibility was used as a taunt when goblins argued, but Juhg felt certain the foul creatures did use dweller bones for barbaric decorations.

Despite his efforts, Juhg did not recognize the designs in the whiskers of the ship's crew. Then he realized that Raisho was calling to him. He glanced over his shoulder.

"To port," Raisho urged with quiet desperation. "To port. The ship there. Quick-like."

Taking a firmer grip on the oar in his hands, Juhg pulled the skiff toward the nearby ship. His heart hammered. He felt the iron manacles clamped around his wrists and ankles as if they were still there. He also felt the rough wooden handle of the miner's pick that he'd carried for all those long years of his captivity. His back still bore scars from the whips of the harsh goblin taskmasters and tormentors that had run the mine shifts.

"Back, now," Raisho called. "Ease off on her an' pull her about, now."

Skillfully, due in large part to Raisho's abilities, the skiff tucked in close to the two-master cog. The ship's deck rocked on the tide twelve feet overhead.

"An' blow out that lantern."

Juhg lifted the hurricane glass and blew out the fluttering flame. Nervously, he peered upward, wondering if they'd alerted the ship's crew standing watch over the vessel. If they were spotted, he felt certain the hue and cry of alarm would fill the harbor. At the very least, they would be challenged about their presence.

"Be easy," Raisho whispered. He sat in the skiff's bow, his attention on the goblin ship. His sword lay naked across his knees.

"They're goblins." Juhg kept his voice low and tried to keep his fear under control.

"Aye. I see that, right enough."

"We can go back now."

Raisho nodded.

"Captain Attikus only wished to know if the ship belonged to goblins." Juhg wanted to be back aboard *Windchaser*, snug and warm and safe beneath his cover in his hammock. He trembled in the cold night air, but he knew it wasn't because of the chill.

"Aye," Raisho agreed. "That he did, an' he will as soon as we tell him."

The goblins talked in excited, or possibly angry, voices. A fat goblin in an ill-fitting captain's uniform stepped onto the deck and the crew fell silent. The captain talked for a moment, then the crew swung longboats over the ship's sides on block-and-tackle falls and plopped them into the water.

"An' once we tell the cap'n," Raisho asked, "what do ye think he'll want to know next?"

Glumly, already knowing what his friend was thinking, Juhg kept silent. The splashes of the goblin oars hitting the water as the crews filled the boats rolled over him.

"I'm thinkin'," Raisho said, "that the cap'n will want to know if'n there's truly a book aboard that ship."

"He will," Juhg agreed.

"The way I see it, there's two ways the cap'n can find that out. Mayhap he'll keep 'Chaser here fer a few more days, then follow that ship out into open water an' take her."

Juhg envisioned that with dread. Fighting ship-to-ship was bloody business.

"Or," Raisho said.

With stomach-sinking conviction, Juhg knew that his friend wasn't talking about the paddle in his hands. He also felt certain he knew what the young sailor was about to suggest.

"—or I steal aboard that ship after the crew's leave," Raisho finished, "an' look around to see what's what."

"That would be foolish."

"Ye say 'foolish.' I say *brave*. Mayhap I can keep the cap'n from riskin' 'Chaser an' her crew from takin' this ship later if'n there's no reason to."

"If we get caught, no matter what you call it, we're just as dead."

"Aye." Raisho grinned. "But only if'n we're caught, bookworm."

Juhg swallowed.

"An' it won't be 'we,'" Raisho continued. "It'll be me. An' I won't get caught neither. I'll just ask ye to mind this here boat whilst I'm gone to look fer that book."

Juhg turned and stared at his friend. "Do you even know what a book looks like?"

Raisho scowled and watched the goblins rowing for the piers. He looked back at Juhg. "A lot like that one ye keep scribblin' in."

"No. That's just one way a book can look." Juhg shook his head.

"There's any number of ways an author can assemble a book. Before Lord Kharrion assembled the goblinkin and set to burning libraries and destroying books, authors used all kinds of mediums to record their histories, their philosophical discourses, and their texts concerning the sciences."

"A book is a book," Raisho growled defensively. "Yers wasn't the only one what I ever seen."

"But that's all you've seen," Juhg argued. "You haven't been trained to look for books as I have."

Grandmagister Lamplighter trained Juhg in that task. Seeing that Raisho either didn't grasp his point or chose to ignore it, Juhg threw his verbal sails into the air and tried another tack.

"Did you know that the Kupper elves used to live in this hospitable place?"

Raisho didn't answer.

"They did," Juhg went on. "Before Lord Kharrion, before the Cataclysm reshaped the known world, the Kupper elves lived along the shore of the Frozen Ocean."

"Elves live in forests," Raisho grumbled. "Ever'one knows that."

"Not always," Juhg said. He was surprised at his friend's limited knowledge of the world. Then he reminded himself how narrow his own knowledge of the world had been until Wi—until Grandmagister Lamplighter had taken him into the Vault of All Known Knowledge and begun his true education. "The Kupper elves divided their lives between the sea and the forest. They wrote books with shells and pebbles, and their language was laid out in color and shape and texture and sound."

"I never heard of such a thing."

"The Tordalian humans," Juhg went on, "wove their books into carpets and tapestries. "Their language spoke through thread length and thickness, through skillfully tied knots and patterns. Khroder dwarves carved obelisks with their picks that interlock so tightly no seams can be seen. Reading a Khroder dwarven book requires a knowing hand, and the meaning of the sequence of the pieces, as well as the icons carved on their surfaces, tell the message."

Raisho grunted in disgust.

"So you see," Juhg said, "you might not know the book for what it is even if you see it."

Growling an oath, Raisho shook his head. "Means I got no choice, then, bookworm."

Juhg felt a little relieved, then felt guilty almost at once. He should want to know about the book as much as Captain—

"Ye're gonna have to go with me," Raisho said.

4

The Book

Juhg stared through the shadows at Raisho. The young sailor gestured again, pointing out the length of rusted anchor chain that ran from the goblin ship's stern. Reluctantly, Juhg slowly stood in the cargo skiff and took hold of the rough links of the chain. He started climbing, hauling himself up the chain with relative ease.

Under the cover of the night and with the skiff lantern out, he and Raisho had quietly rowed to the goblin ship undetected. Whatever skeleton crew, and Juhg hated the images that term automatically summoned to mind after having read some of the selections from Hralbomm's Wing that Grandmagister Lamplighter had recommended, remained aboard appeared uncaring about the security of the ship.

Of course, Juhg said, *few people try to sneak aboard a goblin ship.* He grabbed another handful of rusty chain and pulled himself up farther.

Only a short time later, he reached the railing. His arms ached and his body quivered from exertion. He held on with his cramped fingers, his nose barely hung over the bottom rung, and peered across the deck.

The huge ship's wheel stood abandoned, locked in

place by a wooden bar and leather tethers. The furled sails along the 'yards above rattled in the wind. Three goblins stood in the hesitant glow of the ship's forward lanterns. A pot of soup, so ill-smelling that Juhg's stomach threatened to turn, hung from a nearby railing. The goblins filled bowls of the vile concoction, and—occasionally—bones crunched as the creatures chewed.

"Well?" Raisho demanded in a hoarse voice from below.

With his feet wrapped around the anchor chain and one hand securely on the deck, Juhg turned and held up three fingers.

"Three guards?" Raisho asked, rising to a standing position in the skiff. "That's it?"

Juhg put his forefinger to his lips. "That's all I see."

Raisho growled a curse. He rigged a quick harness over his back to hold his cutlass, then tied the skiff to the anchor chain, and climbed.

Mastering the fear that resonated within him, Juhg hauled himself over the ship's side and remained within the stern deck's shadows. He crouched, thankful he was so small and so slight. But he knew that Raisho didn't have those natural attributes. He dreaded his big friend's arrival.

Staying in the skiff, Juhg realized, would have been so much safer. But he knew his own argument about whether Raisho would have recognized a book if the tome were rendered in any other fashion than the written page held true.

And if there was a book aboard the foul ship, Juhg felt beholden to get it. During the Cataclysm, the Old Ones first fashioned the dwellers, rendering them meek and small and weak so that they could better hide the books from Lord Kharrion. He had his heritage to live up to, as well as his Librarian training.

He calmed himself, drawing his breath in through his nose and pushing it out through his mouth, using a technique developed by Mathoth Kilerion, a noted human tactician who had raised fierce guerrilla armies to face the goblin hordes when Lord Kharrion had threatened to dominate the world.

The effort worked a little, but Juhg still felt frightened. At least, he felt a little better until he spotted Raisho's hand appear and grab the railing. Lantern light glinted against his dark eyes and the silver hoops in his ears.

The three goblins guarding the ship stayed occupied with conversation and the meal.

Silent as a cat, Raisho vaulted the railing and landed on bare feet on the stern deck. He drew the cutlass in one smooth motion, reversing his grip on the handle and keeping the blade low. No light reflected from the blade due to the way the metal had been cast. The cutlass was a fighting man's weapon, and Raisho took pride in his possession.

"Captain's quarters," Raisho whispered.

Before Juhg could object, the young sailor took two lithe steps and vaulted the railing from the stern deck leading to the main deck amidships. He disappeared below the stern deck's edge at once.

Heart in his throat but determined not to let Raisho down, Juhg dropped to his hands and knees and scuttled to the stairs leading down to the main deck. He expected to hear startled shouts from goblins that Raisho might have inadvertently surprised with his bold move.

Juhg halted at the railing beside the steps, his hands wrapped around the rungs, and peered down.

Raisho was already on the move, racing for the door set against the stern castle. Broad in the beam as the goblin ship was, the vessel afforded larger quarters there, as well as a steadier ride across the rough seas. Captains always kept their private quarters there, if the ship was large enough to provide the necessary space.

Pausing at the door, Raisho glanced up. He pointed to his eyes with two fingers, then in the direction of the goblin guards.

Juhg understood immediately and nodded. He hunkered down in the shelter of the stairs, staying high enough to watch the goblins.

Raisho sheathed his cutlass between his shoulders, then knelt and removed something from the rolled-top boots he wore. He leaned into the door and worked on the locks. After a moment, he looked back up at Juhg with a grin on his face. He motioned to Juhg, calling him down.

Juhg's hopes that the locks would force Raisho to give up sunk. He wouldn't have been too badly disappointed if the locks had proven too much for Raisho. The dweller forced himself up again, crouching on trembling knees as he went down the steps. Once on the main deck, he joined Raisho at the door.

"I see that Herby isn't the only one with dubious skills," Juhg whispered.

Shrugging, Raisho replied, "A knack. Something I picked up in me youth. Merely a passin' fancy." He drew his cutlass again, then pushed against the door.

Juhg remained to one side of the door. His heart seemed like it was going to explode. He fully expected something to rush at them from the darkness of the captain's quarters.

"Can ye see anythin'?" Raisho whispered.

A dweller's vision at night, like an elf's and a dwarf's, was better than a human's. That was one compensation the Old Ones had endowed the other races with after providing humans with such a capacity for reproducing and tastes for conquering and exploring. At least, Vodel Haug had put forth that possibility in his *Treatise on the Races: The Lasting Impact of Wars and Poetry.*

Hesitantly, Juhg peered into the cabin. "No goblins," he announced.

"Good." Raisho strode into the room with his blade in his fist. "Come on."

Juhg forced himself to follow. Cold wind blew in from the sea and crossed the back of his neck. He shivered.

Raisho lifted the glass on the lantern hanging on the wall.

"What are you doing?" Juhg demanded.

"I can't search this room in the dark." Raisho pulled up the wick.

Hurriedly, Juhg closed the door and stood with his back to it. He watched in disbelief as Raisho used his own tinderbox to light the lantern.

Yellow light filled the room and brought Raisho's face out of the darkness in gleaming relief. Smoke twisted in tiny threads up to the cabin's low ceiling and pooled there briefly before spreading and thinning away. Cargiff oil wasn't completely smoke-free. After spending hours trapped in a room lit by lanterns aboard *Windchaser,* Juhg wistfully remembered the sweet smell of glimmerworm juice that lighted the halls within the Vault of All Known Knowledge. Now, however, he was glad for the oil stink because it helped cover up the stench of the goblin captain's quarters.

Buckets of bones and refuse sat at the foot of the captain's unmade bed. Weapons adorned the wall, and Juhg knew from past experience that goblin commanders and leaders all had stories to tell of the weapons in the creatures' possession, of how the goblin had killed warriors in glorious battle. Most of the weapons came from junk the goblins picked up and passed off as trophies of war. Cloaks and outerwear lay strewn across the room and filled four sea chests.

Raisho wasted no time searching the room. The young warrior plowed through the personal belongings in short order.

mel odom

Juhg took a more sedate approach, even though a screaming voice in the back of his mind kept worrying him with the possibility of discovery. He didn't cover as much of the room as Raisho did, but he was thorough. Unfortunately, that thoroughness required coming in contact with the crawling vermin that lived within the goblin captain's things.

"I don't see how these creatures can live like this." Raisho dusted an army of insects from his clothing. The bugs crunched underfoot. "If'n I was a bug, I'd choose somewheres else to live, I would."

"Ships are worse than the houses goblins choose to live in," Juhg said. "Goblinkin can move from house to house, abandoning each in turn, or live out in the forest if the tribe chooses. But a ship is a considerable investment." He shook meal weevils from a pile of garments. "Goblins won't just leave a ship because they're too hard to replace. The creatures don't build them, and dweller slaves don't know enough to build them."

Raisho glowered at the room. "There's no book here."

"There are often hiding places." Juhg got down on his hands and knees. "Didn't you notice that we also didn't find any valuables?"

"Ye mean, aside from them dog bones what's in them buckets by the bed?" Raisho's tone was sarcastic.

Juhg shuddered. "You didn't look closely at the bones." He ran his hands across the dirty wooden floor.

"I looked close enough."

"Those aren't all dog bones or rabbit bones or cat bones or fish bones." Juhg shoved more refuse out of his way. He forced himself to breathe through his open mouth so the stench wouldn't gag him. "There are also dweller bones in that bucket."

Looking into the bucket, Raisho cursed.

Even though seeing the bones of his people in the bucket hadn't surprised Juhg, simply speaking the fact left him chilled and even more nauseous.

"Goblins are a blight," Raisho whispered in a voice hoarse with disbelief. "Ought to kill 'em all."

Even after everything he had been through, Juhg couldn't find it within himself to be so hateful, even toward goblins. The creatures remained feared and ferocious enemies, but Juhg would rather have seen goblinkin put in places where the tribes couldn't prey on the rest of the world. Before Lord Kharrion had organized and led the goblinkin, the creatures hadn't multiplied to such vast numbers or lived in areas that could sustain a tribe well enough to allow those large numbers to thrive.

Rapping against the wooden floor with his knuckles, Juhg located a hollow spot beneath the planks. "Bring the lantern here."

"Ye found something." Raisho caught the lantern up in one hand and approached.

"Perhaps." Juhg dug at the plank with his deft fingers. Calluses covered his fingertips from years of working with a quill. He'd taught himself to write and draw with both hands, something that few Librarians at any level could do. He sought for unevenness but couldn't find it.

Without a word, Raisho slipped one of his boot knives free and handed the weapon over.

Juhg pressed the finely honed point between two of the suspect planks and levered one of them up. The plank rose from the floor with a sucking noise caused by the semisoft tar that lined the fitting.

"A neat enough little hidey-hole," Raisho commented as he moved the lantern over to reveal the contents of the hidden space.

Once uncovered, the hidden space was nearly as long as Juhg's arm and as wide across as the span of his hand. Light gleamed over a handful of silver coins, two gold ones, a few pieces of jewelry, and three small black cloth bags.

"Not exactly a treasure trove," Raisho whispered, grinning. "But 'twill do good enough." He reached into the hole.

Alarmed, Raisho grabbed his friend's hand. "What are you doing?"

"Helpin' ourselves to a little windfall, of course."

"Stealing from the goblin captain?"

Raisho looked puzzled. "Unless it's some other creature what hides its belongin's in the cap'n's quarters, then aye, I'm takin' it from the cap'n."

"But . . . but . . . that's stealing!"

"Course it is. Now, leave go of me hand so I can be about it an' we can be on our way."

"We didn't come here to steal."

"An' if'n there'd been a book in this here hidey-hole, then?" Raisho raised his eyebrows.

"But there is no book."

"So maybe the story about the book was a false alarm, right enough, but I can't see any reason why we shouldn't be a-helpin' ourselves to a goblin cap'n's ill-got gain. All that ye're a-lookin' at there, why, it's probably twice-stole already. Us takin' it will at least put everythin' here back out of goblinkin hands where it belongs."

The young sailor's argument held flaws, but Juhg was too enervated to sort through it all now. He released his friend's hand.

Raisho started scooping the contents from the hiding place. "Whyn't ye busy yerself tryin' to find another one of these?"

Knowing that neither of them could leave the captain's quarters till the room was thoroughly searched, Juhg turned his thoughts from what Raisho was doing and concentrated on finding more hidden areas. He rapped plank after plank with his knuckles.

"Well, now," Raisho said with pleasant surprise. "Looks like we'll be havin' new wealth to continue our merchantin' investments."

Glancing over his shoulder, Juhg stared at the jewels spilled across Raisho's rough palm. Even from the distance, Juhg noted the flaws in the gems. "That isn't the fortune you think that it is. Several of those stones aren't worth much."

Raisho closed his hand over them and grinned with true larceny. "We'll be leavin' with more'n we came with. That'll make me happy enough."

Juhg only hoped that leaving proved as easy as his friend described the effort. He continued his search.

"Well," Raisho said, "this'n is a superstitious one, right enough." He held out a fistful of carved toe bones blackened with runes.

A knot of distaste rose to the back of Juhg's throat. He knew where the goblins had gotten the toe bones.

"An' treachery, it appears, weren't never far from his heart neither." Raisho revealed the stoppered glass bottles of green-blue powder. "Know what this is?" He shook the bottle, causing the contents to slide back and forth.

"Ratter's rot," Juhg answered without hesitation. "Poison. Some goblinkin captains use it to poison the water supply of the ships when those creatures intend to cut part of the crew out of the cargo profits." Even the goblinkin didn't condone such practice.

Raisho carefully replaced the bottle of poison in the cloth bag he'd gotten it from. "An' ye were a-worryin' yerself about a little bit of stealin' from such a despicable creature." He shook his head and clucked.

Only a few minutes later, he was convinced that the hiding place he'd found was the only one in the room. Raisho's agreement with the assessment relieved him.

"Ready, then, bookworm?" Raisho asked.

"To go back to the ship?" Juhg asked hopefully.

Raisho grinned. "Now, I have to admit that I'm sorely tempted to go knockin' timbers throughout the rest of this vessel, especially since the cap'n an' his crew seem bound an' determined to go tavern crawlin'."

Although the taverns along Kelloch's Harbor never closed as long as coin purses remained open, Juhg knew they had no idea how long the goblinkin would be gone. "The goblinkin could be back at any moment. The creatures could already be on the way back." Images of the goblins even now rowing for the vessel filled his head and reignited the terror that stayed poised to scream through him.

"Aye," Raisho admitted ruefully. He took one of the cloth bags from the pouch at his hip. "But maybe we can make a trip to the ship's water barrels afore we leave."

Horror dried the back of Juhg's throat. He hated the goblins with fierce passion, but the thought of pouring ratter's rot into the water barrels to poison the crew made him nauseous.

"No," he said, and he wanted to point out that getting off the ship in one piece was the most important thing they could do. Captain Attikus needed to know that the goblin ship held no book as Herby's cooper had said. *Maybe it was only a story.* But he knew that Raisho would see through his falsehood.

Raisho grimaced as he surveyed the bag of ratter's rot. "Those goblinkin deserve it. But I've got no stomach for killin' like that either." He tossed the bag to the captain's ill-kept bed, then blew out the lantern's flame.

Plunged once more into the inky blackness that filled the captain's personal quarters, Juhg stood by the door. In the space of two drawn breaths, the foul odor of the cabin—no longer held at bay by the burning lantern wick—flooded his nostrils.

Raisho eased the door open and peered out. Positioned below his tall friend, Juhg peered out as well.

No one walked the main deck. Above the top of the prow deck railing, the heads of the goblins remained together near the lanterns. All of the creatures were accounted for.

Without a word, Raisho opened the door and stepped out onto the deck. He held his cutlass in one hand and waved to Juhg with the other.

Pushing his fear down tightly inside him, Juhg ran for the stairs to the stern deck. Fleet of foot, he reached the top quickly, feeling the vibration of Raisho on his heels.

Lantern light moved out onto the deck from one of the hatches leading belowships.

Juhg froze, watching terrified as a tall robed figure pushed the lantern ahead as he stepped out onto the deck. Before Juhg could recover, Raisho put a big hand between his shoulder blades and pushed him down onto the deck. He thumped, but the sound was lost in the thudding of his heart roaring in his ears. Raisho lay on top of Juhg, holding them both down behind the railing.

Spindly and cadaverously thin, the figure paused as if scenting the air. Arcane symbols decorated the man's robes. Lantern light caused the symbols to glow, awarding them an inner fire, or perhaps only revealing the power they already contained.

A human! Juhg recognized the ancient man at once for what he was. He cringed a little more. Humans and goblins sometimes traded goods, generally when the goblins found something the tribe couldn't use and the humans wanted it. More often than not, the only humans who spent much time in the company of goblins were outlaws and brigands. Even thievery couldn't make friends of the two races.

But a human traveling in the company of goblins? That was the mark of a wizard who practiced evil and dark magicks, the kind that got them banished from human cities and towns. Dark magick was blood magick, and blood magic, required sacrifices to maintain power.

Juhg's heart hammered inside his chest as he surveyed the spindly figure and hoped that the wizard didn't ferret out Raisho or him. Wizards possessed keen senses of smell and knowing. During his time at the Vault of All Known Knowledge, Juhg had witnessed the Grandmagister's wizard friend Craugh employ such powers.

Not much escaped wizards.

But wizards also meant something else, Juhg knew. Wherever wizards were, so too were books. If not tomes and treatises written by others, a wizard at least carried his own spell book. Those volumes often borrowed sections and passages from other books.

Not every Librarian at the Vault read from wizards' spell books that had fallen into their hands over the years. Reading spellcraft was a demanding and risky bit of business. Grandmagister Lamplighter and a handful of First Level Librarians told stories about those who had mistakenly read from spell books without first recognizing them for what they were. Librarians had gone up in flames, turned into toads, or had vanished—never to be heard again. There were a lot of other nasty surprises, but those were the main ones that thundered through Juhg's feverish mind.

The wizard went forward. He climbed the stairs to the prow slowly, as if lifting his feet was all that he could do.

The three goblins at the prow moved away from the old man. The creatures' hands drifted to weapons, but it was obvious the goblinkin feared the wizard.

The wizard spoke in a dry voice and looked toward Kelloch's Harbor. One of the goblins answered him. The wind blew the wizard's beard and long hair about. Whatever the question and whatever the answer, the wizard seemed content to stand in the open.

Raisho tapped Juhg on the shoulder.

The unexpected contact almost made Juhg yelp in surprise. He clapped both hands over his mouth in an effort to still the sound before it escaped his throat. He looked up at Raisho clad in the darkness.

"Belowdecks," Raisho whispered.

Keeping his hands in place because he didn't trust himself, Juhg shook his head. Belowdecks was the *last* place he wanted to go—or they needed to be.

"That's a wizard." Raisho pointed at the old man. "Wizards have books."

Juhg couldn't argue with that.

Light from the stern lanterns highlighted Raisho's black skin, warming the color to dark molasses. He stared at the prow and let out a tense breath. "Then stay here. Yell a warnin' if I need one." He looked at Juhg. "Can ye do that?"

Despite the fear that rattled his insides, Juhg knew he couldn't let his friend go alone. The same reasoning—that Raisho might not recognize a book if he saw one—held now.

Juhg forced his hands down. "I'll go."

"Then step lively." Raisho shifted toward the stern castle stairs. "An' don't be heavy-footed. Might as well toss up a shot of Grekham's Fire if'n ye do."

Grekham's Fire isn't exactly the best comparison, Juhg thought. Humans had invented Grekham's Fire. As a race, humans were known for their ability to bend the wind and water to their will, and for their borderline suicidal impulses for creating weapons of war. Elves and dwarves contented themselves with skills and a few magical weapons, goblins took whatever they could find, but humans went out of their way to invent arsenals that were as potentially dangerous to themselves or their compatriots as they were to their enemies. Grekham's Fire was a prime example.

Designed for catapult loads for siege missions against castles and fortified cities, Grekham's Fire was a concoction of pitch, sulfur, suet, and lye soap. Formed in large balls for catapults or in fist-sized chunks to rain like hail, the loads were fired and hurled against their opponents. When great balls of Grekham's Fire landed on buildings, flames spread throughout.

However, the catapult loads didn't always stay lit, and using the loads also proved dangerous because the flames frayed the catapults and caused launches to go awry so that often the loads landed on nearby armies. In addition, many times the warriors assigned to loading and firing ended up drenched in the stinking concoction and going up in flames.

When the human navies sought to use catapults loaded with Grekham's Fire at sea, the disasters grew even larger. There was often nowhere to go from a burning ship in the middle of the ocean.

By the time Juhg got to his feet, Raisho had already reached the stairwell. The dweller hurried after his friend. He stayed so low his knuckles sometimes knocked against the ship's deck and dragged.

The wizard continued staring toward the town nestled into the crooks and crannies of the ragged-edge shore while the three goblinkin watched on fearfully.

Amidships, Raisho stepped into the hold the wizard had emerged from. Juhg followed. His large feet found the ladder leading down into the hold with accustomed grace. After so many days at sea, crawling through the innards of *Windchaser,* he moved by instinct.

Most cargo ships of similar size tended toward a similar layout. With a ship's shape, there were only so many designs that allowed comfortable usage of all available space.

The goblin ship held three decks. The upper, the waist, and the hold. Cargo went into the hold, jammed in to fill every conceivable space. Crew's quarters occupied either end of the mid-decks. General sailors rode crammed into the prow, where the ride aboard was less generous. In the event of rough seas, the prow oftentimes took a beating.

Cabin space for officers and for important passengers occupied the stern.

Raisho immediately turned his attention to the stern. He kept his sword in hand as he went.

Fearfully, Juhg trailed behind the big sailor. He took heart in Raisho's reasoning. The wizard's quarters had to be located in the stern, but Juhg didn't know how the man had withstood the stench that permeated the ship.

Perhaps he used a spell, Juhg reasoned. He opened his own mouth to breathe and only felt the impact of the stink lessened in a small degree. His bare feet left tracks in the creeping sludge and slime that coated the deck. At that moment, he was grateful for the care and work that Captain Attikus put into *Windchaser.*

Never once, even with all the cargo the ship shifted, did Juhg remember *Windchaser's* decks ever feeling like the grunge he now walked through. He felt certain that his poor feet would never be clean again or be free of the putrescence of goblinkin filth. At the very least, it would take a flensing knife to whittle the flesh from his foot bones to—

Raisho stopped at a locked door. Two others he had tried had opened at his touch. He produced his lockpick again and felt for the lock.

"Careful," Juhg said, striving not to let his teeth chatter. "There might not just be a lock on the door. The wizard could have an alarm warded onto the wood. Arch-mage Kulkinny in *The Foul Master of Heart's Bane* often left his door ensorcelled to tell him when someone tried to—"

The lock clicked open.

Raisho froze.

For a moment, Juhg thought a spell had struck his friend and rooted him to the spot. He didn't know what he was going to do. He couldn't carry his friend to safety and he couldn't leave him either.

Then Raisho shifted and pushed the door open with his free hand. He kept his cutlass crossed in front of him to parry any attack that might come.

Drawn by the innate curiosity that had lured so many dwellers to their doom, Juhg peered around his friend. Peeking into places where he hadn't been, *especially* if he wasn't supposed to go there, was catnip to a dweller.

Warm yellow light filled the small room. Opposite the door, a sagging bed occupied the wall beneath built-in shelves. Robes, some of them plain and unadorned, shared space on the right with other, more wizardly, garb. A heavy leather traveling cloak showing years of hard use lay across a small chair.

A desk sat on the left side of the room. A narrow trough held a capped inkwell and a sleeve of goose quills.

There were no books in sight, but Juhg's interest peaked instantly. Whenever you find ink and quills, books are not far away. Forgetting himself for the moment in the fresh flush of discovery, he moved forward around Raisho.

The big sailor stopped him with a hand on his shoulder.

"Hold up there, bookworm," Raisho ordered in a hoarse whisper. "Ye don't know what mayhap be waitin' on ye in that room. An' it were yer own warnin' ye were all set to forget about."

Chastised, Juhg put aside the excitement that screamed through him and stopped at the door. He stared longingly at the desk, wondering what secrets the drawers might hold. Still, a wizard's quarters couldn't be a safe place.

With cautious care, Raisho stepped across the threshold and into the room. He looked almost surprised that something didn't immediately leap on him.

"Didn't expect it to be this easy," he said.

And you may have just cursed us with that bold statement, Juhg thought. But he didn't retreat. "We probably haven't got much time."

Raisho nodded. "I'm likin' this less as we go."

"There's a desk."

"I don't see no book."

"It's probably inside the desk. The wizard wouldn't leave it out where something could happen to it."

Raisho scowled. "Like as not, he wouldn't leave it in a desk where it can be so easily pilfered neither."

"The goblins wouldn't want it. They'd have no use for it."

"They could sell it." As always when it found its own way, Raisho's mind turned to profits.

"And risk a wizard's wrath?"

"Which is what ye an' me are doin' here now, I might remind ye."

The reminder, Juhg thought, was a very unhappy one, though timely. He gazed at the desk. "Let me try the desk. I can be very careful."

Raisho hesitated.

"You can keep watch at the door," Juhg pointed out.

"An' we'd probably be the better for it," Raisho said. "At least, I can keep me mind on lookin' out for goblins an' the like."

Juhg ignored the comment. Quelling his fears, he crossed to the desk. He focused on the evil ways of the goblinkin and those who worked with them. No book should ever be kept by goblins.

He ran his fingers over the desk, searching with nimble alertness for tricks and traps. Wizards were a crafty and canny lot by nature, and the more evil they were, the more crafty and canny they were. He found nothing untoward. Quick as a wink, though, he filched the inkwell and quills from the desktop. Writing utensils were hard to come by along the mainland too.

With the inkwell and quills inside the kit he wore at his waist, Juhg tried the middle door. Although it stuck and seemed jammed into the desk somewhat crossways, the drawer pulled out.

Inside was a book.

The sight of the book took Juhg's breath away. The book was slim and tidy in appearance, standing out at once against the crusted grime that littered the drawer. A blue handkerchief provided a bed for the book. Maroon cloth bound the book. Black writing of a language Juhg couldn't read and couldn't immediately identify—which was strange because he was well versed in several languages and trained to recognize scores of others— scrawled across the front. A black lithograph of a small cottage on a hill filled the lower right cover.

He studied the book for a moment, still wary of the wizard's possible magicks. If the volume was the wizard's personal spell book—and Juhg doubted that because most wizards' books tended to be invisible to normal eyes or hidden away in pockets of *otherwhereness* until such time as the wizard called them forth—it was much too slim to hold much in the way of spells.

Probably a discourse or a treatise, Juhg told himself. The Librarians at the Vault who still labored to sort out all the books gathered after Lord Kharrion rose to power among the goblinkin often began their initial separations based on heft alone when those decisions couldn't be made based on language or interior illustrations.

But so many important things arrived in the pages of discourses and treatises. Scholars with a true talent for words could unveil so many large mysteries with only a few well-chosen words. Secrets to crafts and metallurgies and healing herbs had gotten lost during the Cataclysm. The Librarians worked hard to rescue those processes and applications from the books they studied.

And histories, Juhg reminded himself. Normally, histories came fat and unwieldy, no matter what the language. Paper books weighed in by the ream and books like the Vuwelchel Shark People's shell books rolled along in wheelbarrows. But every now and again, a slim book detailed a monarch's rule or a year of trade that brought so much understanding of a culture. He loved histories because the more skilled writers painted such bright and vivid pictures of lost lands and countries and peoples that might never be seen again.

"Juhg," Raisho called.

Juhg's mind snapped back to the moment. He realized he'd forgotten to breathe. He did so now, and the sounds of the ship lying at anchor—the lap of the waves against the hull and the creak of the timber and the clank of the chain—all returned in a rush.

He reached for the book.

Movement froze Juhg in place like a mouse that had spotted a hawk. Then he realized that the movement rippled along the desk's top surface.

The wood rolled and drew up airy and light like bread dough. It twisted and shifted, becoming an open-mouthed viper the same color as the dark wood of the desk, just as stained and just as scarred, but bearing the unmistakable markings of scales.

The wooden snake's mouth looked big enough to swallow Juhg's head. Fangs stood out prominently in powerful jaws that dripped green-blue venom. Cold light danced in the ink-black eyes.

The creature lunged at Juhg.

5

Blowfly

uhg flung himself backward, hoping to escape the snake's lunge but knowing in his heart that he couldn't match the magical creature's speed. He was dead, and though he didn't accept that, he wished that his passing might be quick and painless.

Even as the snake's distended mouth and gleaming fangs seemed to fill all of Juhg's vision, he saw Raisho already in motion. The young sailor strode forward and swung his cutlass.

The keen blade caught the wooden serpent behind its wedge-shaped head and knocked its strike to one side just as Juhg tripped over his own feet in his panicked haste and fell to the floor. The serpent's fangs embedded in the ship's deck with a thunderous *crunch*.

"Get up!" Raisho stepped in front of Juhg. "Hurry afore it kills ye!"

The serpent lifted its head. The eyes looked cold and indifferent, but Juhg saw now that they also contained intelligence.

As he pushed himself to his feet, the snake wrenched the rest of its body free of the desk. The massive coils, at least twenty feet of them and as big around as Raisho's thigh, plopped to the wooden floor. Another snake's head formed on the desk and started stretching to free itself from its prison.

Raisho set himself and swung as the first snake struck again. The cutlass swept overhead and crashed down on the snake's head. Splinters flew like chaff and the dull *thunk* of a blade meeting wood filled the cabin.

The second snake wriggled and squirmed, reaching almost five feet long as it bumped its head against the ceiling.

Holding the snake's head pinned with the cutlass, Raisho swung a boot around and slammed it onto the creature's snout. He looked up at Juhg. "Go!"

"The book," Juhg protested. He looked longingly at the desk that contained the coveted prize.

"Leave it!" Raisho freed his blade and stood precariously atop the snake's head. The creature writhed and jerked, working its massive body toward the young sailor. *"Now!"*

Hurling himself from the room, Juhg slid across the hallway and banged into the wall on the other side of the narrow stern corridor between two rows of cabins. The vibration of the snake's struggle to get away from Raisho echoed in Juhg's feet.

The second snake struck without warning, uncoiling and launching itself from the desk.

Raisho ducked the second snake's attack and slapped his free hand against the underside of its throat as the head passed. Moving quickly, he leapt from the first snake and sped for the doorway. The snakes gathered themselves in his wake and pursued at once.

In the hallway, Raisho spun and caught hold of the door, barely pulling it closed. The two snakes slammed through the door like arrows driven from a Bramblethorn elf warder's war bow. The resounding impacts echoed in the mid-deck hallway.

"Run!" Raisho grabbed Juhg by the shoulder and shoved him forward.

Juhg ran, but his breath burned short and quick in his lungs. He glanced over his shoulder and saw the snakes slithering through the holes in the shattered door. Coils of wooden snake filled the hallway behind them.

Raisho grabbed the lantern from the wall and flung it back toward the snakes. The lantern burst against the snout of the lead snake and showered cargiff oil over both magical creatures. Luckily, the wick stayed lit, though it didn't at first ignite the oil.

Juhg caught the ladder and hauled himself up. He missed the first rung with his foot in his haste, barked his shin painfully, then curled his toes around it on the second attempt and hurled himself up. By the time he reached the upper deck and started to pull himself through the hold, the wick caught the oil aflame.

Blue and yellow fiery tongues gave chase to the wooden snakes in a slow, liquid rush. The snakes moved in a zigzag fashion, throwing their heads back and forth, then twisting their coils to follow.

"Move! Move!" Raisho grabbed onto the ladder and clambered up after Juhg. The ladder shook under the young sailor's weight.

Juhg threw himself from the hold and turned to watch his friend, afraid that the quickly moving snakes were fast enough to catch him.

With a seaman's ease, Raisho fairly ran up the ladder and flung himself from the hold. As he came clear of the opening, Juhg peered down and saw the snakes coiling around the ladder. The flames caught up with the creatures, zigzagging along the oily paths they'd left. Greedily, the fire rolled over the snakes and enveloped them. Juhg didn't know if the magic that animated the creatures would protect them from the fire and he was curious.

"C'mon!" Raisho called. "Ye've got goblins fit to skewer ye!"

Glancing up, Juhg saw the three goblinkin racing pell-mell across the deck. The creatures carried harpoons and short swords. Behind the goblinkin, the wizard held his hands out and chanted. Blue sparks flickered in the wizard's palms. Ozone crackled in the air.

Although he hadn't often been around magic, Juhg recognized evidence of the arcane art. Hair stood up on the back of his neck. He turned and fled and a harpoon rattled against the deck where he'd just been standing.

Up the stairwell as quick as he could go, Juhg spotted Raisho beside one of the two stern lanterns that marked the ship for all to see. The young sailor yanked one lantern free of its moorings.

"Wizard!" Juhg yelped, pointing and running at the same time. The efforts didn't complement each other. Before he knew it, his legs went out from under him and he sprawled across the deck.

"I know." Raisho threw the lantern amidships.

Pushing himself up again, Juhg watched the lantern arc out onto the deck as a flaming snake's head thrust up from the hold. Obviously in pain, the magical creature cracked open its maw and bellowed.

The goblins stopped, pointed at the fiery snake, and shrieked in terror.

The captain had left the three in charge of the ship. If the flames spread and the ship burned to the waterline or even only suffered major damage, the captain would deliver the goblins' executions on the spot.

Then the lantern Raisho had thrown smacked into the starboard side of the deck. The glass shattered on impact and oil spilled in a long, ropy puddle. Caught by the wind, the flames quickly danced across the surface of the oil pool.

The goblins shrieked in terror again, pointing at the new threat.

"A diversion," Raisho said. "C'mon, now. Unless you've a mind to hang around until they get those fires out."

At the prow of the ship, the wizard threw his sparking hands forward. A fireball formed in the air only inches from his fingertips. While sailing through the air, the fireball grew in size till it was almost as big as Juhg.

"Down!" Raisho roared, but by then Juhg was already facedown on the deck and striving to be as small a target as he could manage. The fireball screamed over his back. The heat drenched him, so hot that at first for a moment he feared he'd gotten caught up in the conflagration.

Then the fireball was past him, catching the stern railing and setting the wood there alight before *whoosh*ing into the cargo ship astern. The fireball smashed against the ship's mainmast, spreading into a thousand fiery bits that dropped to the merchant ship's deck. In the space of a drawn breath, as Juhg watched in horrified disbelief, flames spread along the ship's deck and climbed the ratlines and rigging to the furled sails.

78

Raisho got to his feet. "Juhg!" He waved anxiously as he moved toward the stern.

Juhg glanced back toward the ship's prow, checking to make certain the wizard didn't have another fireball up his voluminous sleeve. Instead, the wizard was crossing the deck, moving arthritically. Evidently his spell had cost him dearly.

The three goblins pointed at the flaming stern as well. Terror etched the creatures' ugly faces.

On his feet again, Juhg followed Raisho. They clambered over the ship's side and made quick work of sliding back down the anchor chain.

At the bottom, Raisho snared the cargo skiff with his foot and pulled the tiny craft close enough to jump on. He held the skiff steady while Juhg leapt the short distance. Together, they lifted the oars and stroked away from the burning goblin ship.

mel odom

Already frantic and frenzied cries of alarm rose from the cargo ship blasted by the wizard's wayward fireball. Ship's crew raced with buckets of water and wet sand to extinguish the blaze. From the looks of things, the goblinkin would spend their efforts in vain because the fire claimed ground quickly.

Juhg pulled his oars vigorously as Raisho aimed the skiff for the promising shelter of the shadows of a ship on the port side of the goblin vessel. Despite his best intentions, Juhg glanced up and searched the goblin ship till he spotted the wizard through the smoky haze given off by the burning merchanter. The two wooden snakes burned like dry branches but writhed across the decks like they truly were the creatures they resembled.

Despite the fact that he and Raisho were lucky enough to escape, Juhg couldn't help thinking about the book they had left behind. A book in the hands of goblins; it was unforgivable. But he set his feet and pulled harder on the oars till the ship they passed blocked the view of the goblin ship.

"So ye went an' had yerself an adventure, didja? An' here ye was, a-sayin' that ye wasn't wishful for such a thing."

Reluctantly, Juhg turned his attention from the activity he was watching out in Kelloch's Harbor and glanced at Herby. The boy had come to Juhg's side so quietly that he hadn't heard him. Of course, the fact that activity out in the harbor had captured the dweller's attention so completely might have aided in his distraction.

"It wasn't an adventure," Juhg said. "It was foolhardiness."

Herby cocked an eye skeptically. "I warrant the cap'n might not like hearin' it called that. Seein' as how it was hisownself what sent ye an' Raisho onto that ship."

"Only to find out if there was a goblin ship," Juhg said. "Deciding to climb aboard her, that was Raisho's doing."

"So he says. He's tellin' big stories over breakfast down in the galley. How the two of ye faced down thirty or forty goblinkin, squared off against a den full of magical wooden snakes, an' took on an evil wizard."

Juhg started to interrupt, then decided not to. During the brief interlude between the dregs of the night and dawn, he'd set down the events in his journal. He'd transcribed an accurate accounting of the sortie aboard the goblin ship, which was adventurous enough in its own right, but he'd been with *Windchaser*'s crew long enough to enjoy a proper whopper of a story. He decided to let Raisho's tale stand.

"It isn't something I'd like to repeat in the near future," Juhg said. "Or any time ever."

Herby shook his head and sighed as he leaned against the ship's railing. "I can't believe ye had to leave all them jewels an' gold behind."

"Jewels and gold?"

Nodding, Herby said, "Raisho's tellin' everybody about the treasure that ship carried. Why, half the crew's ready to pick a fight with them goblinkin just to have a chance at all them riches."

"That," Juhg said, "would be dangerous."

"Aye." Herby's eyes gleamed with larceny. "An' a prize worth takin' the chance for." He wiped his nose with the back of his hand. "Accordin' to the cap'n, we may well get that chance, too."

"What are you talking about?"

"The cap'n's got his spies out an' about. Medgar an' Toryn. Out there spyin' on the goblinkin. Findin' out what they can about her business."

"They could get caught."

Herby grinned. "Aye, they could. An' that's what makes it all excitin'. But they won't. They's the best spies what the cap'n has. 'Cept me. But he don't see it that way."

"The captain told you this? That we might try to take the goblinkin ship?" Juhg kept his voice low so it wouldn't carry far across the water.

During the night, the goblins had managed to put the fire out aboard the ship. As it turned out, Raisho and Juhg had only just missed the return of several of the ship's crew bringing supplies. Under the cover of darkness, Juhg, Raisho, and Captain Attikus had watched the goblin crew extinguish the flames.

The corpses of the three goblins who had served guard duty last night still hung from the 'yards. Pelicans and seagulls warred over their flesh with clacking beaks, raking talons, and flapping wings.

The ship struck by the wizard's fireball had suffered a similar fate. Unable to save their ship, the crew had abandoned the vessel and left her to a brutal death. The flames had consumed her down to the waterline until they burned out. Precious little cargo was saved, but the captain had put crews in skiffs out to do what they could. Her blackened husk sat out in the harbor while small sailing vessels lashed chains to her so they could drag her from the harbor.

The goblinkin worked hurriedly on their ship, making repairs as best as they were able. But goblins, though seafaring in their own right, had never mastered the true hand of sailors. The ship was patched together right enough that she could sail, but Juhg would have hated to trust her out on the open sea.

"The cap'n," Herby said, "why, he didn't tell me, of course. But I heard it just the same."

"You were listening at his window again."

Herby lifted his shoulders and dropped them. "I just like to be kept informed, is all. I draw a ship's pay from 'Chaser same as ever' other man on this ship."

Juhg eyed the goblin vessel doubtfully. *Windchaser* had a seasoned crew aboard her and the promise of riches would draw her sailors' courage.

For himself, he could scarcely keep his thoughts from the mysterious book. If the book were the prize, would he go willingly to attack a goblin ship? The itch inside him to see the book, to peruse the pages, grew strongly and deeply.

Despite his fatigue, Juhg labored in the heat of the day. He sat on the rat-lines spun like an immense spider's web along *Windchaser*'s prow and worked in his book with charcoal. Traveling with Grandmagister Lamp-lighter had trained him to work with a fine hand in ships while at anchor or at sea, though he hadn't thought the skill or compulsion would continue long after he'd said his goodbyes at the Vault of All Known Knowledge. As an added benefit, working in charcoal was generous, allowing him to blend smudges into the illustrations he so feverishly drew.

He framed the pages in his journal quickly and neatly, working one after the other while he munched sandwiches of jerked taupig, sliced cucumbers, tangy peppered lemonfrass, and drizzled with sweet apple-mustard. He didn't try to fill the images he drew with details, just applied enough lines and shading to get the overall image blocked out so he could better render them later. He let his mind roam, picking the memories he intended to capture of the events last night, as well as what he saw going on aboard the goblin ship now.

Three pages held eleven images of the wizard. Juhg drew the man in profile, as well as full frontal and from the back. He added as many of the arcane symbols as he could, feeling that he dared much because one of those icons of power on the wizard's robes might inadvertently rise from the page and strike him dead for daring such an affront.

Or perhaps one of those symbols might afford the wizard the ability to spy on him through the book. Juhg didn't know. But he felt certain that if he could remember enough details, Craugh might be able to identify the man from his robes. Despite the fact that the world seemed to teem with humans, only a few of them became wizards, and fewer still of those ever managed power enough to fling fireballs.

A few of the pages showed pictures of the mysterious book as he had seen it. He drew pictures of it by itself, and of the way it was placed in the drawer. A historian oftentimes never knew the true significance of what he chose to record.

He copied the writing he'd seen on the front as best as he could, but he couldn't be certain how much of it, if any, was correct. Looking back on things now, he wished he'd chosen to study the book better before reaching for it and triggering the magical defenses the wizard had placed on the book. But the book had lain right there, seemingly his for the taking. A quick flight up the ladder and he could have been gone with the book.

 Juhg sighed at his own impatience.

In times past, Grandmagister Lamplighter had urged caution before moving too swiftly through a thing. The Grandmagister had tempered his remonstration through examples of his own past ineptness, which was only one of the things that had won Juhg over to him. Besides being the Grandmagister, Edgewick Lamplighter had also been very much a simple dweller. But he hadn't lived a simple life since the crew of *One-Eyed Peggie* had shanghaied him all those years ago.

Taking a break for a moment, Juhg finished his last sandwich, then dropped the crusts and crumbs into the water. Fish that had gathered in the shadows on the lee side of *Windchaser* puckered their lips and took the crumbs with gulping kisses. He glanced up at the goblin ship and watched her crew lower her sails. The wind brought the canvas to full bloom in heartbeats.

The fire aboard the goblin ship had left soot patterns that stained the canvas, but the sails caught and held the wind easily enough.

mel odom

Rising to his feet, surefooted among the ratlines after all his time at sea and possessing a dweller's innate sense of balance and movement, Juhg closed his journal and shoved his stick of charcoal into the cloth bag that held his writing instruments. As far away from other ships as they were, there was little chance that any ship's crew in the harbor could have seen what he was doing.

Slowly, the goblin ship came around in the harbor. She tacked into the wind, maneuvering back and forth until she could properly come about. Once the other ships' captains had a proper chance to see how badly the goblins handled their craft, a few of the nearer ones moved away, giving the goblin vessel more room to maneuver. Hoarse shouts and curses drifted across the harbor water, and sailors hung out from the rigging to yell imprecations at the goblin crew.

Coming about to starboard, the goblin ship slid into a merchanter stern hard enough to crack timbers. Still, the goblins kept their vessel turning till she nudged free of the other ship and put her head more properly away from the wind. The merchanter's crew ran astern to check out any possible damage. Their ensuing curses told Juhg that the goblins had splintered her rudder.

Once the ship was pointed out to sea, the goblin crew turned her sails to catch the wind. The dark patterns of smoke stood out against even the grimy and tattered canvas the ship carried. But she moved.

The ratlines under Juhg's feet shifted as they took on weight. He glanced over his shoulder and spotted Raisho coming forward to join him.

"The goblin ship's under way," Juhg said, feeling the need to say something.

"Aye." Raisho nodded. "That she is."

"Does Captain Attikus know?" Juhg caught himself. Of course the captain knew. Captain Attikus was a fine sailing man. "I mean, did he know she was about to set sail?"

"The cap'n knew, right enough. Medgar an' Toryn brought him word of it. Them goblins, they took on supplies an' hired out some of the ship's repairs." Raisho grinned. "After last night, 'pears her cap'n didn't have the stomach to stay an' risk another thief."

"A thief?"

Raisho shrugged. "That's the scuttlebutt bein' told in the harbor. Course, nobody believes a goblin ship would have anythin' worth stealin'.

If'n they did, why, they'd be back on their way to a goblin city port down South where the weather's better an' they could spend their ill-gotten gain like proper pirates."

Quiet concern filled Juhg as he watched the goblin vessel sailing away. "They were here for a reason."

"Aye, but Medgar an' Toryn, they didn't get a glimmer of what that reason were."

Juhg watched the goblin ship sail through the narrow confines of the harbor mouth. "What about the book?"

"No one knows. Since we got back with the news last night, the cap'n assigned Medgar an' Toryn to watch over *Blowfly*—"

"*Blowfly?*"

Raisho nodded toward the departing ship. "That's her name. *Blowfly*. Ye ask me, they done went an' named her fair an' proper, 'cause she's got the stench of a corpse about her."

"Where's she bound?"

"Don't know. Medgar, he figgers the crew don't know either. Otherwise them goblins would have been talkin' it up. He was listenin' to the crew rail an' rave in the taverns." Raisho glanced at Juhg. "Wouldn't be the first time a goblin cap'n kept its crew not knowin' nothin' about where they was headin'."

A forlorn feeling swelled within Juhg. He felt as though he was letting Grandmagister Lamplighter down. "They're getting away with the book, Raisho."

"No." Raisho showed him a white mirthless grin. "Them goblins, why, they ain't gettin' away with nothin', bookworm. Cap'n Attikus, he's givin' 'em a lead, is all. Lettin' 'em build their confidence afore he takes it all away. *'Chaser,* she can cleave through the water faster'n that dirty pig ever thought of sailin'." He glanced up at the sun and squinted. "Won't be much longer afore we take off after her."

"We're going after *Blowfly?*" The possibility spun crazily in Juhg's mind. He'd been part of ship-to-ship fighting in the past, seeing decks that ran red with blood and hearing the constant ring of steel against steel and screaming men's voices, but years had passed since then. It was not an experience he was looking forward to repeating.

"Aye. We are. An' we'll catch her, right soon enough."

"What about the wizard?"

"Wizards ain't nothin' but men." Raisho spat into the water. "Some of 'em take a little more killin' than others, but they die." He winked at Juhg. "An' if'n they wasn't afeared of dyin', why, they'd stay in the thick of things instead of hidin' themselves away in castles an' big houses an' caves an' islands an' the like. No, them evil wizards don't live among most folks 'cause they's afeard of gettin' a knife 'twixt their shoulder blades when they ain't lookin'. Keeps 'em honest in town. To an extent."

Uneasiness bounced in thick, greasy globs in Juhg's stomach and made him feel sick. He was certain they'd barely escaped with their lives last night, and Raisho's overly confident manner made him fearful for his friend. Confronting a wizard was never a good thing.

85

6

Pursuit

ear dusk, when *Blowfly* was at least half a day out to
sea, Captain Attikus called a meeting in his cabin.
His quartermaster, a quiet man of middle years named
Lucius, and first mate, Navin, who was only a few years
older than Raisho and was normally boisterous and outgoing, joined the captain.

Juhg and Raisho also stood in attendance.

The captain's mood was somber. "We'll weigh anchor
and ride the eventide out to sea in just a bit. Make sure the
men are fed proper and bundled up when they're about
the deck. I want them looking sharp as can be."

"Aye, Cap'n," Lucius said, and Navin echoed him.

Captain Attikus glanced at his mate. "Navin, you'll
take first shift. Keep the men on short watches. Rotate
them so they stay rested and ready."

"Aye, Cap'n," Navin replied. His hand fiddled idly
with the cutlass he wore at his side. The scars he bore on
his face spoke of past battles, but they didn't say whether
he had won them or lost them.

"And remind them that hard tasks, like taking that
goblin ship soon, are part of what they signed on to do
when they took ship's articles."

"I will, Cap'n," Navin declared. "But I won't be havin' to remind them much. This ship, Cap'n? Why, we've been bloody before, an' we know we'll be bloody again. You look around durin' a boardin', you won't find a man in this crew what's takin' a lackluster step."

"I'll hold you to that, Navin," the captain said in a gruff voice. "And tell the men that I'm proud of them."

Juhg looked at each man in turn, studying them so that he could easily sketch the scene in his journal when time permitted. *How can they so easily talk of possibly going to their deaths?*

Even after reading treatises and biographies of warcraft and battles, Juhg struggled to comprehend what drove warriors, humans most of all, to seek out violent confrontations. The goblinkin were an easy study. Those foul creatures knew no other way of life, even among their own kind.

"Lucius, you'll take the men after first watch," Captain Attikus went on. He reached into a hidden compartment in the wall behind his desk and took out a sealskin container. Reaching into the container, he took out maps of the area. Only sailors who sailed the seas to protect Greydawn Moors and the Vault of All Known Knowledge had maps.

(During his tenure at the Library, Juhg had drawn maps. Grandmagister Lamplighter insisted that every Librarian know cartography well.)

Captain Attikus checked through the maps, then unfurled one across the desk. The paper was thick and limber as cloth, specially prepared down in the bowels of the Vault of All Known Knowledge, and held inks in the same color and same thickness as the day they were applied. The formula for making the paper had come from the books in the Library, one of the first things rescued from the higgledy-piggledy mess left by the armies that had delivered the books by the wagonload and shipload.

Lucius reached for the small lantern and raised it over their heads so the light might better strike the map.

"For now, we'll assume *Blowfly* made for south," Captain Attikus said. "If after two days' sailing we haven't caught up with the goblin ship, we'll turn back north."

"Ain't much in the way of north," Lucius commented. "Just colder an' more miserable. Can't see them botherin' to head up that way."

"Agreed." Captain Attikus studied the map. "But we still don't know what *Blowfly* and her captain are doing in these waters."

"Or the wizard." Only when the other men looked at him did Juhg realize he'd spoken aloud. Embarrassment flamed his cheeks.

"I haven't forgotten about the wizard, Librarian Juhg," the captain said, gazing at him levelly. "If getting that book wasn't impressed as important to me by my standing orders, I wouldn't hasten to chase a wizard. I don't much care for magic, and I've yet to find a seafaring man who does."

"This wizard's weak," Raisho said. "He only had the one fireball in him last night."

Captain Attikus shifted his attention to the young sailor and waited a beat before speaking. "Aye, Raisho, but I also see that one fireball was responsible for a lost ship this morning. I don't mean for my ship to be counted as the next. And you don't know if a fireball spell is the only thing that wizard is capable of."

Raisho gave the captain a curt nod.

"I've studied the map and I know these waters," the captain continued, glancing back at the parchment lying across the desk before them. "Goblinkin don't trust sailing as a general rule and have only learned what they have of it for the plunder they can take." He traced a finger along the coast of the mainland.

Juhg followed the captain's directions. Much of the map Juhg already knew from his own journal he'd prepared for his journey back to the mainland.

"The goblinkin will hug the coast, never wanting to be far from it." Captain Attikus' finger stopped at a cluster of islands only a short distance from the coastline. " '*Chaser*'s fast enough to outrun them. We'll hug the coastline, too, and beat them to the Tattered Islands."

Juhg's heart took a dive. He knew about the Tattered Islands and all the evil that was supposed to cling to them.

"The Tattered Islands," Navin repeated with a small nervous quaver in his voice. "That's a dangerous place, Cap'n. Full of jagged rocks an' coral reefs."

"I know," Captain Attikus agreed. "Most captains swing out wide of the Tattered Islands, following along them rather than the mainland to avoid those rocks and those reefs. There are plenty of ships that lost their bottoms there and went down. I'm guessing that *Blowfly*'s captain will do no differently." He studied the map. "We're going to sail through the Tattered Islands."

"Cap'n," Navin protested. "Them reefs an' them rocks, why, that ain't all they say is in them waters there. I've heard any number of stories about the stalkers that—"

Horrid illustrations, all fangs and blood and curved talons, filled Juhg's mind from the books he'd read while in the Vault. The Tattered Islands had existed before the Cataclysm, a place of some unknown doom that had been forever changed and forever cursed. A number of volumes in Hralbomm's Wing recounted at length the adventures of hapless heroes and dastardly villains who spent their last breaths upon those broken shoals.

Captain Attikus interrupted Navin, cutting in with a tone that brooked no argument. "I'm sure you've also heard stories about the endless piles of pirates' loot that decorate the coasts of those islands."

"Aye, an' I have," Navin replied. "An' I've never once hoped to go a-huntin' there, Cap'n. Them islands, why, they're a fearful place. I've talked with ship's mates what's been near to them an' they've had plenty to say about all the wailin' fer a man's blood what goes on there."

The captain held up a hand. "I've been through the Tattered Islands. Seafarers from Greydawn Moors have marked passages through there. I've used those islands as hiding places before—and I've endured more than enough of the superstitious twaddle about undead things living there—to elude pirates with more ships than I could fight."

Juhg could tell by Lucius and Navin's reactions that the men clearly were not happy with the captain's choice of action.

"We'll sail on through to the other side of the islands," Captain Attikus stated. "I'm guessing two days will put us there ahead of *Blowfly*. If our luck holds, they'll cross those waters early in the morning and we'll catch sight of them." He tapped the map at the outermost island's edge. "There's anchorage here on Jakker's Hold where fresh water can be taken on. We'll stop there when we've finished our business with the goblinkin, then—once we have the book—head back to the Blood-Soaked Sea and Greydawn Moors."

"Return to Greydawn Moors so soon?" Navin shook his head. "We only just got shut of the place, Cap'n. There's profits to be made from the investments the crew has made in the cargo we're carryin'. Some of it's perishable. You're askin' them men to take a loss against their good faith."

Juhg knew the first mate was more concerned about his own investments. Navin tended to be a gambler of the first order, always seeking the highest profits to be made.

"You men who came aboard my ship," Captain Attikus spoke levelly, "took an oath to first defend Greydawn Moors and the hiding place of the Vault of All Known Knowledge across the Blood-Soaked Sea."

Navin had trouble meeting the captain's penetrating gaze. "Aye, Cap'n. That we did."

"Then I'm going to hold you to that."

Navin's jaw firmed. He clearly didn't like how things were going, but he knew his place. "Aye, Cap'n. I was just thinkin' that maybe that book—" The mate said the word like it was a curse, a thing to be despised. "—might could wait awhile. Till we finish the journey we've planned. To go a-chargin' back across the Blood-Soaked Sea like that, why, we're like to call attention to ourselves, we are. An' ye know we shouldn't have none of that."

Captain Attikus raised his eyes to meet Juhg's. "Explain it to him, Librarian Juhg."

Feeling a little embarrassed, and a little challenged because few people of any race outside those that lived on Greydawn Moors truly understood the significance of books, Juhg said, "If the goblinkin haven't destroyed that book by now, and it's in the care of a wizard, it has to be an important book."

"Ye saw the book," Navin accused. "Don't ye know if'n it's important or not?"

"The book's important," Raisho growled. "If'n it wasn't, the wizard would never have wasted an enchantment to protect it."

"Ye don't even know if they still have the book. Fer all ye know, that goblinkin captain mighta traded it back in Kelloch's Harbor."

"They did their pirate trading with the cooper that young Herby told us of," Captain Attikus said. "A cooper would have no use for a book."

"Then why bring it all this way?" Navin persisted. "Don't make no sense, is what I'm sayin'."

"The book belongs to the wizard," Raisho replied. "Them goblins talkin' about the book, why, them creatures was just talkin'."

Navin thrust his whiskered jaw out defiantly. "Then how did the cooper know the book was on the goblin ship?"

Juhg had to admit the man was clearheaded enough to point out that discrepancy in the story. How did the cooper know the book was coming into port? Juhg hadn't thought up an answer that satisfied him yet.

"Mayhap we could go back an' ask the cooper," Raisho growled. "*After* we finish this bit of business."

the destruction of the books

Navin sighed and shook his head. "We're gonna be spillin' blood, that's all I'm sayin'. Our own, as well as that of them goblinkin. I just gotta know how many men's lives a book is worth."

Anger ignited within Juhg. How many times had he ventured into dangerous and inhospitable lands with Grandmagister Lamplighter to retrieve a book from ruins or some other hidden place? How many times had they gone just to investigate a rumor that had been carried by the friendly pirates working the Blood-Soaked Sea? He didn't know. But men, elves, and dwarves had died in those efforts.

"The worth," Juhg declared in a much stronger voice than he'd intended, "depends on the book."

Navin looked up at him. Surprise gleamed in his eyes.

Juhg suddenly felt nervous and he almost stopped speaking, but his anger was upon him and the silence between the humans watching him drew the words out. "We don't know what a book's worth until we read it. Even then, that worth might be a long time in coming." He fidgeted, feeling so small with the four of them looking down on him. "So many people think the Librarians hoard information they glean from the books they read. Shopkeepers even along the Yondering Docks in Greydawn Moors talk with each other about fabulous fortunes the Librarians know about because of their studies."

92

Windchaser heeled over a little bit as the crew worked the sails topside and she caught a crossways breeze.

"Once," Juhg went on, "an attempt was made to kidnap Grandmagister Lamplighter when he was still a First Level Librarian. They wanted him to find the Lost Tower of Jeludace, where, rumor had it, a king's fortune awaited discovery."

"I heard about that," Lucius said. "The Grandmagister barely escaped with his life."

Juhg nodded. "There was no fortune waiting to be won. But there were books."

"Then what's the use of 'em?" Navin demanded. "They've laid there for years, some of 'em rotted."

The idea of books languishing so long they'd given up and departed the mortal coil pained Juhg. During their travels, he and Grandmagister Lamplighter had occasionally found small, personal libraries that had decayed and been forever lost.

"Because books give us our ties to the past," Juhg said. "They help us rebuild the world that once was."

"An' that world will never be again," Navin argued. "So what's the use of that?"

"They help us to better understand who we are now," Juhg went on. "They tell us how to do things, arts and sciences that were lost during the bloody years of Lord Kharrion's war."

"Men learn what they need to learn," Navin said. "That's the way it's always been."

"It takes time to learn," Juhg said, striving to make himself understood. "That's why books are written. To carry on information others have already spent their time to learn. Animal husbandry. Gardening. Even sailing and building ships."

Navin shook his head. "Ain't never need to know nothin' me da didn't teach me. Was I to need somethin' past that, I learned from those around me. Ye want knowledge? If it's somethin' worth knowin', why, most folks already know it. All that other stuff ye're talkin' about, why, it ain't worth the time it takes to read nor write."

"Navin," Captain Attikus admonished, evidently fearing the first mate had gone too far.

The man's attitude aggravated Juhg. So many of the inhabitants of Greydawn Moors felt as Navin did, that the Library and all its Librarians were a waste of time and resources better spent elsewhere. Even Grandmagister Lamplighter's father hadn't wanted him to work at the Vault of All Known Knowledge.

"It's all right, Captain," Juhg said. His eyes never left Navin's. Although dwellers as a race tended to be meek and mild, he knew the melancholy and anger at the events that had shaped his life marked him differently. That was what had finally driven him from the Library and from Greydawn Moors: No matter how hard he had tried, he had never quite fit in.

Navin looked a bit triumphant. He smugly folded his arms across his chest.

"Do you remember the sickness that ran through Greydawn Moors last year?" Juhg asked.

"Aye. Me sister's snot-nosed brats came down with the fevers an' them chilblains."

The sickness had reached near epidemic numbers on the island last spring. Grandmagister Lamplighter had traced its cause back to one of the pirate ships that had come in unknowing with the sickness.

"Do you know who found the cure to the sickness?" Juhg asked.

"The apothecary," Navin answered. "Was him what fixed up the herbs an' such that fixed everybody up."

"It weren't the apothecary," Lucius stated with a quiet grin. "Mayhap he made up the herbs, but 'twas the Librarians what told him how it was to be done."

"That's right," Juhg said. "When the sickness broke out through the port area and climbed up into the foothills of the Knucklebones Mountains where many outlying homes are, it was the Librarians who searched for an answer to the sickness in those books that you're so ready to shovel out with the barn muck."

"That sickness had never been seen on the island," Raisho said. "Like as not, everybody in Greydawn Moors might well have died from it had the Librarians not found the cure."

Navin scowled. "There's still a powerful lot of nonsense that the Librarians take pride in that ain't needed."

"Not in your life," Juhg replied. "But in the lives of others?" He shook his head. "That's not for a Librarian to say. A Librarian serves best by making sure the information is kept up with."

Navin blew out his breath. "All right, then. It wasn't like we had any real choice about fetchin' that blamed book. I just hope it's worth the trouble, is all."

So do I, Juhg thought.

"Since we're all in agreement now," Captain Attikus rumbled dryly, making it clear that no chance had existed of the situation going any other way, "this is how we'll do it." He tapped the map. "When that goblinkin ship rounds Iron Rose Island, the southeasternmost of the lot, and if it's morning when they do, we can get onto them quick. Coming out of the morning sun as we'll be, they won't see us until we're right on top of them." He paused, staring at the map, then lifting his eyes to the men around him. "That should give us all the edge we'll need to take that ship."

Even with the edge, though, Juhg knew men were going to die in the attempt.

"Raisho," Captain Attikus said, "I know you're probably wondering why I asked you here."

"Aye, Cap'n."

For that matter, Juhg thought, *so am I.* The fact that the captain would have a war council before taking up the pursuit of *Blowfly* was no surprise. Captain Attikus was a thorough man.

"I'm thinking," Captain Attikus said, "that mayhap those goblinkin, or at least the wizard, might suspect we're after the book. More than likely, the book is the only thing of worth on the whole vessel." He glanced at Raisho. "All the tales of gold and riches notwithstanding."

"Aye, Cap'n," Raisho apologized. "Tellin' of all that made for a good tale, though."

"I'm sure it did, Raisho, and there will be no few who will be disappointed—"

"Or downright mad," Navin put in, then glanced hurriedly at Captain Attikus. "Beggin' the cap'n's indulgence for speakin' so out of turn."

Attikus nodded. "You'll have to make amends for your stories, Raisho."

"Aye, Cap'n," Raisho stated glumly.

Juhg knew that no young human ever liked to have to go back and change a story once told that brought glory and interest to him. And the tale of the trip they'd made aboard *Blowfly* last night had delivered a considerable amount of both to him.

"Of course," Captain Attikus said, "it's possible that the goblinkin vessel spent or gambled away all their riches. Or were even serving the wizard to pay off a huge debt or buy an ensorcelled object." He didn't look at the young sailor.

A canny look fitted itself to Raisho's face. He gave a slight nod, but said nothing.

"In the meantime, Raisho," Captain Attikus said, "it may well be that we can't take the goblinkin ship without sinking her. Besides the damage we'll undoubtedly inflict while taking her, she appears none too steady anyway. I'm certain the fire damage from last night did her no good."

A cold apprehension suddenly started across Juhg's shoulders as he realized where Captain Attikus was headed.

"Librarian Juhg," the captain stated, "I'll have to ask you to be part of the boarding party."

"Me, Captain?" Juhg couldn't believe it. "But—but I'm no warrior." He'd fought in the past, when he'd had to and where he'd had to, but never because he'd *wanted* to.

"It may be that we don't have the book from the goblinkin ship at the time she goes down," the captain explained. "You'll go aboard and seek to find the book, should time grow short once we've started boarding the enemy vessel."

"Me, Captain?"

"You," Captain Attikus stated emphatically. "I'm sure that your Grand-magister would demand no less of you."

No, Juhg was certain of that as well. Grandmagister Lamplighter had often risked his life in pursuit of books that had avoided collection during the Cataclysm.

"Raisho," the captain went on, "you'll be personally responsible for Librarian Juhg, should he have to take on the mantle of a hero to go after that book."

"Beggin' the cap'n's pardon," Raisho said, "there's any number of men what's able to nursemaid—to *look after* the bookworm. Ye need me up front, Cap'n. Where all the fightin' is. That's when I'll be at me best."

"You're a capable man, Raisho, despite your youth and your arrogance. And you're friends with the Librarian. I know you won't be tempted to leave him to his own devices in the heat of the moment." Captain Attikus placed his hands together behind him. "This is going to be done as I wish it to be done, gentlemen. That's all there is to be said about the matter." He looked around the room. "If there are any more questions . . . ?"

There were none, though Juhg firmly wanted to lodge a protest. Raisho would be busy enough taking care of himself without spreading his defenses thin to protect another person who didn't belong on the front line of a boarding party anyway.

Midmorn streaked the horizon a day and a half later. The stabbing fingers of the newly rising sun didn't make much headway against the storm front moving in from the east across the Frozen Ocean. Whirling clouds fought for space in the dark sky, looking like black roses blossoming time and time again against a field of black velvet.

Juhg sat in *Windchaser*'s crow's-nest, sharing space with Ornne, the young sailor whose eyes were sharp as spyglasses. Ornne was gangly and short, all arms and legs and a head that looked much too big for him. Next to Ornne, Juhg had the best eyes among the crew.

Nervously, Juhg scanned the eastern horizon. Pushed by the storm coming in to land, the dirty slate-gray waves rolled tall and white-capped. Spotting sails, especially *Blowfly*'s soot-streaked sails, would prove hard against the dingy sky and ocean almost the same color. Occasionally, jagged rips of lightning burned across the sky, and the crack of thunder—loud as a blacksmith's hammer while working old iron—rolled over the ship.

The crew stood ready on *Windchaser*'s deck. They were clad in leather armor that barely offered any protection for the head and chest. Heavier armor couldn't be worn: If they lost their footing and fell from the ship during the planned boarding, they'd sink like stones and the crew wouldn't be able to pull them back aboard. Many of the crew didn't know how to swim.

The storm presented an ill omen, and sailors had always believed in omens more than anything else.

Windchaser rested uneasily at anchor as if shying away from the forbidding chunk of rock that stood against the storm's fury. When he'd first seen Iron Rose Island during the night, Juhg was convinced that it was as desolate as the others he'd had a chance to observe as the ship sailed between the Tattered Islands and the mainland.

But even in the false early morning light presented by the storm, he knew that wasn't right. A city had once existed on the island. All that remained of that city now were remnants of buildings that stood close to the ground—where they stood at all.

When first constructed, the buildings had resembled black roses. Iron framework held the lines of nearly all the buildings and even the modest houses. The exterior of those structures consisted of black slabs of rock cut like rose petals. Where the iron framework showed bereft of stone, the design stood out in bold relief.

Once, Juhg knew, the city filled the foothills of Iron Rose Island with beauty. He wished that there was time to go ashore and study the architecture and the grounds more thoroughly, but the captain had forbidden that. However, the ululating wails that came from the island caused no little apprehension and probably would have held Juhg from making such a landing on the beach anyway.

Navin and a few of the other sailors who had stood watch on deck and listened to the wails insisted the Stalkers made them. No one on watch saw anything in the water or on land all through the night, but the men who talked so long and so loud of the Stalkers insisted that the creatures lived in underwater pockets along the shore. The living arrangements, if they were true, reminded Juhg of crayfish, and he couldn't help picturing the Stalkers as that. With his imaginative eye, he saw the Stalkers as human-sized crayfish with skull-like features and dead-white flesh. But hands had shaped the iron frameworks and black stone slabs, not pincers.

The sailors also held forth that only blood in the water would make the Stalkers leave their desolate island. Like sharks, the Stalkers were supposed to be able to smell the blood in the water for miles. Juhg desperately hoped that weren't true.

Ornne shifted beside Juhg, catching his arm in his hand and tugging to get his attention.

Following the boy's line of sight, Juhg spotted the soot-streaked sails standing proudly aboard the ship that rounded the southeastern tip of Iron Rose Island.

"Do ye see the ship?" Ornne asked in a quick, nervous voice.

"I do," Juhg agreed. "It's there." Fear took a proper hold of him then, stronger than anything he'd felt through the night.

Ornne lifted his voice, shouting, "Sails! Sails ho, lads!" and *Windchaser* became a bustle of activity as she prepared for war.

 98

7

"Boarders Away!"

attle stations!" Captain Attikus roared from the stern deck. He stood solid and unbending, a force now rather than a man, and Juhg knew when the time came to write of this battle—provided he lived through it, of course—then he would describe the man as that. "Raise the sails! Fill those 'yards with canvas!"

Navin repeated the captain's orders, bellowing them out in his stentorian voice and adding colorful threats to individual crewmembers as he strode amidships with a cutlass in his hands. Gust trailed along through the rigging above the first mate's head. The monk shook his gnarled hand threateningly, in an exact mimicry of Navin's efforts.

Instantly, the ship's crew pulled the ropes that raised the canvas and stretched it tight between the halyards along all three masts. Luck stayed with them in spite of the inclement weather: Most of the wind drove from the east, spitting rain toward the west so that the ship could run full-out toward the goblin vessel.

As the wind caught the rising canvas and pressed it out full-bellied, *Windchaser* surged forward, straining at her anchor. The prow nosed down and the stern threatened to come about as she twisted to be free.

"Haul that anchor!" Navin crossed the deck at a full run and oversaw the crewmen winding the great wheel that drew up the heavy anchor. Timbers creaked, splintering the noise of the canvas cracking in the wind, and whitecaps retreating from the mainland hammered the ship's stern so hard that the ship shuddered.

"Hard to port," Ornne yelled through his cupped hands. "Hard to port. *Blowfly*'s makin' good time, she is, an' she's runnin'."

"Has she seen us yet, Ornne?" Captain Attikus demanded.

"No, Cap'n, but she's makin' a good head all the same."

"Let me know the instant those goblins see us."

"I will, Cap'n."

Navin roared the order to pull the sheets to port louder. The canvas crew adjusted the sails. *Windchaser* heeled over hard to port as she was torn between wind and water and the dead weight of the anchor pulling free of the seabed.

Ornne turned to Juhg, but his sharp eyes never left the goblin ship. "Ye get along on, now. I can keep track of our prize, right enough, me-ownself."

Juhg hesitated, glancing down the rigging and seeing the ship's deck so far below. *Windchaser* twisted and fought to gain her head with all the canvas throwing her forward. As he looked down, an unaccustomed feeling of vertigo slammed through Juhg.

"Get on with ye," Ornne growled, pushing at Juhg's shoulder with an open hand. "Just mind yer step on the way down an' ye'll be fine." He grinned with childlike delight. "It's not that fall ye have so much to worry about, Juhg. It's that sudden stop what's at the end."

Juhg sincerely believed the young lookout's sense of humor was misplaced. Asking the Old Ones to watch over him, since they were supposed to have some mercy toward dwellers because they'd created them and given them such mild natures, Juhg grabbed the lines and prepared for the descent.

He swung a leg out over the crow's-nest and started down the rigging. Pouring through the square openings of the rigging, the wind clawed at Juhg in a frenzy. He'd never been aloft in a blow, and even though this was not truly a blow now, he had never before felt the wind so strong. The rough hemp chewed at his hands like rat's teeth. Hours of working with inks and quills hadn't given him the calluses the other sailors had.

Moving quickly, only slipping once so that he dangled above the deck so far below and scraped one cheek against the rope, Juhg made his way down. At the bottom, he dropped to the heaving deck and had to catch himself with his hands.

Peering west-southwest, where he knew the goblin vessel was, Juhg only saw the heaving sea looking like it towered nearly as tall as the mainmast. *Windchaser* occupied the bottom of a trough of a wave. Blown by the wind and going out with the tide, the wave retreated and brought the ship along with it.

Then the wind caught the sails more surely and pushed *Windchaser* up from the trough onto the wave's back amid the white curlers. The ship crested the wave, hanging high for a moment so that Juhg glimpsed *Blowfly* in the distance. Juhg stared at the goblinkin ship and tried to push all the old fears and memories back wherever they'd come from.

I won't be a goblin slave again, he promised himself. *No matter what else happens in my life, I'll never suffer that again. I would rather die first.*

Then, with sickening speed, *Windchaser* crested the wave and slammed back down onto the front side of the wave. The deck tilted sharp enough that every hand aboard her had to grab hold of support to keep from tumbling.

Juhg made his way to the mainmast, staying beneath the main boom and the lines as the sails crews kept the canvas tight and in the correct position to best take advantage of the wind. He crouched by the mast, one hand around it to steady himself. The polished wood felt wet and cold.

"Archers, make ready!" Captain Attikus roared, and the command was picked up at once by the first mate.

Immediately, the men aboardship who were designated archers took their mighty Ardynwood bows from oilskin pouches. They braced the bows against the deck and used one hand to bend the bows and the other hand to string the weapons, working from bottom to top. They'd kept the bows and the strings dry so they would not stretch out in the humid weather. The bowmen showed skill, and if it hadn't been for the fact that goblin archers would shoot back, Juhg would have felt more relieved to witness the practiced maneuvers.

Raisho stood among the archers. He reached over his shoulder and took a cloth-yard shaft from the quiver he wore. With practiced ease, he nocked an arrow to string and waited with his knees slightly bent so he rode out *Windchaser*'s movements easily.

Watching his friend, Juhg knew that when the battle was done and he could write of the experience, he would draw Raisho as he saw him now. He just hoped they all survived.

Windchaser cleaved the water, running full-out now. Even though the waves retreated before them, the ship overtook the water and spray burst over the prow. Juhg tasted the wet brine on his lips and felt it burn his eyes. Fearing the worst, he felt his heart hammering inside his chest.

"Cap'n!" Ornne squalled.

"Aye," Captain Attikus roared back.

"*Blowfly*'s done went and seen us, Cap'n!"

Peering ahead as *Windchaser* crested another wave, Juhg watched goblin activity suddenly boiling on *Blowfly*'s deck. They came to port to stare out at the approaching vessel.

"Cap'n," Navin called up. "Shall we show 'em our colors?"

Captain Attikus nodded gravely. "Run them up, Navin. Declare our intentions and let's see if any of those goblins have a spine."

They have a wizard, Juhg thought glumly. He remembered the heat of the fireball two nights ago when it narrowly missed him.

Navin bellowed out more orders. Four sailors ran to the aft mast while another retreated belowdecks. *Windchaser* kept her pirate's flag stowed in a hidden compartment below. A few cities along the coastline, most of them human, maintained a harbor patrol that required searches of all arriving ships. Trading in those ports was necessary, and Captain Attikus didn't want to have to explain that they weren't quite pirates. And he couldn't explain about Greydawn Moors anyway because the island's—and the Vault of All Known Knowledge's—existence had to remain secret.

102

The sailor reappeared from belowdecks in a moment. The black flag was attached to the line, then ran up to flutter in the galling winds beneath the stormy sky.

The grinning skull and crossbones stood out proudly on the field of black. An eyepatch covered one hollow socket, and two gold teeth marked the grin.

"All right, laddies," Navin bellowed above the howling wind, "it's pirates ye be, an' proper pirates too. Up agin them despicable goblinkin, ye are, an' I'll not tolerate any man shirkin' his bounden duty to create despair an' sorrow among them awful creatures."

The crew shouted in excitement, but Juhg saw fear in some of them too. He'd seen that emotion among human crews in the past. Humans, at least on the surface, seemed so warlike. Many of them, of course, were, but they knew fear as well. Dwarves lived to fight, and showed no real fear, accepting death as part of the price that was paid for being warriors. Elves, smug in their arrogance, did not believe they could be bested in physical prowess or cleverness until their deaths were upon them.

The dwarves and elves seldom fought, only over matters that truly concerned them: land holdings and border disputes primarily, and against goblinkin, because those races detested each other, and when their senses of honor compelled them to take up axes or swords or bows against those who would sully them.

However, even dwarven and elven battles with goblinkin occurred only after long and careful consideration of the potential outcomes because of the cost in lives. That was one of the reasons the wizards who had organized the defense of the lands and the building of the Vault of All Known Knowledge had trouble rallying the elves and dwarves to their cause.

But humans, with their fiery tempers and short span of years, fought for almost any reason at all: out of anger, pride, jealousy, fear, want, need, and love. In the Library, Juhg had studied many histories, and he best loved those of the humans and their toils. Sadly, human historians rarely maintained a properly long view of an epoch or an era. Their lives were simply too short and their vision too narrow.

Dinraldo, one of the oldest sailors aboard *Windchaser,* raised his voice in song. He was a long, thin reed of a man with iron-gray hair down to his shoulders, a scarlet kerchief tied round his throat, gold earrings, and the weathered walnut skin of a man who had known only life out on the salt.

Gather round, me hearties,
An' stan' up straight an' true,
'Cause they ain't no sailin' man
What comes rougher'n tougher'n you!

The crew cheered and supported the old sailor's song.

Don't want to go down on me dyin' day
Lyin' abed an' a-wastin' away.

So give me a blade an' a fair wind
An' I'll take up piratin' agin!

So stan' me to a drink an' gi' me a blade
An' I'll fight aside ye, dogs, I'll fight aside ye!
Until them goblins or this ol' seadog is daid,
Ye can count on me to give 'em a lick or three!

Give 'em a lick or three! The crew sang the refrain, going through it again and again while the waves crashed liked thunder against the bows as they neared their prize.

Juhg knew the crew's voices carried across the water and that the goblins could hear them. Part of him couldn't help but take pride in the crew, but he was afraid for them at the same time. During the long days of the voyage, he had ended up sketching everyone in the crew and telling them stories of far-off places and deeds of derring-do. He knew them, and he had listened to their stories of places and people they had met over their years of voyaging.

Occasionally, he had even told them of voyages he had accompanied Grandmagister Lamplighter on, although he changed the names because the Grandmagister didn't like for many to know everything he had done or where he had traveled. During those times, the crew had surprised Juhg by their insistence that the two Librarians in the story were so brave. For one, they were—of course—dwellers, which made bravery an awfully rare thing. And second, the "adventures" were fraught with peril and hardship, and so well detailed that it was hard to think of them simply as stories.

During those times—then, as now—Juhg's only consistent thought was of a way to survive. But he couldn't help thinking of the book the goblins held captive on the ship. He wrapped his arms around the mainmast and held on. The book couldn't be allowed to stay with the goblins.

As *Windchaser* crested the next wave, the sound of throbbing drums echoed in Juhg's ears. The basso pounding sounded ominous and threatening and discordant, and a moment later the noise was punctuated by the wild screams of the goblins stoking up to a battle rage, which was a terrible thing in a goblin when that goblin had nowhere to escape. Each ship's crew tried to drown out the other and earn a psychological advantage.

To Juhg, the efforts were all barbarous, little above the keening and growling of animals.

Despite the threatening noise made by the goblin crew, *Blowfly* tried to run for the open sea. She turned and made haste to the west, giving up hugging the coastline for the moment. The goblin crew wouldn't run too far, Juhg knew, because the goblinkin weren't as adept at steering by the stars as the humans. As soon as the creatures became afraid of getting lost, the goblins would reverse direction and speed toward the rising sun.

"They're runnin', lads!" Navin whooped, raising his cutlass high.

Juhg clung to the mainmast and felt dry-mouthed. His stomach flipped over as *Windchaser* rose and fell with the ocean. *Blowfly* appeared and disappeared as the waves separated the two ships. But Juhg knew it was only a matter of time till *Windchaser* caught her prey. *Windchaser* was a faster ship and more expertly handled.

Captain Attikus remained calm in spite of the goblin crew's rising bloodlust. He called out orders, which Navin relayed, and brought *Windchaser* smartly up behind the goblinkin ship. In a short time, *Windchaser* slid into place behind *Blowfly* and stole her wind. When the goblin ship's canvas started to collapse and hang limply from the 'yards, a thunderous cheer rose from *Windchaser*'s decks.

"Ornne," Captain Attikus called.

"Aye, Cap'n."

"Do you see that wizard?"

"No, sir."

The mere mention of the word *wizard* caused Juhg's stomach to curdle. If a fireball took them at sea and they couldn't put the flames out, they'd burn down to the waterline. Out on the open sea as they were, there was nowhere to go. Iron Rose Island was too far away unless some of the longboats survived.

"Archers," Captain Attikus ordered, "prepare to fire on my order."

Raisho and the other archers drew back till the arrow fletchings touched their cheeks.

The goblins raised bows too, and a few of them fired prematurely. Most of the heavy shafts were poorly aimed or didn't have the necessary distance to reach *Windchaser,* but a few thudded into the ship's prow or tangled in the forward sails.

"Helmsman, bring us to her port side," Captain Attikus ordered.

"Aye, aye, Cap'n." The helmsman yanked on the great wheel as sail crews yanked the booms and adjusted the 'yards to present the canvas so the ship turned hard to port.

Blowfly, without the favor of the wind, appeared dead in the water. The goblin crew pushed and shoved against each other in the stern as they fired their bows.

Arrows flew all about *Windchaser.* Several caught in her canvas or struck her side. Juhg glanced up at Captain Attikus, wondering when he was going to give the order to shoot.

"Ornne," the captain called up. An arrow struck the stern deck only inches below his feet. In the next second, two more arrows lodged in the wood of the railing that fronted the stern deck. Captain Attikus stood his ground. Juhg knew the captain had no choice. If he elected to hide or flinch, his crew would lose faith in him and themselves.

The goblins had the distance now, but still lacked skill as true archers.

Elven bowmen, Juhg knew from experience, could have been at three times the distance and picked off their targets easily even as the sea rose and fell. He slid around the base of the mainmast, putting the thick column of wood between himself and the attack. Arrows slapped into the wood and Juhg felt the vibration of the impacts against his back.

"Ornne," Captain Attikus called. "Find me that wizard."

"Cap'n," Ornne protested from the crow's-nest, which was festooned with arrows, "mayhap that wizard ain't with them."

Two sailors aboard *Windchaser* went down with arrows through them. They yelled in fear and agony as they flopped on the deck.

"Cap'n," Navin called back, pacing nervously at the back of his crew. "We need to strike back."

"Patience, Navin," the captain said, his gaze never leaving the goblin ship. "Would you rather face a wizard or a goblin crew?"

Navin scowled and cursed beneath his breath.

Back to the mainmast, Juhg peered at the goblin ship. The two ships rode nearly the same wave now, but *Blowfly* remained ahead of *Windchaser,* rising on the crest for a little while longer. By the time *Windchaser* came down after the goblin ship, her position on the wave put her almost on top of the other vessel. Several times while gazing over the ship's side, Juhg had the distinct belief that *Windchaser* was going to crash down on top of *Blowfly* and crush both ships.

"There!" Ornne screamed. "In the stern, Cap'n! The wizard's in the stern!"

Wiping the stinging brine from his eyes, Juhg stared at the goblin ship's stern. As he watched, the wizard trudged up the stairs leading to the stern castle. The goblin bowmen separated around the wizened figure in arcane robes.

"Archers," Captain Attikus ordered instantly, "take aim!"

"Aye, Cap'n," the archers responded.

The goblins continued to unleash uneven volleys of arrows. Three more sailors went down, one of them transfixed through the throat. The sight of the mortally wounded man pushed the fear inside Juhg to a fever pitch.

Another arrow struck Captain Attikus in the shoulder, driving him back a step.

For a moment, Juhg thought the arrow had pierced the man's heart.

Gathering himself, though obviously in pain, Captain Attikus reached for the arrow and snapped off the fletched end. Blood soaked his blouse, but his gaze rested unerringly on the goblin ship. He was a hunter in that moment, and the only thing that mattered was the ship he pursued as prey. "Steady, lads. Just hold steady." His voice betrayed no hint of fear or pain.

Windchaser steadily climbed out of the latest trough. With *Blowfly* dead in the water, *Windchaser* was in danger of pulling past the goblin ship on the port side.

107

"Steady," Captain Attikus urged. "Just hold steady and true, lads, and I'll see you through this."

Juhg watched, helplessly hypnotized by the action about to take place. Every archer in the *Windchaser* group stood tense as a bowstring, the fletchings pulled back nearly to their ears now.

Then *Windchaser* was over the wave, descending on the goblin ship like a fisherhawk diving for a fat prize just below the ocean's surface. She was still ten feet above *Blowfly*'s decks when Captain Attikus gave the order.

"Fire!"

Almost as one man, the archers loosed their shafts. Deadly and true, the arrows feathered the goblins and drove them back and down.

The wizard flung up a hand and something blurred in the air before him. Arrows stopped in mid-flight less than two feet away from him, then clattered to the stern deck. The wind tore at his hair and beard, but he stood irresolute.

"Archers," Captain Attikus yelled. "Fire at will!"

The archers already had their second shafts nocked and were picking out targets.

"Boarding crews," the captain bellowed, "prepare grappling hooks. I don't mean to miss that ship and let her have at our backside."

A dozen crewmen stepped forward with iron grappling hooks at the ends of chains. Regular grappling lines were made of hemp and could be thrown farther, but Captain Attikus preferred chain because even a sharp axe couldn't sever the heavy links on a first blow. Usually, even an axe drove the links deeply into the wooden railing.

The human archers fired again and again, spending their arrows with a miser's care but as quickly as they could pull the bowstring. The shafts fell with telling accuracy among the goblinkin. Squalling and cursing with utter ferocity and crudity, the goblins gave ground and fell back.

"Stand and fight, you blasted creatures!" the wizard snarled as he stood on the stern deck with imperious dignity. "I am Ertonomous Dron, and I will have your loyalty or I will have you dead!"

The goblin crew halted the mad scurry from the stern, but the creatures didn't appear willing to once more take up the fight.

"By the Dark Lord," the wizard thundered. "You'll not ignore my wishes." He lifted a skinny arm and pointed his wand at the nearest goblin.

 A pulse of almost invisible movement roiled over the hapless goblin and stripped away its clothing and flesh in a flash of eldritch blue fire, leaving only a gory skeleton standing in the boots it had been wearing. With the next heave of the waves, the skeleton came apart and loose bones clattered across the deck.

More properly motivated now, the goblins once more took up the battle, surging forward to try to be the first at the railing.

The display also somewhat weakened the resolve of *Windchaser*'s crew and gave hesitation to the archers. Juhg saw that effect in the slack-jawed look of amazement on the men's faces. No one—human, elf, dwarf, or goblin—wanted to get crossways with a wizard. Nearly everyone luckless enough to get in one's path or earn his ire didn't live to tell the story.

Or else they spend the rest of their life as a toad, Juhg thought. The wizard Craugh, who was a personal friend of the Grandmagister's, was reputed to have increased the populations of toads in several places where he was made unhappy or found villains working to thwart his designs.

"Grapplers," Captain Attikus commanded. "Heave the lines!"

Immediately, the sailors holding the grappling hooks hurled them at the other ship.

Wide-eyed, Juhg watched the hooks sail over the goblin ship's railing. The heavy hooks fell onto the deck, all save for one, which ended up over a goblin's shoulder. Tines scraped fresh white scars across the wooden deck as the sailors hauled the chains back. The hook that had fallen on the goblin buried itself in the creature's flesh, leaving it squalling and crying as it was spitted like a specimen in a butterfly collector's case.

"Free those lines," Ertonomous Dron shouted. "Keep those people back from this ship." The wizard paced behind the pack of howling goblins.

"'Yards," Captain Attikus called. "Away with you!"

Instantly, the dozen sailors who had been up in *Windchaser*'s rigging after furling the sails stepped forward and revealed themselves. Ornne bailed out from the crow's-nest, running confidently across the topmost 'yards to join the rigging crew.

The rigging crew perched at the ends of the 'yards like ungainly birds, waited for the pitch and yaw of the two ships to favor them, then launched themselves across twenty feet of open water and landed in the rigging of the goblin ship, catching fresh holds with uncommon skill.

Goblin archers wheeled to deal with the first wave of the invasion that was to come. As the goblins did, the creatures became targets for *Windchaser*'s archers. Arrows slammed into the goblinkin creatures and knocked them down.

The grappling crews aboard *Windchaser* secured the other ends of the chains that bound them to the goblin ship. The two vessels rubbed hulls with thunderous poundings that Juhg would have sworn meant they were both coming apart at the seams.

One of the grapples pulled free, tearing through a weakened section of railing that snapped like kindling. The goblin pinned by the grappling hook fought to escape but couldn't. Even so, when the goblin went slack in death, the grappling hook found no solid purchase and yanked the creature's corpse over the side. Still, ten grappling hooks held, binding *Blowfly*'s fate to *Windchaser*'s own.

"Boarders," Captain Attikus roared, "away!"

In quick order that showed practice and cunning, the sailors hoisted themselves up and threw themselves from *Windchaser*'s railing onto the goblin ship's deck. Swords flashed between the two crews, and the blades suddenly turned crimson.

High above the deck, the sailors in the goblin ship's rigging worked with sharp knives, slashing through the ropes and dropping the huge sheets of canvas onto the deck and crew. Even if the boarding attempt failed, *Blowfly* would be in no shape to try to evade *Windchaser* without effecting serious repairs. Quite possibly, the goblin crew wasn't even trained to restring the rigging and would end up at the sea's cold mercy.

At the back of the boarding party, the frown and frustration on his face clearly showing that he didn't like where he was, Raisho dropped his bow and quiver, then raked his cutlass from his sash. He turned to Juhg.

"C'mon, then, bookworm!" Raisho grinned. "Don't you want to be a hero?"

No, Juhg thought. Most heroes were dead heroes, and they never truly met easy ends. He'd learned that from all the history chronicles he'd read. The books from Hralbomm's Wing that Grandmagister Lamplighter treasured so much guaranteed a much happier end for heroes.

Juhg put his fear aside, concentrating on the idea of the book in goblin hands. He crossed the heaving deck, made even more treacherous by *Blowfly*'s drag, and stood behind Raisho. There was no time to wait, because as soon as Juhg arrived, the boarding party's wave of movement had reached Raisho.

Without hesitation, Raisho jumped lithely to the railing and held on to a ratline. He yelled in warning, then threw himself onto the other ship.

Juhg climbed to the top of the twisting railing more warily, not at all sure if he could leap the distance to *Blowfly*. He rocked with *Windchaser*'s motion, finding his balance despite the ship's heaving because he was a dweller and possessed incredible balance.

Raisho landed on the deck and fell into a swordsman's crouch immediately. The cutlass flashed in his right hand and he used a long knife in his left to parry. A trio of goblinkin confronted him as he surged forward to make room. Shifting quickly, Raisho disemboweled one goblin and continued spinning to the left. He parried a heavy slash aimed at its stomach with the dagger, driving the goblin's cutlass to the deck, where it tore out a chunk of wood. Then Raisho struck again, lopping the head from the third goblin. Still moving, he lifted his right foot and drove it into the face of the second goblin before the creature could free its cutlass from Raisho's dagger.

In an eye blink, a space was clear on *Blowfly*'s deck. Blood stained the wood, reminding Juhg of the cost that had been paid so far and yet remained to be paid still.

"Juhg!" Raisho barked, looking back over his shoulder.

8

Death in the Water

*g*alvanized into action because he knew his friend would stand there and be a target, Juhg took two lightning-fast steps across the nearest grappling chain, felt the links beneath his bare feet, and hurled himself onto the deck.

As surefooted as he'd been crossing the chain, though, he wasn't nearly as graceful meeting *Blowfly*'s shifting deck. It came up as he was going down, tripping him neatly and sending him sprawling.

Not, Juhg thought ruefully, *exactly a hero's arrival.* But his embarrassment was short-lived. When he rolled over, he discovered he'd gone several feet past the area Raisho had cleared. On his back now, he stared up at a goblin that grinned down at him.

"Come all this way to up an' die, did ye, halfer?" the goblin taunted. It took a two-handed grip on its cutlass and swung.

Juhg tried to move, but the bloody deck beneath him didn't allow him to get his footing. His hands slid out from under him and he sprawled again.

Then a cutlass intercepted the goblin's blade, sliding under it with a shriek of metal. Still, Juhg knew the blade was going to get him after all and split his skull because the cutlass couldn't halt the power of the downward swing. But the cutlass continued forward, catching the goblin's blade on the hilt, then the curved point dug into the deck on the other side of Juhg.

Staring up at the blade that had halted only inches from his head (because the defending cutlass had used the deck as a fulcrum to turn the blow), Juhg couldn't believe he was still alive. The goblin couldn't believe it either. An angry grimace melted the triumphant smile the foul creature had worn prior to the defense.

The goblin pulled its blade back and turned to face Raisho. Before the goblin could get set, Raisho spun and kicked his opponent in the face. Propelled by the blow, the goblin flew backward and toppled over the ship's railing. It squalled for an instant, then *Windchaser* and *Blowfly* came together in another thunderous *boom* as the hulls met.

Lying on his back, his attention focused on the railing area where the goblin had gone over, Juhg thought, *Squished. Now, that's a horrible way to die.*

Raisho grabbed him by his blouse and yanked him to his feet. He thrust his face into Juhg's and spoke loudly. "Are ye all right, Juhg?"

Juhg nodded and tried to speak twice before he could make any sound come out. "Yes."

"Good." Raisho released him. "Then see that ye stay that way. I'd not have the good Cap'n Attikus vexed at me 'cause I'd gone off an' let ye get skewered."

Juhg didn't want that either.

Beyond them, the fight continued. *Windchaser*'s crew slowly made headway against the goblins. The sailors weren't pretty in their swordplay as Raisho was. They were fierce fighting men, but not true swordsmen. Mainly, they hacked and slashed their way across the deck with brute force and some canny skills, working together and presenting a solid front. Goblins fell and gave ground before them.

High above the deck, the sabotage crew started clambering down. They cut ratlines and rigging free, swinging down to join the fray. With surprise, Juhg noted that Herby and Gust were among them. The young thief and the monk threw sections of rigging down over the goblin group, entangling them and causing no end of problems.

Navin stepped back from the boarding party and glanced up at the stern castle, where the wizard stood surrounded by a dozen goblins. "The wizard!" he shouted. "Get the wizard!"

A group of sailors split off from the main boarding party and hurried up the stairs. The goblins raced to intercept them. In a moment, the sailors' running advance was slowed to a crawl of inches.

Raisho growled and stamped his foot.

Juhg knew his friend longed to be part of the action.

Angry and frustrated, Raisho turned to Juhg. "The book. Will the wizard have the book?"

Steel on steel clanged around them and distracted Juhg terribly. He gazed up at the wizard, aware that the man stared at him.

It's my imagination, Juhg told himself. *That's what it has to be. This ship is so filled with enemy sailors, the wizard wouldn't notice me at all.*

But the wizard did. More than that, the wizard stretched out his arm and mouthed words as he pointed his wand.

"Raisho!" Juhg knew the young sailor hadn't seen the threatening move because he was engaged with a goblin that had fought through the main line. Juhg threw himself at Raisho's back and bore his friend down.

The goblin battling Raisho grinned maniacally as it assumed it had the upper hand. Raisho struggled to get his blade lifted for a defense, and for a moment Juhg thought he'd gotten the young sailor killed in spite of his efforts.

115

Just as the goblin swung, a green lightning bolt sizzled through the air where Juhg and Raisho had stood. Caught by the lightning bolt, the goblin exploded into splotchy gray-green chunks of burned meat and broken bone. Gore covered Juhg's face, letting him know how near a thing the encounter had been.

Raisho moved instantly, pushing himself once more to his feet. He caught Juhg's collar with his dagger hand and yanked the dweller to his big feet.

"That wizard must have recognized what a fierce fighter I am," Raisho growled, peering up at the stern castle.

Juhg didn't bother to mention that the wizard had directed the lightning bolt at him and Raisho happened to be in the way. *Why would a wizard target me?* Juhg wondered. Then Raisho pushed him into motion and rescued him from another goblin's cutlass.

Raisho fought quickly, outmatching the goblin in a few short, clanging strokes. When the goblin fell back, its head split open by a wicked cutlass blow, Raisho turned to Juhg.

"Do ye think the wizard has the book, then?" Raisho demanded.

The book. Somehow in the heat of the battle, Juhg had forgotten the reason he was there.

On the stern castle, the small group of sailors fought past the last of the goblin defenders. They raced toward the wizard, who stood his ground fearlessly. When they were almost upon him, the wizard mouthed more words, then swept his arm toward the sailors.

Arcane power blurred the air between them. The sailors fell back, great cuts opening across their bodies as if the same sword blow had hit each of them. They turned from a pack of fighting men into a group of dead and dying.

Juhg recognized all of them and felt their loss. Tears sprang to his eyes as he realized that he would no longer listen to those men's stories or songs, nor have the chance to regale them with his own.

Raisho cursed and started toward the stern castle.

Catching his friend's arm, Juhg said, "The wizard won't have the book."

Torn, obviously angry and hurting over the loss of so many of his friends, Raisho glared at Juhg. "Ye don't know that."

"I believe it to be true," Juhg said. "The book is under the wizard's care, Raisho. It doesn't belong to him. Otherwise he would have had it on his person that night in the harbor."

Raisho took a fresh grip on his sword and looked determined to scale the stern castle himself. "He killed them, Juhg! He killed them all!"

The dead sailors' bodies sprawled across the stern deck. Unseeing eyes stared from their pain-wracked faces.

"I know," Juhg said. "I'm sorry. But you can't do anything for them."

"I can avenge them."

Juhg stepped in front of his friend, aware that they were targets on the deck. Navin and the rest of the boarding party held back the goblin crew, pressing the creatures toward the ship's prow as they fought through the tangle of fallen sails.

"Avenge them by taking the prize," Juhg said, locking eyes with his friend. "That's what they died for." He glanced back at the stern castle,

afraid that at any moment the wizard would blast them to bits with another lightning bolt.

Ertonomous Dron, however, appeared weakened. Though he alone
stood alive on the stern deck, he leaned back against the railing and seemed
to struggle to stay on his feet on the heaving deck. *Blowfly* continued to
strain against the binding chains that held her fast to *Windchaser*. Juhg had
no doubt that the ride aboard *Windchaser* was no easy thing either.

"The wizard has spellcast himself to weakness," Raisho argued.

"Or he's playing possum," Juhg pointed out.

"He killed our *friends*," Raisho growled.

Juhg looked at the young sailor. "And I'll not suffer the loss of another
if I can help it. This ship is a dead thing, Raisho. Even if we don't kill the
wizard, he won't make it out of these waters alive. Not without a ship's
crew. Not without a ship."

Two goblinkin broke free of Navin's boarding party. Sailors shouted
warnings to Raisho. Wheeling quickly, the young sailor met the blades of
the goblins with his own, knocking the creatures aside. Moving into the
creatures he stomped on one goblin's knee, breaking the limb with a short,
vicious crack, then slitting his opponent's throat with his dagger as the goblin fell. He made a cunning twist against the other goblin and dropped the
creature's headless corpse to the deck.

Standing, breathing hard and covered in goblin gore, Raisho looked at
Juhg. "All right, then. Belowdecks it is. We'll get that book, an' if that
wizard still lives, I swear I'll make him pay for the lives of our mates."

Juhg shuddered at the ferocity of the oath. He had never truly seen this
side of his friend during the time they had shared together.

Raisho jerked his head toward the middle hold only a few feet behind
the line Navin and the other boarders held. He pushed Juhg into motion
and fell in beside and one step ahead of him.

Blowfly tilted sharply, twisting back toward her stern as she slid over
another tall wave and *Windchaser* held her back. The slippery blood caused
Juhg's feet to go out from under him. He fell, skidded, and caught himself.
Just as he was about to grab onto the hold and heave himself inside, a loose
sprawl of canvas from the fallen sails slid over the hold and covered it to
block the way.

"No," Juhg wailed, pulling at the heavy canvas. The sail proved too
heavy for him to manage by himself. For a moment, he thought the canvas

had been cast there by some spell on the wizard's part, but a glance back at Ertonomous Dron showed the man still holding on to the stern railing to support himself.

Without warning, Gust dropped to the deck beside Juhg. The little monk shrilled and shook his hairy fingers at Juhg, then grabbed the sailcloth and tugged. Unable to move the sailcloth, Gust shrilled angrily and shook his hands at Juhg.

"Move aside," Raisho commanded in a voice strained by emotion. "Ye too, ye flea-bitten imp."

Feeling helpless, Juhg scrambled to one side. Gust leapt up and caught the lowest section of nearby rigging. He chattered the whole time as if disgusted and feeling abused.

Raisho plunged his cutlass into the center of the canvas covering the hold. The blade sliced through the sailcloth easily. The young sailor withdrew the cutlass and slashed again, inscribing a large X that defined the perimeters of the hatch opening.

"There," Raisho said as he drew the cutlass back again.

Juhg peered down into the hold and caught a metallic glint. He dodged back just in time to avoid the spear thrust that nearly caught him in the eye.

"Goblin!" Juhg yelped as the goblin thrust again with the spear.

Raisho lifted his foot, then slammed his boot into the creature's face. Knocked from the ladder, the goblin fell back into the waist.

"Well," Raisho commented, "at least it's not gonna be dull down there." He took a fresh grip on his cutlass. "Ye stay back aways, then, bookworm. I'll clear the way." He swung over the hold's side and onto the ladder, clutching it with his left hand crooked so he could grip with his wrist and maintain the hold on the dagger.

Peering down into the darkened hold, Juhg was suddenly of a mind that perhaps confronting the wizard in the grim daylight provided by the storm conditions might be a better option than running through the narrow confines of the decks below. By that time, though, Raisho had already set off into the waist, heading—no doubt—for the wizard's quarters.

Move, Juhg commanded himself. *You can't let Raisho go alone to brave those enchantments that protect the book.*

Gathering his courage, he threw a leg over the side of the hold and descended into the shadowy darkness below. The goblin that had fallen at the foot of the ladder suffered from a broken neck. Juhg knew that at once by the grotesque twist of the creature's head because it was very nearly looking at its own back.

The stench of the goblinkin ship was almost overwhelming, even worse than Juhg remembered. *Of course, that might have something to do with expecting one of them to come lunging out of the darkness at any moment.* Memory of the sailors felled by Ertonomous Dron's wizardly magic pummeled his thoughts and chipped away at his confidence as he stumbled over *Blowfly*'s uneven deck while the ship pitched and yawed and fought her tethers to *Windchaser*.

Undaunted by anything that had happened, Raisho forged ahead. The lanterns mounted on the hallway walls streamed thin wisps of smoke up against the ceiling.

A goblin charged from the other end of the hallway with an uplifted axe. Another climbed up from the hold below with a lighted lantern in one hand.

Raisho roared a battle cry and rushed forward at once. He caught the goblin's axe with his dagger and halted the weapon's descent. Still pushing, Raisho shoved the goblin back into the creature behind it, revealing yet a third goblin climbing up from the hold.

The lantern light gleamed as it played over the goblins. The realization that the goblins were wet unleashed a new fear inside Juhg.

We're sinking! Perhaps he might have been jumping to conclusions, but he figured that line of thought was much better than thinking everything was all right when in fact it wasn't.

A blood-curdling yell behind Juhg caused him to jump. Glancing over his shoulder, he spotted two more goblins coming from the prow end of the ship.

Raisho had his hands full with the three goblins he'd already taken on.

Knowing he couldn't take the goblins on in armed combat and hope to survive, Juhg ran. A desperate plan formed in his mind as he spotted the door to the wizard's quarters. He only hoped that Ertonomous Dron hadn't relocated in the last two days.

He grabbed the handle and twisted. *Locked!* He tried the handle again with the same result. *Of course it would be locked. And probably better than it was last time.*

By that time, the lead goblin was almost upon him. Juhg turned to face the brute. He lifted his hands before him, knowing that Raisho would not arrive in time to save him.

"Halfer," the goblin grinned as it faced Juhg. The word held all the contempt the goblins had for the dwellers. It pulled its heavy battle-axe back and prepared to swing. "I'm gonna chop you into tiny bits, and then make soup outta what's left."

Always with the speeches, Juhg thought. *They don't threaten Raisho when they fight him.* His thinking skated crazily in his mind, propelled by terror and the certainty that he was doomed. But he prepared himself. Struggling in the goblin mines and venturing out across the mainland with Grandmagister Lamplighter had prepared him to take his fate in his own hands when he had no choice.

And the Old Ones had blessed dwellers with uncommon quickness. Juhg noticed the way the goblin's upper body tensed, then ducked under a horrendous blow that would have cleaved him in twain had it hit. Desperately, Juhg grabbed the goblin's foot while it was off balance and yanked with all his might.

Behind Juhg, the door broke loose from its moorings under the goblin's forceful blow and fell inward. The goblin's foot came up as the creature rocked back with the axe blow, and Juhg kept the limb moving till his opponent fell backward.

The goblin landed on its nether regions and also knocked the nearest goblin down. The felled creature glared up at Juhg with murderous fury. "Now you're gonna die, halfer."

As if that wasn't the plan in the first place, Juhg thought. He regretted the time spent thinking the thought. Sarcasm, as it turned out—even when it was instinctive and quick—cut into the time one had to manufacture one's escape.

Shoving himself to his feet, Juhg bolted for the wizard's room because there simply was no place else to go. *And I've got to be here anyway.* His first step, however, sent him sprawling as he tripped over the broken door knocked off its hinges by the goblin's axe blow.

Juhg landed on his face, bruising his chin terribly and almost knocking himself senseless. He groaned and rolled over weakly, barely managing to keep his mind focused. He glanced up as the first goblin grabbed the doorframe and hauled itself into the room.

"This is the wizard's room," one of the goblins behind the first cried out.

"I know it is," the first goblin said. "Do you think I'm stupid?"

"It's death to be in the wizard's room. The cap'n told us. The wizard himself told us."

"Would you rather go back to the wizard and tell him we allowed the halfer to rummage through his things?"

The second goblin looked perplexed. "No . . ."

"Well, then, let's kill the halfer and be quick about it." The first goblin took its battle-axe in both hands.

"Remember the snakes from the other night?" the second goblin asked. "They almost done for us."

"The snakes are gone."

"There'll be other . . . things."

"I don't see no—" The first goblin suddenly screamed in fear. "It's got me! It's got me! I'm blind! I'm blind, I tell you!"

In total disbelief, surprised that he wasn't already dead, Juhg glanced up and saw that Gust had somehow found his way into the ship's hold. Evidently the monk had seen the danger Juhg was in and chose to do something about it. He squatted on the first goblin's shoulders and held his hands over the goblin's eyes.

"It's a monk," the second goblin said.

"A monk?"

"Aye. A monk."

"Well, get it off me before it puts my eyes out."

The second goblin reached for the monk. Seeing his danger, Gust vaulted into the room and landed on Juhg. Immediately, the monk clambered atop Juhg's head and wrapped his arms tight around his neck and under his jaw.

The goblin drew back the battle-axe again.

Abandoning his attempts to free the monk from around his head, Juhg threw himself at the desk where the book was kept. Confident of themselves against a dweller and a monk, the goblins thundered after him. In front of the desk, Juhg caught the handle to the drawer, felt the tingle of whatever magical spell protected the book, and yanked the drawer open.

All three goblins gathered around the desk. The creatures grinned in wicked anticipation.

"Ah, little halfer," the first goblin said, "you've certainly picked the wrong place to hide."

Juhg, with Gust still wrapped around his head and a hairy arm over his right eye so he could only see from his left, sat on the floor under the desk in mortal terror. He pressed his back against the wall behind him and bitterly cursed the luck that he was having. Evidently the wizard had removed the spell of protection.

"C'mere, halfer," the first goblin coaxed, reaching under the desk for Juhg. "Let me fetch you out of there so's I can get a clean chop. I swears I'll have you outta your misery quick-like."

Gust howled mournfully in Juhg's ear, obviously fully aware that the end of his own existence was at hand.

Just before the goblin's massive hand clutched Juhg's ankle, shadows suddenly twisted inside the room. Memory told Juhg that the only light had been a thick candle on the desk that barely served to beat back the darkness. Against the opposite wall behind the trio of goblins, the bobbing shadows looked massive.

"Oh no," one of the goblins whispered in a hoarse voice as it looked up at the desktop.

Screams out in the hallway let Juhg know that Raisho was still hard at work fighting goblins.

The goblin that had hold of Juhg's ankle looked up as well, then swore a vicious oath. In the next instant, Juhg watched as a snake head the size of a water barrel snapped down and gulped the goblin down to its head and shoulders. The goblin screamed in terror, but it sounded like its voice was coming out of a cave.

The snakes were much bigger than Juhg remembered. Instead of ending the enchantment that protected the book, Ertonomous Dron had obviously strengthened them. Fat coils of impossibly huge snakes started hitting the floor and kept coming.

The snake that had hold of the goblin that had hold of Juhg pulled. The goblin went up into the air and Juhg came out from under the desk.

"Yaaaaahhhhhh!" one of the two free goblins yelled. The creatures pushed at one another in their haste to flee the room. Before the goblins got far, the second snake whipped down and snatched one of the two up. Coils of snake blocked the third goblin's escape.

Screaming in terror himself, Juhg kicked out at the goblin holding him by the ankle and tried to pry the monk from around his neck. Gust had a stranglehold on Juhg that shut his wind off.

mel odom

The goblin's strength, especially when frightened, proved too strong to break, but luckily when the snake opened its venomous jaws to take a bigger chomp of its intended repast, it knocked free the goblin's hand from Juhg's ankle.

Horrified at the sight before him, Juhg watched as the snake's head came low to the floor, then tilted up so the mouth pointed toward the ceiling. The goblin's legs kicked frantically as it yelled for help. Then the snake's head swelled as the jaws slid all the way down the goblin. In the next instant, the goblin's boots shivered just beyond the snake's snout, then they too disappeared.

Juhg grabbed Gust's fingers quite by accident, only because one of them had slipped into his eye and created stabbing pain. Still half-blind, his wounded eye smarting severely, he managed to disentangle himself from the monk. He looked up just in time to bump noses with the giant snake.

The snake's nose was bigger than Juhg's head. In the candlelight, the scales glittered iridescence and possessed an oily sheen. Plumes of heated air from the snake's nostrils pushed into Juhg's face as he sat there hypnotized by the presence of imminent death. Gust was not so enthralled. With a shrill cry of alarm, the monk hurled himself from Juhg's shoulders and dashed toward the door.

Then the snake grinned, or so it seemed, because the jaws widened to reveal the pink and white mouth and the wickedly curved fangs. Just as Juhg was certain the snake was about to swallow him whole, the goblin came surging back up from the snake's throat.

Attacked, quite literally, by a case of indigestion, the snake clamped its jaws shut and swallowed its gorge once more.

The action released Juhg from his stunned state and he stood. Information he'd read came to mind. Two days ago when he'd confronted the snakes the first time, he hadn't been able to think about the source of the spell of protection. During his time at the Vault of All Known Knowledge, he'd read a lot about magic and wizards because the subject had fascinated him. Especially after coming in contact with some of the magical items Grandmagister Lamplighter and he had found over their years of roving. Cobner, the stouthearted dwarf who belonged to Brant's gang of thieves, still carried a magical axe that they had found when they'd gone questing for the riddle of the Quarhavian Toad Emperor. Cobner also still carried the scars that acquiring that axe had given him.

Spells of protection, Juhg knew, depended on an array of tokens infused with power by a wizard. The problem was that those tokens could be anything. However, they had to be things that were the same, each identical to the other so the necessary resonances could be used by the spell's energy.

Juhg's quick eyes scanned the room. There was no hope of escaping through the door because the second snake blocked the way.

"Juhg! *Juhg!*" Raisho called from the door.

From the corner of his eye, Juhg saw his friend valiantly, but ultimately ineffectually, hacking at the snake's body with the cutlass and the knife. Neither weapon truly harmed the magical constructs that guarded the mysterious book.

The snakes continued to move restlessly. The second one snatched up the final goblin and started choking the creature down.

Gust scampered around the room, mad with fright and knowing he was running for his life. His antics drew the attention of the first snake from Juhg.

Then Juhg's quick eyes noted the bright copper coin set squarely under the snake's chin as it swiveled its head to follow the monk. He glanced around the room, looking for copper coins, knowing there had to be some.

Candlelight brought the coins, now that he knew what to search for, into bright relief. One was on the other side of the room, and one was inset in the ceiling almost over the snake's weaving head. Juhg knew more coins had to be placed inside the room to create the protection spell, but he was all out of time.

The snake struck at Gust twice but missed both times.

Knowing he would never get to the other side of the room past the snake, Juhg set his sights on the one inset in the ceiling. All he had to do was pry the coin out. Unfortunately, he didn't have a tool to do the job. He glanced at Raisho, who was still struggling to cut his way into the room.

"Raisho," Juhg called. "I need your dagger."

Reacting at once, Raisho reversed his dagger and held it by the blade. A quick flip spun the knife through the air.

Panic flooded Juhg as he watched the dagger embed deeply into the back of the snake's thick neck.

Drawn by the sudden pain, the snake lost interest in tracking Gust and turned its baleful attentions to Juhg, as if holding him responsible for the sharp pain in its neck. Knowing he had no choice now, Juhg set his fear aside for the moment as he'd learned to do in the mines when the pit bosses had come along to taunt and terrorize the shackled dwellers digging in the deep earth.

The snake opened its jaws and struck, but Juhg was in motion by then. The snake's head smashed the writing desk into a thousand pieces. He put a hand at the side of the snake's jaw and ran forward, vaulting up onto the snake's back. If he'd been wearing shoes of any kind, except perhaps for Jalderrin Stickyfoot climbing shoes made of Vankashin spider's web far to the south and knitted with magical dreamthorn, which could grip any surface, he would have slipped and fallen on the tight, smooth scales.

The snake shifted, though, as it coiled back to view the dweller running up its back. The angle of its back straightened and Juhg couldn't run straight. He dug his toes in and leapt, catching hold of the dagger's haft and hoping scales would hold it fast. Holding on to the dagger, he flipped and scooted up behind the snake's head.

Feeling someone on its head, the snake bobbed and weaved in an effort to dislodge Juhg. He held tight desperately. *I'mgonnadie, I'mgonnadie!* With his legs wrapped snugly around the lunging creature, he took a fresh grip on the dagger haft and yanked the blade free. Bilious blue ichor spewed from the wound, but the bleeding slowed almost immediately as the puncture started closing because of the snake's innate magic nature.

Juhg's effort to get the knife threw him off balance. He slid down the snake's neck, looking at the same time for the copper coin embedded in the room's ceiling. Knowing he had only one chance, he sprang from the snake's back. Faster than Juhg would have believed possible, the snake snapped its jaws open and struck at him.

Great gleaming fangs rushed at Juhg as he drove the dagger at the coin embedded in the ceiling. *Letmehitit! Letmehitit!* He put out his free hand to keep his face from smashing into the ceiling. He shoved the dagger at the coin, missed by two inches, and cut a deep groove across the wooden ceiling. The snake's mouth lay open like a dark fanged pit beneath him. The forked tongue flicked out and caught him in the ear.

Then the dagger's point caught the edge of the coin, slid into the deep wood, and the coin spun free. The snake didn't disappear immediately as Juhg had thought. As gravity overcame him and he fell, he dropped into the snake's mouth, felt the cold and wet rush of reptilian flesh around him, and knew he wouldn't stop plummeting till he reached the thing's gullet.

125

the destruction of the books

He closed his eyes. *That's what you get for thinking you know so much!*

Then he landed flat on his back on the floor hard enough to knock the wind from his lungs. He opened his eyes and looked up at the ceiling, realizing only then that he wasn't in the snake's belly as he'd feared he would be.

Without warning, Raisho leaned in over him with a worried expression.

Startled by the unexpected sight of his friend, Juhg yelped in fear.

Pumped up by his own battles and the near thing that had just happened, Raisho yelled back, thinking he was under attack from behind. He whirled with his sword in his fist. Gust, frenzied from being chased around the room by the huge snake, chose that moment to leap on Raisho's shoulders from the cabinet space he'd taken refuge in. Evidently the monk believed Raisho was an island of safety in a suddenly insane world.

Raisho yelled again and grabbed the monk. He drew back his cutlass as he swung the monk around.

"No!" Juhg said, scrambling to his feet. "It's just Gust!"

Chest heaving from his exertions and the panic that had seized him, Raisho managed to stay his hand. Held by the scruff of his neck, the monk dangled and whimpered with his hands over his eyes.

"Stupid monk," Raisho growled. He opened his hand and Gust dropped to the floor on all fours.

 Gust retreated quickly and hid under the wizard's bed. He leaned out from under the edge of the bed and shook his fists at Raisho while screaming monk imprecations.

Raisho quickly surveyed the room, searching for enemies and surprises. Then he looked at Juhg, hugged him tight for a moment, and grinned. "Ye're alive."

"I am." Juhg, still somewhat stunned by that fact, ran his hands over his chest to make sure he was still whole as well.

"Where did the snakes go?"

"I broke the spell."

"An' ye know magic now, do ye?"

"Not exactly." Juhg grimaced as his hand found a big glop of what appeared to be snake spit running down his side.

"Careful with that," Raisho advised. "Could be poison."

Now, there's a cheery thought, Juhg thought. He took his hand away and grabbed some of the bedding from the wizard's bunk.

Raisho took a fresh grip on his cutlass and picked up the dagger Juhg had dropped when he'd slammed against the floor. "Will them snakes be back?"

"No." Juhg turned and looked back at the shattered debris of the writing table. A patch of red fabric caught his eye and filled his heart with hope. "With the enchantment broken, they're banished back to whatever place the wizard called them from."

"Why didn't ye think of breakin' the enchantment the other night when we was runnin' for our lives?"

"Because we were running for our lives." Juhg crossed to the patch of fabric and dug through the debris. He felt a smile spread across his face as he uncovered the book. The tome was unharmed despite the snake's fierce blow. "Surviving can be very distracting."

"Hmph," Raisho snorted. "I'm just sayin' that if ye could break the enchantment, it would have been better, is all."

"And we'd still have had the goblin crew to worry about."

"Aye." Raisho looked up. "Well, we got yer book. Let's get back topside an' see how we're doin'."

The reminder about the battle going on there dimmed Juhg's feelings of success. Carefully, he tucked the book away inside his blouse and followed Raisho. He stopped at the door long enough to call for Gust. If the monk didn't return to the ship, Herby would be heartbroken.

Reluctantly, Gust emerged from under the bed and bounded across the room. He latched onto one of Juhg's legs, wrapping his arms and legs as well as his tail around the dweller's limb. Burdened by the weight of the monk and unable to persuade the creature to let him go, Juhg limped down the hallway after Raisho.

The young sailor immediately started up through the hold.

Juhg dashed past the ladder.

Halting just under the deck, Raisho peered down. "Where ye goin'?"

"To check the hold," Juhg replied, racing past a dead goblin in the hallway toward the hatch that led down to the cargo hold. "Those goblins that came after me were wet."

"Ye think *Blowfly* is leakin'?"

"Has to be. Have you ever heard of goblins bathing?"

Raisho scowled. The idea of goblins bathing was disturbing on two fronts. For one, gobins *never* bathed unless the creatures were caught out in a rainstorm. And two, goblins were hideous enough dressed. A naked goblin had to be truly stomach-wrenching.

Juhg took a lantern from the hallway wall on his way. The goblin ship listed hard, and the thunderous cannonade of *Windchaser*'s hull slamming into her again filled the hallway. He bounced off the wall, painfully jarring his shoulder. Then, reaching the hatch, he dropped to his knees and held the lantern out over the opening.

Twenty feet and more below, water rushed from *Blowfly*'s prow to her stern, mirroring the movement of the ship in the water. Crates and barrels floated on the water, hinting at the depth the vessel had already taken on.

"She's holed." Raisho peered over Juhg's shoulder. "Looks like her bottom's busted up somewhere, though I can't see where. We'll have to tell Cap'n Attikus. If *Blowfly* rips loose all at once, she could drag *'Chaser* down with her."

Gust shrilled and shook one tiny fist.

Raisho clapped Juhg on the shoulder, nearly knocking him down. "C'mon, then. I'm sick to me stomach over this blasted stench."

Worrying, knowing that the waters around the Tattered Islands were filled with hidden reefs and sandbars, Juhg followed Raisho back to the ladder. Raisho climbed swiftly to the top, and Juhg trailed along as best as he could with the monk wrapped fearfully around his leg.

Raisho halted at deck level and shoved the slashed sailcloth out of the way. "It's clear," he advised, then hauled himself up.

Struggling, Juhg crawled out onto the deck as well. Once more in the open, Gust released his leg and scampered into the ship's rigging. Dread filled Juhg at once as he stood on the heaving ship's deck.

Dead goblins and sailors sprawled in all directions. *Blowfly*'s sails and rigging hung in tatters. To port, *Windchaser* strained under her own weight, as well as the additional weight of the foundering goblinkin ship.

Even with their losses and having being outnumbered at the onset, the pirate crew had defeated the goblinkin. The survivors clustered in the ship's stern with their swords as they faced Ertonomous Dron. Despite being cornered as he was, the wizard showed no fear.

Raisho ran forward, leaping and dodging bodies of friends as well as opponents.

Not feeling nearly as heroic or driven, Juhg hung back. Finding a new home in a snake's gullet had been a near thing. Still, he was drawn reluctantly to the action.

The bodies of the sailors slain by the wizard's invisible blade earlier lay in a half-moon around Ertonomous Dron. Wind clawed at the old wizard's iron-gray hair and beard. Several of the sigils on his blue robe glowed with inner fire, but more of them were dull and lifeless.

Five archers aboard *Windchaser* loosed arrows. Imperiously, Ertonomous Dron waved his hand and reversed the course of the arrows so they struck the archers and drove them back down onto the pirate ship's deck.

"Any man that seeks to touch me dies," the wizard promised.

The sailors hung back as their foe held them off with his steely gaze. Superstitious by their very nature, sailing men wanted nothing to do with anything that smacked of magic unless it promised good luck.

Raisho strode forward. "Yer ship lays a-dyin', wizard. Even now she founders, an' she's gonna go down. Unless ye can sprout wings an' fly away, ye'll go down with her soon enough."

"Mayhap," the wizard threatened, undaunted, "I'll just turn you into the giant popinjay that you are and fly away on you." He pointed his wand.

All of the sailors, including Raisho, drew back.

"Avast there," Captain Attikus called from *Windchaser*. He stood on the pirate ship's stern deck. Blood streaked his clothing from the arrow in his shoulder. He clung to the railing and Juhg felt certain it was as much for support now as it was to stand against *Windchaser*'s pitching deck. "You've got nowhere to run to, wizard. I'll negotiate your surrender. If you're willing."

A feral grin lighted the wizard's face. "I think not, Captain. No matter what you say, I don't believe your offer would be overly generous."

"I'd see you live," Captain Attikus replied gruffly, taking a little offense at the wizard's pointed declaration.

"On your word of honor?" Ertonomous Dron curled his lip in a cold sneer. "How quaint. Do you know what a sense of honor is, Captain? It's a vulnerability. A chink in a man's armor. No, I don't live my life as an honorable man, nor will I hold others to such a thing."

"'A man who knows honor recognizes it in others,'" Captain Attikus said.

The quote of Seldorn the Gracious, king of Coppertop and author of

The Art of Chivalry, surprised Juhg. He knew the captain wasn't a man of letters, so Attikus must have heard the quote at some point.

"I see no honor," Ertonomous Dron said. "Nor do I seek it. I've always been a man who has made my own way in this life." He turned abruptly and pointed the wand at Juhg, calling out commands in an inhuman tongue.

Before he could move, Juhg saw the near-invisible force surround him. Then whirling winds lifted him from the deck and sailed him through the tangled mess of rigging and 'yards. In a moment, he hung suspended before the wizard.

Ertonomous Dron's eyes widened in surprise. "A dweller."

Juhg wriggled inside the whirling winds that held him but couldn't escape. He was trapped.

"I was told one of the brigands who stole aboard this ship the other night was a dweller," the wizard said. "I even thought I saw you myself, but I knew it couldn't be."

"Let him go," Raisho yelled, stepping forward.

Ertonomous Dron whirled on the young sailor. "Or what? You'll die before him?"

"If ye kill the little man," Raisho growled, "ye'll perish right after him."

"Let me get this straight," Ertonomous Dron said. "If he lives, then I live?"

The arrogant tone the wizard wielded like a weapon echoed over the deck, drowning out the creak of timbers and whine of rigging.

"All right," Ertonomous Dron said. "You drive a hard bargain, but I'll do it. I'll let the little dweller live, though I do loathe the vile creatures, so that I may live. But I must admit, I hate being blackmailed into such an agreement by men who were only moments ago offering me honor."

Juhg pitched and strained against the force that held him. Unfortunately, his efforts only succeeded in setting him to spinning inside his invisible cage. He clawed the air frantically in an effort to stop his wild, head-over-heels gyrations.

The wizard gestured again and Juhg stopped whirling.

"What were you after the other night?" Ertonomous Dron mused. "Even pirates usually have better things to do than rob vessels crewed by goblins. Unless they've come to rescue family members or friends who were taken on as slaves."

Juhg's heart pounded. The wizard hadn't been taxed as much as he'd believed.

"And since when do dwellers travel so easily among humans? Hmmmm?" the wizard asked. He smoothed his beard with his free hand. "There is more to you than meets the eye, dweller." The wizard gestured with his free hand.

Movement stirred in Juhg's chest. For a moment, Juhg believed the wizard had worked a spell that yanked his heart from his body. Then he saw the red clothbound book spin free into the air in front of him.

A frown furrowed Ertonomous Dron's weathered face. "You were after the book?"

Juhg tried to think of a lie, but his skills weren't that good. He knew any falsehood he tried out would be immediately known for what it was.

"Are you a Librarian, dweller?" Ertonomous Dron demanded.

Fear stilled Juhg's tongue, but he felt that he was going to throw up. From the corner of his eye, he saw Raisho duck away quickly, fading back into the crowd of sailors. Juhg felt terribly betrayed. He couldn't believe Raisho would so handily abandon him.

"Did you hear me?" Ertonomous Dron asked more forcefully. He gestured with the wand.

Inside the bubble of magical force, Juhg shook and spun. The air turned thick as syrup and wouldn't move from his lungs. He couldn't breathe.

"For years I've heard the stories of the Librarians." Ertonomous Dron stepped closer, examining his captive with renewed interest. "Dwellers who know how to read and write. Hmph. It's always been my experience that trying to pass on any kind of higher learning to a dweller was wasted effort. Put them at the end of a pick or a hoe, or leave them a pile of dirty dishes that need cleaning. That's the kind of work dwellers are best suited for. If you can get them to work at all."

The harsh words stung Juhg's pride. After all the years he'd spent swinging a pick in the mines under goblinkin supervision, he knew he had grown and changed under Grandmagister Lamplighter's expert tutelage. Mainland dwellers didn't even have rudimentary written language. They didn't know about the existence of the Vault of All Known Knowledge on Greydawn Moors.

"A bunch of poppycock are what those stories are," Ertonomous Dron announced. "Just stories a few meek dwellers tell themselves to make themselves feel better about their lot in life."

What dwellers? Juhg wanted to know. But he couldn't speak.

Over the years, only a few dwellers ever left Greydawn Moors. Most believed there simply was no better place in the world—at least, not for dwellers. The warders, sailors, craftsmen, and merchants who traded out of Greydawn Moors all believed in the great Library and would not betray its secrets. They were all watched like hawks. If loyalty didn't keep them in check, then the elven warders assigned to keep prying eyes away from the island would find them and execute them.

"Where are you from, dweller?" the wizard asked.

In that moment, Juhg knew that the wizard believed all those stories that he had heard. The question was a trick, designed to get the location of Greydawn Moors from him.

"Why would you steal a book?" the wizard asked. "Do you work for Craugh?"

The question surprised Juhg. He hadn't known that Craugh was known outside of Greydawn Moors. However, a number of times Craugh had accompanied Grandmagister Lamplighter on forays out into the mainland. Or, at least, had started the Grandmagister out across the Blood-Soaked Sea.

"I'll have your secrets, little dweller," the wizard promised in a low and threatening voice. "There are people who would pay dearly for what I believe you know."

"Hey," Raisho called as he stepped out from the crowd carrying a fishnet in his arms. "Wizard."

Irritation filled Ertonomous Dron's face as he turned toward Raisho. Before he could say anything, Raisho threw the fishnet.

The wizard threw up his hand. The fishnet slowed in midair but didn't stop advancing. Juhg thought maybe it was because the net wasn't a projectile weapon because some magic only turned edged attacks or objects the wizard who cast the spell recognized as potentially lethal. Or maybe it was because the net was larger than an arrow or spear.

Whatever the case, the net belled out like a jellyfish, then fell over the wizard. The net wasn't heavy enough to bring the wizard down, but it staggered him. The bubble around Juhg dropped a few inches, and for just an instant the thick, syrupy air in his lungs became breathable. Then the bubble tightened with bone-breaking strength and the air returned to syrup.

"You'll pay for that, you insolent fool," the wizard threatened. He shoved his free hand through the net and gestured as he called on whatever dark powers he'd ascribed his allegiance to.

A shimmering wave of force smashed into Raisho and knocked him reeling. He flew backward and landed hard enough against the stern castle railing to crack several of the boards.

Ertonomous Dron used his free arm to pull at the net. But the net refused his efforts, becoming increasingly entangled around him.

Three other sailors darted forward, intending to take advantage of the wizard's weakness. Juhg could have told them—if he could have only spoken through the heavy liquid that gurgled in his lungs—that they were wasting their time. Ertonomous Dron curled his fingers, then snapped them forward. The three sailors jerked back as if pierced by harpoons. Blood gushed from wounds that suddenly opened up on their chests.

"Now," Ertonomous Dron said, turning his angry attention on Raisho, "now you're going to—"

"I don't think so," Raisho said. The young sailor leaned forward suddenly. A throwing knife magically appeared between his fingers.

For a moment, Juhg thought his friend was going to waste his time and his life by throwing the knife at the wizard. But Raisho whipped his arm away from his foe.

Straight and true, the throwing knife flipped through the air twice and hit the release lever for the stern anchor. Hammered by the strength of the knife throw, the lever jerked back into the unlocked position and chain began paying out from the wheel with loud clanks.

At the same moment, a coil of rope jerked to life between the wizard and Raisho. Captivated by the unfolding events, Juhg watched first in perplexion, then in wide-eyed understanding of the thing that Raisho had done.

One end of the rope was attached to the anchor chain, which pulled the rope down, and the other end was attached to the fishing net. The wizard realized what was going to happen as well and began frantically yanking at the fishnet.

Before he could free himself, the slack in the line disappeared and the rope drew taut. The weight of the anchor and chain yanked him from his feet. He screamed hoarsely, and Juhg thought that was horrible because Ertonomous Dron didn't sound like a wizard at all, but like an old man afraid of dying.

Scrabbling like a cat falling from a leafy perch in a tree, the wizard flailed for a handhold on the stern castle railing but sailed past it without pause. He followed the chain and the line down into the water, disappearing under the dark gray-green brine.

That was when Juhg realized the spell that the wizard had cast over him had remained in effect. Horrified, he tried to yell for help but couldn't get his voice to escape the thick sludge in his chest.

Then Raisho was there, leaping toward him and wrapping his arms around the invisible bubble. The young sailor used his weight to propel them to the deck and prevent Juhg from going over the side. The bubble burst, and Juhg wasn't sure if it was because he'd gone past reach of the wizard's spell or because the wizard had lost sight of him, things that were both important, according to books on high and low wizardry.

It could also have been because somewhere in the depths Ertonomous Dron met his final doom.

All Juhg knew was that Raisho had saved him from being pulled into the ocean and meeting whatever fate the wizard had met. And he could breathe again. He took a deep draught of air.

"I've got ye, bookworm," Raisho said. "Ye're safe enough now."

"I know," Juhg said. "Thank you."

Raisho got up and shoved a hand out to help Juhg to his feet.

"Hey, Raisho," Navin said, wiping blood from a cut on his face. "That were a neat trick with the fishin' net. Ye shoulda thought of it sooner."

"Well—" Raisho said, his chest puffing up.

Then a horrendous crash of splitting timbers rent the air. *Blowfly* shuddered and heeled abruptly. Caught by the grappling chains that still bound the two ships, *Windchaser* slammed against the goblinkin ship. More breaking timbers sounded and the deck beneath Juhg's feet actually split asunder.

"Raisho, ye great lummox!" one of the sailors cried out. "Ye didn't happen to think about what that there anchor would do when she hit sea bottom, now, did ye?"

Juhg could tell by the look on his friend's face that Raisho indeed had not thought that far ahead. Not that he faulted the young sailor. His quick thinking had saved several of them from the wizard's wrath.

But *Blowfly* was utterly doomed.

"Take leave of that ship," Captain Attikus ordered.

Windchaser slammed into *Blowfly* again and again. Each collision broke the goblinkin ship to pieces. In the space of a drawn breath, *Blowfly* dropped eight feet as her hold filled with water and the sea drank her down.

A patch of red cloth skidded past Juhg as the deck sharply tilted. *The book!* The realization struck him almost too late to save the mysterious tome from the water lapping over the rear of the stern castle. He ducked down and grabbed the book only inches from the water and shoved it back inside his blouse.

Under Captain Attikus' urging, the sailors stopped and collected their dead. They ran to the ship's side and struggled to get them across. That task was made easier—and more dangerous—because *Windchaser* kept banging into the goblinkin ship as both fought against the restraining pull of the anchor.

Raisho paused in the stern long enough to break loose the anchor wheel and cast it over the side to free both ships. But by that time the sailors walking on the midships were swamping through a foot of water and had dropped below *Windchaser*'s deck.

When all the human dead were cleared of the goblin ship and once more back aboard *Windchaser,* Juhg climbed up the rappelling chains. By the time he reached the deck, he was all but done in. Still, he helped stow the grappling chains.

The last of the sailors, Raisho among them, stepped from *Blowfly* while even her stern and prow decks were submerged. For the moment, only the natural buoyancy of the wood and possibly a few air pockets in the hold kept the failing ship afloat.

Windchaser fought the undertow created by the sinking ship. She'd taken quite a beating as well. With dead sailors in addition to wounded scattered across her deck, she looked like she as well might not survive the encounter.

Captain Attikus, haggard and pale from blood loss and pain, ordered the sails put up again. Staggering fitfully as though she were wounded herself, *Windchaser* slowly pulled away from the sinking goblin ship.

Aloft in the 'yards, handling the sails with the rest of the crew, Juhg felt pain over the loss of so many of the pirate crew. And he felt guilty because his mind wandered again and again to the book in his blouse. What secrets did it hold? And was it worth the lives of so many of his companions and the defenders of Greydawn Moors?

138

9

An Uncommon Gift

s he gonna live?"

Juhg brushed perspiration from his forehead as he worked on the arrow that had pierced Captain Attikus' upper chest. Raisho knelt at his side, helping with the surgical tools, hot water, and clean towels. Thankfully, the captain slept on his bed in his quarters.

"He'll live." Juhg examined the captain's wound. The broken end of the shaft jutted up from the puncture. "Judging from the placement of the arrow and the fact that the captain's breath remains free of blood and he's not coughing any up, I'd say the arrow missed the lung."

"An' that's good."

"Yes," Juhg said. "That's really good. If the arrow had pierced the lung, I wouldn't be able to save him."

"If the arrow hit the lung, ye couldn't save him?"

Juhg shrugged. "I might not be able to save him. There are other ways. It's just that I've never done them."

"But you've done this?"

"Yes. Three times before. Once, I had to take an arrow out of my own leg when I was stranded in the Bleak Marshes. The trick then was not to leave a blood spoor behind so wolphurs could track me." The memory still sometimes haunted Juhg in the still hours of the night.

"You've been in the Bleak Marshes?"

Juhg pressed a thumb against the arrow and found it moved with sufficient force. *Good. The muscles haven't contracted around it and locked it into place.* Getting the arrow out under those conditions would have been harder, and Attikus would have been laid up longer for recovery.

"Yes. Twice. Neither time because I wanted to go."

"Ye went with Grandmagister Lamplighter, then."

Juhg nodded.

"What was it like?" Raisho asked. "I've never been to them marshlands."

"Swampy. The woods were filled with things that existed only to kill you and eat you if they got the chance. And then there were endless mosquitoes as big as my fist."

"Did ye go there for treasure? I heard there was whole cities what was sunk out in them marshlands."

"We found three cities." Juhg took up one of the clean towels. "Lift the captain up a little and roll him onto his side."

Raisho leaned forward and performed what was asked, holding the captain effortlessly. "Three cities." He paused. "Did you find any treasures in 'em?"

"Yes. But we had to leave them in a hurry when we inadvertently provoked the people who lived there. And that wasn't what we went there for anyway."

"Ye went for a book."

The arrow stuck out Captain Attikus' back less than two inches. The arrowhead was a smooth one, not a broadhead. A broadhead, with its four razor-sharp edges set in an X, would have created more damage as well as a wound designed to stay open so the target would bleed to death.

Juhg took up a pair of tongs from the ship's medical kit. As quartermaster for the ship, Lucius was supposed to tend to all the medical needs. Unfortunately, Lucius had fallen as one of the first casualties. His body lay on the deck bundled in sailcloth, as were all the others. As it turned out, Juhg was the next crew member with the most medical experience.

"Yes. We went for a book. We found nine of them, in fact." Juhg took hold of the broken arrow with the tongs.

"Did men die them times?" Raisho asked in a quieter voice. "Men that went with ye an' the Grandmagister?"

"Yes." Juhg pulled on the arrow. Captain Attikus moved with it. "Raisho, I need you to hold the captain more securely. I'm going to take the arrow out now."

"Won't he start bleedin'?"

"A little. But the amount can be controlled with pressure. We waited this long so the body could start shutting off the blood to the wounded area."

"Yer body does that?"

"Of course it does. Haven't you ever noticed a scratch you might have gotten and the way the blood stops going to it?"

"Course I have." Raisho braced the captain.

"If your body didn't stop itself from bleeding, you'd die from even a small scratch. It would just take longer." Juhg took hold of the arrow and pulled. He didn't yank because that might have done more damage and even cost the captain the use of his arm. Slowly, the arrow pulled through the captain's chest. Blood followed, pooling on his hands and on the tongs. He breathed through his mouth, in order to keep from being sick. Even after everything he'd done, after everything he'd seen, he was still squeamish for this kind of work.

"Did an apothecary teach ye all this?" Raisho asked.

"I learned some of what I know from different people," Juhg said. "Apothecaries. Herbalists. Barbers who also treated wounds. Most of what I learned, though, I learned from books. Like the captain's wound. I've seen men die with arrows through their chests."

"Through their hearts?"

"Those too. But they die quick. A man shot through the lungs dies slower."

"Like a deer," Raisho said. "Ye shoot fer their lungs, an' while they lay dyin' a hunter cuts their throats so they pass on peaceable."

"Yes." Images spun in Juhg's mind of two men he'd seen die slow deaths as he'd described. Some of the things he'd seen while traveling with Grandmagister Lamplighter had been as horrible as the things he'd seen in the goblin mines.

The broken arrow shaft pulled free. Captain Attikus moaned.

Worried that he'd done something wrong, Juhg glanced at his patient.

After a moment of discomfort, Captain Attikus passed back into a deeper sleep.

"We lost a lot of good sailors today," Raisho commented a short time later.

"I know." Juhg tried not to think about it, but couldn't help himself. Mending the captain was his first priority, but there were others awaiting attention. He didn't want to do it. He knew two of the sailors would probably die during the night despite his best efforts. No matter what he knew, the thing he knew most of all was that he didn't know enough.

I'm a Librarian, not a doctor.

"All fer a book that ye can't even read," Raisho said.

His friend's words wounded Juhg deeply.

"I'm sorry. I shouldn't have said that," Raisho mumbled.

"It's all right," Juhg replied, though it really wasn't. But he knew a lot of the crew felt the same way as they trimmed the ship and effected repairs and tended their wounded shipmates.

"Mayhap that book will turn out to be important after all," Raisho said. "After all, a wizard was guardin' it."

That only made Juhg feel more useless. If the book were so important that Ertonomous Dron had enlisted a goblin ship to protect it, his inability to read it stopped him from taking any kind of action. Not that he could take any real action. The book had to go to Greydawn Moors, which was where *Windchaser* was now headed. But if he'd had the skills, he could have read the book and been prepared for Grandmagister Lamplighter. Together, they could have decided what to do about it.

And that's only if it doesn't turn out to be a cookbook, Juhg told himself sourly. If the book turned out to be something like that, or a made-up tale fit only for the shelves in Hralbomm's Wing, Juhg knew he would never live down the disgrace.

His only consoling thought at the moment was that a wizard would not guard a cookbook with a spell of protection.

Unless Ertonomous Dron didn't know what the book contained either.

"Could be the book is about a treasure," Raisho said hopefully.

"I don't think so." Juhg filled the captain's wounds with Krylik's weed to offset infection and help keep the bleeding to a minimum. He'd already had Cook prepare some Fosdin's tea to help with pain and fever. "Books about treasures usually come with maps."

142

"The book has no maps?"

"None. That means it's probably not a book on history, a biography, or science. All of those tend to have illustrations. Likewise, the book is not about mathematics, otherwise there would be formulas and such. Even if whoever wrote the book chose to use different symbols than the numbering systems we've discovered at the Vault of All Known Knowledge, it would look differently on the page."

"If ye don't know what it is an' ye've never seen the like of it before," Raisho pointed out, "seems like the Vault of All Known Knowledge is some'at mis-named."

"I know," Juhg quietly agreed. "When the Elders built the Library, they intended for it to store all the world's knowledge. Even the human, elven, and dwarven armies couldn't save all of the libraries scattered throughout the nations Lord Kharrion and the goblinkin laid siege to and plundered. So much was lost." He scooped up the bandages and quickly bound the captain's wounds.

When Juhg was satisfied with the job he'd done, he gathered his medical supplies and quit the captain's quarters. He stood on the deck and squinted up against the bright sun and the blue sky.

Out on the open ocean now with the Tattered Islands behind them, *Windchaser* rode free and easy. If it hadn't been for the dead lying across her deck awaiting burial and the wounded lying abed belowdecks, the day would have been an enjoyable one.

"Now that the cap'n's seen to proper-like," Raisho said, "I'm gonna see if Navin needs some help fixin' *'Chaser* back into shape. If you need somethin' else, let me know." The young sailor went toward the stern castle, where Navin occupied the captain's place.

With a heavy heart and feeling somewhat abandoned, Juhg turned his steps toward the hatch to go belowdecks. Thoughts of the book, what the writing on the pages might mean, stayed uppermost in his mind. He was angry with himself because his greatest desire was to go off by himself and see if he could decipher the writing.

"Mother Ocean," Captain Attikus said in a strong voice that only betrayed a little of the weakness Juhg knew the man had to have been feeling, "we commend the bodies of these brave sailors who have been graced by your presence and at times fought you with all their resources. Please take them gladly into your embrace and show them the secrets of you that they never knew in this life."

Juhg stood on deck with the other sailors in the twilight hour after all the wounded had been tended. One of the men Juhg had bandaged as best as he could had died before regaining his senses. Juhg hoped the man's passing was as peaceful as it looked.

Seventeen bodies lay swathed in sailcloth. The drain on the ship's resources was considerable. Throwing away good sailcloth wasn't something any good captain wanted to do. Captain Attikus would have been within his rights to simply heave the bodies overboard and been done with it.

But they were shipmates, men who had spent time together and protected the secret of the Vault of All Known Knowledge on Greydawn Moors.

One by one as the crew sang their farewells to the dead, the seventeen fallen sailors were tossed into the sea as *Windchaser* continued to run west toward the Blood-Soaked Sea. Rocks from the ballast lining the bottom of the ship's hold were wrapped in the bottom of the sailcloth so the bodies would drop to the sea bottom.

To Juhg's way of thinking, burial at sea was a horrible thing. Once on the ocean floor, crabs and fish would start eating on a person's body till only bones remained. He shivered slightly at the thought and knew that his dreams that night, if he slept at all, would not be restful.

When the ceremony was finished, the sailors returned to their appointed tasks. A lot of work remained to make *Windchaser* shipshape again.

None of them spoke to Juhg, and he knew that all of them blamed him for the deaths of their comrades. In fact, *he* blamed himself because he was a Librarian and they'd felt compelled to honor their sworn duty because he was among them.

All for a book that he still couldn't translate.

"Librarian Juhg."

Hearing the captain's voice, Juhg looked up at the stern castle. Captain Attikus stood at the railing, his left arm in a sling to protect his wounded shoulder.

"Yes, sir," Juhg replied. Rigging creaked and sails cracked overhead.

Windchaser ran through the sea like a racehorse, completely in her element under the clear skies and across the smooth sea.

"You could eat that down in the galley, you know."

Juhg carried a plate in one hand and a mug of chulotzberry tea. The plate was piled high with sweet breads, nuts, grain cakes, jerked pork, and cheese. He carried two apples tucked inside his blouse. It was too late for breakfast actually and too early for lunch, but it was his first meal of the day because he'd slept late after working into the wee hours by lantern light. His eyes still burned and were light sensitive from overwork and lack of sleep.

"That's all right, Captain," Juhg said. "The morning light is better out here." That wasn't the real reason he wasn't eating in the galley and they both knew it. Despite the passage of three days since the attack on *Blowfly,* the crew still kept their distance from him. He had become an outcast on what was essentially a very small island in a huge ocean.

It didn't help that he had been released from shipboard repairs, which turned out to be considerable down in the hold, where caulking threatened to come loose and temporary patches had to be made to fix hull timbers where they had cracked. *Windchaser* was taking on water, but not at an alarming rate and not anything that the pumps couldn't handle.

"A moment of your time if I may, Librarian Juhg."

Reluctantly, knowing the captain would be asking about his progress on translating the book seventeen men, threescore or better goblins, and one wizard had given their lives for, Juhg trudged up the stern castle stairwell. The book rested inside his blouse, along with his journal and the fresh book he'd made from packing supplies aboardship.

"How is it going, Librarian?" the captain asked. His gaze continually scanned the horizon ahead of them. The gray-green water was starting to take on the red-purplish hue that had given the Blood-Soaked Sea its name.

"I've not given up on the book, Captain," Juhg responded, deciding to cut to the crux of the matter because it would save time for them all.

"No, I hadn't thought that," Captain Attikus said.

"And I haven't made any progress either."

Captain Attikus gave a short nod. "That distresses me, Librarian. I had hoped to give the men some news of the book's contents that might make the losses of their fellow crewmen easier to bear."

Secretly, Juhg doubted that was possible. Not many "pirates" who protected the Blood-Soaked Sea were often called upon to spend their lives. Usually the crews of those ships put up the skull and crossbones any time an outside ship showed up in the area and scared off potential discoverers of the island.

"I understand," Juhg said.

"It's a hard thing to lose good men."

Juhg couldn't think of anything to say about that.

"There is one other thing, Librarian." Captain Attikus kept his gaze out to sea. "If you should discover that we've only managed the rescue of a cookbook, I'd rather the men not know that. Even while we're in harbor at Greydawn Moors." He paused. "Are we clear on that?"

"Yes, sir," Juhg replied.

"Then I'll talk to you when you have more news."

"Yes, sir." Summarily dismissed, Juhg trudged back down the stern castle stairwell and went forward. The encounter almost robbed him of his considerable appetite, one in which he felt would truly match his dweller heritage.

No one has any faith in you. Juhg knew that. After three days, no one believed he could decipher the book. And if he did, they fully expected it to be only the crassest sort of joke.

He made his way to the prow rigging and climbed up into the ropes. Sitting cross-legged in the netting, he placed the heaped plate in his lap and tried to summon his appetite again. He studied the water around them, amazed at how peaceful it was at the moment, like a plate of the finest glass.

The mid-morning sun hung behind the ship. Shadows from the taut sails fell over Juhg, and the absence of direct light almost made the loose blouse and breeches too flimsy to wear in the chill. In the distance, Juhg noticed the first faint wisps of the fog that rolled constantly over the Blood-Soaked Sea.

An unfamiliar feeling coursed through Juhg as he looked at the fog and knew that Greydawn Moors lay only a few more days' sailing beyond. The feeling was bittersweet. He was going home after weeks away from the city and the Library and the Grandmagister, and he wanted to be there, to be in familiar surroundings after all the atrocities he'd witnessed.

He'd been a fool to leave. He should have stayed. He saw that now. During the days before he'd left, Grandmagister Lamplighter had tried in vain to get him to see that.

Well, I see it now.

He only hoped he translated the book, or at least got a start on the translation before *Windchaser* dropped anchor in the harbor at Yondering Docks. Going back to the Vault of All Known Knowledge and to Grandmagister Lamplighter with a puzzle he couldn't unravel on his own after all the time the Grandmagister had invested in him would be almost more than he could bear after everything he'd been through.

Sailors worked aloft today. He heard their voices behind him, and that simple thing reminded him how far apart he was from them. He remembered Grandmagister Lamplighter's own tales of his first voyage aboard *One-Eyed Peggie,* of how the Grandmagister had gone from potato peeler to pirate in just a matter of days.

But Grandmagister Lamplighter had saved lives aboard the pirate ship. When the Embyr had alighted in the rigging, Grandmagister Lamplighter had gone and talked to her, convincing her that she didn't want to harm them or the ship.

He saved lives, Juhg thought bitterly, *and I set my friends upon a course that took them.* During the few hours of sleep he got a night, dreams of the killings aboard *Blowfly* haunted him, shocking him awake in a cold sweat in his hammock where he slept on the main deck.

He picked up a grain cake, mixed with honey and cinnamon to bond it, and nibbled, hoping to work up some kind of appetite. He had to eat. He needed his strength. As he ate, he reached inside his blouse and took out the red clothbound book.

He felt the tingle of *something* again. It felt like something alive, though he knew it couldn't be. The only explanation he could think of was that some innate magic remained within the book and he was sensitive enough to "feel" it.

That was a scary probability. A few Librarians at the Vault of All Known Knowledge had inadvertently tried reading tomes of magic that were meant only for wizards' eyes and had ended up dying hideous deaths. Specialists were trained who perused such volumes and hid them away until such time that Craugh came visiting.

Juhg flipped open the cover and started scanning the first page again, looking for some clue as to who had written it. So far he hadn't even ascertained which race had authored the book. Juhg spoke a couple dozen languages, most of them dead after the events of the Cataclysm, which had driven nearly every race to learn a new language together, one that allowed them to work quickly and efficiently together.

After the Cataclysm, after Lord Kharrion and the goblin hordes had finally been beaten, although many of the lands remained inhospitable to man or beast as a result, the races had kept the common tongue they had devised during their decades-long wars. So many languages had been lost during that time. At least, the oral versions of them had been lost. The written versions still existed within the Library.

As he ate, forcing himself now when he had so been looking forward to the meal only moments ago, Juhg studied the pages of writing, trying to discern something—a pattern or a few words—that would give him the key to unlocking the language that bound the secrets in the book.

Juhg roused from a nightmare, feeling embarrassed because he knew he'd been crying out as dead men and goblins rose from *Blowfly*'s decks and came after him. He blinked up at the night sky, feeling his heart hammering inside his chest.

Overhead, Jhurjan the Swift and Bold, the greater of the two moons, burned a red glare across the dark heavens. He would cross three more times during the night at this time of year. Farther to the south now, Gesa the Fair showed pale blue and was in her shy phase when she could hardly be seen at all due to Jhurjan's magnificence.

"Ease up there, bookworm. You're all right."

Juhg turned at the sound of Raisho's voice and saw the young sailor sitting in the rigging over the prow only a short distance away. A nearby lantern occupied a spot on the prow railing.

Two more days had passed and Juhg had not broken down any of the language in the book. Nor had the crew broken down their standoffishness against him.

Suddenly aware that he was hanging out over the dark ocean as *Windchaser* sailed along under the night sky and that it was only a short drop into the brine and a quick disappearance with no hope for rescue for a man with a knife, Juhg shifted warily in the rigging. Raisho always carried plenty of knives.

"What are you doing here?" Juhg asked.

Raisho shrugged. "I have missed ye."

"I've missed you too," Juhg said, "but I wasn't the one who chose to stay away." He couldn't avoid placing the blame where it lay, though he wished he were a bigger person than that.

"No," Raisho admitted, looking a little guilty. "No, ye weren't. Were me. Were the crew too, but they ain't seen the error of their ways yet." He paused. "Give 'em a little more time an' they'll come around."

Sitting up, Juhg wrapped his arms around his knees. "They judged me harshly, Raisho. They found me responsible for the deaths of their friends. Of *our* friends."

"Aye, they did at that. As did I." Raisho glanced out to sea. "Them men we lost, they were good men. It shouldn't have happened."

Silence stretched between them for a moment, fragile and intense, then Juhg broke it. "If I could take it back, I would."

"An' if'n ye did, why, then ye wouldn't have that book what's the cause of us runnin' back to Greydawn Moors as we are."

"That's something else no one is happy about."

"Mayhap. But one thing I know, sailors is a lot that likes to gripe. Show me a sailor what ain't gripin' about how his lot in life is an' I'll show ye a sailor what ain't givin' this job his all." Raisho grinned.

In spite of his despair and anxiety and wariness, Juhg smiled back.

"Ye know what really brought me around to remember that ye ain't just no Librarian?" Raisho asked. "That ye were also Juhg, me friend?"

Juhg shook his head, not wanting to offend in any way. And he did not have a clue.

"Was Herby," Raisho declared.

"Herby?"

"Aye. This afternoon I was talkin' to Herby. He told me about yer book." Raisho opened his hands and showed Juhg his personal journal.

Juhg felt uncomfortable about Raisho having the journal until he remembered that the young sailor couldn't read. Then he felt inept because he'd left out all the books, the one they'd found in the goblin ship as well as the copy of it he had so diligently made, in the knapsack he kept his tools in.

"Herby talked about all them stories ye told him about the men who died," Raisho said. "Heroes, ye made 'em out to be."

"They were heroes," Juhg said.

Raisho flipped the thick journal open to some of the latest entries. The lantern light turned the parchment pages golden brown. Ink drawings of the crew embroiled in battle with the goblinkin filled the pages. Other pages held pictures of the dead crewmen as they sat around tables in the galley or did shipboard chores, and even images of the funeral that had taken place aboard *Windchaser*. Some of the pictures were clearer, more detailed than others, but all of them were recognizable.

"I suppose I never have realized what it is ye do with all yer scribblin'," Raisho admitted. "I've seen ye spend hours on end scribblin' an' drawin' in yer book. Now an' agin, I looked upon them pictures ye drawed, an' I listened to them stories ye told. I thought ye had a fair hand at drawin', but I never once put it all together an' seen what it is ye really do."

Juhg shook his head. "I don't understand."

Raisho sighed with feigned irritation. "Why, ye're savin' them men. Turnin' them into forever heroes is what ye're doin'." He hesitated. "See, me an' the rest of the crew, why, we'll tell stories about them men. But each time the story gets told, among ourselves an' even to other people, why, that story will change. In just a short time, them stories about these men an' what happened aboard *Blowfly* an' what we lost will be nearly all made up. Nothing will remain of them men the way they really was. But this book—" The young sailor shook the book and the moonslight showed unshed tears in his eyes. "—why, it's a permanent thing an' the story in it will never change, never become less or more than them men were. It'll be a fair an' accurate accountin'. I know that 'cause I know the way ye are."

Embarrassed at the sentiment that he heard in Raisho's words, Juhg had no idea what to say.

"Ye've got a fine an' uncommon gift, bookworm," Raisho said. "I don't think I ever appreciated what you do as much before as when I was sittin' here lookin' at them pictures an' seein' all that scribblin' by 'em. I'd almost be willin' to learn to read if 'n only to read about them friends we lost."

"I could teach you." The words were out of Juhg's mouth before he knew it. He knew he'd made a mistake. No one outside the Vault of All Known Knowledge and Greydawn Moors was taught to read. The skill was considered too dangerous, considering all the books that were left out in the world. But Juhg didn't think about that. He'd come from outside Greydawn Moors as well, and the Grandmagister himself had trained him to read and write and think a thing through.

"Mayhap." Raisho nodded his head. "Mayhap ye will. But fer now, ye just get ye some more rest. Don't ye be worryin' about them night haunts nor nothin' else. I'll be right here, an' I'll protect ye from them."

Cautiously, still not quite trusting Raisho because of his own past problems, Juhg lay back down. He remained quiet, not wanting to offend his friend, and feigned sleep, intending to be prepared just in case this was a trick and a way to get rid of him. But somewhere in there he went to sleep, and he didn't rouse again until the sun was warm on his face and someone was yelling, "Land ho!"

10

Greydawn Moors

curious feeling filled Juhg as he stood in *Wind-chaser*'s rigging and looked out at the small port city that appeared in the thick fog looming over the Blood-Soaked Sea. The feeling was one that he had never felt before, even when he'd returned from trips with Grandmagister Lamplighter. He felt like he was coming home.

"Well," Raisho said, "ye've got a smile on yer face, ye do."

"I know." Juhg clutched the rigging and stood tall as the gentle winds that swept the natural harbor played over him.

Greydawn Moors occupied the northern foothills of the Knucklebones Mountains, the curious ridges that shoved toward the sky at the island's highest point and looked like the hard knuckles of a closed fist. But that fist was impossibly large, containing caverns and the immense buildings that housed the Vault of All Known Knowledge. Below the Knucklebones ran an almost perpendicular set of ridges called the Ogre's Fingers which looked disturbingly like a hand closed around the wrist of the fist that made up the Knucklebones. Once that image had settled in, the viewer couldn't help but think of the mountain range as the hands of two gigantic warriors forever locked in battle, their bodies sunk in the rocky island.

Legend had it that the Old Ones created the island from the bodies of two monsters: an ogre and a champion who had held the ogre off while the island was made by magic. According to those stories, the giants' toes had dug into the bedrock of the ocean floor and anchored Greydawn Moors when they were turned to stone.

Juhg didn't know if those legends were true, but what he had learned from the books in the Vault of All Known Knowledge and his travels with the Grandmagister was that every legend and lie had a seed of truth somewhere.

The city occupied the coastal area. For hundreds of years, Greydawn Moors had existed in protective isolation at the edge of the Blood-Soaked Sea. The population had increased only gradually and some speculated that number was also managed by the same magicks that had created the island, hidden it from the rest of the world, and enshrouded the area with perpetual fog.

And filled the Blood-Soaked Sea with monsters, Juhg thought as he heard one of the massive creatures call out farther out to sea. The monsters were real, but they didn't linger around the island much.

Three wooden docks ran out to sea, all of them short and compact to handle the infrequent sea traffic. Few merchants made their way to the island to trade, and then only those who had been born on Greydawn Moors and promised the allegiance to the island and to the secret of the Library.

Mostly, the citizens of Greydawn Moors saw to their own needs from the arable lands to the south and east that the farmers tilled. They also took deer and coneys from the woods, but the elven warders given charge of taking care of the island's needs tended to those numbers.

The populations of the deer and the rabbits were carefully husbanded and parceled out. Only elven warders hunted in and took meat from the forests, and those bounties were traded for meager supplies the elves needed or wanted. All of them had taken vows to protect the island. The few dwarves that worked Greydawn Moors' two forges to provide needed hardware had taken the same vows and traded under the same circumstances.

Most of the town's population was made up of dwellers, and from their numbers the Librarians came. The dwellers, though, came with increasing reluctance over the years because being a Librarian was the hardest and most demanding occupation on the island.

Only a few buildings made up the small city. The Customs House to the east, where goods were logged in and out, was the tallest and most impressive. The lighthouse on the craggy finger of land extending out into the harbor was the second tallest. Two bright lanterns spun in the windows, their dwarven gears spun by the incoming and outgoing tide so that captains familiar with the water could tell at a glance whether the tide was rolling in or rolling out.

The market area, at the western end of town with its handful of small permanent structures supplemented by tents of all sizes and colors, spread across the most area. *Windchaser* arrived home early in the morn, so a number of traders were in evidence at the market area, bartering their harvests so they could get back to their fields or shops after the midday meal.

The rest of the buildings in the town proper were mercantiles, taverns, the school where all dwellers were taught the rudiments of reading and writing, and a stable for the horses of a few of the businesses, as well as corrals for the few head of livestock—mostly cows, pigs, and chickens farmers raised—that were sold or traded to the various ships. The animals were purchased and butchered on the spot, then salted and loaded onto the ships in barrels. Occasionally, new livestock were brought onto the island to keep the herds supplied with fresh blood.

155

Houses sprinkled the foothills leading up from the shore and the town. The homes were mostly dweller shacks, made up of whatever the owners found that came to hand. Pieces of ships that had come back from battles in the Blood-Soaked Sea too battered and broken to be repaired, crates no longer necessary to hold cargo, wood from past buildings that had finally collapsed, and lumber harvested by the elves from the forest made up the houses. They all looked as though a strong breeze might blow them down, but they looked bright nonetheless because dwellers tended to favor bright colors and the dwarves made paints of all hues. Oddments and other items that other people might call junk became treasures that the dwellers used to accessorize their homes.

In sharp contrast, the dwarven homes were neat and tidy, with sharp corners and straight walls. White fences, which dwarves claimed made good neighbors of dwellers because they didn't feel so inclined to take something they saw because they were certain the dwarves living there didn't truly appreciate enough that item's worth, defined yards and gardens that were carefully tended. The elves made their homes in the trees and farther up into the Knucklebones.

The humans on the island, their numbers much fewer because there weren't as many of them and the fact that humans by their very natures were wanderers, lived wherever they chose. Most of the humans were sailors and fishermen, always pitting their skills against the wind and the sea. And every so often, as if their lives weren't short and fleeting enough, those humans gathered into a monster-hunting party and went after one of the great beasts that resided in the Blood-Soaked Sea. To keep the numbers of the monsters in check, they claimed, but Juhg had the distinct feeling that they mainly just wanted to see if it could be done, then if it could be done again.

The Barrel of Ale tavern, which was a human establishment, boasted the head of one of the monsters that dwelt out in the Blood-Soaked Sea. On those rare occasions that the monster hunters returned with a prize, the Barrel of Ale served up monster steaks. Juhg, for the life of him, didn't know why anyone would want to eat anything as repulsive—and possibly as *poisonous*—as one of those forbidding creatures.

But that was Greydawn Moors, lost in time and in place to the mainland, and it was truly the only safe place Juhg had ever known.

The wind blew out of the south, snapping across the Knucklebones, then plunging to fall over the forested lowlands. Juhg stared into the teeth of the wind and felt the chill that often lingered in the mornings. The cold came from the sea, and there was never a time in Greydawn Moors when people went long without their cloaks.

Having grown up in the South on the mainland, where goblins tended to congregate the most, Juhg longed for the warmer climes that he remembered. The chill, not actually an uncomfortable cold, was a constant reminder that he was not a native to the area.

Even after twenty years of living among the people of Greydawn Moors, he still felt like an outsider. The citizens' fear of outsiders seemed almost bred into them. But not an elven, dwarven, human, or dweller child who grew up on the island didn't know the horrifying tales of Lord Kharrion and the goblinkin that had almost destroyed the world.

The island people knew the ships' captains and crews that came to trade there, and nearly all of them were born of the island. Very few outsiders were allowed into the ships' crews. No outside traders were allowed into Greydawn Moors.

Strangers in town meant the worst kind of danger. If the wrong person shipped aboard with a crew that sailed to Greydawn Moors, then went back to the mainland and told of the existence of the island and the Vault of All Known Knowledge, all the work that the warriors who had stood against Lord Kharrion and the goblin hordes would be undone. The goblins would brave the Blood-Soaked Sea to find the island and not be afraid of sailing over the edge of the world as they generally were.

The harbor patrol put out four sleek ships manned by human, elven, and dwarven warriors. Their lanterns burned through the fog. The ships were small two-masters built with shallow keels so they skimmed the ocean quickly, and constructed with round bodies to better afford fighting decks. Giant crossbows and ballistae occupied their decks.

Warning bells clanged as the small ships appeared. Archers stood on the decks, their bows nocked.

Captain Attikus stood on the stern deck and awaited their arrival.

"Ahoy the ship," one of the officers aboard the closest harbor defense vessel shouted. "Furl yer sails an' identify yerselves."

"We're *Windchaser*," Captain Attikus roared back through the wisps of fog that darted between the ships. "These are our home waters. I know you, First Mate Faggul, and you should know me."

The burly dwarf standing in the ship's prow motioned the archers to put their weapons away. He grinned a little and put his massive war hammer over his shoulder. "So ye do, Captain Attikus. But ye weren't expected back here fer a time, if 'n I recall rightly."

"There have been problems," Captain Attikus said.

A sour look knotted the dwarf's face. "Come ahead on, then, an' we'll get 'em sorted out soon enough."

"What a sorry homecomin' this is," Raisho grumbled in a low voice as he threw out a line.

Looking at all the people thronging the dock as *Windchaser*'s crew cast off lines and tied the ship up, Juhg had to agree. They held lanterns filled with smokeless and sweet-smelling glimmerworm juice, which was a product unique to Greydawn Moors. Bearing the lanterns was the custom, but the crowd was somber instead of talkative as was usual. Normally when a ship came back in to harbor after being gone on an extended trip, families turned out to welcome loved ones home with food and gifts.

Feasts were sometimes set up at the market and hours of revelry ensued as sailors delighted or frightened their listeners with tales of the outside world that few in Greydawn Moors had ever seen. Of course, the stories grew bolder and scarier in the telling, and the sailors' own courage in the face of grim obstacles grew larger with it.

And the wit the sailors exhibited, with their cutting remarks and careful attention to detail about mythical beasts and whatever puzzles they swore they encountered that kept incredible treasures just out of their hands, was nothing short of the kind of brilliance staged by the elven playwrights of Delkarrian Falls. Those scribes wrote stories designed especially for the branches of trees where they performed, using the placement of the branches as a military tactician might use the lay of the land.

Some of the families onshore were already crying, having heard some of the news of the seventeen who had died as *Windchaser*'s crew had talked with the harbor guards as they made their way to the free dock. Others anxiously awaited to find out if one of their kin had been among those lost.

Through it all, Juhg knew he was responsible for the sadness that would grip the community.

 Bells continued to ring out in the harbor as the small cargo skiffs plied their trade among some of the outlying ships. Greydawn Moors maintained a small navy of merchants and pirates. The clangor carried across the waves lapping at the rocky edge of the shoreline and sounded too loud to Juhg.

"Where ye gonna be later, bookworm?" Raisho asked in a quiet voice that didn't carry.

"Probably at the Library," Juhg said. "I'll have to find the Grandmagister and show him the book." He paused, his heart heavy and leaden inside his chest. "He'll have to be told of the circumstances we recovered the book under. And I want to tell him of those men who gave their lives to get it."

Raisho shook his head. "I'll not be comin' to the Library for ye. They'd never allow the likes of me inside them walls."

Juhg knew that wasn't true. Over the long years of its history, the Library had entertained any number of guests from all walks of life. Of course, most of those had come there at the invitation of the reigning Grandmagister at the time. And none visited that did not have business there. Many still told frightening stories about the dreadful secrets the Librarians sometimes uncovered that claimed the lives of those who beheld them.

"But if 'n ye're back in town afore we set sail," Raisho continued, "ye'll find me in one of the taverns. I'd be proud to share yer company. I'll be stayin' at the Sails Inn."

Juhg looked at the people lining the harbor and felt thankful for his friend's generosity. "I'm grateful for your offer, Raisho. I doubt there's many who would feel that gracious after they hear I was responsible for their losses."

"Wasn't ye, bookworm." Raisho dropped a big hand on Juhg's shoulder. "Was just bad luck. An' it were our bounden duty to get that book after we heard of it. An' it wasn't just them what lost kin an' friends. Was us, too. Me an' ye."

"I know. But it will cause another rift between the Library and the town."

"Won't cause one. But 'twill remind them again of their separate natures." Raisho shook his head. "That has nothin' to do with ye. The Library's always been here as long as Greydawn Moors, an' there's been a passel of Librarians afore ye. That's what's always been, an' what's always will be."

The long-standing feud between the citizens of Greydawn Moors and the Vault of All Known Knowledge had started roughly when the first stone was put into place for the Library. The dwellers who had been placed on the island had relished the idea of being cut off from the goblin hordes, and hadn't minded dedicating some of their young to become caretakers to the vast amounts of books placed for safekeeping in the caverns that had first housed the Library's holdings. But they had resented the fact that the Grandmagister held sway over so much of what their everyday lives were like.

Many shopkeepers and merchants disagreed with how the Grandmagister got a small percentage of their profits for the support of the Library, even though that amount was meager and small because the Librarians were trained to make do and tend to their own needs. Over the years, the townsfolk had tried to separate themselves from the Librarians, feeling that the Vault of All Known Knowledge was a strain on their resources.

"Besides all that," Raisho said with some of the humor that was so characteristic of him, "I still think ye're the onliest one what can make a rich man of me." He clapped Juhg on the shoulder again, dropped to his knee, and said his goodbye with a hug that two warriors blooded in battle together might give.

Juhg's heart soared for just a moment before it came crashing down when he remembered how they'd come to be blooded together. Most of the rest of the crew said goodbyes as well, but Juhg knew they thought themselves well shut of him.

The harbor guard ran out gangplanks from the dock. Captain Attikus made the work assignments, deferring them for the next day after he graciously accepted the help offered by the harbor guard in watching over *Windchaser* while the crew debarked to see their families and comfort those families that had lost members. The humans at Greydawn Moors were a close-knit group. Even Herby and Gust gamboled down the gangplank and were welcomed into the crowd, though Juhg guessed that no few of them would soon find themselves relieved of small trinkets and coins.

Torn in what he had to do and knowing how much he dreaded that, Juhg went to report to the captain, who still remained at his familiar position at the stern castle despite the entreaties of his family. He begged off, saying he wanted to do a final inspection of the ship before leaving her. The captain stood with his arm still in a sling, but his back was ramrod straight.

"Well, then, Librarian Juhg," Captain Attikus said, "I expected you to be the first one off ship. That book is important."

"Yes, sir, and I'll be on my way as soon as I finish up here."

The captain waited.

Juhg hesitated, not really knowing what he had come to say, but knowing he had to say something all the same. He feared what he was about to ask, and he couldn't turn away from it because he knew he had to ask.

"Librarian Juhg," the captain said in a softer voice, "I know what troubles you."

"You do, sir?"

The captain nodded and looked out at the people gathered in the harbor. "Of course I do. Command is not an easy thing to handle."

"Command, sir? But I'm not in command." That wasn't the issue at all that Juhg had in mind.

"You're a Librarian," the captain replied. "Of course you're in command. Perhaps you only call it being responsible, but the feelings are the same. You could no more ignore the call of that book than I could foreswear the oath I took when I stepped upon this vessel as captain." He cut his gaze to Juhg. "There will be many who fault you for what happened when we encountered *Blowfly*. Perhaps some of them will be survivors who made it through this voyage. But that isn't where the ultimate blame rests. If anyone is to truly be blamed, Librarian Juhg, it is I."

"But, sir, I—" Juhg didn't understand how the captain could possibly see the matter that way.

"I should have been better prepared, should have found another way to take that ship, should have been better able to protect my men." Captain Attikus was quiet for a moment. "Those things are in my purview, Librarian Juhg, and I'll not allow anyone to say elsewise in my presence."

"Captain—"

"Nor you, Librarian Juhg. I won't have it." Captain Attikus adjusted his shoulders. "You have your mission before you, as I have mine to get this vessel once more shipshape and back out on the salt."

Juhg felt a glimmer of pride at the captain's words. *Taking the book to the Grandmagister* is *a mission.* And it was one that he had trained for. If only he had succeeded in making sense of the text he'd found on those pages.

"Now, if there's anything I can do to help you, let me know," Captain Attikus said. "Otherwise I expect you to get on with your duty."

"Yes, sir. Thank you, sir." Juhg turned and started to leave, then turned back around. He had to ask what was uppermost on his mind. "If I should get the chance to ship with you, Captain—"

"You'd be most welcome, Librarian Juhg. I've enjoyed our dinner conversations. Take care of yourself. Till we meet again."

"And you, sir." Juhg walked down the gangplank with his pack over his shoulders and the book heavy inside his cloak.

Cracked oyster shells lined the winding road that led up from the docks. They shifted and clacked beneath Juhg's bare feet. He breathed in the scent of the town.

Fresh bread still baked in the bakeries that serviced the taverns and sailors' inns that were kept for those seafarers who never truly made a home in Greydawn Moors and remained only welcome transients. Spiced meats hung in the windows of the butcher shops. Smoke from fireplaces in homes and fire pits in inns and taverns tickled his nose.

He'd missed those things out on the ocean. Cooks were always baking in the Vault of All Known Knowledge. Dwellers liked their meals. When they could schedule them, they liked them six and seven times a day. The galley had come as a weak replacement for those things.

But though the smells were enticing, Juhg found he had no appetite. He'd eaten a little aboard *Windchaser* because he had trained himself to do so while working in the goblin mines. A weak dweller who couldn't lift his pick or help pull an ore cart was a dead dweller by dark.

He pulled the traveling cloak a little more tightly around him as the wind gained in intensity as he reached the top of the last hill that led to Raysun Street, the thoroughfare that cut through the heart of the town.

Shopkeepers and townsfolk stood outside the buildings and gazed down at the harbor. All of them were talking, and Juhg knew they talked of the ship's ill-fated voyage and the Librarian who had been among the ship's crew. Some of them pointed in his direction, thinking that he did not see them.

A cart clattered by him. The iron horseshoes of the pair of matched mares pulling the vehicle cracked the oyster shells. A dweller man and his wife rode on the springboard seat, and three small children huddled in the back among barrels and sacks.

Rounding the corner where the shipwrights had their building yard, Juhg gazed up the long road that led out of town, through the forest and the foothills of the Knucklebones. At the other end of the long road that wound so torturously through the broken terrain, the Vault of All Known Knowledge sat surrounded by high walls covered in thorny bushes. The natural barrier, tended to by the elven warders, layered over the man-made barrier.

In case the Library was ever attacked from without, the walls offered proof against its enemies. A standing guard of dwarven warriors stayed at the Library in shifts.

If goblins did discover the island and the Library, they would have to fight their way up from the harbor. Getting through the dwarves and pirates and sailors in the town would be difficult. Beyond that lay the forests, where the elven warders promised quick and silent death from their hiding places and from the great hunting cats and fierce falcons they had trained to fight with them.

Fog hid most of the Vault of All Known Knowledge from view at the moment. Perhaps at midday it would burn off, but even on the best days the Great Library wasn't very visible. The buildings were constructed to blend into the Knucklebones Mountains behind them, flowing along the natural lines above the Ogre's Fingers. The distance was also great enough that only a keen eye without a spyglass could pick the buildings out.

"First Level Librarian Juhg," a happy voice exclaimed.

Surprised at such a greeting, Juhg halted his steps and turned in the direction of the voice.

A plump dweller dressed in the white-fringed light gray robe that was the official color of a Third Level Librarian stood beside a lamppost. He carried a basket under one arm.

"Don't you know me?" The plump dweller let a car rattle past, then crossed the street.

Juhg thought he did recognize the other Librarian, but he wasn't certain. Camaraderie in the Vault was somewhat limited, and he'd never truly gone out of his way to meet other people. Having grown up on Greydawn Moors as they had, few of them really felt comfortable talking to Juhg.

Then the name clicked into Juhg's mind. "Third Level Librarian Thelf."

"Yes." Thelf was partially out of breath from his run across the street. His face was florid and pink from spending so many days in the subterranean haunts where nearly every Third Level Librarian spent years sorting the crates, boxes, and chests of books that had been heaped into the caves during the first arrivals. "I only just heard you'd returned."

"Yes. I was on my way to the Library to see the Grandmagister."

"Then your journey will be a short one, and it won't be up to the Library."

"The Grandmagister is in town?"

Thelf nodded. "Yes. He came to the Customs House for a bit of business and decided to stay to break his fast."

Juhg's stomach churned. In a way, it would be good to get the book off his hands and where it would no longer be his responsibility, but seeing the Grandmagister also meant having to admit to all the deaths for which he was at least partially to blame.

"Where can I find him?"

Thelf pointed down the street. "At Carason's Eatery."

"You're certain he's there still?"

"I only saw him but moments ago, First Level Librarian."

"Then I'll thank you for your assistance and be on my way." Juhg

changed directions and headed down the street. He kept his steps hurried, aware of the attention he got.

Word had already spread ahead of him. He knew that from the looks and the whispered words and the faces clustered together at the windows of the shops.

Carason's Eatery was one of the Grandmagister's favorite places to dine when in Greydawn Moors and away from the spectacular kitchen in the Vault of All Known Knowledge. Juhg had eaten with the Grandmagister there a number of times, generally on the outset of a new voyage to the mainland or a return home from such a trip.

The dining establishment was a small building with a commonplace atmosphere. Whitewashed stone walls made the business a permanent fixture, but it hadn't always been Carason's Eatery. The human who owned and operated the eatery was from the mainland, a companion gathered on one of the Grandmagister's adventures with his friends Brant and Cobner and the Friends' Circle of Thieves, which they had become known as. Of course, that was before Brant had become Baron Brant of Sweetgrass Valley after taking his hereditary lands back from the goblinkin in a vicious war where the Grandmagister had played a significant part.

Carason had been a wanderer and a sometime fighting man of average skill, but a wonderful chef. And he'd enjoyed the attentions of Dyeran, a female wizard who Craugh had trained for a time. Dyeran was from Greydawn Moors, and she often lived there when she wasn't exploring the mainland for wizardly pursuits and chasing forgotten knowledge.

Latticework windows allowed brief glimpses inside the eatery at the tables filled with patrons, but Juhg knew that Grandmagister Lamplighter as a habit held a table in the back. The eatery's door stood open, and Carason— as well as his most consistent patrons—said that the open door was the best advertisement that he could have for his business.

The smell of sweet-and-sour praline-melt, the tangy aroma of peppered chozt loaf, and the promise of lemon-sprinkled strawberry yams were like no other. On any other day, Juhg knew his appetite would have been an undeniable force.

Three steps led up to the veranda, where people waited on long wooden benches to enter or spent time after dining, wailing that they were too stuffed to move. Lanterns hung from the eaves, and the light blue glimmerworm juice was mixed with spices that made a delicious aroma all their own that further whetted the interest of passersby.

A young dweller maid met Juhg just inside the door. "Greetings, traveler," she said. "I hope you brought a full appetite."

She doesn't recognize me, Juhg realized. He felt embarrassed. He'd been there dozens of times with the Grandmagister and even knew her name was Xhandree. Suddenly aware that he had the hood of his cloak up, Juhg pushed it back.

"Ah." Xhandree's face lit with a smile. "First Level Librarian Juhg."

"Yes," Juhg agreed, grateful for having seen a friendly face.

"I was not aware your ship had returned."

"Only just," Juhg said.

"Much earlier than she was expected."

"Yes. There was some . . . trouble." *How do you call the loss of seventeen men trouble?* Juhg felt ashamed of himself, yet he did not want to frighten the young maid.

Her face darkened with worry. "You are all right?"

"Yes. Thank you for asking." Juhg stood on tiptoe and peered through the crowded room. If she didn't know *Windchaser* had returned, there was a good chance he'd beaten the news to the Grandmagister.

"Grandmagister Wick is here," Xhandree said. She had always referred to the Grandmagister in a familiar way. A number of people who liked the Grandmagister did, but Juhg had never felt so inclined. "Will you be joining him?"

"If he'll have me," Juhg assured her.

"Of course. Follow me." Xhandree took a lighted scented candle from the shelf along the wall beside the door, then walked across the packed floor.

Tables and chairs filled every conceivable space, and even late as it was for the farmers and herdsmen, all of those tables and chairs were occupied. Humans, dwarves, elves, and dwellers all ate at Carason's. Appetite knew no racial boundaries, and if it had, Carason's bill of fare would have quieted it.

Grandmagister Lamplighter sat at the back table in the corner. He was diminutive even by dweller standards, nearly a handful of inches shorter than Juhg, and maintained a decidedly slender build for a dweller, much less for a Librarian. Most of those tended to look much like Third Level Librarian Thelf.

The Grandmagister's red-gold hair also set him apart from most of the other dwellers in Greydawn Moors. He wore charcoal gray robes with black piping that clearly marked his station for all to see. Food heaped the plate in front of him, but his hands idled with the carving of a few quills that lay in a neat stack at one side.

Three books occupied a corner of the table. All of the books had cloth ribbon bookmarks. A neat, handmade journal with leather covers and the mark of the Grandmagister embossed upon it lay atop the books. The eatery was one of the Grandmagister's favorite places for casual reading.

Dressed in homespun but wearing an apron, Carason sat across from the Grandmagister. Tall and heavyset and scarred from his days as a warrior, the human had gone gray over the years that Juhg had known him. Despite the winter in his hair and beard, though, many a rowdy sailor who'd come into his own on the seas and thought himself grown enough to run roughshod over the eatery because it was small and conservative had learned that Carason had hard-knuckled ways about him. No few of them had ended up thrown into the oyster shells that covered the street in front of the building.

"Grandmagister Wick," Xhandree called as she neared the table. "Look whom I have brought to see you."

The Grandmagister turned with a smile on his face, but that expression slipped a little. Confusion and a wistful look warred with the gentle smile. The Grandmagister hadn't wanted to see Juhg leave the Library or the island, but was now immediately concerned that he was so quickly returned. "Juhg."

Over the years, the Grandmagister had always called Juhg by his given name rather than his title in relaxed surroundings. That practice anywhere in Greydawn Moors had been somewhat unsettling to Juhg. Things were just done differently when they were aboardship or questing through the dangerous territories of the mainland.

"Grandmagister," Juhg replied, inclining his head out of respect for the man and for the office. "I'm afraid I've arrived with a mixed bag of news." He heard his voice break as emotion slammed into him. Visions of the dying sailors and of the funeral aboardship twisted through his mind and knotted his stomach.

"Well, then, let's have a look at it." Grandmagister Lamplighter left his seat and threw his arms around Juhg. "No matter what it is, lad, we'll see it through, right enough. You're not alone. Never have been as long as I've known you." He released Juhg, patted him on the shoulder with only the kind of reassurance that the Grandmagister could give, and pointed to the seat Carason vacated.

"Right here, First Level Librarian." Carason put both big hands on the chair and offered the seat. "I'll have something to eat brought right out for you."

"No," Juhg said. "Really. I'm not hungry."

"A dweller not hungry?" Carason shook his shaggy head in disbelief. "I've never heard the like. Next you'll be telling me glimmerworms can fly. And wouldn't we all be in trouble if that were so." He went off, always a bundle of energy when he had a set course before him.

Juhg started to disagree, even though the food on the Grandmagister's plate looked tempting.

"No," Grandmagister Lamplighter advised in a quiet voice as he resumed his seat. "Do not turn down the generosity of a meal. You know Carason will not hear of it. You'd be better served shouting into the eye of a hurricane."

Juhg sat in the chair and shivered. His traveling cloak was still damp from the sea spray, and sitting idle seemed to draw the chill through him. And, too, he knew that he hated having to tell the Grandmagister of all his considerable failings.

"What was it that brought *Windchaser* back?" the Grandmagister asked.

"This." Juhg reached into his pouch and took out the red clothbound book.

Reverently, the Grandmagister took the tome. His quick, knowing fingers slid along the binding and the edges, learning what he could of the book's manufacture and origins before ever opening it. Over the years, Juhg had seen the Grandmagister identify books from the binding, the texture and scent of the paper, and from the thickness of the lines of ink laid down on the pages. His skill as a Librarian was nothing short of phenomenal.

Finished with his cursory examination, the Grandmagister adjusted the candle on his side of the table, careful to keep the flame inches away from the pages. He opened the cover and peered at the pages. "And what is this?"

Ashamed, Juhg said, "Grandmagister, I don't know. The language was beyond me."

The Grandmagister flipped through the book. His face remained impassive. "Rest assured, Juhg, that I am no master of this writing either."

Juhg released a pent-up breath.

Looking over the book, the Grandmagister asked, "Are you relieved?"

Immediately embarrassed, Juhg started to say no, then thought better of it. In all the years they'd spent together, he'd never lied to the Grandmagister and had felt that the Grandmagister would have known immediately if he ever did.

"Yes," Juhg admitted. "The language defeated me at every turn. Some words, some phrases, even some of the handwriting seems familiar. But every time I tried to grasp it, the understanding darted away like minnows, just slipped right through my fingers."

The Grandmagister leaned back in his chair and took out his pipe. He stuffed the pipe with pipeweed and lit up at the same time Carason set a large plate of food in front of Juhg.

"Eat up," the Grandmagister advised. "I'd like to ponder these pages awhile longer."

After thanking Carason, Juhg used the fingerbowl at the side of the plate to clean his hands, then eyed the choices before him. He was surprised at how famished he felt, in spite of everything in his head. Still, he could not find the will to put one morsel in his mouth for a moment. *You don't deserve a meal this grand, Juhg. You got those sailors killed. If you had simply gotten that book the first time you were aboard* Blowfly— He pushed that thought away, desperately needing an answer to the questions he had.

"Grandmagister, forgive my intrusion."

"Yes." Grandmagister Lamplighter looked up.

Unable to figure out any other way to ask the question, Juhg blurted, "That isn't a cookbook, is it?"

The Grandmagister hesitated for just a brief spell. Then he shook his head. "Without knowing for certain, I couldn't say. But it is my feeling that this is not a cookbook of any sort. There are no—"

"No headings," Juhg said, jumping in because he was unable to stop himself. "There are no subdivisions. There are no ingredient lists." He finally stopped himself. "I apologize."

"I have," the Grandmagister admitted with a rueful look, "upon occasion risked my life to recover cookbooks. Even books on beauty care. At the time I didn't know what they were, nor would it have mattered if I had. A book is a book, Juhg, and as such is a treasure unique unto itself. As well as a danger that must be controlled. That was one of the very first things I taught you."

"I know. But I've got something I must tell you, Grandmagister. Seventeen sailors—men known to me as friends or at least acquaintances—perished while taking that book from the hands of goblins."

"Goblins?" The Grandmagister's brow furrowed in consternation.

"And a wizard."

"Perhaps you had better tell me more of this book's discovery."

Before Juhg could speak, the door to the eatery burst open and a group of angry sailors pushed into the building. They looked around for just a moment, then one of the sailors Juhg recognized from *Windchaser* leveled an arm at him and pointed.

"There he is!" the sailor declared. "There's the Librarian what led us to our dooms!"

Like a pack of wolves, the sailors crossed the room, baring iron fangs, from knives to swords, and bore down on Juhg.

11

Craugh

ear slid greasily through Juhg's stomach and chilled his heart as he watched the mob coming straight for him. Many of the sailors had been drinking. He knew that from their flushed faces.

When not working on the ships, sailors tended to gather in taverns and drink too much. The harbor patrol at Greydawn Moors didn't put up with much rabble-rousing if situations got out of hand, but those situations seldom did. Sometimes fights broke out, but those were quickly stopped and disbanded.

On extremely rare occasions, sailors and townsfolk subjected Librarians to vile invective, but they had a long history of not approving of the Vault of All Known Knowledge or the Librarians' work there.

But never had Juhg heard of a lynch mob forming to come after a Librarian. Still, his past instincts served him well because he immediately chose to flee. He stood.

Before he could flee, the Grandmagister's hand hit him in the middle of the chest and toppled him back into the chair. "Stay seated, First Level Librarian Juhg. I'll handle this."

"But Grandmagister—"

"No." The Grandmagister's voice barked authority.

Watching Grandmagister Lamplighter as he squared himself in front of the mob that had shoved through the seated customers, Juhg could not believe that the Grandmagister had ever been as timid as he claimed he once was. Perhaps he was not a physical force or a threat to the sailors quickly approaching them, but he stood firm and proud. He wore the authority of his office well.

Curses and imprecations followed in the wake of the sailors, but none of the farmers or herdsmen or townsfolk who had come for a quiet meal lifted a hand to help. No one went running for the harbor guard.

Juhg sat helplessly. Carason's had no back way out. There was only one entrance. Except for the stairs that led to the upstairs floor where Carason kept his personal quarters and warehoused supplies. Juhg knew he could flee through the windows and across the rooftops of the buildings. He had done that before.

But where would I go then?

Across the rooftops, even quick as he was, he was certain he would only be a target for an archer or a harpooner. No, the group of drunken sailors had come to draw blood and no one could stop them.

"You men will stop," Grandmagister Lamplighter declared.

In spite of the sheer inebriated state the men were in and the anger that fueled them, the sailors halted.

"Get out of our way, Grandmagister," a beefy human sailor ordered. "We'll be after havin' that one hung from a yardarm, we will, an' ye too if ye vex us."

"You won't hang anyone, Ganthor Hemp," the Grandmagister replied.

Carason came from the bar at one side of the eatery. He carried a longsword and scabbard in one hand. Without a word, he stood at the Grandmagister's side. His meaning and intent were clear.

"That—that—*Librarian* of yours," Ganthor thundered, his beard trembling and spittle flying in his rage, "got honest an' proper sailin' men killed chasin' after a trap he done laid for 'em!"

"A trap?" Grandmagister Lamplighter's rage was apparent in his flashing eyes.

Juhg was impressed. Even after all their adventures together seeking out books from hidden places along the mainland, he'd seldom seen the Grandmagister so set on following a course of action.

"I've not yet heard the events of those sailors' deaths," the Grandmagister said, "but I know this Librarian. He set no trap to cost the life of any man. I'll vouch for him."

"Do ye, now?" Ganthor roared drunkenly. "Why, from what I hear, that there Librarian came from the mainland. He's probably workin' for the goblins like he was afore he come here."

"First Level Librarian Juhg," Grandmagister Lamplighter said in a clear voice that contrasted sharply with Ganthor's angry tone, "was a slave in the goblin mines. He lost his family to those foul creatures, and he spent years toiling with a yoke of iron around his neck while he tried to stay alive and escape." The Grandmagister took a step toward the human, and it could be plainly seen that he was barely half the man's height. "Not one of this crowd has ever been in such dire straits."

Ganthor leaned forward, towering over the Grandmagister threateningly. Carason slipped free his blade from the scabbard, looking grim and deadly earnest the whole time. His message to Ganthor and the others was clear: If any of them touched the Grandmagister, he would spill blood.

And you're the reason for this, Juhg told himself. *Whether you mean to be or not, you're the reason the Grandmagister stands so defenseless before them. You're not one of these people.*

"He's an outsider," Ganthor accused.

"He's been in service to the Library for twenty years," Grandmagister Lamplighter argued.

"For all the good it's done any of us."

"You can't even begin to understand what a Librarian's job is," the Grandmagister replied.

"They's wastrels an' thieves by any other name." Ganthor looked around the room seeking support.

All of the sailors agreed and some of them gave voice that Ganthor should get on with what they came there to do.

Juhg had no doubt that Grandmagister Lamplighter was setting himself up to be killed. Even with Carason at his side, and what little help Juhg himself could provide, the sailors would plow through them like hail through a spring hay crop.

He couldn't imagine the Grandmagister taking such a firm stance, although they had faced down horrible foes in the past. Their major endeavor in those times had been to flee and escape whenever possible, which most of the time had been the case. At other times, Brant and Cobner had been with them, as well as other agents who the Grandmagister had enlisted to his cause, and the Library's, over the years.

Juhg stood, intending to give himself over to the sailors and hope that they came to their senses.

Without turning around, the Grandmagister stuck an arm out and blocked Juhg's path.

"No one here much cares for ye or yer little Library," Ganthor stated with a mocking sneer. "Ye're a parasite what thrives off superstition an' what ye can suck outta these good people here. I ain't the only one what thinks that."

"Then you're a fool," the Grandmagister declared. "And all those who think that way are fools with you." He looked around the room, somehow seeming taller than he was. "Greydawn Moors was put here to house the Library, to hold dear the knowledge that Lord Kharrion and the goblinkin tried to take from the hands of humans, dwarves, and elves in those long-ago Dark Years. You people who live here have been blessed to never know the hardships of the mainland. Those of you who have crewed aboard the ships know that I speak only the truth."

"Speak fer yerself," Ganthor roared. "I've come near to spillin' me life's blood more'n once a-carryin' out them orders what comes from the Library. I'll never—"

"You'll never," the Grandmagister stated in a voice that might have blown fresh off the ice of the Frozen Sea, "have to worry about such an event again, Ganthor Hemp. You'll never crew aboard a ship from this island again. As is my rightful decree as Grandmagister of the Vault of All Known Knowledge and executor of the estate of the island of Greydawn Moors, you are banned from ever setting foot from this place again. You shall live out your days on this island, never to go forth and risk seditious and treasonous acts against the Library, and never to hold a position that would require the trust of the Vault of All Known Knowledge. Your fate will now and forever be sealed with that of this place."

For a moment, silence echoed across the eatery. Then the whispers started as the patrons as well as the sailors recovered from the astonishment of the Grandmagister's order.

Everyone knew of the power of the Grandmagister, and there were even tales of past Grandmagisters who had caused some to be locked up for a time for heinous acts. But no one had ever been made an outcast on the island and a prisoner at the same time.

"Ye can't do that," Ganthor roared. A quaver of fear sounded in his voice despite his bluster.

"It's been done," the Grandmagister said in a level, unemotional voice. "All of the good folk here are my witnesses."

"Aye, I witnessed it," Carason said. "And all those who work for me or who intend to keep eating at this establishment heard it as well."

Ganthor turned back to the crowd of sailors pressing at his back. "We don't have to take this. It's just a lot of guff an' hogwash. Ain't nobody happy with the way the Grandmagisters have been runnin' things. Them that come before this 'un was at least human an' knew their places. We sure ain't gonna have to listen to no halfer who's gotten bigger'n his britches."

Most of the sailors raised their swords in agreement, but Juhg noticed that a few of them had started slinking away.

"Well, then, halfer," Ganthor sneered, turning back to the Grandmagister, "what do ye got to say about that?"

"Only this," a deep, stentorian voice announced. The words carried throughout the eatery from the front door, and they brought with them a sense of the power and regal bearing of the speaker. "Would the Grandmagister like you better as warty toads or as bigmouth bullfrogs?"

"Craugh!" someone croaked.

Gazing through the sailors and the wide area they'd left open behind them that led to the door, Juhg saw the individual standing in the door-frame. Juhg recognized the man at once.

At six and a half feet tall—and that was without the pointed hat that made him near a giant—and slender as a reed, the wizard Craugh was imposing and threatening simply standing idle. He was not idle now, nor was he mentally self-involved as he often was unless in deep conversation with the Grandmagister.

Worn russet-colored traveling leathers draped an innocuous brown homespun shirt that had seen better days and a pair of dark green breeches. No one knew how old Craugh was. Stories went back a hundred years and more, even though he was human and should have been long dead. Magic, it was well known, added years to a human's life. Provided, of course, that those forces didn't kill a wizard outright, or sooner rather than later.

His long gray beard trailed down his skinny chest and framed a narrow face that looked sharp as a blade or a prow on a fighting vessel. That face, Juhg swore, could break through ice floes or shear forests. Craugh's bright green eyes flashed with the power he wielded. He carried a gnarled wooden staff only slightly taller than him and had a crook on the end of it for lifting things.

Without fear, Craugh walked into the eatery. Even the people still sitting at the tables moved away from him in fear. He fixed his gaze on Ganthor.

"You drunken popinjay," the wizard stated in a heated voice, leaning down to thrust his face into the ringleader's. "How dare you talk that way to the Grandmagister! Especially *this* Grandmagister whom I have known these many years and know firsthand has risked his life and limb dozens of times over to keep both this island's knowledge intact as well as its secrets. His efforts have gone far beyond those of other Grandmagisters before him. And there you stand, Ganthor Hemp, throwing accusations like a chittering squirrel high in the branches of an oak tree."

Ganthor shriveled.

Craugh did not stop until he, too, stood at Grandmagister Lamplighter's side. Under other circumstances, the sight of the two standing so close together might have drawn laughter. Craugh was nearly twice as tall as the Grandmagister but seemed even taller because of his thin build.

"Well," Craugh said as he faced the would-be lynch mob, "you've heard the Grandmagister's pronouncements. What are you waiting for? *Begone!*" He stamped his staff against the wooden floor.

The thudding sound resounded throughout the building, growing in intensity. Eldritch green flames jetted from Craugh's eyes. He raised his empty left hand and threw it out before him.

Wind rose inside the building from nowhere and whirled through the room, blowing out all the candles and banging the shutters on the windows.

Shrieking and yelling for mercy, the drunken sailors ran from the room. They pushed and shoved against each other in their haste to escape the wizard's wrath, then sprawled into a drunken mass out in the street. They were quickly up again and running as if for their lives.

Perhaps, Juhg thought as he stared at the wizard, *they are.*

The flames exuding from Craugh's eyes faded. He turned and looked at Grandmagister Lamplighter. His eyes crinkled as he smiled and smoothed his ratty beard. "Bless me, Wick, I think that went about as well as could be expected under the circumstances."

"It was good that you came when you did, old friend," the Grandmagister said, smiling as well.

"I daresay, you had the situation well in hand. I should have let well enough alone, but you know how I love to make an entrance."

Juhg watched as Carason's staff went about relighting lanterns and candles, and righting overturned chairs and tables. He suspected that the building couldn't withstand many more such exits.

"It's been a long times since you last visited," the Grandmagister said.

"I have missed you, too, Grandmagister. But many events have been happening along the mainland and in the goblinkin countries that needed watching. I have learned a great many things, not all of them pleasant."

The two hugged, though Craugh quickly worked to regain his aplomb and his pointed hat, which had come dangerously close to falling off. The wizard turned his attention to Juhg.

As always, Juhg had a hard time meeting Craugh's blazing gaze, even though he and Craugh had always gotten along well together. Still, Craugh was the Grandmagister's friend, not his.

"And you, apprentice," Craugh said, sizing Juhg up at a glance, "I heard down in the harbor that you've come across a book under strange circumstances."

"Yes," Juhg said. Craugh had never called him anything but apprentice since Grandmagister Lamplighter had found him and taken him under his wing. "I was about to tell the Grandmagister the tale."

"Then you can tell it to us all." Craugh gazed at the table, eyes lighting on the plate Juhg had left. "Those ruffians interrupted your meal. Get back to it. The sooner you finish, the sooner we can talk at length about this. I have tales of my own to tell. Even with a full day before us, we might not get it all done."

"I can wait to eat," Juhg volunteered.

"No," Craugh and the Grandmagister and Carason said at the same time.

"A traveling adventurer never knows when his next meal might be coming," the wizard added.

"You'll need to keep up your strength," the Grandmagister announced.

"And you won't want that when it's cold," Carason said.

"Seeing the wisdom in a meal," Craugh said as he reached out and took up a nearby chair with deceptive ease because he was much stronger than he looked, as Juhg well knew, "I'll take a plate myself, innkeeper."

"As I've told you before," Carason grumbled, "I'm not an innkeeper. I'm a chef."

"A *full* plate," Craugh said, ignoring Carason's reply. "I'll settle for quantity—and hot—rather than quality from some would-be meat burner with grandiose ideas. I've just come in on a small ship that boasted only water and hardtack by voyage's end."

"I've never seen a ship come into Greydawn Moors in such a shape as you describe," Carason protested. "You're just a picky eater. And like as not, you skipped eating so you could come in here and eat for free as you normally do."

"Well, then," Craugh said with a grudging smile, "are you going to feed me or are you going to try to talk me to death?"

Still complaining about the lack of gratitude in wizards in general and Craugh in particular, Carason stepped into the back kitchen to see to the food himself.

As soon as the plate hit the table, Craugh thanked Carason and began eating with grim ruthlessness. "Well," he said, glancing at Juhg, "tuck in. When I'm finished, you're finished. There's not going to be any lollygagging about during this meal."

That was something of a challenge as well as a threat, Juhg knew from past experience. Craugh loved to eat, and could eat surprising amounts that his skinny frame denied, but he wasted no time on the enjoyment of any repast set before him. Juhg set himself to the task.

They ate mostly in silence, the calm quiet that those who have shared the road in dangerous times and in dangerous places know. And it was mostly silent because every herdsman and farmer who had witnessed Craugh's show of wizardry had left.

"Ertonomous Dron." Craugh repeated the wizard's name after Juhg finished telling of the battle against *Blowfly* that had gained *Windchaser* the mysterious book that the Grandmagister held. "I think perhaps I've heard the name in my travels, but I've never met the man. From what I recall, he was an evil and despicable man." He puffed on his pipe. "Are you certain that he's dead?"

"He was left at the bottom of the ocean near the Tattered Islands," Juhg said. "Even if he survived, it's a long way to the mainland. Or even to the Tattered Islands."

Craugh stroked his beard. "Still, you'd be surprised at what wizards can live through." He smiled grimly at past memories. "The Old Ones know the fits I've given some of my enemies when they thought they'd killed me. Eh, Wick?"

The Grandmagister nodded as he turned pages in the book. "Yes. I do remember the Falmorrean Gargoyle quest in particular. Even I thought you were dead that time."

That adventure, Juhg knew, was one he had not been privy to in conversation or in the Grandmagister's journals he'd read, and he'd read all of them that were available. The Grandmagister had not allowed all of his personal journals of his travels to be entered into the Library. Still, he had used those narratives as resources and contributed several monographs on historical sites, biographies of people long dead, and discussions of architecture and constructions that hinted at the places he had gone and the things he had seen and done on those missing travels. He also had not given any indication why those narratives of those journeys were missing from the Library stacks.

"That was a dicey bit of business," Craugh said.

"If there ever was." The Grandmagister kept turning pages, only halfway paying attention to his friend. "I thought we were both dead." He puffed contentedly on his pipe, then took it from his mouth and used the stem to chase sentences across the page. "I can't believe as widely read as I am that I can't at least guess at the origins of this language."

"You don't know everything, Wick," Craugh said. "At least, you don't know everything *yet*."

Juhg heard the emphasis and his curiosity pricked immediately. There was some kind of hidden communication between the wizard and the Grandmagister. On past trips, he had seen and heard evidence of the same thing. Neither Grandmagister Lamplighter nor Craugh were given to let everyone in on his secrets.

"Mayhap someday I will," the Grandmagister mused. He sighed, then looked at the wizard. "You said you had news of the mainland."

Craugh nodded and breathed out a wreath of smoke. "The goblinkin are massing along the South. They're growing stronger every day."

"Why?" the Grandmagister asked.

The news left a chill in Juhg's heart. He had been imprisoned for all those years in a mining colony in the South.

"I don't know." Craugh frowned. "Oh, I've heard rumblings of a

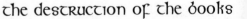

council of goblinkin going to form, and even that some new prophecy has come into being among the tribe clans."

"A prophecy?" the Grandmagister asked.

Craugh waved the possibility off with a hand. "The same folderol the goblinkin trot out every so often. At least, when those creatures even think to remember to do so. That Lord Kharrion will rise to lead them again."

"Something is bringing the goblinkin together."

"Yes. I've traveled there, Wick. Seen them myself. They are massing down near the Quartz Sea. I've stayed up in the mountains and spied upon them through the eyes of a falcon—not very settling to the stomach after a while, I must tell you. There are valleys and hills and dales filled with those noxious hide tents goblinkin use when those creatures march in the field instead of out in the ruins of one town or another."

"Have you identified any leaders among them?"

Craugh shook his head. "Oh, you'll see one goblin talking big one day only to see another run that one through the next day."

"Usually that will set one tribe against another."

"Mayhap it still will. But for now, they seem content not to try to kill each other in great masses. That, in itself, is a frightening thought: that we can't depend on the goblinkin to simply destroy each other over pillaging rights." Craugh puffed on his pipe. "You do know the tale of the Quartz Sea, don't you?"

The Grandmagister nodded. He reached for his current personal journal, opened it to the bookmark ribbon, then took out a fresh quill and a bottle of ink. With a deft, sure hand that Juhg was so familiar with after years of experience, the Grandmagister worked.

A map took shape across the fresh, clean page. The shoreline looked like a crescent moon. Patches of rock formed as well. The Grandmagister moved smoothly, picking up ink with the quill and adding lines, then back to the ink before the last line faded too much.

"I know about the Quartz Sea." A troubled look settled onto the Grandmagister's brow.

"We've never talked about this tale," Craugh said. "I didn't know if you were aware of the legend."

"I am," the Grandmagister said. "And I'm convinced that's all it is: a legend."

"Hmmpph," Craugh snorted. "It's only a legend till it crawls out of the night or the shadows and bites you on your nether regions."

"There's nothing crawling out of the Quartz Sea," the Grandmagister insisted. "That place is dead."

"Have you seen the Valley of Broken Bones that lies in the foothills of the Mountains of Despair near the Quartz Sea?" Craugh asked.

"No."

"Then would it surprise you to learn that the valley is now covered in verdant growth and game is in goodly supply?"

The Grandmagister looked up. "Yes. Yes, that would surprise me. The Quartz Sea was one of the worst damaged areas during the war. One of the worst damaged that the Unity of dwarves, humans, and elves caused, at any rate. From the descriptions I'd read of the place, nothing would ever grow there again."

"They said the same thing of Teldane's Bounty," Craugh replied. "You saw for yourself all those years ago when you were sold in the slave auction at Hanged Elf's Point that regrowth was taking place there."

"As well as the massing of the goblinkin," Juhg said, remembering the Grandmagister's account of those times.

"That was because of the slave market," the Grandmagister said, dismissing the similarity. "And because of the protection Fomhyn Mhout and his Purple Cloaks provided in the area."

"While Fomhyn Mhout researched the dark magicks he pursued," Craugh agreed. "We almost didn't catch that."

"*We* didn't," the Grandmagister said. "Brant did."

"They say the Gut-Twisting Catacombs still lie beneath the Quartz Sea and that dead creatures roam the tunnels," Craugh stated in a quiet voice. "No one of the Unity has ever seen the place."

"No, and no one ever will. The wizards of the Unity sealed the place off, remember?"

"Things that have been sealed," Craugh said, "have a way of coming unsealed." He pointed his pipe at the book on the table. "Just as you intend to ferret out the secrets of that book."

Grandmagister Lamplighter thumbed the book Juhg had taken from *Blowfly* again. Juhg couldn't clearly identify the Grandmagister's motivation as interest or irritation.

"No book has ever defied me before," the Grandmagister said.

Juhg knew the claim was not false, nor born of pride or self-aggrandizement. Grandmagister Lamplighter had become the wisest of all the Grandmagisters who had ever served at the Vault of All Known Knowledge. Of course, no Grandmagister before him had ever possessed as keen an understanding of all that the Library held, or had traveled—and traveled extensively at that—throughout the mainland.

"Nor will this tome stand long in your way," Craugh said.

The wizard's apparent belief in the Grandmagister made Juhg feel proud of his mentor's accomplishments. Grandmagister Lamplighter had labored hard during his tenure of service to the Vault of All Known Knowledge. Over the years, Juhg had also been surprised to see Craugh—for all his wizardly accomplishments—defer to the knowledge that the Grandmagister possessed on occasion. Of course, the information and learning the Grandmagister kept in his mind had served to save them all a number of times throughout their adventures.

"If I didn't know better, I'd swear this was written in no language that was known to men, elves, or dwarves before Lord Kharrion massed the goblinkin and attacked the world."

Sharp interest flashed in Craugh's green-as-frog-skin eyes. "If this isn't one of those languages, Wick, then what are you saying it is?"

"A new language." The Grandmagister's pipestem chased a line of writing across the page. He tapped the page with authority. "I know that's what this must be. I can feel it in my nose." He tapped his nose.

"How can that be?"

"Someone," the Grandmagister said in a low voice as he focused on the writing, "invented it."

"Invented a language?" Juhg couldn't believe what the Grandmagister said. And he couldn't believe how casually the Grandmagister advanced the possibility.

"Yes."

"How?"

"Believe it or not, First Level Librarian," the Grandmagister said dryly, "there was a time when no language at all existed. At one point, all the languages had to be invented. Otherwise dwarves would have continued to draw on cavern walls, elves would have continued to shape trees to tell stories, and humans—well, humans would have forgotten much more than they ever learned."

Juhg's mind boggled at the concept. *A new language.* The possibility fired him with excitement, but at the same time filled him with dread.

"Nor were those languages all invented at the same time," the Grandmagister continued. "They emerged over the centuries as people traveled farther from home and traded more, as they needed them. A means had to be created to keep track of things. Where goods could be bought, when they could be found there, who gave the best prices, when was the best time to travel according to the weather and the markets at the other end of the voyage. That sort of thing."

Juhg knew that. The birth of the languages lesson had been one of the first the Grandmagister had taught him. That had been back during the time when he hadn't believed that the Grandmagister could truly read. At first he felt that the Grandmagister believed he'd forgotten even those simple lessons, then he realized that the Grandmagister was only talking out loud, seeking to convince himself in his line of pondering.

"Lord Kharrion sought to push the world back to those primitive days," Grandmagister Lamplighter said, lost in the memories of the battle he still fought to keep ignorance from claiming all the lands, "to strip our knowledge from us, and to force us to live once again in caves and be afraid of natural things instead of understanding them." He paused.

The words sounded ominous to Juhg's ears in the quiet of the eatery.

"The Goblin Lord very nearly did that thing," the Grandmagister said. "To know how close Lord Kharrion came, all you have to do is look to the mainland, where stories of books and people being able to read are considered myths at best and bad luck to mention at worst, if not outright foolishness that will incite tragedy."

"But with all the languages that have been used, with all those that have already been invented," Juhg said, "why invent another?" During their travels, he'd often acted as the Grandmagister's sounding board. He fell into the routine naturally.

"To keep secrets," Craugh said, stepping into the conversation and addressing the Grandmagister. "Wizards are rife with secrets while seeking to pillage the secrets of others."

Grandmagister Lamplighter gazed at the wizard. "And you, old friend, do you share those feelings?"

A cold smile twisted Craugh's thin lips. "Upon occasion, Grandmagister, I have been known to succumb to those siren calls. The mysteries of the world, how they work and why they work, call out constantly to the likes of me."

"You're a meddler," the Grandmagister accused, and the declaration was only half in jest. The matter was an old but good-natured argument between them. "You can't be satisfied with just knowing. You have to test things and alter things as well."

"How else is one to truly know something," Craugh countered, "without testing and altering?"

"Acceptance," the Grandmagister replied. "One can learn acceptance."

"Hmmmph." Craugh snorted his obvious displeasure with that suggestion.

"But this is a wizard's book," Juhg pointed out, wanting to draw the conversation back to the matter at hand. "Wizards know languages. It doesn't make sense that Ertonomous Dron would invent a language simply for his own use."

"If he had his own personal secrets he wished to keep," the Grandmagister said, "he would have done such a thing."

"No," Craugh disagreed. "I must beg a difference of opinion, my old friend. Many of the forces that wizards invoke lie in the first language the Old Ones gave those who would borrow magick from the land and the oceans and the heavens. Even those goblinkin sorcerers that practice the dark magicks drawn from fire use that language. You can't change that fact."

182

"You're both assuming that the book is the wizard's," the Grandmagister said. "That could be a mistaken perception. It's possible that it was not Ertonomous Dron's book."

Juhg blinked, thinking about that. He'd recognized no wizard's sigil or mark anywhere in the book. And those would have looked no differently than any owner's mark. No claiming design existed.

Dracol's Principles of Logic," the Grandmagister reminded. "Juhg, you should remember that. The Laws of Assumption?"

" 'Clearly state only the known,' " Juhg said. " 'Clearly state the questions that are to be answered. And remember that logic, like a river, doesn't have to flow straight and true; only get to where it's going.' "

"But it will never double back on itself or contradict itself," the Grandmagister added.

Juhg nodded.

"The wizard had possession of the book," Craugh said. "That's a fact."

mel odom

"Yes. Although a case might be made, under the circumstances, for the book having possessed him." Grandmagister Lamplighter nodded. "Why did Ertonomous Dron have possession of this book? Or vice versa?" He lifted the volume with his fingers.

"It wasn't by accident," Juhg said, carefully adding a known fact. "He took pains to guard it."

"Or," Craugh said, "at least to protect himself from it. Which makes a case for it being something that he didn't wish to have around and was possibly afraid of."

The Grandmagister picked the book up. "It doesn't appear dangerous."

"Neither does a threet fingerling," Craugh said. "But if you get stung by one during spawning season, you're a dead man."

Threets, Juhg knew, were vicious predators that hatched in the bodies of corpses. They were most dangerous when they were newborns, fingerlings.

"I'll take your word for that," the Grandmagister said, "and be glad that I've never seen a threet, fingerling or full-grown."

"A birthing of a swarm of threet fingerlings," Craugh said in a tight voice choked with memory, "is something that is not easily forgotten."

"Ertonomous Dron traveled with goblinkin," Juhg said.

"Why?" the Grandmagister asked.

"I will state that it wasn't by choice," Craugh said. "Even the most evil wizard will not travel with goblinkin if he has a choice."

"Fomhyn Mhout allied himself with goblinkin in Hanged Elf's Point," the Grandmagister reminded.

"Mhout used the goblinkin who infested the city only as a barrier to keep his enemies away from his fortress," Craugh stated.

"We'll agree to disagree over that one," the Grandmagister said.

The wizard nodded. "So why travel with the goblinkin with the book?"

"Because the book had to be transported," Juhg said.

"Why not just transportation for the wizard?" the Grandmagister asked.

"If Ertonomous Dron wanted transportation only for himself," Juhg said, warming to the mental work at hand, "he would have traveled on his own. More than likely *without* the goblinkin escort."

"Perhaps not," Craugh said.

"He might not have had a choice," the Grandmagister pointed out. "The book could have held them all in thrall."

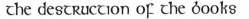

"All right." Juhg nodded. "But Ertonomous Dron wouldn't have traveled with the book if he feared for its safekeeping."

"What would he have done with it?"

"Stored it," Juhg answered. "Put it in some wizardly secret hiding place that only he knew of."

"Such places have been found," the Grandmagister said. During the years, he had found a few of those places scattered across the mainland.

"Yes, but not easily. And the book was more exposed during travel than it would have been in hiding." Juhg thought for a moment. "Kannithon's *The Slight of Sleight: A Beginner's Guide to Pick-Pocketing.*"

Craugh looked at the Grandmagister. "You have a book like that on the required reading lists for Librarians?"

"Only for some First Level Librarians," the Grandmagister admitted. "I found the work a fascinating study. A tremendous supplement to Yahweg's *A Warrior's Art of Defending Others, and How to Take Their Lives in the Event You Are Not Paid So That Your Reputation Grows.* Kannithon held to a basic premise of exposing a target, whether it was an object or a human being, then acting. Many successful assassins used his book."

"You make that sound like a good thing."

"Kannithon was a master at his craft. His skill was an art, and the book was a treasure trove of information not only about assassination, but about the times and the cities in which he lived. There were several cities and countries, and all are elegantly brought to life in his words. Though, of course, the dark alleys and seedy bars and docks are by far the most covered."

"Remind me to take a look at the lists you are putting out these days," Craugh commented.

"The point is," Juhg said, "that Kannithon felt a moving target was a more vulnerable one. So the question now is whether Ertonomous Dron moved the book because he chose to—or because he was afraid not to."

"Meaning that the book was of worth to him," Craugh said. "And that others were after the book."

"Yes." Juhg nodded. "And that it was no longer safe where it—or where *he*—was."

"Possibly." The wizard drew on his pipe in quiet contemplation.

"There is a definite way to quickly find out if this book is magical in nature," the Grandmagister said in a soft voice. His finger idly played with the stitched binding that held the book together.

Craugh looked at him.

Without another word, the Grandmagister pushed the book across the table to the wizard.

A sour expression filled Craugh's face. "You know how much I hate messing about with another wizard's magicks. I've told you that on any number of occasions."

Grandmagister Lamplighter nodded solemnly. "As I recall, you always say that only the worst kinds of things can happen."

"Tampering with another wizard's spells is not a simple thing, nor a safe thing."

The Grandmagister sighed and said, "You're right, of course. I'll take this book back to the Vault of All Known Knowledge. We'll puzzle over it for years, seeking answers when there might not even be a need for them. Or, quite possibly, missing the window of opportunity our having it might give use."

"Not a need for this book?" Craugh echoed.

Grandmagister Lamplighter looked at the wizard. "It could be a cookbook."

"A cookbook?" Craugh snorted his disbelief. "And it guarded by goblinkin and a wizard?"

"A very *important* cookbook," the Grandmagister agreed.

"By the hoary beards of the Old Ones, you're baiting me, Grandmagister," Craugh said.

Grandmagister Lamplighter steepled his fingers. "Is it working?"

Craugh fumed and puffed on his pipe in stony silence.

"Seventeen sailors from *Windchaser* gave their lives to get this book this far," Grandmagister Lamplighter said. "First Level Librarian Juhg almost lost his life getting this book."

Craugh glanced askance at Juhg.

Juhg nodded. "It's true. The book was well protected."

Craugh was silent for a moment. Juhg took his lead from the Grandmagister, who sat silent and still.

"Oh, all right," Craugh grumbled. He stretched out a hand and murmured a few words in a sibilant language that Juhg was surprised he did know. Craugh held his palm over the book. Tentative blue sparks dropped like snowflakes from his hand to touch the book.

Almost immediately, a roiling gout of red flame flashed up from the book, growing large enough to cover the table in less than a heartbeat.

Juhg felt the heat of the fireball as it rushed upward and was sure that he was going to die.

12

The Trap Is Sprung!

efore he could move to even attempt to save himself, Juhg saw Craugh lean toward the fireball. Firelight carved the wizard's face clean to the bone. At least, that was the way it seemed at that instant. Actually, the harsh red color of the fire drained Craugh's skin of color, matching it to the flames themselves till it seemed they met and meshed.

Craugh thrust his hand into the fire. A frenzy of harsh, sibilant language fell from his lips. As Juhg watched, astonished, the flames receded from the wizard's flesh. Wondrously, Craugh's skin wasn't burned and blistered as Juhg had expected.

The flames surged again, though, only this time they butted up against a bowl of force Craugh had evidently conjured up with his magic. The flames licked the sides of the invisible container that the wizard had conjured up.

"Get back," Craugh advised. "I don't know if I can contain the energy that's been unleashed here."

Juhg sprang from his chair and moved back several feet, instinctively going to the Grandmagister's side so that he might protect him. *If that is even possible,* Juhg thought, watching the whirling flames inside Craugh's invisible vessel grow more frenzied and brighter. Even ten feet from the table and the book now, Juhg still felt the heat of the spell rush over him.

Heated winds somehow escaped the prison of force that Craugh had woven around the spell. The wizard's hat blew off, but almost lackadaisically he caught it on the end of his staff. His gray hair blew back in the fury of the power being expended, and his clothing plastered against his front as though he stood in a gale storm.

Grandmagister Lamplighter gazed helplessly upon his friend. Concern etched his features.

Juhg truly believed the wily old wizard had met his doom. All the majestic power that Craugh commanded seemed unable to release him, and there was no chance for the cunning that so many of his enemies had witnessed just before he had bested them.

"Grandmagister," Juhg pleaded, pulling on the Grandmagister's arm. "We need to leave this place."

"No." Grandmagister Lamplighter stood his ground. "I will not leave Craugh. He will not let this thing beat him. He's too prideful and stubborn. But you may go, Juhg. I'm quite capable of standing here on my own."

Juhg held tight to the Grandmagister's arm but made no effort to move away. "If you believe in Craugh, Grandmagister, then I believe in him." *But I think we're both fools.*

Craugh's hand started to tremble. The quaver ran up his arm and intensified. The old wizard set his jaw in determination. Green fire returned to his eyes.

Then, with a clap of thunder that popped Juhg's ears, the table beneath the flames shattered. Burned boards and ashes dropped to the hardwood floor, but the flames winked out inches from hitting it.

Craugh drew his hand back and tucked it into the folds of his traveling cloak, obviously aware that he was shaken. "Well, now, *that* was exciting." He let out a loud sigh that sagged his narrow shoulders.

"What happened?" Juhg asked.

"Obviously the book was booby-trapped." Craugh glanced around and saw Carason standing nearby with a bucket of water. "You won't need that water now, Carason, though I feel the need for a mug of mulled wine, if you don't mind."

"Of course," Carason said. "I'll see to it straightaway."

"What of the book?" Grandmagister Lamplighter asked, moving

closer. He took a lantern from the wall and peered closely at the inches-deep pile of gray and white ashes.

"You'll want to be careful mucking about in that," Craugh advised in a hoarse voice. "That was a powerful spell—and treacherous. I wouldn't put it past whoever worked that nasty bit of magic to render the ashes poisonous to the touch."

Juhg slipped a knife from his boot, one that Raisho had given him to seal the agreement they had made to trade together. "Let me, Grandmagister."

"Yes," Craugh said. "Let the apprentice do it. You still need both your arms, Wick."

That, Juhg thought, *is not positive support.* He knelt and dug through the ash and kindling with the point of his knife. To his surprise, he found the book whole, more or less.

"It survived," the Grandmagister whispered, sounding just as astonished as Juhg felt. "Quickly, Juhg, fetch the book up and let's see what's been done. Perhaps we can save most of the pages."

As carefully as though he were handling a loathsome swamp toad that might leap at him at any second with a mouthful of venomous fangs, Juhg pulled his hand into the sleeve of his cloak and used the material to keep from touching the book. Of course, he knew from studying toxicology that any number of poisons transferred through material—and even a fair number killed by scent alone. Remembering that, he breathed more shallowly.

"Craugh," the Grandmagister said.

"Hasn't your curiosity caused enough damage?" the wizard demanded petulantly.

"Doesn't a book that was filled with such raw magic make you the least bit curious yourself?" the Grandmagister asked.

"Yes."

"Then tell me if the book is safe to touch."

Craugh leaned down and pointed his staff at the book. As the wooden length came closer, Juhg turned his face away and closed both eyes. He expected nothing less than getting his head blown off.

"It's safe enough," the wizard declared. "And no poison either."

Quick as a wink, the Grandmagister snatched the book from Juhg's hand.

Breathing out in relief and feeling more than a little light-headed, Juhg pushed himself to his feet. Movement at the eatery's front door and windows let him know that the explosive nature of the spell had attracted a crowd.

"The book didn't exactly weather the spell well," Grandmagister Lamplighter observed. "The one it contained or the one that you used to banish the trap."

Craugh brushed at some stubborn embers that still burned orange in his clothing. "It should have been destroyed. I held nothing back."

Juhg stared down at the burned and crumbled remnants of the heavy wooden table they'd dined on and knew that the wizard was right.

"It wasn't meant to be destroyed," the Grandmagister said. "That spell was designed to kill anyone who used magic on the book. Maybe there was a word that released the spell without setting it off."

"Or perhaps the book was not meant for wizards," Juhg said.

Craugh harrumphed his displeasure at the suggestion. "Books and wizards go together, apprentice, just like books and Librarians."

Juhg knew that was not true, but he also knew well enough not to argue with Craugh while he was in a particularly grumpy mood. Wizards read books only to learn what they wanted about powers and things with power and—on occasion—about treasures to finance further searches for things with powers. Librarians read for the education promised with the opening of each book.

Despite his harsh beginnings among the goblinkin mines, Juhg had experienced those same feelings when he lifted a book's cover. Grandmagister Lamplighter had taught him to read while they had traveled together after Juhg's rescue from the mines. They had spent weeks aboard, running from enemies deep in the goblinkin-infested Southlands.

Juhg still carried the very first journal the Grandmagister had made him, the one he had scrawled his first letters in, then words and sentences and paragraphs. The Grandmagister had also taught him to draw, to render people, places, and things so those could be captured in more than words.

"There was some damage," the Grandmagister said, flicking a fingernail under a heat-blistered and -cracked section of the cloth binding. He also riffled the pages. The heat had caused them to draw and wither, much like water damage. "But I think it remains legible." He opened the book.

Juhg glanced at the front of the eatery and wanted to be out of the place. The eatery still stank of ozone in the air, stronger than even a close lightning strike. And the crowd outside was growing larger with each passing second.

How long is it going to be, Juhg wondered, *before someone suggests that we are to blame for this? That the Librarians are to blame for this?* He reconsidered. *Well, we are to blame for this. A little.*

"Look!" the Grandmagister exclaimed. He held high the lantern he'd taken from the wall. The book lay open in his free hand and he shined the soft light over the singed and rippled pages.

Craugh leaned closer and surveyed the pages. "What?"

Juhg saw the difference at once. "The writing," he whispered, feeling the awe at what was revealed before him. "The writing has changed."

A smile spread across the Grandmagister's face. "I knew there had to be a secret other than just a made-up language. It just didn't make sense for a book to be written that no one could read."

Craugh caught Juhg's eye and nodded toward the crowd gathered outside the eatery. "Perhaps, Wick, you'd like to read the book in the Library."

Before someone gathers a howling mob and comes in for us, Juhg thought. *A ship nearly lost at sea, seventeen sailors dead, and now magic spells thundering in the local eatery. No one in Greydawn Moors is going to like that.*

"Of course," the Grandmagister said. He licked his forefinger and thumbed through the pages.

"Apprentice," Craugh directed as he clapped his pointed hat back on his head and turned for the door.

Understanding the wizard's unspoken command, Juhg took the Grandmagister by the elbow and guided him in Craugh's wake. The wizard led the way out of the eatery as the Grandmagister continued turning pages. The crowd drew back from the imposing wizard, but unkind words followed them.

Juhg sat in the back of the cart as it rumbled up the Knucklebones Mountains. Craugh drove the team of mules while the Grandmagister continued to read through the mysterious book that had held two secrets.

Two secrets so far, Juhg reminded himself, watching the Grandmagister meticulously making notes in his own journal, despite the way the cart rocked back and forth. *Both of them dangerous. And this last secret of all, Grandmagister, will it be the death of us? Or will it be a fantastic treasure?*

the destruction of the books

Juhg tried not to worry, but the attempt was doomed to failure. He could still see the sailors' bodies dropping into the ocean only a few days ago, and he had a few flashburns and blisters from the magical fire that had vomited forth from the book back in Carason's Eatery.

The clatter of the mules' iron-shod hooves against the worn stone trail rang out over the mountains and made the whole world sound empty. No soil remained on the winding path up into the mountains where the Vault of All Known Knowledge sat, leaving only the naked bone of the earth.

Huddled in his traveling cloak because he still was not rested and because he was still not over the fear that had filled him with first the lynch mob and then with the magicked book, Juhg leaned back against the seat in the port corner of the cart bed. He smiled a little at his mental reference to his position. He'd been on a ship long enough to pick up ways that would be hard to get shut of.

He wondered if Raisho had heard of the excitement in the eatery. And if his friend had, what Raisho thought of it all.

That led Juhg to the realization that *he* didn't know what to think of it all. Questions assailed his mind, and from time to time he watched the Grandmagister reading and nodding his head as if in agreement with something he found in the pages of the mysterious book. Still, Juhg bided his silence because he knew from experience that the Grandmagister wouldn't acknowledge him till he was ready.

Instead, Juhg turned his attention to the hard granite mountainside on his starboard, and the wide-open spaces of the forest far below. They had come up beyond the treeline in short order, and the wind turned colder still.

With the rhythmic slap of the mules' shoes and the creaking of the rocking cart, Juhg found himself lulled to sleep before he knew it. He awakened with Grandmagister Lamplighter's hand on his shoulder.

"Wake, Juhg," the Grandmagister said gently. "I know you're tired, but there's a lot we must do to solve the riddle the book poses."

"Riddle?" Juhg repeated.

"Yes." The Grandmagister nodded. "This book lists volumes of texts that had secret messages embedded in them. We have to look up passages in other books to get the full meaning of this one."

"Couldn't the author of that book simply list whatever secrets he had hidden?" Juhg grumbled. "After all, the book was magicked several times over."

"This book," the Grandmagister said reverently, "was one of the last written during the Cataclysm. Whoever the author was, he couldn't be certain that it wouldn't fall into the hands of the goblinkin and Lord Kharrion. It hints at a secret weapon that could be used against Lord Kharrion."

"Evidently it wasn't needed," Juhg observed. "The warriors of the Unity put an end to Lord Kharrion."

"True," the Grandmagister replied, "but the thought of some great weapon of destruction lying about out there is unsettling."

"Does the text mention what that weapon might be?" Craugh asked.

The Grandmagister looked at the wizard with suspicion. "No."

"Pity," Craugh commented. Then he clucked to the mules. "What about the location of the device? Does it mention that?"

"I'm certain it does. But to get that information we'll have to decode the hidden messages."

"And to do that, you'll need the books in the Library."

"Yes."

"How could the author of that book know you, or the reader, would have access to a library of books?"

"I would think," the Grandmagister replied, "that an assumption on the author's part would be the correct thing. If anyone could decipher the book, anyone could find the weapon. Right? He wouldn't have wanted just anyone to find it. He would have wanted it in the hands of people who were civilized. And civilization, as everyone knows, includes written records. A collection of them."

"A *library*," Craugh said derisively.

"Yes."

Juhg knew the wizard didn't mean to be offensive. He was just irritated. And the fact that the Grandmagister gave more respect to the tomes within the Vault of All Known Knowledge than to the power a wizard wielded rankled Craugh to some degree. Craugh was used to respect everywhere he went. If he didn't get respect, he earned an opponent's fear.

"Not everyone who could read in the old days was civilized," Craugh countered. "You know there are a few scattered across the mainland who can read who aren't civilized."

"Yes," the Grand Magister agreed, "and most of them are wizards."

"Are you saying I'm not civilized?"

"At times," the Grandmagister replied immediately, "you are not. You have your own agenda in all things. Even for your presence in Greydawn Moors today."

For a moment, Juhg feared that Craugh would take offense and that in the next moment the Vault of All Known Knowledge would have a warty toad for a Grandmagister.

Then Craugh chuckled. "Point taken."

"Your saving grace," the Grandmagister said in a lighter tone, "is that you have always cared about the world and other people. From what I've seen of most wizards, that isn't always true."

"I suppose," Craugh replied grudgingly. "After all this time, the weapon is probably gone. Perhaps it was even used in the struggle against the Goblin Lord."

"Perhaps," the Grandmagister agreed. "But I've never been one to let a secret pass me by."

"Pain in the rump dweller curiosity, if you ask me," Craugh grumbled. "Though I'm loath to hold you accountable for the egregious parts of your nature."

"A dweller's curiosity is second only to a wizard's lust for secret things," the Grandmagister said in an even tone that relayed he'd taken no offense at his good friend's pronouncement.

"Even if the weapon is there," Juhg asked, hoping to distract both of them from finding fault with the other (in case dire warty and toady things happened), "what would be the use of looking for it? Lord Kharrion is gone."

"Items of power, especially magical power," Craugh said in a grim voice, "if true, should not be left lying about for anyone to discover. Usually a high and painful price has been paid to bring such objects into the world, and they are fashioned for specific purposes. The world would be a terrible place indeed if all the things wizards conjured up were allowed in the hands of just anyone. When not used for good, many things created by wizards end up in the hands of evil men and fools only to beget atrocities."

"If it is still there, if it can be found," the Grandmagister said, "then we must find it."

"And then what?" Juhg asked.

Grandmagister Lamplighter hesitated for a moment. "I don't know. Yet. We'll know more, should we find the device."

Out of the fog clinging to the upper reaches of the Knucklebones Mountains, the Great Library started to take shape. Squat towers and turrets of blue-gray stone shot through with white sprinkles along the defensive wall jutted up from the steeply sloped mountainside only a few yards above the Ogre's Fingers.

Juhg wiped sleep from his burning and blurry eyes and stared forward. Craugh headed the mule team toward the huge twenty-foot stone gates that sealed the entrance to the Vault of All Known Knowledge. There on the doors in bas-relief were the images of a giant quill and an inkwell. The title VAULT OF ALL KNOWN KNOWLEDGE ran in deep and richly cut letters across the tops of the two doors.

Despite the years that he'd lived within the edifice, though probably helped by the fact that he had been gone from the place for weeks, the sight of the Great Library took Juhg's breath away. Carefully mortised as they were, the main tower and four outlying towers looked like they'd sprouted from the mountains at their feet, stolid and proud, with mortared seams that did not show at that distance. Windows showed through the patches of fog now, many of them filled with sparkling stained glass depicting the arts and the sciences in dazzling gem-bright blues, greens, reds, and yellows.

Besides being a great storehouse, over the years under the loving attention of the Librarians, who lived there their whole lives, the Library had come to be a work of art. Yet it never lost the air of being a place of learning and education.

Craugh brought the mules to a halt in front of the gates just as three dwarven warriors in full armor stepped out of the gatehouse in front of the mammoth doors. The dwarves carried halberds at their sides and battle-axes slung over their shoulders.

The dwarven guards met the cart where the trail was still narrow. Enemies, if ever anyone dared attack the Library, could be easily forced from the trail and down the steep side of the Knucklebones Mountains to the Ogre's Fingers a bowshot distant. No enemy could mass the gate and hope to get through without pouring blood for the effort. Coming up the mountain undetected, even in the dead of night, because a moonless night made the stone trail plain as well, was impossible. A large group could be seen coming for over a mile.

"Grandmagister," the lead dwarf called out in a deep gravelly voice. He stepped up beside the mule on the right and fisted the mule's bit so he could control the animal.

Juhg knew the move was a habit because he knew both Grandmagister

Lamplighter and Craugh. The dwarves who guarded the Library had all taken oaths to lay down their lives in the defense of the books and the Librarians.

"Varrowyn," the Grandmagister replied, then smiled.

Shifting his gaze from the Grandmagister, Varrowyn looked more closely at the wizard. His greeting wasn't quite as warm. Dwarves didn't care for magic as much as humans, who were drawn to the power, or elves, who were curious about how magic worked with natural things. "Hello, Craugh."

Craugh acknowledged the greeting and sat with the harness reins in his hands.

Varrowyn stepped back and waved to the other dwarves guarding the gate. After a moment, the massive gates moved, pushing outward and rolling on specially designed stone tracks. The present wall and gate had replaced the earlier one, which had been made of a jumble of rock.

Slapping the reins across the rumps of the mules, Craugh guided the cart inside the Library grounds.

Anticipation filled Juhg as he took in the landscaped grounds. As much attention had been given to the outlying area of the Library as the inside.

The front of the Library was for show, to entertain the few guests that made the trip up from Greydawn Moors. Neat flower gardens and fruit trees, all of them planted in holes dug into the stone and in earth that Librarians in the past had laboriously brought up into the Knucklebones Mountains, lay neatly between paths of bare stone left from the mountainscape. The plotting and planting rendered intricate geometric shapes that were as pleasing to the eye as the stained-glass windows.

In several places, black, white, yellow, and rose stones made up the patterns. Ships' captains in the past had thrown out ballast on the south side of the island that had come from all over the mainland. Most of those stones were not indigenous to the island. Over the years, Librarians had transported choice stones to the Library and used them to build rooms, the outbuildings, and the patterns.

Craugh brought the cart to a halt at the foot of the steps leading up to the main doors. "Well, Wick, you're home again and of a piece."

The Grandmagister nodded, slipped his finger inside the book to mark his place, and turned to look at Juhg. "Get up to your old room. You'll find robes in the wardrobe that will fit you." He turned and slid down from the cart's seat.

"What?" Juhg asked.

Looking impatient, the Grandmagister said, "Robes, First Level Librarian. You must wear robes if you're going to be working throughout the Library. We stand on tradition and decorum in the Library, and I'll not see that put aside." In a flurry of his own robes, the Grandmagister turned and scurried up the steps.

Juhg marveled at his mentor. He turned and looked at Craugh, who sat still in the cart and watched the Grandmagister pass through the doors. The Grandmagister's appearance alone was enough of a rebuke to three Third Level Librarians who were lazily going through the books they'd brought up from the undeclared sections of the Library to classify that they got to work in a frenzy.

"He is a strange one, isn't he?" Craugh asked.

Juhg refrained from replying, thinking silence was surely the most certain and safest course.

"Many people take one look at Wick and misjudge him," the wizard went on. "But if you know what to look for—and I do, young apprentice, because I've had a friendship with him that has lasted years—you can see seeds of greatness in him. His passion for what he does is all-consuming." He shook his head. "By the Old Ones, Wick would have made a fine wizard had anyone but started him on that path."

Juhg didn't know about that, but he did know that he hadn't ever seen the like of the Grandmagister in his life.

"Of course, that same passion is what sets a donkey apart from the rest of livestock." Craugh handed the reins to a Novice who showed up to take care of the animals and the cart.

Juhg dropped over the cart's side and landed on his feet. Craugh stepped down lightly and with surprising alacrity for someone his age. The Novice led the team and cart toward the stables along the eastern wall, out of sight behind the main building.

Craugh took out his pipe and glanced at Juhg. "Well, what are you waiting on? There're mysteries to be solved. Do you want the Grandmagister to solve them all by himself?"

"No," Juhg said, and he stepped away from the wizard and hurried into the Library.

———

"What are you doing back?"

Straightening his robes, Juhg glanced at the open doorway of the room he'd gotten twelve years ago when he'd made First Level Librarian. All Second and Third Level Librarians had to share rooms. Novices bunked four to a room.

First Level Librarian Randorr Cotspin stood in the doorway with his arms folded and a disgusted expression on his face. He was heavyset, even by dweller standards. His arms and legs looked like sticks pushed into his body. Heavy-lidded eyes peered from an oval oblong face whose longest circumference was from side to side rather than up and down, almost succeeding in masking his pinched nose. Hairy eyebrows stood up in pugnacious spikes, mirroring the twisted tangles of black hair and the wisps of a beard he was still desperately trying to grow to make him look more intimidating.

"Hello, Randorr," Juhg said. While he had been at the Library, Randorr had always carried a grudge against Juhg, whom he claimed was the Grandmagister's favorite when the Grandmagister wasn't supposed to have favorites.

"Well?" Randorr snapped.

"I came at the Grandmagister's request." Juhg carefully folded his traveling cloak and his outerwear, then stored them in the large oak chest at the foot of the simple bed. Even though he'd lived alone, the room was small.

 Librarians didn't live the lives of luxury that so many townspeople in Greydawn Moors accused them of living. Copies of famous paintings of places Juhg would have liked to have seen before they were destroyed in the Cataclysm hung on the walls. He'd made the copies himself, eliciting comment even from the Grandmagister on occasion at how fine his hand was.

It was unusual, however, to see the small bookshelves and desk devoid of books. He'd always had several projects going on at once, those of his own choosing, as well as tasks the Grandmagister had assigned to him. One of the hardest things he'd had to do before leaving the Library was give some of those tasks, his own and the Grandmagister's, to other Librarians. Grandmagister Lamplighter had helped in the choosing of some of the Librarians who had taken over for him, but it still had not been easy letting go.

"I thought you'd left Greydawn Moors," Randorr stated petulantly.

"I did."

"Now here you are."

"Yes." Juhg felt like quoting from Janse Aschull's *Obviousness and Its Tiresome Wear: A Guide for Those Who Want to Master the Lost Art of Conversation Among the Elite and Those Otherwise in Possession of Their Senses.*

"The Grandmagister insisted you would be back," Randorr said.

"If it's any consolation," Juhg said, "my return is as much of a surprise to me as it is to you."

"Not just a surprise," Randorr said. "Your arrival is also quite displeasing." He entered the room and walked around without being granted permission. The act broke several tenets of the Librarians' Code of Behavior regarding the treatment of another Librarian's privacy.

"I'm sorry you find my presence here displeasing."

"Oh, don't go acting so naïve." Randorr looked out both windows of Juhg's room. Most rooms only had one window. Juhg's possession of two windows had always struck Randorr as a personal affront. "You knew I didn't like you, even before you left the Library."

"Yes," Juhg admitted. "Though I've never understood why."

Randorr put his sticklike arms behind his back, folded his hands together, and peered out the window. "I don't like you because your presence here is a distraction."

"A distraction?"

Turning to face Juhg, Randorr said, "The Grandmagister should devote his energies here. To the Library. He should not be haring about the mainland as he seemed so intent on doing since he discovered you in some goblin's mine pit."

Anger surged within Juhg. Randorr wasn't just insulting him; the other Librarian was also insulting the Grandmagister.

"Grandmagister Lamplighter," Juhg said in carefully enunciated words, "had a habit of going to the mainland, even before he found me."

"You made it worse."

"How?"

"You gave him companionship. In no time at all, the Grandmagister was going more and more frequently—and dragging you off with him."

"The Grandmagister searched for books," Juhg protested. "He read about small libraries and collections that were left behind during the Cataclysm in journals and notes of generals and educators that were found in the Library. Not all of those were there, but enough of them existed that he took chances on carefully researched information."

"The Grandmagister made other trips to the mainland as well. When his friend the thief—"

"Brant," Juhg supplied automatically.

"Whatever." Randorr waved the name away, as if it was insignificant. "When his friend the thief got into trouble in some far-off place—"

"In his homelands. He fought against the goblinkin that had held his people and his family lands. Not only did he fight them, but—with the Grandmagister's help—Brant succeeded in reclaiming those lands."

"That was wasted effort. The Grandmagister should have been here at the Library. He's given his time away too freely."

"The Grandmagister cemented a relationship with an ally. He had been Brant's friend since their adventures in the Broken Forge Mountains, but once Brant was returned to the barony, those people became friends as well."

"Do they know of the Library?"

"No. The Grandmagister has never let that information out." Brant and the others knew, but they had kept the secret between them.

"Then how do you know they are friends of the Library?"

"They would be," Juhg said stubbornly. "In times of trouble."

Randorr paced the room like a general marshaling his troops. "We don't need any relationships with the mainland. That is why the Unity established Greydawn Moors out in the Blood-Soaked Sea. No one is supposed to know about the Vault of All Known Knowledge."

Juhg took a deep breath to calm himself. "The Library was hidden in the beginning, when the goblins ran rampant in the world and darkness covered the lands and seeped into the seas. The elves were chopped from the forests. The dwarves were buried in the earth they mined. And the humans had their ships shattered at sea. The Unity did not know if they would survive against the Goblin Lord. They wanted only to preserve the knowledge that the goblinkin warred so hard to destroy."

"To preserve it, you must protect it. And to protect the Library, you must keep it secret."

"The Library isn't supposed to be kept secret forever," Juhg said.

Randorr snorted. "Oh right! And we're supposed to catalogue, restore, copy, and care for this Library, only to give it away at some point? We're just custodians, then, with no glory of our own to earn? Once we give this knowledge back into the world, we'll be nothing. Don't you realize that?"

The naked hate in Randorr's voice surprised Juhg. For years he had known the other Librarian sought attention and wanted to improve his station. Randorr had often vocalized his demands to the Grandmagister that the townsfolk of Greydawn Moors be forced to acknowledge the debt of gratitude they owed the Librarians for being allowed to live on the island.

"The Librarians were given the task of keeping and sorting the information," Juhg said, "but only until the world was safe enough to entrust the knowledge back among the people." He remembered how Raisho had said he would like to learn to read, and his own immediate impulse that such teaching couldn't happen. He felt guilty now.

Stubbornly, Randorr shook his head.

"And we wouldn't be giving it away," Juhg hurried on before the other Librarian could interrupt. "We'd make copies of books that were given away, train people to read, and make available knowledge of other books, other resources."

"It's not theirs. It's ours. It was given to us."

"It's not ours," Juhg pointed out. "Many people lost their histories when the goblinkin destroyed their books and schools. We were entrusted with the books. We can give that back to them. Let them reconcile their pasts with the present they now have." He paused, knowing he was baring so much of his personal belief—and part of the reason he had left Greydawn Moors. He and the Grandmagister did not see eye to eye on these issues. "We could give those people brand-new futures."

"Those people along the mainland," Randorr stated, "will *never* be ready to trust with the knowledge that we hold."

"They might."

"Listen to yourself! What colossal tripe! Can you imagine the kinds of problems those people would create if they knew as much as we do? If they had access to all the knowledge we guard so fiercely? There was a reason that knowledge was removed from them!"

Juhg bridled at the vicious nature of the other Librarian's attack and the narrow-minded view. Before he could stop himself, he crossed over to Randorr and stood in his personal space. That was Lesson One from Kalberd's *Intimidating Presence and the Vanquishing of Enemies Without Fisticuffs.*

"Those people," Juhg stated in a harsh voice, "are the ones who observed laws and science and events, experimented till they understood what they saw, and recorded their findings. That knowledge has never been ours. They paid for it in blood and sweat, and we were fortunate enough to be given a role to play in the safeguarding of it."

Randorr grunted, "Eeeep!" and stepped back quickly. He raised his sticklike arms over his head.

Juhg let the other Librarian go. With the anger running through him and the fact that he as a Librarian was responsible for the deaths of so many sailors aboard *Windchaser,* he didn't trust himself. He had never committed violence against another Librarian, though he had fought for his life a number of times on the mainland.

"You speak as though we don't make a difference," Randorr whined.

"We've only made a difference," Juhg said in a more measured tone, "when we're able to go back among the races along the mainland and give the knowledge back to them."

Randorr avoided Juhg, giving him a wide berth as he made his way back to the doorway. Once through the door and safely out into the hallway, Randorr said, "You're as insane as the Grandmagister. I don't know which of you has infected the other worse. Edgewick Lamplighter should have never been made Grandmagister. That position should have gone to Gaurilityn."

Gaurilityn was a human Librarian. Since all Grandmagisters of the Library in the past had been humans, everyone at the Vault of All Known Knowledge had expected Gaurilityn to be named Grandmagister. Grand- magister Lamplighter's appointment to the position by the previous Grand- magister, Grandmagister Frollo, had surprised everyone in the Library. First Level Librarian Lamplighter had maintained an adversarial relationship through much of his career with Grandmagister Frollo.

"Out!" Juhg ordered. "Get out of my sight before I do something we both regret."

"You're a barbarian," Randorr accused. "A mainlander. Perhaps Grand- magister Lamplighter took you from those savage environs, but he didn't exorcise the savagery from your nature."

Juhg walked toward the door and Randorr fled. Out in the hallway, Randorr continued to run away, gathering his robes like an old woman and tottering away in an ungainly manner that Juhg found much more satisfy- ing than he knew he should have. He knew he wasn't a man to be afraid of. He'd met men who inspired fear in others as naturally as a fish breathed, but he knew he was not one of them.

Yet, in Randorr's world, Juhg knew he truly was a savage. That saddened him. He would never be accepted at the Library. Not truly. He had pointed that out to the Grandmagister and received only arguments in return. The Grandmagister had remained certain that Juhg's history would soon be overlooked. All these years later, he had still ventured the same argument when he'd tried to dissuade Juhg from shipping out with *Windchaser.*

And now look at you, Juhg chided himself, *back at the Library only a short time and already at odds with Randorr.* He walked down the quiet hallways, scarcely noticing the happy glow of the glimmerworm lanterns.

He followed the torturous maze that formed the inside of the Library. As the exterior buildings had been constructed on top of the caverns that had served as the first resting place for the vast libraries dumped there by the Unity transport troops, little thought had gone into the design. The way everything fit together came much later. At that time, the dwellers who worked in the Library had labored like ants, building more rooms for the Vault of All Known Knowledge, then shoveling the books into the areas that were delegated for the different categories. As a result, Novices were constantly getting lost in the labyrinth, forgetting that sometimes it was necessary to take staircases up and down to get places.

This one last task, Juhg promised himself. *Once you're finished with helping the Grandmagister find the solution to his latest puzzle, you're going back to the Yondering Docks. If* Windchaser *won't have you, there are other ships.*

Nearly three hours later, Juhg was winded and his back felt near to breaking as he carried the latest stack of books into one of the Library's Great Rooms.

"Is that the last of them?" Grandmagister Lamplighter asked across the room.

"Yes." Juhg placed his burden on the floor, then placed his hands on his knees to stretch his back and shoulders like a cat. He felt so light after carrying the books that he thought he might actually float up from the floor.

"Did you find Darg Tarkenbuul's *Treatise on the Lives of Inner Selves?*" The Grandmagister moved slowly through the three hundred and nineteen volumes they had gathered from throughout the Library.

"Yes." Juhg massaged his back, thinking that it would surely never be the same again. "Dissitan had it. Just as you remembered."

When the book had turned up missing from its shelf, Juhg had been

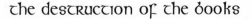

convinced the search for it would take considerable time. Instead, even though the book wasn't assigned to anyone—which required paperwork to be filled out, the Grandmagister had known exactly who'd had it. His knowledge of the Library, as well as the one hundred and twenty-odd Librarians who worked there, was nothing short of amazing.

"Well, then, Juhg, let's be about our task."

Juhg surveyed the stacks of books they had assembled. According to the hidden text in the mysterious book *Windchaser* had salvaged from *Blowfly,* the various volumes named were supposed to be gathered for quick reference and passages read and interpreted from them.

"Do you see anything among these books that immediately stands out?" the Grandmagister asked.

Looking at the titles, nearly all of them books that he had read at one point or another, Juhg shook his head. "Not really, Grandmagister. There are books on different sciences, different histories, plays, and adventures."

"One thing I have noticed," the Grandmagister said. "All of these authors are from the Southlands. And no two books are by the same author."

Juhg glanced around the room, suddenly feeling too warm in his robes. The glimmerworm lanterns glowed against the walls, giving off enough light to illuminate the huge expanse of the room. Several shelves holding often-used books shared space with dozens of chairs and tables. The Grandmagister had cleared the room of Librarians when they had started to work.

However, Randorr and a few of the other Librarians had peered down upon them from the second-story walkway that ran around the inside wall. Evidently the whole Library knew about the Grandmagister's latest project.

Craugh came through the main doorway. He carried a lantern and walked at a brisk pace that was almost a run. He had retired to the Library's kitchens while the book gathering was going on. The Grandmagister was supposed to send for him when they were ready to begin.

"Wick!" the wizard called. *"Wick!"*

The Grandmagister turned toward his friend.

"What have you done?" Craugh demanded.

"Nothing," the Grandmagister replied. "Only finished gathering these books."

Craugh marched through the room like a hound scenting the air. "There's magic in this room."

"Only the spells that protect the books," the Grandmagister said.

"No," Craugh said in a harsh voice. "This is something different. I know those protective spells. I helped put some of them in place. This—" He scented the air again in a deep draught. "This is something different. There is a new spell in this room, and it's growing stronger." He held out a hand toward the books. "It's coming from the books."

Even before the echo of the wizard's words disappeared from the cavernous room, a shudder ran through the whole Library and a hole ripped into view in the air above the books. A violet sky streaked with crimson lightning blazed into view through the hole, but a gigantic bat-winged beast that flew through the hole and into the room quickly blocked the sight of that.

Broad-bodied and sporting horns, the creature looked a bit like a bull, but only if bulls stood as tall as a human at the shoulder. It breathed out huge gusts of gray vapor that immediately filled the Great Room with the stench of death.

A four-armed warrior dressed in full battle armor sat astride the strange beast. He carried a bow with an arrow already nocked back, and took aim at Juhg. He carried an axe and a shield in his lower two arms. Inside the helm, there were no features, only the grinning jaws of a bleached white skull and empty eye sockets with a hint of spectral crimson fire.

"You will die!" the warrior roared in a voice that sounded like splintering wood.

The arrow leapt from the bow and came straight at Juhg, who stood frozen, knowing only that the enemy had finally found the Library.

13

The Bellringer

efore Juhg could move, Craugh swung his staff with blinding speed, with no more apparent thought than he might shoo away a fly. The staff broke the speeding arrow in twain and both pieces hurtled harmlessly by Juhg.

"Move!" Craugh commanded in that steely tone Juhg had heard on occasion before. "Move if you would save your life, apprentice!"

Juhg threw himself to one side and dodged behind the stacks of books. *The treacherous books,* he couldn't help thinking. Whoever had designed the trap had constructed it well enough. If there were ever to be any wooden horses of Phamscrifa brought into the Library, a book was surely the vehicle to deliver those enemies in. He placed his back against a stack of books and peered back toward the center of the room.

Craugh stood with both hands on his staff. Galing winds from wherever the monstrous beast and its terrifying rider had come from whipped at the wizard's robes. The beast snarled, threw its head back and whipped it forward, spitting a line of fiery liquid.

Arcane words Juhg had never heard spilled from the

wizard's lips. Juhg had never seen the language anywhere, and had often felt certain if he ever did find examples of it that he would never want to read it. Wick had mentioned more than once that the older wizards, and Craugh was certainly one of those, had their own language.

Some said the language was from the Dark Times, even before Lord Kharrion had gathered the goblinkin and brought about the Cataclysm. Others said that the truly powerful wizards took their power from some other place, a world removed from the one most people knew, a place of terrible beasts and men where horrible events took place every minute of every day.

It was said that a wizard, a truly powerful wizard, was exposed to that world—like Annealis who was dipped into the River of Time as a baby by his mother so that he would be forever immortal, except for the ear that his mother held him by—for only a short time. The time was supposed to be long enough to gain the power, but not long enough to go mad.

Many of those who sought to wear wizard's robes were dipped too long or not long enough. Very few were dipped just right. Wizardwork was a very hazardous calling, and not much appreciated by anyone.

Until you have need of a wizard, Juhg thought, watching as Craugh caught the flaming spit in one bare hand and threw it back into the creature's face.

Smashed full in the face by the seething mass of flames that clung to its obscene features, the creature reared straight up. Evidently the creature could contain the fire inside itself but not endure it the way that dragons could, or perhaps Craugh's magic altered the flames in some way. Blisters, huge and weeping, appeared on the animal's face sacked in thin green skin.

Driven by the rearing creature, the four-armed warrior slammed into the room's tall ceiling. Stone shattered and a crack ran half the length of the room. Dazed by the impact, the warrior slipped from its mount and fell against the stone floor with a resounding clangor of metal. The warrior did not immediately get to its feet, and Juhg was heartened.

But even as Juhg thought they all might quite possibly survive the encounter, two more creatures bearing riders stepped through the impossible gate that had formed in the room. The riders fired arrows at Craugh, who stood his ground and called on the forces at his command. Green lightning blazed from the wizard's eyes. One of the arrows caught in the wizard's robes. The second came so close to hitting him that the broadhead sliced hair from his beard and the stiff fletching sliced his cheek from his nose to his ear. A line of crimson blood oozed out.

"Juhg!"

Drawn by the Grandmagister's voice, Juhg glanced in Wick's direction.

The Grandmagister stood behind one of the thick stone columns that supported the ceiling. Embers caught in his robes and his red hair.

"Go get the dwarves!" Wick yelled. "Ring the alarm bell! Tell them that we have Dread Riders and Blazebulls inside the Library!"

Dread Riders and Blazebulls! Juhg wanted to kick himself. He should have known what the beasts were. He had read a few books about the fearsome riders and their merciless beasts. Of course, all of those books had come from Hralbomm's Wing and had been at the Grandmagister's suggestion to lighten Juhg's "too scholarly" approach to his reading.

It was the Grandmagister's contention—Grandmagister Lamplighter's and not Grandmagister Frollo's, nor the contention of any Grandmagister who had gone before, most of the Librarians said—that reading the incredible adventures and romances in Hralbomm's Wing also gave insight to a culture's beliefs and histories. Juhg had believed that because the Grandmagister had told him so. Too often, though, the tales twisted too much the events and people that inspired the romantic accountings. Where Wick seemed to grasp with ease the allegory and subtlety of the stories and fathom the hidden meanings, Juhg had struggled. 209

But Dread Riders and Blazebulls were something Juhg felt he should have known. As far as anyone knew, the creatures did not exist in the world. They were reportedly from some other place, a hidden place filled with horror and wickedness. Some even said that dragons had once lived there but had made their escape into the world.

But, Juhg thought, staring wide-eyed as Craugh brought his staff down against the stone floor with a mighty crack that should have sundered the surface, *they are* real!

Lightning leapt from Craugh's staff as he stood against the two newest beasts and their riders. Bolts of blazing green power shot across the room and blew great chunks from the Dread Riders and the Blazebulls. For a brief moment, their attack was battered back like an incoming wave against a rocky shoal.

Then small shadows crept in between the rearing, snarling monsters.

The new arrivals were shorter, even than dwellers. The color of black ink, so dark that none of the lantern light or the Blazebulls' flames reflected from them, the creatures had huge bulbous heads a full third of their body length that made them appear almost waiflike. But one look at the close-set malevolent black eyes encircled by pools of venomous yellow and the snapping jackrabbit teeth shattered that impression immediately. Their limbs were blade-thin, harsh lines devoid of muscle or fat, and the joints were heavy knobs. The hands and feet were three sizes too large for their spindly, featureless bodies. They wore no clothing, and their skin, as Juhg remembered from his reading of *Veskheg Versus the Hordes of Shadow*, was hard and slick as a beetle's carapace.

"*Grymmlings,*" Juhg whispered, giving a name to the terror the small creatures evoked. The few stories he'd read of the beasts left him trembling.

Despite their bulbous heads, the Grymmlings had no rational thought patterns. No one could communicate with them. At least, as far as Juhg knew, no one could communicate with them, but that couldn't exactly be true because they were here now working with the Dread Riders and the Blazebulls. The general thinking was that Grymmlings were no more coherent than insects and worked through a group consciousness, a hive mind. Like locusts, they descended in droves to devour everything in their path. They were omnivorous, eating plants and meat, and seemed possessed by—not of, as the romance writer Iligurl had pointed out no less than seventy-three times in his story of Veskheg—*by* an insatiable appetite. They carried foot-long crystal blades spun from gossamer crystal by giant Laragan spiders they kept as pets in their lairs.

"Juhg!" Grandmagister cried out.

Embarrassed at having been caught so flatfooted by everything that was transpiring, Juhg glanced back at his mentor.

"Go!" the Grandmagister ordered.

Out in the center of the floor, Craugh backed up three paces. His voice sang with fury and the raucous sound of a file rasping along a rough edge not yet ready for fine work. He thrust his staff up before him in both hands, stamping forward with his left foot.

In response to Craugh's movement and the magic he commanded, the three hundred nineteen books that had been brought into the room leapt from the floor and swirled into the advancing line of attackers. The heavy books bludgeoned the invaders, knocking the Grymmlings back like tenpins and even thudding swiftly enough to dissuade the three Blazebulls that had entered through the mystical gate from continuing on inside the Library.

"No!" Grandmagister Lamplighter wailed. "Craugh! Not the books!"

But the wizard gave no heed, gesturing again to send the books once more against their opponents. Several of the books burst their bindings in the second assault. Pages from paper and vellum books flew into the air, turned into fiery crisps in a heartbeat as the Blazebulls breathed flames on them. The pages swirled in circles, propelled by the winds that blew in from wherever the creatures had come from.

Other pages—stone pages from books made from a single rock, glass pages blown by glassmakers and fused with a dozen different colors, delicate seashell pages hung together by seaweed strings and turtle sinew, snake scale sash books that told histories of individuals and events, and a dozen others—shattered, broke, and fragmented in a rush across the stone floor. Several of the pieces pierced the huge feet of the Grymmlings, but if the creatures cared, they didn't slow a bit. Bloody footprints, black as squid's ink, followed them.

Juhg caught the Grandmagister's eye.

"Go!" Grandmagister Lamplighter ordered again. "Get to the bell! Call the dwarves! You are faster than I am!"

Juhg knew that wasn't the truth, though. He might have been a little faster than Grandmagister Lamplighter, but Juhg knew the real reason the Grandmagister stayed behind was to stand with his friend. The Grandmagister had never been a brave soul, and tended more toward cautiousness, even after years of adventuring along the mainland and surviving dozens of close calls.

"Now!" the Grandmagister commanded. "Before those horrible imps catch your scent!"

That fact had slipped Juhg's mind. Grymmlings were noted in the annals he'd read of being expert trackers. Once they had locked onto a potential victim's blood spoor, they did not deviate from that victim until one or both of them were dead.

Juhg pushed himself into motion, crossing the room as quickly as possible. His movement attracted the attention of a half-dozen Grymmlings. He saw their black, black eyes focus on him, their black tongues ooze between the yellowed jackrabbit teeth, and felt their unwanted attention, their hunger.

One of them threw itself at him. As it closed, hurtling like an arrow launched from a bow, it swept the gleaming crystal knife out at his throat.

Juhg ducked.

Out of control, the Grymmling slammed into a chair, bowling the chair over and spilling in a tangle of arms and legs. Another leapt for Juhg's legs, arms outspread and jackrabbit teeth open wide to bite deeply.

Leaping into the air, Juhg watched the Grymmling shoot past beneath him. Juhg landed on a study table, knocking over other stacks of books as he skidded across the top. He slipped off the other side before he was ready and dropped to the floor. He landed off balance, gave in to gravity and fell forward, and rolled, coming up on his feet once more. The robes hampered his movement and he shed them as he ran.

Three Grymmlings slammed into the table behind him. They made vicious little noises that sounded like paper cuts might if given voice. The buzzing, burning, irritating chatter filled Juhg's ears. His lungs filled with deep draughts of air, and he tasted the smoke of burning paper.

Before he reached the door, one of the enchantments laid upon the Vault of All Known Knowledge by the Builders activated. Fire was a problem to any building made up of wood, or even any building made of stone that was shored by wooden timbers. But a fire inside the Library was thought to be the worst thing that could ever happen.

Until the Dread Riders, Blazebulls, and Grymmlings arrived, Juhg thought as he ran for the door.

Many of the enchantments laid on the room were designed to protect the books. Water was the first line of defense. Drawn from the southern shores of the Blood-Soaked Sea and pulled by magic through the countryside and the stones of the building, water wept from the ceiling inside the room. By the time Juhg reached the door, the condensation that had begun the protection effort had turned into a monsoon, evidently reacting to the intensity of the flames the Blazebulls breathed, as well as Craugh's own use of that fire.

At this rate, the spell will drain the Blood-Soaked Sea, Juhg thought. He caught the edge of the door and peered back, watching as Craugh grudgingly gave ground before the fierce aggressors. Then a Grymmling jumped onto the wall almost at Juhg's face, clinging there with its strong fingers and prehensile toes.

Unable to stop a cry of surprise, Juhg stumbled back in shock, tripped, and fell on his backside. Three more Grymmlings appeared in the door, their yellow eyes vacant and hungry, their crystal blades scraping across the stone floor.

Juhg got himself up and ran, trying desperately to remember which way the alarm bell that would summon the dwarves stationed within the Library as well as those presently on leave down in Greydawn Moors.

In all the history of the Library, the great bell had never rung before. He was going to ring it—the first ever. If he lived.

"Gangway!" Juhg yelled, barely able to part with the breath that it took to force out the warning. "Gangway! Grymmlings!"

He wanted to shout out everything, to tell the Librarians wandering the dimly lit halls of the Vault of All Known Knowledge that the Great Library was under attack. He wanted to tell them that Dread Riders, Blaze-bulls, and Grymmlings ran rampant. That the Grandmagister's life might already be forfeit and even Craugh, when Juhg had last seen him, wasn't faring so very well.

But he didn't have the breath. And he didn't have the time.

Librarians by their very nature were not slow creatures. They had a tendency to size up situations quickly. Although none of them had ever seen Grymmlings, at least a few of them recognized the deadly little creatures for what they were.

"Grymmlings!"

"Grymmlings!"

The shrieks roared through the long hallway Juhg was presently running along. He had at last gotten his bearings and remembered where the great alarm bell was located.

Six Librarians ahead of Juhg took up the cry, froze in their tracks for just an instant, then fled in the other direction.

No, Juhg reflected grimly, *if you show a Librarian a Grymmling, they know at once what to do.* He tried to suck in a deeper breath, and couldn't. He tried to cry out again to say that the Grandmagister needed help and couldn't. Desperately, he tried to lift his knees higher to lengthen his stride, or more quickly to hasten his frantic pace, and couldn't.

The Grymmlings remained just behind him. The low, growling buzz of their tiny voices pursued him relentlessly.

Despite their quick uptake on the situation, the Librarians weren't as fleet of foot as Juhg was. He caught up with them and passed them, feeling instantly bad when the Grymmlings caught up with the Librarians in the next breath. He shoved and pushed his way through the Librarians.

Juhg shut their piteous cries out of his head. He couldn't stop. If he fell, the great bell would never be rung and the dwarves would not know that Death had found its way into the Library. Down in the mines, he had sometimes been forced to chop the leg off a dweller who had died of overwork and starvation. Chains had bound them all together, and dragging a dead body around till the end of a shift put an impossible drain on the rest of the chain crew.

Three times during his long years in the goblinkin mines, Juhg had chopped the legs off dwellers who had fallen. They'd also had to carry the leg of a fallen friend back with them each time, to show that the dweller free of the chain hadn't simply escaped. The average goblinkin wasn't overly bright, but even they had known that dwellers came with two legs.

Behind Juhg, cries for help became cries of agony. He ran, leaving the cries behind him, but hearing the steady skittering of chitin-hard, overly large feet slapping against the stone floor of the hallway behind him. Unable to help himself, he turned to look.

Lantern light glinted from the crystal knives two Grymmlings carried as they continued their pursuit of Juhg.

Frightened, knowing that his fatigue was slowing his step, feeling the iron bands that had seized up tight around his chest, Juhg faced forward again just before he took a nasty spill down a flight of stone steps. Unfortunately, he knew he would never be able to slow in time to manage the long flight without tripping and falling, quite possibly to his death.

And then there would be no one to ring the bell.

Trusting to his dweller's surefootedness, Juhg leapt to the railing to the right of the stairs. Only when he gained the railing did he realize he was along the portion of the underground section of the Library most referred to as the Pit.

When the Builders had formed the island during the Dark Years of the Cataclysm before any of the races became certain their warriors stood a chance against Lord Kharrion and his goblinkin army, they had drawn up the earth they had used to make the island from the sea floor. Whatever magic and skills they had used had left a long, vertical pit in the center of the Knucklebones Mountains.

The pit was thirty feet across and, at least from where Juhg stood, ninety feet straight down. The Librarians drew their water from that pit. The salt of the Blood-Soaked Sea—and whatever other revolting stuff lurked out there in those crimson depths—was strained out by the limestone roots of the island.

Heart in his throat, Juhg ran along the railing, telling himself he would not fall. One misstep, he knew, and his race would be run. Rocks waited at the end of that long fall at the bottom of the Pit. Even if he survived the fall and somehow found the small opening that allowed egress into the heart of the mountains again in the complete darkness below, and if the water level was high enough at the moment that he might reach that opening, he would never be able to sound the bell in time.

Despite the Grandmagister's seeming confidence, Juhg held no real hope that even the dwarven warriors would be able to hold back the things that walked into the Library through the mystical gate. But he ran, fleet of foot, through the dim glow provided by the occasional lantern. This part of the Library generally required a Librarian to bring his own light, as the Librarians he'd heard fall behind him had done.

Reaching the bottom of the railing, he leapt to the floor. No sooner had he landed than one of the two Grymmlings that pursued him landed across his shoulders. Evidently the creature had taken the same route while its companion tumbled and bumped down the stairs.

Cruel teeth bit into Juhg's right shoulder. Blood coursed, warm and thick, down his side under his blouse. Pain exploded inside his skull as he screamed in fear. Off balance, he fell heavily to his right, slamming into the railing next to the Pit just as he managed to lever his right arm under the Grymmling's chin and start pulling.

The railing caught Juhg in mid-chest. More pain burned along his ribs as he bent over the railing. However, the sudden stop worked even less in the Grymmling's favor. The creature tore loose from Juhg, leaving a wake of ripped clothing and long scratches along bruised flesh.

The Grymmling made no noise as it hurtled out into the darkness in the center of the Pit. The last thing Juhg saw of the creature were the venomous yellow eyes and the gleam of the crystal knife as it dropped from sight.

Then the other Grymmling plopped onto the floor in a fetal ball.

Gasping for air, certain his heart was about to explode into a million pieces, Juhg watched as the creature unfolded its limbs, looking like a spider as it shoved out its arms and legs. Then its head popped up and the jackrabbit teeth flared open as it squeaked menacingly.

Juhg pushed himself from the railing and ran the final distance to the door to the alarm bell. Every floor had access to the stairwell that led up to the curving steps that snaked up to the top of the alarm tower. Thankfully, the Grymmling was too stunned to follow at speed until after Juhg grabbed the lantern from the wall outside the doorway, then started up the stairwell.

The Grymmling howled its eerie buzzing noise.

Inside the stairwell, Juhg wasted a moment to look for a latch to lock the door behind him. Then he realized that he was back in the Vault of All Known Knowledge and that no one locked doors inside the Library.

He turned and started up the stairs. His knees protested at once. He felt light-headed and couldn't quite catch his breath, which tasted like heated brine anyway.

But he made himself go. He had spent years in the goblinkin mines. That experience had not defeated him, only made him stronger in mind and in body than he had ever truly realized before now.

He went, two and three stairs at a time, round and round to the right, so fast that he felt dizzy. The lantern bounced in his other hand and the light whirled around him. He thought he was going to be sick, but he forced himself to keep going, charging into the gloom ahead of him while a lethal shadow nipped at his heels.

At last, just when he was certain that his legs would burst into flames and he couldn't go another step, Juhg spotted light ahead. Breathing in shuddering gasps, black comets whirling in his vision, he raised the lantern high at the end of his trembling arm.

Around the next turn, he spotted a beautiful stained-glass window showing Enloch standing tall at the Bridge of Loronal, one of the key conflicts during the final push against Lord Kharrion during the Year of Hope Redeemed, which would have been named the Year of Shattered Courage if Enloch and his group hadn't managed to hold the bridge till the majority of the Unity's armies could draw back to fight again. Enloch had died during that battle, but the second battle fought the next day had helped break the back of Lord Kharrion's army.

Juhg chose to take the stained-glass representation as a good sign. His lantern light reflected against the stained-glass panes, and only then did he realize that sunset had fallen outside. They had worked so long to gather the three hundred nineteen volumes named in the book *Windchaser* had recovered that they had lost the day.

Only night lay outside the walls of the Vault of All Known Knowledge, Juhg realized. Most of the town sleeping below the Knucklebones Mountains would be abed. His heart sank. His feet faltered. He fell and bruised his shins against the sharp stone corner of the step.

Before he could get to his feet again, the Grymmling caught his ankle and pulled.

Juhg's chin impacted against the step with enough force to almost knock him out. He screamed and yelled, knowing the whole time that no one could possible hear him. Images of Grandmagister Lamplighter's poor torn body flashed through his mind.

No! he told himself with grim determination. *That has not happened! I will* not *allow that to happen!*

He rolled into the side of the staircase in an effort to dislodge the loathsome creature. It clung to him stubbornly. The insane buzzing chatter filled his head. The jackrabbit teeth bit into his ear and more blood spilled down the side of his face.

The Grymmling drew back its blade and drove the weapon home into Juhg's side. New pain scalded the dweller's mind. He drew his arm forward and brought his elbow back in a manner Master Pohkem taught in his book on martial arts, *The Unarmed Warrior Bares His Knuckles and Teeth and His Heart, and Other Things.*

His elbow popped into the Grymmling three times. The creature tumbled backward, but not before managing to shove the crystal blade into Juhg's arm once for good measure.

Spinning, knowing for all his efforts that he had only earned a moment's respite, Juhg swung the lantern into the Grymmling. The lantern shattered at once. Glass fragments and glimmerworm juice flew over the creature and the wall behind it. The wick remained lit and landed at the Grymmling's foot. Although glimmerworm juice burned cool, it also burned easily, soaking into a wick as if the two had been separated and were only then reunited.

Flames spread along the Grymmling. The creature buzzed and shrieked in agony and fear, jerking and jumping. Then, as if realizing that it couldn't put the flames out, the Grymmling turned its yellow eyes on Juhg. Madness dawned there, fueled by the clinging lummin juice.

On his back, Juhg shoved his feet forward and caught the nearest step, propelling himself up the staircase. The steps bruised his back, but he got enough distance to flip over and use his hands to push himself up and run again. He didn't run, though, so much as he managed to fall up the stairs a very long way.

He reached the platform where the bell was and saw the coil of rope wound round a great iron hook set into the wall. Dust and spiderwebs covered the rope and the great bell. The Librarians tended not to be overly interested in cleanliness unless a certain state of dishevelment could be directly attributed to a particular Librarian.

Summoning the final dregs of his strength, near-to-passing-out because he couldn't catch his breath, Juhg dove for the bell rope and clung with both hands. Incredibly, the bell didn't move. Aghast, he glanced up and saw that the clapper and the spindle the bell was mounted on had evidently rusted in place.

 The great bell had been forged by Thomak-Oolufsin, one of the Burning Iron Forge Dwarves during the early days of the Library. Thomak-Oolufsin also designed and smithed much of the wrought iron in the common rooms where the Library was expected to entertain guests. Since there were so few guests that came to the Vault of All Known Knowledge, much of Thomak-Oolufsin's final works went unviewed.

Juhg had always considered that a sad thing, but the saddest thing at the moment was that no one had seen to the great bell more often.

The flaming Grymmling forced its way up the steps. The creature no longer moved quickly, but that it moved at all let Juhg know he was not long for the world. Even though it was smaller than him and still burning in some places, although the chitinous outer skin made that hard to discern in most places, he knew from grappling with it earlier that it was stronger than him.

Thinking quickly, first—guiltily—of his own survival, then of how he was to ring the bell, Juhg spotted a lantern filled with lummin juice hanging on the wall. The Library was filled with lanterns because Librarians often didn't pay attention to how much lummin juice they had left in their lanterns and often got stranded in the dark.

As a result, the Librarians who were responsible for filling the lanterns again when it was their turn did not miss a lantern. Although the great bell was not ready—and Juhg had to admit that no procedure existed for testing the bell—the lantern was full.

The bell hung twenty feet above Juhg. He dug his nimble toes into the rope and shoved himself upward, using his free hand. After all of the countless hours climbing *Windchaser*'s rigging, climbing the rope was simple. However, the Grymmling climbed just as easily. Fiercely, the deadly little creature followed him, its knife tucked securely between the jackrabbit teeth.

At the top of his climb, Juhg reached up, caught the edge of the bell, threw his feet against the wall, and walked up to the bell by pressing his hands against the bell while he pressed his feet against the wall. He carried the lantern in his teeth.

The Grymmling didn't possess arms long enough to continue its climb. It hissed and buzzed inside the bell.

Safe for the moment, Juhg held on to the top of the bell, knowing if he fell the creature would be all over him. Bracing himself on his elbows, almost strained to the limit, he opened the lummin juice reservoir and reached up to pour the liquid over the spindle that held the bell in place. He poured more through the hole at the top where the clapper was affixed.

In addition to burning with a cold flame that didn't often prove combustible to other mediums, Grymmling chitin proving one happy exception at least, lummin juice also combatted rust with a vengeance. Before Juhg could secure his hold again, his weight forced the freed bell into motion.

He fell, tumbling and squalling in fear, flailing with both hands until he grabbed the bell rope. No sooner had he seized the rope and stopped his fall than the clapper smacked into the side of the bell and released a huge, clangorous note that felt like it turned his bones to jelly. He lost his hold on the rope and fell again.

Hitting the stone floor below almost knocked Juhg unconscious. The impact did knock out what little air he had in his lungs. Before his senses fully returned, something landed on his chest. Curious, and a little afraid because he thought he knew what the lump might be, he looked up into the yellow eyes of the Grymmling.

The thing grinned, obviously a little woozy from the bell's clangor as well. But it definitely had murder in mind as its hard-knuckled fist closed on the crystal knife.

Then the bell *bonged* again, filling the bell tower with even stronger noise than the first time. The vibrations shuddered through Juhg and disoriented the Grymmling.

Taking advantage of the creature's hesitation, Juhg slapped his palm into its face and shoved it from his chest before it could sink its blade into his heart or its teeth into his throat. The Grymmling rolled backward, but came to its feet again as Juhg did.

The creature threw itself in one of those incredible jumps its kind was able to perform. Juhg ducked, putting up a hand into the creature's stomach to keep it off of him. It slashed at him in its passing, though, and the blade drew blood from the back of his hand.

Juhg turned, expecting the thing to bounce off the wall behind him and hurtle itself at him once more. Only it didn't strike the wall; it struck the stained-glass window.

Delicate and fragile, pieced together from hundreds of shards of glass mounted in a delicate framework, the stained-glass window shattered outward at once. Silver moonlight caught dozens of pieces of glass and rendered them into gleaming jewels spread out in a long spray of color.

The Grymmling vanished from sight, headed for a very long, very hard fall down the north side of the Knucklebones Mountains.

Shaking and weak, almost overcome by fear and his exertions, as well as blood loss, Juhg walked to the window and peered down. He saw the Grymmling, parts of it still covered in flames, lying against the unforgiving stone below. The creature did not move.

Just as Juhg caught a breath of fresh night air that constricted his lungs, light invaded the bell tower. He turned, holding his hand up against the bright light that leeched the darkness from the tower.

The bell continued to bong hollowly, making any other sounds impossible to hear.

At first, Juhg had feared the worst, that some other creatures had followed him from the research room where the mystical gate had opened. Then the man holding the lantern held it to one side so that his features were revealed.

"Varrowyn," Juhg cried, and knew the dwarf had not heard him because he could not hear himself over the clanging bell.

The dwarf reached out and took Juhg's arm, turning the limb slowly to examine it under the lantern light. He glanced back up at Juhg and his lips moved.

Unable to hear because of the bell and unable to read the dwarf's lips because of his fierce beard, Juhg pointed through the broken window at the body of the Grymmling. Juhg doubted greatly that the dwarf knew what the creature was, but he was certain Varrowyn knew it didn't belong in the Vault of All Known Knowledge.

Varrowyn growled and spat. Then he clamped a hand like a vise of iron on Juhg's upper arm so hard the dweller lost the feeling in that limb, and marched him down the same stairs that Juhg had fought so hard to climb up with the Grymmling at his heels.

Juhg protested the harsh usage at first, because the grip hurt his arm so badly and he was already hurting, but he remembered that life hadn't looked all that rosy for Grandmagister Lamplighter and Craugh the last time he had seen them. He only wished that they weren't dead.

The bell renewed its clangorous assault on Juhg's hearing. He glanced back and saw that one of Varrowyn's dwarven warriors was pulling the bell rope mightily. Two score more, all of them dressed in plate armor and carrying battle-axes and pikes, followed Varrowyn.

At first Juhg didn't know what Varrowyn was doing. Then he noticed the dwarven leader's attention riveted to the steps. In the next instant, he realized that Varrowyn's hunter's eyes followed the blood trail back the length of the hallway.

At the bottom, before the Grymmling had leapt onto Juhg and bitten his ear so that the blood flowed even more easily, the blood drops were farther apart, but the trail remained. Varrowyn lengthened his stride. Juhg tried desperately to keep up.

14

The Destruction of the Books

s the gate still open, then?"

Juhg shook his head. "I don't know, Varrowyn. Perhaps Craugh has closed it by now." *But I don't see how.* If the wizard were going to do that, he would have done it immediately. *Maybe.* Juhg had to admit that he was no wizard and had no idea of what wizards could do in circumstances like they had just witnessed.

Varrowyn still maintained a merciless grip on Juhg's left arm as he followed the Librarian's directions back to the research room. Not much direction had been needed, though, for the dwarf had a keen eye and the lummin juice burned brightly in his lantern. Blood splatters led back a long way.

Juhg had evidently torn a long scratch along his right leg when he'd slid across the table in the research room to avoid the Grymmlings that had pursued him. Blood still ran freely from that wound as well.

After years in the mines, Juhg had learned to ignore his wounds, even though they scared him. One of the first things having a goblinkin overseer did was make a slave realize what was only a wound and what would kill him.

"The books were used to open this gate?" Varrowyn asked.

"Yes," Juhg said. "But it wasn't the Grandmagister's fault."

Varrowyn shook his head. "I reckon not. But there's gonna be them what blame the Grandmagister fer them deaths that we can't stop in these halls all the same."

Glumly, Juhg realized that what the dwarven guard said was true. Despite how tightly their origins tied with those of the Library, the people of Greydawn Moors considered themselves a separate entity. Families, like Grandmagister Lamplighter's own, considered it a hardship to let one of their own don the robes of a Novice Librarian to serve the Library.

Another few feet and the party of dwarven guards came upon the Grymmlings that had given up chasing Juhg after finding easier prey among slower-moving Librarians. The lanterns glinted against the evil yellow eyes of the monsters. Blood smeared their lipless, razor-edged mouths.

"All right," Varrowyn growled, pushing Juhg back, "let's see how much fight these here beasties gots in 'em to give." He took up his two-handed battle-axe and set the lantern on the ground. The light played over the horrible scene ahead, and Varrowyn's shadow loomed tall and long as he strode in front of the lantern.

Other dwarves kept shoving Juhg to the rear of the pack, then placed their lanterns down as well and joined their leader.

Mindless and greedy, the Grymmlings attacked, even though they were outnumbered.

Numb with horror but with a part of his mind screaming that they needed to hurry, that they needed to find out what had happened to the Grandmagister, Juhg watched as the dwarves divided into four-man groups called *anvils,* setting up two by two.

Under the strict leadership of a tight-fisted military leader, the dwarven anvil was a deadly thing. Stacked two by two, the anvil worked defensively, double-teaming any enemies that came within reach of their weapons, taking care not to break formation.

Once the anvil had broken the brunt of an enemy's attack, the dwarves formed into the *axe,* a formation that had one dwarf in the lead with two following and then one more to guard their backs so that the axe could move forcibly through a hesitant or stagnant enemy line at either end.

If the dwarven advance was broken and the axe blunted, they fell back into the anvil, forming up two by two again, with the forward dwarf

dropping into the right front slot so that when the axe formed again a new
warrior who had not been taking the brunt of the attack was at the forefront. For thousands of years, opponents on battlefields everywhere had
learned to fear the anvil and axe of the trained dwarven military fighter.

Juhg had sometimes watched Varrowyn and his dwarves do field exer-
cises. At the time he had been amazed by how fluidly the dwarves moved,
each change in placement like a dance almost. Even on defense, dwarves
never hesitated to attack. But he had felt certain that Varrowyn and his
dwarves trained only for pride, that they would never truly see battle until
they left the island, which would never happen because they and their families had sworn to give their lives for the Vault of All Known Knowledge.
Seldom had a dwarf given his life for the Library, other than in longevity of
service.

One of the Grymmlings launched itself at the dwarves. However, they
stood prepared. Varrowyn had questioned Juhg relentlessly on how the
creatures fought during the few minutes it had taken to return down the
hallway from the bell tower. Juhg had been hard-pressed to keep enough air
in his lungs for the rapid movement and the questions. The only thing that
had saved him was that the dwarves moved in full plate mail, clanking and
thundering down the hallway. Every time he told Varrowyn something a
lieutenant on Juhg's other side turned, called, and relayed his words back to
the rest of the dwarves.

Varrowyn's great battle-axe flashed through the air, intercepting the
leaping Grymmling as lazily as a toad took a fly. Halves of the evil creature
fell to either side of the dwarves as first blood spilled over their shiny armor and shields.

The dwarves had two sets of armor. One set was dull and combat-
scarred, mail that wouldn't reflect light easily and allowed them to walk un-
noticed in the dark of night or in the shadows of the forest. But the set they
wore now proclaimed whom they were and what they were there to do.

With hoarse battle cries, the dwarves ran at the Grymmlings full-tilt.
The dwarves were merciless in their killing. In seconds, dead Grymmlings
fell to the ground, sharing space with the half-eaten corpses of the Librarians.

"Juhg." Varrowyn lifted his visor and wiped blood from his eyes. His
shield and his breastplate showed deep scars where the Grymmling's crystal knives had scored the metal.

Stumbling a little, his eyes drawn to the horribly mutilated bodies of dwellers he had known only a short time before, Juhg stumbled forward. He breathed shallowly because of all the blood stink, but that worked against his need for air and made him lightheaded.

"Steady him," Varrowyn commanded.

One of the dwarves grabbed Juhg, clamping down in very nearly the same place as Varrowyn had.

"How much farther?" Varrowyn asked.

Juhg grew aware that he stood in the blood of the Librarians, as well as that of the Grymmlings. He thought for a moment he was going to be sick.

"Juhg." Varrowyn's voice was sterner.

In the distance, Juhg heard the pealing alarm bell. Surely, more of the dwarven guards would be on their way up the mountain to reinforce those in the Vault of All Known Knowledge. The pirates who sailed the Blood-Soaked Sea would surely follow because part of their sworn oath was to protect the Library at all costs from all enemies. In addition, the elven warders would come, bringing their wolves and bears and other creatures they had bonded with.

A small army occupied Greydawn Moors, in addition to the navy that stayed in the harbor or out to sea.

"Yes," Juhg responded.

"How much farther?"

"Only a short distance. The first research room ahead on the right."

Varrowyn started off in that direction again. He wiped blood from his axe blade with a Librarian's robe, which Juhg found at once distasteful but also realized the need for the weapon's cleaning.

He also understood why Varrowyn had to ask directions. The dwarves didn't spend much time in the Library and they didn't know their way around. Their defensive plans hinged on the terrain outside the walls of the Vault of All Known Knowledge. No one was supposed to be able to penetrate the walls. If an enemy did, that meant all the dwarves outside the Library's main buildings had perished in the attack

They hadn't trained for an enemy that struck from within the walls of the Library itself. Noisily as before, the dwarves took up a rapid pace in spite of the plate mail. Juhg was swept along in their center, deathly afraid of falling and getting trampled beneath their iron boots.

mel odom

The dwarven war party didn't reach the research room because four Dread Riders and Blazebulls blocked the hallway. Dozens of Grymmlings and other noxious creatures spread out around the four Blazebulls, careful of the animals' stomping hooves.

Standing on tiptoe, Juhg peered anxiously over the shoulders of the dwarven warriors. He looked for Grandmagister Lamplighter and Craugh's bodies, then he looked for pieces of their bodies, thinking they had fallen and been ripped to pieces by their hideous foes.

"How many of 'em did ye say there were?" Varrowyn growled as he took up his battle-axe once more in his hands.

"I didn't," Juhg replied. "There weren't this many when I was ordered to ring the alarm bell by the Grandmagister."

"Mayhap that thrice-blasted door still remains yet open," Varrowyn said, "an' maybe more of those creatures are even now pourin' into the Library."

The idea made Juhg sick to his stomach. He felt cold and shaky, fully aware that this sensation came from the wounds he had suffered and the fact that he had not recovered from either mad dash through the Library.

The jerking yellow lights that filled the hallway beyond the creatures aligned against the dwarves told Juhg that fires still burned inside the re-search room in spite of the magical safeguards. Perhaps the fiery liquid the Blazebulls hurled was mystical in nature as well. Juhg didn't know. No one had done a treatise or even a monograph on the ecology of Blazebulls.

Scraps of paper and burning embers floated out into the hallway, dying before they reached the stone floor. Water gushed by the bucketful from the room, proof that the defensive spells still worked. The water sluiced across the floor, already spreading out into the hallway.

Had the Builders thought of that? Juhg asked himself. *Had they ever considered that a magical fire might take place in the Library and lock the spell on till the Blood-Soaked Sea itself sat drained and the Library was filled to the tiptop with water?*

Lantern light and the fiery breath of the Blazebulls reflected in the wa-ter already pooled on the floor.

How much damage has been caused? Juhg wondered. *How many books have been destroyed already? You can't read ash. Not if it's not kept nice and tidy.*

Several of the books brought into the Vault of All Known Knowledge all those years ago had suffered all kinds of damage. Water had soaked pages. Oil had stained pages. Many had been burned to one degree or another. Using painstaking methods, the Librarians had recovered or gleaned most of the knowledge that was almost lost. Burned pages could be recovered through delicate acids, even if it meant a Librarian had to soak the burned page and immerse it in vinegar to lift the ink to the page's surface once again, then transcribe the page by hand.

But if the ash were broken, as so many of the embers floating through the air offered mute testimony to, then a part of a page or a page or several pages or a book was lost. It was almost as disheartening as walking back through the goblinkin mines at lock-up time and having to carry the leg of a dweller who had succumbed to the harsh life of a slave.

The Dread Riders commanded their fearsome mounts in a clacking tongue that sounded like sticks rattling together. Instantly, the Blazebulls snorted flame.

"Set anvils!" Varrowyn commanded.

In response, the dwarves in the lead hunkered down behind their shield mates in the front row. Only a third of the dwarves carried shields; the rest used two-handed battle-axes, like Varrowyn, or pikes.

Juhg remained standing, dazed as to what they were doing, until one of the dwarves dropped a heavy mailed fist on his shoulder and yanked him down to the flat of his back. Instinctively, he tried to struggle back to his feet.

The dwarf cursed at him.

"Stay down or die, Librarian," the dwarven warrior shouted above the roar of the Blazebulls.

Flames singed the air where Juhg had stood. He squinted his eyes against the brightness. The scent of hot metal filled his nostrils. Glancing forward through the tight ranks of the dwarves, he saw the fiery breath of the Blazebulls crashing against the dwarven shield.

As quickly as it had come, the fiery breath died away.

Juhg gasped, only then realizing he had ceased breathing.

"Axes!" Varrowyn roared.

The dwarves rose as one. The warrior closest to Juhg reached down to haul him up. "C'mon, Librarian. Don't want to leave ye behind as we rout these unpleasant beasties."

Juhg nodded and stood on quaking legs as the dwarves surged forward. Arrows spiked the air as the Dread Riders released their bowstrings.

Grymmlings came on, screaming and gibbering like mad things, their evil crystal knives flashing in the lantern light that filled the hall.

At first, the crushing might of the dwarven axe formation drove the invaders back. Axes, short-hafted as well as the two-handed weapons, cleaved Grymmlings in twain and left body parts scattered in the wake of the dwarves. Even the Dread Riders and the Blazebulls were beaten back as the pikemen dragged one of the Riders from the saddle while others twisted their pikes between the legs of its mount. The axe formation followed to finish the kill.

Fearing for his life but unable to go without knowing the fates of Grandmagister Lamplighter and Craugh, Juhg followed behind when every dweller instinct in him cried out to take cover and save himself. But he couldn't leave the dwarves. If the battle suddenly turned against them, they might not be able to find their way to another staging area to rally, or—if the tide of the battle truly turned against them—find their way out of the twisting maze that was the Library.

The battle raged, and the combatants fell. Juhg passed two dwarves, their faces frozen in expressions of disbelief, as if up until that very moment they had thought themselves invulnerable.

One of them Juhg knew. Artip was a young dwarf, only newly come to the Library Guardsmen.

Once, when Juhg had worked on copying a book in the outer courtyard—on a seldom day when there was no wind to blow dust or dirt into fresh ink and the Library had seemed uncomfortably remindful of the goblinkin mines he had grown up in—Artip had glanced at the pictures in the book. Juhg had reproduced the pictures flawlessly in the new copy of the book he worked on.

The book had been a work on close-quarter pikework, used for tripping great beasts of war used by enemy cavalry. The dwarves had used many of those tactics to bring down the great Blazebull in the Library. Drawn by the pictures, Artip had asked questions of how the fighting was done. Because he'd had to figure out the moves to properly render the instructional images on the page, Juhg had been able to show the young dwarven warrior, which had caused considerable consternation among other Librarians out in the courtyard as they saw one of their own working the pike to further elaborate the methods. Artip had learned quickly, knowing things of the movements that Juhg had stumbled with. Of course, Juhg's rudimentary skills quickly paled when compared to the dwarf's. Even Grandmagister Lamplighter had stuck his head out from one of the high windows to watch the training.

Afterward, whenever Juhg had watched the young dwarven warrior practicing the moves he'd learned that day—and especially when he was teaching those moves to another dwarven guardsman—he had felt proud of his part in teaching Artip a new skill. It had felt good to pass on part of the learning Juhg had discovered, and better still that someone had found a use for something he had read in a book and so laboriously worked to make a copy of. And Artip had praised Juhg for his knowledge for days afterward, something that most Librarians never heard outside of their own circle.

And now his brave friend Artip, with his dreams of being a mighty warrior about whom songs would be sung in dwarven taverns long after he was gone, was dead of a Grymmling knife to his throat and crimson staining his body under his armor.

Juhg's eyes brimmed with tears. All of it was his fault. The seventeen sailors aboard *Windchaser* and the two dwarves who lay fallen in the hallway owed their deaths to him. The book had been his to find, and with it came all the foul luck that had been carefully woven into its pages.

Slowly, though the dwarves fought valiantly and held nothing back, they inched up the hallway to the door of the research room where the

mystical gate had opened. The ring of steel on steel and the hollow *thump* of axe blades and pikes striking flesh filled the hallway.

Juhg peered anxiously at the door, wondering if the gate were still open and whether creatures still poured forth from it.

"Down!" Varrowyn roared.

Too late, Juhg looked forward as three Blazebulls lumbered forward. Flames curled from their black noses. Then they expurgated, hurling fiery liquid toward the dwarven war party again.

The dwarf nearest Juhg swept his feet from under him just as the Librarian started to move. Juhg fell head over teakettle and just managed to keep his face from striking the stone floor.

"Up!" Varrowyn commanded.

The dwarves surged up again, following their brave leader.

"Pikemen to the axe!" Varrowyn yelled.

In response, the pikemen advanced to the front of the axe formation. The shieldmen and dwarves with battle-axes stood to either side and fought off the Grymmlings that tried to overwhelm them by sheer numbers.

A half-dozen Grymmlings overpowered one of the dwarves, tangling his feet and dragging him down. Their knives descended mercilessly, turning crimson and spreading blood all over the floor and walls. The dwarves in the fallen warrior's axe fought to defend their friend, but Juhg knew from the blood and the grim looks of anguish and anger on the dwarven warriors' faces that they were too late. None of the Grymmlings escaped alive, and the dwarves' attentions were as merciless as the foes they fought.

When the dwarves drew even with the door to the research room, Juhg pushed through their ranks, avoiding the quick hands that tried to stop him. He had to know what fate had befallen Grandmagister Lamplighter and Craugh. Twenty dwarves, their numbers already lesser by three and their inability to hold up their attack against innumerable enemies, had barely made this distance.

Even with Craugh's wizardry, Juhg held little hope that the two had survived. He rushed into the doorway, taking cover as long as he dared, then peered around the corner. A mournful cry escaped him as he saw what had happened.

There, in the center of the room amid the three hundred nineteen books—at least, where those books had been—a huge jumble of broken rock stood.

For a moment, Juhg did not know where the rock had come from. Without the lanterns to light the room, mostly shadows filled the great expanse. Then, as his eyes—keen dweller's eyes that could see in the dark almost as well as elves and nearly as well underground as dwarves—adapted to the lack of light, he spotted the huge gaping hole in the ceiling.

Awe filled Juhg at the thought of the sheer magnitude of force that had been necessary to rend the thick stone separating the research room from the upper one. His agile mind, filled with the different paths through the various rooms that had been honeycombed throughout the Knucklebones Mountains, quickly let him know that the upstairs room had been one of the twenty-nine that had been devoted to elven histories.

Then he saw the books spread over the rubble. The volumes lay torn and scattered. The violence done to the books had spread them like confetti. A few of them showed burning embers, as did the crushed mouth of a Blazebull almost buried under the fallen rock.

Looking at the carnage, knowing the loss the Library had suffered, Juhg felt his knees go weak and his stomach twist sickeningly. So much had been lost.

And all of it irreplaceable. The realization haunted his thoughts, making him numb even to the bell still clanging in the distance and echoing through the Vault of All Known Knowledge and the sounds of battle out in the hall.

Only then did Juhg realize that the mystical gate extended beyond the room where it had originated. Crimson lightning streaked the violet sky revealed through the gate that stood above the heap of broken rock and destroyed books that reached almost to the point where the ceiling had once been. In that same instant, he realized further that the rock couldn't have fallen in such a pile, that it had been deliberately shaped and stacked to block the mystical gate.

Craugh, Juhg thought.

Shapes slithered and shadows leapt from the gate in the room above. More and more of the creatures continued to enter the Library. Most of them flooded the upper level across a massive dead tree that someone or something had shoved out into the Library from whatever world they came from.

But, his luck holding true, Juhg was spotted by some of the evil creatures. Grymmlings scampered and skidded down the pile of rock toward him. Their yellow eyes turned on Juhg and their jackrabbit teeth clacked. A Dread Rider turned its Blazebull from the makeshift tree bridge and guided its mount down the massive hill of broken stones. Others followed, including other creatures that Juhg did not recognize.

Darting back out into the hall, Juhg found that the dwarven war party had advanced thirty feet onward, never realizing that they had left their flank open to the attack only now coming from the research room. Their axes and pikes flashed as they fought by the dim light of the lanterns strung along the way. Three more of their number lay unmoving in the hallway.

The buzzing drone of Grymmlings' voices filled the room behind Juhg. He ran, ignoring the painful twinges of his legs, hoping only that they did not fail him.

"Varrowyn!" he yelled. "Varrowyn!" He was almost upon the dwarves when the last one in the group turned to him. When the dwarf's eyes turned hard and his massive jaw dropped slightly, Juhg knew the warrior had seen the threat.

"Our flank!" the dwarf yelled grimly. "To our flank!" He turned around and raised his bloody pike.

Other dwarves at the rear of the war party turned with him. In seconds, the dwarven advance was crushed as two groups stood fore and aft to face them.

Juhg hesitated only long enough to pick up a short-hafted single-bitted axe shieldmen used to cleave the skulls of their opponents or grab onto their opponents' shields and strip them away, leaving them open to another dwarven fighter.

The axe felt heavy and uncertain in Juhg's hands, but he made do. Long years of working in goblinkin mines, lifting rock and a pickaxe for years, had left him with strength. Though years had passed since he'd done those things, he was still strong enough to lift the axe. At least for a while. Looking at the foes arrayed against them at either end, Juhg felt certain that his life's blood would give out long before his strength did.

Varrowyn divided the dwarves into four anvils, two facing either way. Juhg was placed in the rear of one of those formations in place of a missing dwarf. He raised the axe and tried very hard not to be afraid, but he failed.

The two enemy forces suddenly realized they had the upper hand. The Dread Riders took command of their groups, speaking in the harsh clacking tongue they had. Three of the Grymmlings darted forward anyway. At a signal from one of the Dread Riders, a Blazebull snorted fire over the three small predators and crisped them on the spot. Their blackened bodies tumbled to the stone floor.

"Stand yer ground!" Varrowyn growled, holding his two-handed axe at the ready. Blood leaked down from his helm, proof that the Grymmlings' blades had found flesh behind the armor, and black soot stained the plate where he had not always been able to take cover behind a shieldmate.

One of the Dread Riders urged its mount forward. Its fierce gaze raked over the dwarves standing almost shoulder to shoulder in their formations. The Blazebull, cut and bleeding from a dozen wounds, stamped its feet impatiently. Fire curled from its black nose.

The Dread Rider lifted its head as if stretching its throat. When it spoke, it spoke in the common tongue that all the races knew.

"You do not have to die today," the Dread Rider said in a cold, flat voice.

Varrowyn spat in disgust. "Today is a fine day to die."

The Dread Rider worked its throat again. The language was obviously known to it, but it was unfamiliar in its use. "You are a fool."

"Mayhap," Varrowyn replied, "but I'll die a courageous fool with me honor intact if 'n that's what it takes."

The other dwarves cheered and pounded their armor or shields with their weapons in support of their leader's bold declaration. But they never dropped their eyes from those of their enemies.

"You would have died anyway," the Dread Rider promised. "Your passing would have been easier."

Juhg quaked where he stood. He couldn't help it. Even after the harsh life he'd barely lived through in the goblinkin mines, he had a hard time facing the certainty of death. Always before there had existed a chance, however small it was, that he might escape and—

Someone grabbed his ankle.

Startled, Juhg stepped back and peered down. He drew up the axe and got ready to bring it crashing down, thinking that one of the Grymmlings had sneaked through the dwarves' defensive line. The uncertain light, most of it cast by pools of flames spat out by the Blazebulls that clung to the hallway walls or sat in fat puddles on the floor, made it difficult to see who had grabbed him.

Instead of a Grymmling hand as he had expected, Juhg saw a dweller

hand glowing ghastly green flare open. A muffled voice said, "Juhg! Give me a hand!" The hand reached forward, exposing more of the arm.

Recognizing Grandmagister Lamplighter's voice and trained by years of friendship as well as work, Juhg bent down and caught hold of the hand. The Grandmagister's flesh felt cold but strong.

"Pull," the Grandmagister said.

Juhg pulled, and as he pulled, Grandmagister Lamplighter oozed through the stone floor. Marveling at the sight, suddenly aware of what the spectral form glowing green and translucent before him must mean, Juhg exclaimed, "Oh, Grandmagister, they have killed you! I am sorry! This is all my fault!"

"Juhg," the Grandmagister said in a fierce tone, "I am not dead."

Studying the green glowing figure before him, Juhg said nothing. He was confused. *Do I believe what I see before me, or do I believe the Grandmagister?*

"Craugh worked a spell," the Grandmagister said. "The gate extends all through the Library. It has taken root like a carrot and driven down into the levels from top to bottom. We have viewed all the floors."

The three dwarves who made up the anvil Juhg currently stood in stared at the glowing figure of the Grandmagister with confusion and some trepidation.

"Stand ready!" Varrowyn yelled to his troops.

The Dread Rider marshaled its troops. The Blazebull shifted and moved like an earthquake beneath its loathsome master, stamping its feet and snorting great clouds of bright orange embers from his black nostrils.

"Hold fast to my hand, Juhg," the Grandmagister ordered.

Juhg squeezed the hand tightly.

"Varrowyn," the Grandmagister called out.

"Yes, Grandmagister," the dwarven commander replied.

"Have your men link hands," the Grandmagister instructed. "You'll die if you stay here."

"Well, now," Varrowyn said, shifting his axe between his hands, "we're not afeared of dyin', Grandmagister Lamplighter."

"Oh, and wouldn't that help with all the problems facing the Library now," the Grandmagister stated reproachfully. "Here I am, needing every person I can get, and you're willing to die."

Varrowyn blinked at the Grandmagister. Juhg marveled at the dwarf's skill, for Varrowyn never took his other eye from the assembled enemies before him.

235

The Dread Riders held their forces in check, obviously wondering what the Grandmagister's sudden and strange appearance held for them. The Grymmlings crooned and buzzed their bloodthirsty song of want.

"Grandmagister," Varrowyn said, "I just—"

"You'll just live," Grandmagister Lamplighter declared impatiently, "until such time as I can no longer help you do that. I've lost too many friends and too many Librarians I was responsible for today to willingly allow anyone else to die. Now, take hold."

Varrowyn gave the command. One of the dwarves grabbed Juhg's hand in a mailed fist. Excruciating pain shot through Juhg's hand, but he didn't say anything.

Evidently growing less fearful of what the spectral figure in the midst of the dwarves might do, the Dread Rider gave the order for the groups massed on either side of the Library's defenders to attack. They surged forward.

"Craugh!" Grandmagister Lamplighter yelped.

In the next instant, Juhg felt the floor beneath his bare feet turn as mushy as lime-flavor salted seafoam cake batter. The Grandmagister sank through the floor like a man sucked deep into the deadly embrace of a marsh muck pit. Before he could even cry out in alarm, Juhg sank through the floor as well. Frozen in fear, he watched as a thrown spear came right at his chest, then passed on through, leaving only a cold tingle that washed through him the way the incoming sea did when he was checking lobster pots out in the harbor.

Then he was within the stone floor, feeling the rasp of the rough rock somehow, even though it never touched his skin.

 236

15

"Our Enemies Have Struck Us a Grave and Serious Blow"

a flickering torch held the darkness at bay in the hall-way under the one where Juhg had been trapped with Varrowyn's dwarven guards. He stared in disbelief at his new surroundings as he floated toward the floor. Grandmagister Lamplighter suddenly jerked away from him, as if caught in the fierce talons of some fearful beast, and his hand jerked free of Juhg's grip.

Then Juhg stopped floating and started falling. He thudded into the floor almost on top of the Grandmagister. The impact dazed him for a moment, but Grandmagister Lamplighter was already up, hooking his fingers into Juhg's hair and jerking him into motion.

"Get up," the Grandmagister ordered, pulling Juhg. "Hurry. The dwarves are falling and their armor will in-jure you."

Glancing up, twisting through the pain of the Grand-magister's uncompromising grip in his hair, Juhg watched as the dwarves—all of them spectral green—dropped through the floor. As soon as each was clear from the stone ceiling that had been the floor above only moments before, that dwarf took on a flesh and blood appearance again. And they fell like rotten fruit.

One after the other, as noisy as hailstones on a tin roof, the plate-mail-clad dwarves dropped onto the stone floor hard enough to chip the surface in places. Sparks flashed from their armor. Varrowyn was the last to drop, and he only held on to the hand of the dwarf before him. However, a Grymmling had hold of the dwarven commander's leg and was pulled partially through.

"Up!" one of the dwarves cried in warning, forcing himself to his feet. "To arms! They're comin' through after us!" He raised his pike.

Varrowyn landed flat on his back with a growl of pain. He never lost his grip on his battle-axe.

Then a green mist breathed out of the stone ceiling. The wriggling Grymmling suddenly stiffened and mewled in terror or pain. With the buzzing drone the thing made, even afterward Juhg was never sure what that awful noise was.

A moment later, the Grymmling relaxed in death and hung limply from the ceiling. Its crystal knife fell from its limp fingers and shattered against the stone floor below. The yellow eyes narrowed in a vacant stare.

"They can't come through," Craugh declared.

Following the voice, Juhg saw the wizard striding toward the group from the left. A spinning green-white light glowed at the tip of his staff. A handful of scared Librarians followed in the wizard's wake, all of them huddled together.

"This was yer magic then, wizard?" Varrowyn asked, lifting the face-plate of his helm. Blood stained his features, and some of it was his. He blinked his eyes and crimson tears ran down his cheeks.

"Yes," Craugh answered. He looked worn and haggard. Scratches marred his face. His robes showed burned places, as well as long, bloody rents. Juhg knew immediately that not all of the blood was the wizard's. The old man simply could not have bled that much and still yet live.

Varrowyn shook his head. "Ye called us out of the battle just as we had 'em right where we wanted 'em." He sounded gruff and confident.

"Tell your tales in a tavern some other time and be glad you're there to tell them," Craugh said. "I saved your lives and I know it."

Even though Craugh was much more friendly and predisposed to let others live than any other wizard Juhg had met during his adventures with Grandmagister Lamplighter, Craugh possessed no false sense of modesty or even a grain of humility. The old wizard chose his own path long ago at a price that he sometimes alluded to but had never described. He claimed all the glories that came with that choice and his skills.

Varrowyn bristled and took a step forward.

Juhg watched in disbelief, even though he had seen countless times that dwarves loved to fight over anything, and would fight even more quickly over honor and against disrespect. How could the dwarf even think of taking up weapons against the wizard when enemies stood inside the Library destroying everything all of them had sworn to protect?

Grandmagister Lamplighter stepped forward, moving between the dwarf and the wizard. "Varrowyn."

Reluctantly, the dwarf halted, but only—Juhg sensed—because Varrowyn would have had to walk over the Grandmagister to reach Craugh. All who dwelt within the halls of the Vault of All Known Knowledge respected the Grandmagister.

"We've much to do," the Grandmagister said. "Lives are at stake. I would rather join you for a cup of ale and sing your praises after this bit of business is over than to lament over your shortcomings in your chosen responsibility to protect the Library."

Angrily, Varrowyn blew out his breath.

Craugh took no pride in his victory. He had simply stated fact.

Cries of pain and anguish sounded distant down the hallway in either direction. The pealing alarm bell kept up its frantic dirge.

"I understand, Grandmagister," Varrowyn said. "As I give me word all them years ago, I stand ready to serve ye an' this great Library in whatever way ye see fittin'."

"The Library—" The Grandmagister's voice broke, then he began again. "The Library is lost to us. There are too many enemies that have come through the gate and still continue to come through it."

The sense of loss that screamed through Juhg was unbearable. He had left the Library only months ago, intending to seek out his own life and try to find whoever remained of his family, but he had always known that he would be able to return to the Vault of All Known Knowledge any time he wished. No matter where he had gone or what hardships he would have had to endure, he had known that the Library would be there.

But to lose the Library— The thought was unthinkable, yet here he was, staring into the face of that grim eventuality.

"Even though we lose the Library," Grandmagister Lamplighter went on, "I won't lose any more Librarians than we have to."

The Grandmagister motioned to the four Librarians cowering behind Craugh's robes. "Divide up your warriors, Varrowyn. I want them to accompany these Librarians. Your warriors don't know the Vault as well as the Librarians do." He looked at the Librarians, addressing them now. "I want every level cleared of Librarians, and I want as many books carried out of this place as we can. Work your way from bottom to top till you reach one of the hallways out of the Library. Take whatever books you can find, but try to pick up the histories first. We have learned more from the histories than we have any other books."

How many books, Juhg wondered, *could a Librarian carry? Especially when fleeing for his life?* But he knew the answer was simple: A Librarian would carry all that he could—because the Grandmagister had asked him to.

Varrowyn shook his head and the helm creaked. "Fleein' fer our lives as ye say we must, Gran'magister, why, burdenin' them Librarians down ain't gonna make that none easier, nor them any faster."

"I didn't say that it was easy. I only said that it must be done." The Grandmagister took a breath. "I don't ask you or your men to carry any books, although the extra hands could surely make a difference."

Doubt still clouded Varrowyn's blood-streaked features.

Grandmagister Lamplighter kept speaking before the dwarf could give voice to his thoughts. "Varrowyn, our enemies have struck us a grave and serious blow. Books—wonderful and possibly unique books—that might never be seen again have been destroyed and will continue to be destroyed." He slowed his voice and made the words deliberate. "I would have as many of those books saved as I can."

Nodding, Varrowyn said, "It shall be as ye say 'twill, Grandmagister. Ye have me word on that."

"Thank you, my friend." The Grandmagister turned again to the Librarians. "I want the others found, and I want them to leave the Library. Have them wait farther down the Knucklebones. At the trading place near the Ogre's Fingers."

The trading place was little more than a shack with a straw roof to keep off the sun. Most people in Greydawn Moors didn't like the idea of trekking up the mountain at the Library because it was hard to show resentment of a place if someone went there. However, a number of merchants and craftsmen from the town, as well as from the ships, regularly came up to the trading area to swap and barter and sell to the Librarians, who did not want to trouble themselves with traveling down the Knucklebones or who had eclectic tastes for foreign goods.

Still others brought pieces of art, sculptures, and paintings for trade. Art from before the Cataclysm was almost as rare as books, but there were new artists—painters, sculptors, and weavers—that were starting new concepts. Grandmagister Lamplighter, unlike any Grandmagister before him, had assigned such studies to First and Second Level Librarians, giving them the task of matching current techniques with those described in books from the pre-Cataclysm days.

Art, Grandmagister Lamplighter had said on numerous occasions, was as important as anything they could study and was a true and revealing language that remained handed down—father to son and mother to daughter—for generation after generation. Several times through the study of those things, the Librarians had been able to identify tribes and clans and houses of trade that had vanished in the turmoil of the Goblin War. On some of his quests, the Grandmagister had gone into those areas and taken oral histories that furthered the knowledge the Library held. Over the years, Grandmagister Lamplighter had transcribed hundreds of books in this manner.

"Hopefully," the Grandmagister said, "reinforcements will come from Greydawn Moors and from the forest below."

"The dwarves an' the elves will come up," one of Varrowyn's warriors muttered. "Mayhap the humans who might be lurkin' about. But ye can bet that won't none of the dwellers be makin' that long climb up this mountain tonight."

Juhg felt ashamed, knowing that the dwarf was speaking the truth. But a dweller acted in the fashion that the Old Ones had made for him: fearful and unwilling to risk his life or limb for anything outside his own survival or—if the aberration were great enough—for greed. Curiosity was also a weakness, but dwellers who heard the alarm bell ringing would know that only Death awaited at the top of the Knucklebones.

If he had not believed in the Library so much more than himself—and come to believe in it even more over the passing years—Grandmagister Lamplighter had often admitted he would have been no better than most of the other dwellers. Juhg had never truly believed that. Grandmagister Lamplighter was destined for greatness. Even Craugh had said that on seldom occasion.

"No," the Grandmagister agreed without remorse or embarrassment. "Dwellers won't come to our rescue."

The dwarf who'd spoken his thoughts looked guilty and didn't dare meet the Grandmagister's eye.

"And the help coming from town will more than likely be too late," the Grandmagister said. "Mayhap the elven warders who live in the forests will reach us first, and perhaps even in time." He took in a breath and released it. "For now, we save ourselves, and we save everyone else that we can. I want the Librarians out of here, and I want as many of the books taken as we can get our hands on."

"It will be done as ye say, Grandmagister," Varrowyn promised.

The Grandmagister turned to the four Librarians hiding behind Craugh and gave them quick instructions. As he listened, Juhg understood that the Grandmagister had divided the Library into quadrants, already taking into account the four best escape routes and making certain every floor received adequate warning.

He dismissed the Librarians and the dwarves and turned to Juhg. "You will come with us."

Where? Juhg wanted to ask. But he didn't. For one fleeting second, he thought the Grandmagister might be listening to his dweller instincts and intended to flee, then he dismissed that. Grandmagister Lamplighter had run from several fights over the years that Juhg had known him, but only when those fights might be properly avoided. A dwarf or possibly a prideful elf, and definitely a human who believed Death could never truly reach out and touch him, would never have survived as long as the Grandmagister unless that dwarf, elf, or human were well and truly blessed by the Old Ones.

Craugh took the lead, holding his staff with its magical light before them.

No, Juhg realized, watching the wizard's grim face, wherever the Grandmagister was presently headed, things were going to be decidedly dangerous.

"This is a very powerful spell," Craugh said, holding his staff high some minutes later and staring in perplexion at the three stairways carved out of the mountain before him.

All three of the stairways led up. The magical light chopped into the dense, dank shadows that huddled there, but none of the creatures that roamed the Library seemed to have found their way to those stairwells yet.

"We need to get to the lowest level of the Library," Craugh said. He held the staff aloft and looked around. "This isn't the lowest level, is it?"

"No," Grandmagister Lamplighter said. "Four levels yet remain below us."

Gesturing to the three stairwells, Craugh said, "Is there another stairwell that will take us down?"

"The ones on the left and in the center go down," the Grandmagister said.

Craugh looked at him. "Clearly, they go up."

"For only a short time," Juhg said, "then they go down again."

"And the one on the right?"

"It goes up," the Grandmagister responded.

Craugh grumbled beneath his breath. "A perfectly foolish way to build a structure, if you ask me."

"The Library wasn't built in a day," Grandmagister Lamplighter declared defensively.

"Of course it wasn't," Craugh snapped. "It takes real planning to organize this kind of chaos." He headed for the stairwell on the left.

"Not that way," Grandmagister Lamplighter and Juhg said at the same time.

Craugh glared at them. "And why not?"

"Because that stairwell doesn't go four floors down," the Grandmagister answered.

"It only goes two," Juhg said.

"And that level doesn't go any farther?" Craugh asked.

"No," Juhg replied. "That level lies to the south. The third and fourth levels lie to the north and west."

"Excavations on the south side below that level hit the water table each time," the Grandmagister said. "The excavations to the north and west allowed the miners to go more deeply into the earth."

"This is nonsense," Craugh said, plunging through the middle stairwell and quickly going down the steps with the staff pointed before him. "You don't have a Library here, Wick, you've got a rather messy clump of rabbit warrens."

Don't have a Library hung in the still air of the stairwell.

Glancing back up, Craugh said, "I am sorry, my old friend. I—as I so often do, I'm afraid—spoke without thinking. That was not only ill-mannered of me, but very hurtful, given the present circumstances. Please forgive me."

Juhg's astonishment caused him to trip on the stairs. He almost plunged headlong down the twisting steps that dug ever farther into the heart of the Knucklebones Mountains. Never in all of the stories, twice-told tales, or outright lies about Craugh had Juhg ever heard of the old wizard asking for forgiveness or owning up to his ill manners.

Craugh swung his staff and stopped Juhg's plunge at once while never missing a step himself. The staff held like an iron bar till Juhg once more had his balance, then it was whisked away.

"These are trying times," Grandmagister Lamplighter said, "and likely even more difficulties lie ahead of us. I know that you will stand with us, Craugh. Your comment is already forgotten."

"And you, apprentice," Craugh said in a lowered voice that barely carried over the slapping of their feet against the stone steps, "you'll forget this conversation entirely, hmmmm?"

The threat wasn't concealed well and the old wizard's eye was sharp.

"Yes," Juhg promised.

Craugh eyed him a moment more, then turned his attention once more to their progress.

They went on, following the twisting and turning path of the stairwell as they descended to the heart of the Knucklebones Mountains.

At the bottom, the stairwell let out into a hallway with six doors. All of the doors were tall and broad and arched. Lanterns glowed on the walls, providing just enough light to make out the surroundings.

"Can't see a blasted thing in here," Craugh grumped as he thrust his lighted staff around in all directions.

Only then did Juhg remember that the wizard possessed human eyes that couldn't see well in the low light. "What are you looking for?" Juhg asked.

"I know what I'm looking for, apprentice," Craugh snapped. "I just can't find my way there." He stamped the staff against the floor and the magical light glowed more brightly. "Ah, that's much better."

"Which way—" the Grandmagister started to ask.

"This way." Craugh plowed ahead, obviously drawn by something neither the Grandmagister nor Juhg could see.

Juhg followed, wondering why none of the Dread Riders or the Grymmlings had risen up from the darkness to confront them, then just as quickly thanking the fates that those creatures hadn't.

"As I said," Craugh spoke as they raced onward, "this is a very old spell. It has taken root inside the Library, as its dark-hearted weaver intended. To remove it, we must destroy the root."

"Will you be able to separate the spell from the Library?" the Grandmagister asked.

Craugh shook his head. "I don't know."

"If you can't, what will become of the Library?"

Craugh didn't answer.

"Craugh," the Grandmagister called.

The old wizard shook his head. "I don't know, Wick. Truly, I do not. The magic that built this place, all the glamours that have been laid since the Foundation Stone was first put into place those hundreds of years ago, all of it is old. As magic ages, it frays, holding still if it was a strongly laid spell, but becoming a little unraveled."

" 'And in fraying,' " Juhg said, " 'the magic ties into the everyday world to maintain itself, drawing on the true essence that lies within a person, a place, or a thing, till the unnatural becomes part of the natural. In doing that, the magic becomes more a part of everything around it till the glamour and the thing or person or place it was laid upon become inseparable.' "

Craugh looked at Juhg with raised eyebrows. "Very good, apprentice. Very well put indeed."

Juhg felt embarrassed. He'd spoken out of turn. "I didn't just know that. That's a quote from—"

"Legorn's *The Existence of Magic Within the Natural World, or Why Ghosts Exist,*" Craugh said. "I am well aware of the book. I'm just surprised that you would read such a thing, apprentice, or have a command of its understanding."

"My only familiarity came at the Grandmagister's urging," Juhg said.

"Still, that you would remember much of it. Legorn's book was written in Esketaryn, an elven language forgotten even before Lord Kharrion rose up to claim the goblinkin tribes. Not many can read that book. Not even many wizards. Or Librarians, for that matter, I suspect."

"There are translations," Juhg said before he thought about it.

"I didn't know translations existed," Craugh said.

"Juhg did them," Grandmagister Lamplighter said. "In three different languages."

"Translated a magic book?" Craugh looked doubtful.

"A book *about* magic," Juhg pointed out, knowing there was a *big* difference between a magic book and a book about magic.

"One of many such volumes," the Grandmagister declared with a measure of pride. "As I have told you on any number of occasions, Juhg is a very talented Librarian."

"Yet he chose to leave the Vault," Craugh reminded. He shook his head. "His heart is not into this place as much as is yours, Wick. No one has ever loved this place as much as you."

"But—"

"No one," Craugh said. "I've known several Grandmagisters during my time in this world. During my visits. I know what I'm talking about."

Surprise spun through Juhg. No one knew how old Craugh was, but everyone knew that a wizard's years weren't measured as a man's were.

 "And you can't fault him, Wick. Juhg is no different than any other Librarian you've taught or guided or mentored. He's just more knowledgeable than most."

The Grandmagister said nothing, but Juhg saw that Grandmagister Lamplighter's eyes reflected his sadness over that truth. The fact that such an emotion could even register in light of everything that had happened in this past hour was amazing and showed how deeply the Grandmagister had cared about Juhg's decision to leave.

Juhg suddenly felt certain he would rather be upstairs alongside the dwarves fighting Dread Riders and Grymmlings while carrying his weight in books than to be in the lowest recesses of the Library with the cantankerous old wizard and the Grandmagister. Juhg did not want to feel guilty about the choice he had made. Living in the Library and serving the secrets it held was the Grandmagister's dream, not his.

Craugh continued leading the way. Juhg glanced at the doors to the rooms he had visited on occasion while serving as First Level Librarian. Now that he looked at those doors, remembering the shelves and shelves of books in each of the rooms, he wished that he'd had more time to find out what was among the stacks.

Perhaps, he told himself with a little hope, *those days and those opportunities are yet to be. Not all of the Library can possibly be destroyed.*

Only a little farther on, Juhg saw what it was that Craugh had traveled to the bottom of the Library to find. In the fourth large chamber they came to, a pulsating web of deep purple magical power permeated the entire room, contracting and expanding in a seemingly endless flow across the ceiling, walls, and floor.

16

Web of Spells

Juhg stayed behind Craugh, fearing that the darkness ahead was filled with Dread Riders and Grymmlings. Instead, nothing moved but the shadows as the web of magic shifted and flickered, pulsing like a heartbeat. The throb of the magical spell sounded like a heartbeat as well, but one that thundered rapidly. Echoes rolled around Juhg.

"What is it?" Grandmagister Lamplighter asked.

"The root of the magic." Craugh pointed his staff at the pulsing web. Purple sparks shot from the shifting design to bite and flash at the magical light atop the wizard's staff. "This is the force that holds open the doors all through the levels above us."

Another spark spat from the web, jumping like an arrow in flight straight at the wizard.

Craugh blocked the spark with his staff. The spark broke into a thousand gleaming pieces and disappeared. "If I can destroy this, all the magical doors to the upper floors will close."

"What about the creatures that have made it through the doors?" the Grandmagister asked.

"Some might yet remain. That fact depends on how

possessive the spell is. If I destroy the spell and the magic behind it is possessive, the spell may very well draw those creatures back to the world they came from. I will try to encourage that." Craugh settled his pointed hat more firmly atop his head and stepped into the room. "Those that remain we will have to track down and kill. But I don't know yet how many more can be sent through the doors."

"Why aren't any of the creatures here?" Juhg whispered, hoping he didn't jinx them by mentioning the lack of enemies bent to spill their blood.

"No door was made here." Craugh pointed at the web of power. "This is the root. The spell took hold of the Library here, leeched into the magic protecting this place, and bent those old magics to its use as well. The root could not allow itself to be disturbed by doors or anything else that might disrupt its pattern." The wizard faced the spell grimly. "That is the spell's strength and it is its weakness." He stepped closer. "And I must find a way to disrupt it."

Winds suddenly whipped up in the chamber, biting cold breezes that ripped at Craugh's robe and beard until he spoke harsh, guttural words. Then the wind seemed to blow right through him because it never touched him again.

But the wind touched Juhg, bringing a near-freezing intensity that chafed his exposed skin and turned his fingers into brittle sticks. He'd never seen anything freeze so quickly. He squinted his eyes against the gale, blinked near-frozen tears down his cheeks, and watched Craugh approach the magical web stuck tight to the sides of the chamber.

Craugh shouted words of power. The wind changed and became filled with the blazing heat of the desert. Juhg sweltered, opening his robe and breathing harshly to try to pull more air into his lungs.

A ball of whirling green light formed in Craugh's free hand. He raised the ball to look at it, as if weighing it or checking its shape, like he was picking out a melon in the marketplace. Then he hurled the ball against the web.

An explosion rocked the Library, even in the bedrock of the Knucklebones Mountains.

Juhg felt the floor shift beneath him, looking on in stunned amazement as cracks shot across the floor and huge sections of stone lifted and bashed against each other like ice floes colliding. The crunching impacts filled the chamber with noise. Juhg fell and pushed himself up again, only to struggle to keep himself from falling back as the section of floor he stood on reared into the air and almost turned perpendicular to the position it had previously enjoyed.

Glancing to his right, Juhg saw that the Grandmagister was experiencing similar problems keeping his footing. The chunk he stood on suddenly upended and tossed him into the air. Out of control, he fell toward a crack in the floor that was already starting to push back together. If he got caught in that, Juhg knew the Grandmagister would be crushed. The purple and green lights from the conflicting magics showed the fear on his face.

Without thinking, Juhg threw himself at the Grandmagister. Despite his modesty and self-confirmed lack of bravery, the Grandmagister had saved Juhg's life on a number of occasions, often putting his young protégé's survival ahead of his own. Juhg could not sit by and watch the Grandmagister fall to his doom.

Throwing out his arms, Juhg slammed against the Grandmagister and carried them both clear of the gaping crack just as it closed again with a deafening *crunch*. They rolled and came up against the wall to the right of the door.

The Grandmagister said something, but Juhg could not hear him over the horrendous roar of the shattering rock. Out of breath from the collision, his heart beating frantically at how he had just risked his life, Juhg stood on shaking knees.

The floor beneath Craugh shattered so hard that plumes of stone dust spat up like a whale pod breaching and blowing. A section of stone only an arm's breadth across twisted like a bucking horse. The wizard nearly toppled from the stone.

Pointing to the stone with his free hand, Craugh snarled more harsh and guttural words. The stone section took on a silvery sheen, then rose up from the floor and leveled off, despite all the turmoil that took place in the space it had vacated.

Power filled the room. Juhg felt the arcane force. The hair on his arms and his head and the back of his neck stood up in response.

Craugh threw both hands forward, chanting the whole time. The wind picked up intensity, whirling and whistling around the great room. For a moment, the purple web swayed, then it pushed back. The waves of invisible power slammed into Craugh and nearly took him from his feet.

Still, the wizard remained unbowed and unbroken. He grinned into the fury of the forces warring against him. He threw his hands forward again, and this time Juhg saw the green power lash out against the purple web. Whole sections of stone broke where the lines of the web touched the walls, floor, and ceiling, spreading cracks across those surfaces. The entire room shook and clouds of stone dust poured down.

Juhg knelt, hiding from the wind as best as he could. The wind picked up small pebbles and stone shards and hurled them like missiles. A few of them struck Juhg with ringing pain and slashed at his face and hands. He wrapped his left arm over his lower face and breathed through the material of his robe to filter out the dust. His eyes teared from the dust and the grit. He barely managed to stand on the heaving surface of the floor. Grim certainty that the Library was about to come plunging down onto them dug into him with fishhooks.

Then the green fury Craugh unleashed tore chunks and strings from the web of purple power. The strands ripped away, stretching and popping and curling in on themselves until they disappeared. In the space of a drawn breath, only the fractures across the floor, the walls, and the ceiling remained to mark the web's existence. A few faint tremors shook the Library—and perhaps the Knucklebones Mountains themselves—then they faded away.

The Grandmagister dusted himself off. His face bled in a dozen different places and one eye was swollen nearly shut.

"Craugh," the Grandmagister called.

His voice sounded strange in Juhg's ears, now that the roaring wind was absent.

Stepping gingerly from the floating chunk of rock, which dropped with a crash to the broken floor as soon as the wizard's foot left it, Craugh stared up at the ceiling. He held his staff tightly and caused the light at the end of it to blaze to life again.

"Craugh," the Grandmagister called again.

"What?" The wizard's voice held irritation.

"Is it done, then?" the Grandmagister asked.

"The spell is banished." Craugh walked around hesitantly, his eyes never leaving the center of the ceiling where the cracks stemmed. "But whether that is the end of it . . ." He shook his head. "The spell was a true one, Wick. Woven strong. It dug deeply into the magic that was placed into the Library. I don't know what the removal of the spell has done to the Library."

"But how would anyone know how to tie that spell in with the magic that is part of the Library?" Juhg asked. Despite his dazed state, his ever-inquisitive mind sought answers. "The magic that helped create the Library is so old that not many remember how to work it."

Craugh glanced away from his survey of the ceiling and smiled grimly at the Grandmagister. "Well, Wick, people will certainly be asking that question over the next few days."

The Grandmagister evaded his friend's penetrating gaze.

Juhg knew that something important was passing between the two, but he couldn't fathom what it was. Evidently the Grandmagister knew more about the attack than was immediately apparent. Although Juhg had known both of them for years, he found he wasn't surprised that they could hide secrets from him.

"You knew," Craugh accused bluntly, "you knew that this might some-day happen. You knew the risks."

"I did," the Grandmagister replied. "I did know the risks. But they were acceptable."

Craugh waved an impatient arm at the destruction around them. "And are they acceptable now?"

The Grandmagister straightened himself with dignity. "What we've lost remains to be seen."

Even though the Grandmagister said those words, Juhg heard no hope in his mentor's voice. The disconsolate sadness in the Grandmagister's words hurt Juhg and made him feel helpless.

"Or perhaps," Craugh ventured, "what you've lost will never be seen again."

The Grandmagister started for the doorway. Chunks of rock lay in the way. Cracks turned the carved arch into a ragged tear through the rock.

"They were after the books," Craugh said. "Not to keep them, Wick, but to destroy them. They started fires in the rooms we were in to destroy the books. Any Librarians they chanced to meet along the way were just bonuses. They came to destroy the Library."

"I know that," the Grandmagister replied heavily.

"You know who did this."

"I don't."

Craugh stamped his staff furiously. Green sparks spurted from the end of the staff and belled in the air before dying out on their way to the floor. "By the Old Ones but you can be stubborn when you've a mind to. You've known about them for years, Wick. The time is well past that something should have been done about them."

The Grandmagister peered over his shoulder, eyes catching first Juhg, then the wizard. "Craugh, please."

The tone was a warning. *The Grandmagister giving a wizard a warning!* Juhg's mind spun wildly at the very thought.

"Faugh!" Craugh clomped about angrily in his boots. "That's your dweller's instinct talking, Wick. You can't just stick your head in the sand and hope that this goes away."

"I couldn't stick my head in the sand here," the Grandmagister said in a weary voice. He kicked a loose stone. "All we have here is rubble."

"They won't give up after this."

"I can't talk about this now."

"You have to."

The Grandmagister halted and turned around quickly. Anger and pain warred across his face.

Instinctively, Juhg took a step forward, certain that he would have to intercede on the Grandmagister's behalf before the wizard turned him into a toad. *And what will that do? Ensure that I get turned into a toad before the Grandmagister? So there will be a pair of toads that go hopping out of this room?*

"They don't know where we are," the Grandmagister said.

"They do now."

"Do they?"

Craugh glowered, evidently set back by the Grandmagister's question. "You have to assume that they do."

"No." Grandmagister Lamplighter looked at the wreckage in the center of the room.

With the shadows draping the room, the damage didn't look nearly as bad as Juhg was certain it would in the light of day. Or even under torchlight.

"The Dread Riders and Grymmlings got here by that spell," the Grandmagister said. "That doesn't mean that they know about this place. Or even about this island."

"Wick, please. You're making a mistake." Craugh sounded almost as if he were pleading.

Juhg remained silent and still, but he was only a step away from placing himself between the wizard and the Grandmagister—if it came to that.

"No," the Grandmagister said. "I can't allow myself to think like that. That way lies . . ."

A rumble started distant and high in the Knucklebones Mountains. Juhg turned his head automatically, tracking the sound as his heart slammed into full speed again.

The rumble grew in intensity and came closer, faster and faster. Stone dust shot through the cracks of the ceiling, spewing out in long, thin clouds that smashed against the broken floor and spread like warm autumn fog.

Juhg tried to yell out in warning, but his voice became lost in the discordant clatter and crash of breaking rock. Grandmagister Lamplighter grabbed the sleeve of Juhg's robe and yanked him into motion. Juhg followed the Grandmagister, stumbling over a broken slab of rock. He stayed upright only because the Grandmagister supported him. Together, they raced for the broken archway. Craugh was but a half-pace behind them.

The rumbled deepened, growing faster and coming closer, till it reached a crescendo and filled the rooms on either side of the doorway, where Juhg stood grim and fearful.

The center of the room's ceiling, where the web had stood, exploded, shattering into a million pieces and pouring into the room, becoming a waterfall of tumbling stone shards, bookshelves, and books. Juhg went deaf with the sound of it. Several stones skidded across the floor and slammed into his feet, shins, and knees with bruising force. He fell, but the Grandmagister and Craugh grabbed his robe and hauled him to his feet again before the growing pile of rock could cover him. He covered his mouth with the sleeve of his robe but still felt certain he was going to suffocate in the swirling sea of dust.

Then, so quick it was unbelievable, the carnage that racked the Library stopped.

Wheezing for his breath, eyes filled with dust and tearing as they tried to clear the debris, Juhg stared at the incredible mass of broken rock that filled the room. So much of the wreckage piled from floors above that the jumble had choked the hole that had opened in the ceiling. Only the fact that the falling stone had gotten bogged down by its own volume saved them.

The Grandmagister was the first of them to move. Slowly, walking as though stunned, the Grandmagister limped forward.

"Grandmagister," Juhg managed with what little breath remained in his lungs.

"Wick," Craugh called out. "Come back from there. It might not be safe. If that pile of stone shifts, you could be buried in a fresh avalanche."

Obviously unable to stop himself, the Grandmagister kept going forward. "It can't have come to this, Craugh. Not this. We simply can't have lost the Library."

A huge hole gaped in the ceiling. In the darkness, Juhg was barely able to see how large it was, but Craugh caused his magical flame to grow larger and chased the shadows away.

"Perhaps it's not as bad as it looks," Craugh suggested.

Juhg knew that was a poor attempt on the wizard's part to allay the Grandmagister's fears. There was no mistaking the damage that the Vault of All Known Knowledge had suffered.

A few stones slid free of the pile, tumbling down with harsh *clack-clacking* clatter. Other stones shifted, offering immutable evidence that the pile of broken stones wasn't in any way stable.

"Wick." Craugh started forward, but one of his legs slid out from under him, obviously injured, and he sat down heavily. In the glare of his magic flame, his face went white with pain. He shifted his attention to Juhg. "Go get him away from there before we lose him, too. We've lost enough today, and we can ill afford to lose him."

Warily, feeling the pain in his legs, Juhg limped forward. "Grandmagister," he called. "Grandmagister Lamplighter."

More stones slid free and tumbled down the pile. Juhg felt the vibrations through his feet, feeling the certainty of an impending shifting that would spill the stones loose again.

How far up did the damage go? A stone bounding across his foot painfully interrupted Juhg's reverie.

"Get him," Craugh growled, trying in vain to lever himself to his feet with his staff.

Weakness showed in the wizard's every move, and Juhg knew that Craugh was all but done in. He ignored the shifting stones, clamped down hard on his own fear that he should run for his life, and approached Grandmagister Lamplighter.

"Grandmagister," Juhg whispered. This close to the stones, at the very edge of them, he feared that even the vibration of his voice might be enough to set them loose. "Grandmagister."

Tears ran down the Grandmagister's face.

Seeing the raw emotion on his mentor's features made Juhg feel as though a huge hand had closed around his own heart and was squeezing the life from him.

Over the years that he had known Grandmagister Lamplighter, Juhg had seen the Grandmagister cry on a number of occasions. Sometimes it had only taken a sad song in a tavern when they'd been far from home in inhospitable lands, because the Grandmagister possessed a tender heart and a great capacity to care for others than himself. And at other times, the Grandmagister had wept over the graves of comrades when circumstances had forced them to bury in lonely places where no one they knew would ever travel.

"Grandmagister." Juhg took his mentor's robe sleeve. "Grandmagister, we have to go."

"Look at what has been done, Juhg," the Grandmagister whispered. "All of this was put on me. It was my duty to protect the Library. I failed."

More stones shifted, rattling and capering down the pile.

"You did all that you could to protect this place." Juhg stared at the books—ripped and torn and scattered into pages and pieces of pages—that lay strewn within the debris.

"It wasn't enough," the Grandmagister whispered.

Juhg barely heard him over the growing roar of the shifting stones. "Grandmagister, please. We have to go." He pulled on the Grandmagister's robe sleeve.

More stones skittered across the floor.

"Grandmagister," Juhg said, "Craugh needs our help."

Reluctantly, the Grandmagister turned his attention from the hole in the ceiling and the ponderous tonnage of stones shifting there. "Craugh."

"He's been injured," Juhg said.

The wizard still struggled to climb the staff.

"Craugh," the Grandmagister said.

More stones shot outward, beginning a slow tide of detrius that tumbled down from the hole in the ceiling.

The Grandmagister turned and ran to his friend. Together, he and Juhg managed to get Craugh to his feet and started rapidly stumbling for the arched door. Behind them, the pile of stones broke loose from the precarious positions they'd been locked in. The tide of stones became a full-fledged flood, a roaring, snarling beast that pursued them.

Craugh grunted in pain as they ran through the doorway into the next room. The tide of stones halted for an instant against the walls while a tongue of debris lapped out at them through the doorway.

The Grandmagister said something that Juhg couldn't understand, but the younger dweller knew that the Grandmagister had hastened his pace. A huge, cracking roar thundered through the room, overcoming the grinding noise that had filled Juhg's ears until then. Unable to stop himself, he glanced backward.

Craugh's magical green flame still dancing atop his staff revealed the sudden destruction of the walls of the room. They cracked and broke, then became part of the inexorable tide of rock shoving through the room.

Rocks rebounded from Juhg's back, causing him to break his stride and nearly fall. But he kept his hold on Craugh and marveled at the wizard's own efforts to escape the brutal death that pounded at their heels. The room shook underfoot. Then they were through the next doorway and turning to the right to gain the stairs they had followed down to the Library's lowest level.

Like the last wall, this one held only for a moment, but a spray of stones followed them into the hallway and ricocheted against the wall in front of them. Juhg fell, nearly bringing Craugh down with him. But the wizard yanked him upright again with strength that belied his frame and his condition. There were many impossible things about wizards, Juhg knew.

 Guided by Craugh's magical flame, they ran up the stairs.

The walls broke behind them, then the stones filled the hallway and began climbing the stairs. If the stairs hadn't been carved from the very heart of the Knucklebones Mountains themselves, Juhg had no doubt that they would have fallen.

The stones eventually slowed as they climbed above the height of the room. Once the room was filled, the downpour stopped. However, the clouds of dust followed, clogging their lungs with thick, acrid air and coating their eyes so they wept grainy tears.

Juhg coughed weakly, all but out of wind and strength to go on. He made himself go on for a little more, then Craugh fell, dragging the Grandmagister down and causing Juhg to miss a step. Juhg fell heavily, barking his shins on the steps. He pushed himself to his knees, his free hand on the wall beside him.

The wall vibrated. At first, Juhg thought the vibration was caused by the mountain of stones that had pursued them from the rooms below, then he noticed that they pulsed in counter-rhythm to the shifting stone, and that the stones below had mostly come to rest.

It's coming from up above!

Fearfully, Juhg glanced upward, watching as a few dozen small stones bounced and careered from the turn of the landing ahead and came down at them. Juhg covered his head with a hand, fearing that the stones were only the heralds for the mass only now starting to come.

But other than the few stones, nothing more came down the stairway.

He stayed crouched and expectant. The Grandmagister and the wizard did the same, all of them fearing the worst.

Gradually, the grinding noise of the stones came to an end. The vibrations that moved the mountains halted. Only the thick stone dust remained, hanging stubbornly in the air.

"Here," the Grandmagister said. He handed Juhg a section of cloth torn from the hem of his robe. "Tie this around your face. Over your nose and mouth."

Juhg did, watching as the Grandmagister offered another section to the wizard, then tore one for himself. Craugh's green light fought back the darkness but had trouble penetrating the shifting dust clouds.

"That," Craugh said in a painful voice, "was a very near thing."

Grimly, the Grandmagister turned his attention to the wizard's injured leg. He pulled Craugh's robes to one side, revealing the bloodstained breeches.

"I think," Craugh said, "it's broken."

"Of course it's broken," the Grandmagister snapped. He looked at Juhg and the younger dweller saw the uncertainty in his mentor's eyes. "You're lucky you didn't lose your leg." He hesitated. "You still might—infection sets in and you don't care for this properly."

"Nonsense," Craugh snorted. "What use is a one-legged wizard? Why, I'd not even be able to sit a horse properly, never mind being able to go the places I've needed to over the years to find the things I've quested for."

"Juhg," the Grandmagister asked, "do you still carry that knife?"

When they were on the mainland, tracking down myths and legends about books and other objects, the Grandmagister seldom carried weapons. But during those times he did carry a magical knife he'd found in the Broken Forge Mountains. While he was in the Library, though, he went unarmed.

The Grandmagister also preferred that Juhg go without weapons as well, but Juhg almost always carried a knife. Becoming a slave again—for goblinkin or anyone else—wasn't something he was going to allow to happen. He was no fighter, but having a knife meant possibly having some way out of a bad situation.

He slid free the boot knife that Raisho had given him to seal their partnership aboard *Windchaser*.

The Grandmagister gave the knife a quick examination out of habit. "Ah, a Hostyn blade by the Burning Anvil dwarves."

"Yes."

"But not the handle," the Grandmagister said, turning his attention to the wizard. "That's a recent addition."

"Yes. Raisho had the blade refitted when the original broke."

"In the South." The Grandmagister slit the wizard's breeches leg, running the keen blade up the seam. "Sharp."

Juhg knelt beside Craugh. His stomach tightened at the sight of all the blood, but he had seen worse in his years as a slave in the goblinkin mines. *And some* much *worse*, he thought, remembering the attack among the upper rooms, only moments ago.

White bone poked through the side of Craugh's leg. The jagged break had left an edge that had punctured the flesh either at the time the leg had broken or during Craugh's attempts to stand and flee.

"A greenstick break," the Grandmagister said.

Juhg recognized the wound as well. Books on medicine remained high on the Grandmagister's reading list for all Librarians. Usually, unless the patient was extremely fortunate, a limb that suffered a greenstick break was lost. Too much infection was allowed into the wound through the torn flesh. Even when the bone was set properly and the flesh healed without infection, the limb seldom recovered full strength.

"I know what it is," Craugh said irritably. "Help me get the bone back where it belongs."

"I don't know if we can—" the Grandmagister began.

"Do it," Craugh growled. "We've wasted enough time as it is. Don't you want to see what other damage has been done to your Library?"

"It's not my Library," the Grandmagister said.

"It would do you good to remember that." Craugh shifted, hauling himself along the step he sat on so that his back rested against the wall behind him. "Are you going to help me with my leg or not?"

The Grandmagister nodded. "Juhg, you've read up on these kinds of wounds."

"Yes."

"Then let's get started."

Taking his knife back from the Grandmagister, Juhg quickly cut lengths of cloth from his robe, then fashioned two harnesses out of them. He tied one harness to the wizard's leg above the knee and the other at the ankle. Together, he and the Grandmagister helped the wizard to the next landing and took a moment to clear the rubble from the area they would need to work.

They made Craugh as comfortable on his back as they could. The wizard turned even paler during the movements and his breath came in short gasps. Still, his magical staff stayed lit and filled the landing with greenish light.

"Grandmagister." Juhg held up the two ends of the harnesses.

"I'll take this end." The Grandmagister gripped the harness attached to Craugh's upper leg, then knelt down at the wizard's shoulder. He touched Craugh's shoulder gently. "We'll be as quick as we can."

"Just get it done." Craugh held his staff and folded his free arm over his chest. He gazed upward, fixating on the lit end of the staff.

As carefully as he could, Juhg sat at the wizard's feet, his legs splayed on either side of the broken limb. He pulled the slack from the harness.

"When you're ready," Juhg told Craugh.

"Do it." Craugh's voice sounded hoarse and far away.

With steadily increasing pressure, Juhg leaned back. The harness tightened around Craugh's ankle, then started pulling the leg toward him.

Unbelievably, Craugh spoke not a word, nor made a sound.

Knowing the pain Craugh handled was incredible, Juhg heard his own heart beating in his ears, certain at any moment that the wizard would give in to the pain and turn him into a toad simply to end it. He kept building the pressure, watching as the Grandmagister shifted to keep his weight behind Craugh's shoulder, holding the top of the leg and the wizard steady.

Caught between the two opposing forces and no longer connected, the wizard's leg stretched longer than normal. The white bone, burning with a greenish cast from the magical staff, retreated into the awful wound, eased back into line with the other section of bone.

"Almost," Craugh gasped hoarsely. "Keep pulling. Don't you dare stop now." Beads of perspiration gleamed on his face.

Juhg pulled, ignoring the queasy feeling in his stomach. He remembered the times he'd had to cut a dead dweller free of the slave chains, then carry the amputated leg back to the goblinkin guards as proof that the dweller had died. Retreating from those memories, he focused on the task ahead of him. Craugh wasn't going to die.

But is having a live wizard who blames you for his crippled walk a good thing?

Without a word, the Grandmagister leaned forward, keeping his end of the harness locked under his knees. Gently, he probed the wounded leg with his fingers. Finding something that interested him, he pressed.

Bone rasped in the deathly quiet that had descended over the stairwell.

"There," the Grandmagister said, drawing back. "I think it's back in place, Craugh." He paused and took a deep breath. "Juhg, take the pressure off your end. Slowly."

Juhg leaned forward, easing the pull he'd maintained on the harness. In a moment, the harness fell slack. He gazed worriedly at Craugh.

Craugh fought to sit up, using his staff and striving to lean forward from the waist. Both attempts failed. "I am getting far too old for this nonsense." He blew an angry breath between his clenched teeth. "Wick."

"I'm here," the Grandmagister replied.

"I'll have need of your assistance, please."

Still on his knees, the Grandmagister got behind Craugh and helped push the wizard to a sitting position.

"Thank you, my friend. I'll need you to hold me for only a short time."

"Of course."

In the distance, clanking echoed in the halls. Juhg wondered if the noise signaled the impending collapse of still more debris.

Craugh stretched his free hand over his bloody leg. Cool blue light emanated from his palm, bathing his wound.

Interested despite his trepidation at looking too closely at the damage or risking invading Craugh's privacy, Juhg leaned forward. As he watched, the broken ends of the shinbone shifted and rotated.

"Wouldn't do to have a crooked foot after this, now, would it?" Craugh asked in a thin voice. His control was tenuous and frayed. "I'll not suffer a limp."

In the space of a drawn breath, the broken ends of the bone fitted themselves together. The blue glow bathed the ends till the break became a line finer than frog hair. When that was complete, the flesh began pulling together, healing.

During his time at the Library, Juhg had read about healing spells, but he had never seen one in action before. Magic was a thing seldom seen outside of destruction and mayhem. Wizards didn't learn spells to do good; they learned spells to acquire power.

"Apprentice." Craugh's voice came as a harsh rasp squeezed out through pain.

Juhg looked at him.

"After this day, after this moment," Craugh said hoarsely, "there's not to be one word about what you've seen here."

"No," Juhg agreed. "Not one word."

The fact that Craugh could handle such a spell, more aligned with the good forces than the evil forces, spoke volumes about the wizard's true nature and contradicted what most people believed of him. Juhg thought of the wizard with newfound respect.

Abruptly, Craugh fell backward without a sound, crumpling against the Grandmagister, who was almost bowled over by the wizard's collapse. The blue light faded and the green light at the end of the staff exploded in a lizardlike hiss.

Darkness filled the stairwell landing.

"Grandmagister," Juhg called, afraid that the wizard had died from his own magical exertions complicating the massive wound he'd received.

Healing spells, from all accounts, drew mightily on the resources of the healer and did not allow magic places or things often to fuel them. Healing, according to Endelsohn's *The Art of the Magical Healer,* was the most jealous magic ever crafted, the most demanding of its caster.

That was one of the primary reasons why those who wielded magic didn't learn those arts. Magic, by its nature, was disruptive. Even a healing spell played havoc with the wounded person who received treatment. Medicines and rest were far easier to give. Craugh, who was already exhausted, couldn't have had much left.

Is he dead? Juhg wondered, holding his own breath while he listened for Craugh to draw a breath.

"It's all right, Juhg." In the darkness, the Grandmagister's voice was calm and comforting. Even dweller vision was useless in complete darkness.

the destruction of the books

Here there were no stars to light the way. "He's still with us. Craugh is too arrogant and too stubborn to leave us like this."

As if to underscore the Grandmagister's words, Craugh drew a deep, shaky breath.

"When he falls," the Grandmagister said in a soft voice, "Craugh will fall in battle. Against someone or something much more devious and dangerous than he is. For now, he only sleeps."

The clanking Juhg had heard earlier came closer. Then pale golden light came down the stairs above. As the sound filled the stairwell, Juhg recognized the noise as armor clanking just before a dozen dwarves followed a Librarian into the area. Half of the dwarves carried lanterns.

"Grandmagister!" the Librarian squealed in delight. "The Old Ones be praised! I felt certain that . . . that . . ."

"That I might not be here, First Librarian Whimplo?" The Grandmagister stood.

Whimplo frowned and licked his lips nervously, obviously at a loss as to how to answer the question. He was plump and out of breath, and Juhg was certain the dwarves had pushed him hard in their efforts to locate the Grandmagister.

One of the dwarves jostled Whimplo to one side. "Aye, Gran'magister. Varrowyn, why, he's worried that ye might not still be with us after this last bit of carnage."

The lantern the dwarf held played the golden light over his face. The illumination revealed the blood spatters and scratches that adorned his features under his helm. He held his battle-axe in his other hand. Notches showed in the keen-edged blade.

The Grandmagister remained with Craugh, holding the wizard's head in his lap. "What of the Dread Riders and the Grymmlings?"

"Gone." The dwarf shrugged and his battered armor clanked. "Most of 'em anyway."

"And the Librarians?"

The dwarf bowed his head. "We got what we could of 'em out, Gran'magister. But fer some of 'em . . ." He shook his head.

"I'm sure," the Grandmagister said in a forced voice, "that you did all you could."

"Aye. That we did. Only wish it could have been more." The dwarf looked at Craugh. "We can fix a litter, carry him on up if ye want."

"No. When Craugh is ready, he'll walk out of this place on his own. He would not suffer getting carried out in any degree of weakness." The Grandmagister smiled a little, though the effort was strained. "He's very vain about his appearance."

The look on the dwarven warrior's face showed plainly that he didn't believe it. "If ye says so, Gran'magister, but I was thinkin' a bed an' a warm hearth might be more . . ."

"I do say so."

"Of course, Gran'magister."

The Grandmagister looked at Juhg. "First Level Librarian, I want you to stay with Craugh. Until he's able to walk. I'll not have him wake with no friend around him. He's done that often enough while trying to help this place and his friends."

Juhg wanted to say no. He wasn't part of the Library any more. Nor did he feel particularly close to Craugh. Also, Juhg didn't want to remain down in the depths of the Library. Some of the Dread Riders and Grymm-lings yet remained.

And the darkness, with the Knucklebones Mountains piled so high and deep around him, reminded Juhg entirely too much of the goblinkin mines. It reminded him of how powerless and weak he had been during those times.

But he said, "Of course, Grandmagister," because there was no other answer he could give.

265

The Grandmagister took his robe off, carefully using it to make a pil-low beneath Craugh's head. He took a moment to pick up the wizard's staff and hat and laid those items close at hand.

"I'll ask you to assign two of your warriors to stay down here," the Grandmagister said to the dwarven leader. "To stand guard."

The dwarf pointed at two warriors. The dwarves stepped away from the group and took up positions.

The Grandmagister looked at Juhg. "When Craugh is ready, accom-pany him up. I only hope he will understand why I am not here."

"He'll understand, Grandmagister," Juhg said. Overcome by everything he'd been through, he sat with his back against the wall, which allowed him to look in both directions. He sat quietly, listening to the falling stones shift-ing throughout the Library, and watched as the Grandmagister walked away.

Craugh slept, his chest rising and falling in the dim glow of the lanterns.

Juhg looked at the dwarven warrior closest to him. "How bad is it?" he asked.

The dwarf gave Juhg a haunted look. "Plenty bad. Bad as I've ever seen. Got dead strung all through the halls. A lot of 'em's Grymmlings an' Dread Riders, but we left plenty of ours among 'em." He shook his shaggy head. "This here place, why, after today it's filled with blood that'll never come out of this stone."

The imagery made Juhg shiver. "I'm sorry for your losses."

The dwarf nodded. "We all lost today."

266

17

The Account

he sound of footsteps woke Juhg.

Panic flared to life within him as the two dwarven warriors shifted. As one, they stepped into the shadows of the stairwell. Only then did Juhg notice that the lanterns they had placed on the floor had gotten positioned with deliberate care to illuminate the stairs in both directions and allow them hiding places in the shadows.

The dwarves lifted their weapons. Juhg knew that only from the sounds, and only then because he knew the dwarves would only move for that reason.

The footsteps halted. The distinct sound of metal scraping leather echoed into the empty silence of the stairwell.

"Juhg," a voice whispered.

Recognizing the familiar voice, Juhg smiled and said, "Raisho?"

"Aye. Tell them dwarves what's down there that ye know me afore they get too anxious. Tell 'em Varrowyn passed me on down."

Forcing himself to a standing position, feeling the pain and agony that accompanied that effort, Juhg said, "He's a friend."

"Tell him to come on ahead," one of the dwarves said.

Juhg still didn't know the names of either dwarven warrior who guarded him. "You heard him, Raisho."

"Aye. That I did. Just ye keep in mind that I ain't comin' empty-handed. I'm bringin' a basket of victuals. Weren't so much dust a-hangin' in the air down here, why, ye'd probably have smelt it long before ye heard me."

Despite all he'd been through and everything he had seen, Juhg was surprised to find he was hungry. Thirst he'd acknowledged some time ago, before he'd somehow dropped off to sleep. Even in the mines, he'd maintained something of an appetite. He supposed after all those years the feeling was more survival instinct than anything else.

Raisho stepped into the soft golden glow of the lanterns. He carried his sword in one hand and a small lantern in the other.

The dwarves revealed themselves, stepping from the darkness.

"Varrowyn yet lives?" one of the dwarves asked.

Nodding, Raisho said, "Aye. From the looks of him, he's a right enough hard one to kill. An' looks like plenty tried him tonight. He's shed some blood, probably more of someone else's than his own, but he's upright an' in charge of the Library's defenses."

"Where's the food ye was talkin' of?" one of them asked.

Raisho sheathed his blade, then reached around for the burgeoning back-pack he'd carried down. "Knew I'd be feedin' dwarves. Brought enough to feed a small army." He grinned and drew himself up to his full height. "Or a short army at the least."

"Human." One of the dwarves jerked a thumb at Raisho as he talked to the other. "All that extra room from the neck up is just wasted space."

Grinning at them, Raisho knelt and opened the pack like a merchanter revealing his wares. "I'll be sure to mention that to the wizard when he wakes. If 'n he don't remember it all on his own. In me travels, I've seen men what could remember somethin' said around them while they slept." He shrugged good-naturedly. "An' a wizard? Somebody like Craugh? Why, I bet he'd come closer to rememberin' somethin' like that more'n anybody I've ever seen."

The dwarves exchanged nervous scowls.

Raisho spread a feast across the landing, setting it all on a thin woolen blanket he'd brought, leaving the items on the cheesecloth wrappings.

Fruits, breads, cheeses, and smoked meats emerged from the pack. He added two skins, one of water and one of wine.

The dwarves, one at a time, helped themselves.

Juhg took a square of cheesecloth Raisho had unwrapped from a loaf of dill limebread and cut portions of meats and cheeses, added fruits and sections of bread, and wrapped the food. He placed the makeshift bag back in the pack.

"For Craugh," Juhg explained. "For when he wakes."

"Ye'll eat, too," Raisho said. "I didn't trek all the way up the Knucklebones, survive a handful of battles, an' descend into the bowels of the earth in the middle of the night just to feed a couple of thankless dwarves."

The dwarves offered unkind and cutting remarks.

"Raisho," Juhg admonished, "these warriors fought long and hard. Don't speak ill of them."

"Aye." Raisho looked at the dwarves and nodded. "I know that they did. We all did."

"We?" Juhg repeated.

"Aye." Raisho cut a slice of limebread, covered it with firepepper cheese and topped that with a wedge of puckerpear so green and tart it would have dried the mouth all on its own. "Them Dread Riders an' Grymmlings spilled down the Knucklebones, Juhg. They met the rescuers what come up the mountains to help out. Several of them would-be rescuers was caught unawares. I hadn't seen the bodies ahead of me, I'd probably have gotten caught standin' still meownself."

Juhg tried to digest that. "How bad is it?"

Raisho's eyes showed a haunting pain. "Bad enough, scribbler. Bad enough so that ever'body what took part in them battles ain't gonna ever forget what they seen an' done up here in these mountains."

"How many came?"

Hesitating, Raisho said, "Enough. Enough to get the job done." He paused. "Most couldn't believe the bell was ringin'. Nobody ever heard it ring afore."

"Were the Dread Riders and Grymmlings stopped before they reached the town?"

"Aye. Dead in their tracks, most of 'em. Heard there was more of 'em for a while, but they up an' disappeared." Raisho gestured to the food in Juhg's hand. "Eat. Gotta get yer strength back up. Got a lot to do around here."

Juhg took a bite of the sandwich. The combination of flavors filled his mouth but didn't take his attention away from the stories he knew Raisho had to tell.

Seated with his back to the wall, Juhg ate from the small store of food Raisho had forced on him while the young sailor talked. Eating, Juhg had learned, kept Raisho talking.

"I was in a tavern when I heard the bell," Raisho said. "At first, I didn't even know what it was I was hearin'. But the tavern keeper, he knew what it was an' he told ever'one." He hesitated. "I got to tell ye, not ever' person in that tavern took up arms to come a harin' up the Knucklebones to spend their blood protectin' the Library."

"No," Juhg said. "I don't think anyone here expected they would."

"Some of 'em, why, they didn't believe what they was hearin'. But others, now, why, they wanted no part of it. Took themselves off to their own ships an' homes an' such. Some was confused because they'd always been told danger would come from the Blood-Soaked Sea."

Raisho continued talking and serving Juhg food. The young sailor told stories of the action he'd seen, describing encounters between the elven warders and their animal companions and battles staged by the dwarves as they'd hacked their way up the Knucklebones to join their comrades as reinforcements. The Dread Riders and Grymmlings had spilled down the mountainside quickly, overtaking some of the Librarians and running headlong into the arriving rescuers.

There were no stirring tales of dwellers who had joined in the battles.

"For a time there," Raisho said, "it didn't look like the arrivals from Greydawn Moors would be enough to hold the Dread Riders and Grymmlings back. Looked like the town was gonna get sacked. For ever' one that was killed, seemed like two come runnin' out of the Library to take the place of the last one." He tore a piece of limebread to pieces in his hands and ate a chunk. His eyes glazed over in memory. "They was about to overcome the line what held the mountain an' prevented 'em from goin' on down into Greydawn Moors. Then a fierce wind seemed to draw up from outta the Library an' pulled most of them back inside."

"That was Craugh," Juhg said. "He broke the spell. He thought the invaders would be drawn back to wherever they came from."

"Well, it didn't pull all of them back," Raisho said. "But them what was left, why, they put up a decent enough fight, but they couldn't stand. Them elven warders, they didn't come up the mountain to get defeated. Fightin' fair ain't something they believe in, not like for a dwarf. For them elves, it's all about survival. An' dwarves? Why, they won't back down from nothin'."

"That's why dwarves were asked to provide protection for the Library," one of the dwarven warriors said with a trace of pride.

"Aye," Raisho said. "An' I'll grant ye that, right enough. But there's also a reason why so few dwarves sign up aboard pirate ships in the Blood-Soaked Sea. That's for the humans what's sworn to protect the Library. We all got our battlefields."

"How badly damaged is the Library?" Juhg asked.

Raisho looked down at the rubble that had partially filled the stairwell below. "Like that. An' worse. Don't know how big the Library is 'cause I ain't ever been here afore tonight, but from what I've seen, aye, it's been damaged all over. Above ground and below."

Juhg couldn't believe that. Images of the Library lying in ruins filled his head, but he couldn't bring himself to believe that they were true. The Library had been built to last forever.

No, he corrected himself. *That is incorrect thinking. The Vault of All Known Knowledge was built to last long enough to give its treasures back to the world. That's all. It was only meant as a repository, not a permanent place.*

But Grandmagister Lamplighter hadn't felt that way.

"Did you see the Grandmagister?" Juhg asked.

"Aye." Raisho nibbled at a bit of sweet honeydew cheese crusted in crushed walnuts and olives. "Talked to him meownself. Let him know I was plannin' on lookin' ye up, makin' sure ye was all right. It was him assigned a Librarian to guide me till I could find me own way."

"The Grandmagister was all right?"

"Seemed to be. Worn an' a little ragged, mayhap. He was organizin' salvage parties when I left him."

" 'Salvage parties'?"

"To get them what survived up outta the Library. Some of 'em got trapped in places when the mountain come apart. An' they're savin' the books, of course. Gettin' all them books up outta places is harder than bringin' up Librarians an' dwarves."

Removing so many books from the Library, Juhg thought, will be an awesome task. But where will they all be kept?

Reaching inside his cloak, Raisho said, "The Gran'magister asked me to give ye something." He pulled out a full-sized journal bound in cloth.

Juhg took the journal and automatically searched for the title and author. Neither existed. He flipped the journal open and found page after page of the best paper made at the Vault of All Known knowledge. Only First Level Librarians got to use that paper.

"What is this?" Juhg asked.

Handing over a small leather pouch, Raisho answered, "The Gran'-magister, he said to tell ye to make a record of ever'thin' that went on last night."

"Last night?"

"Aye." Raisho shook his head. "It's mornin' already, Juhg. Didn't ye know that?"

"No. I didn't." Down in the bottom of the Library, there had been no way of keeping time.

"Was well past mornin' when I come down here," Raisho said. "That's why I knew ye'd prolly be hungry."

Juhg looked at the blank pages inside the book. He felt the weight of the task settle on him. For a moment, he felt inadequate. Writing something like this was a job meant for the Grandmagister. Not a Librarian who had willingly left the Vault of All Known Knowledge.

"The Gran'magister," Raisho said, "he said to be sure an' tell ye that ye weren't to hold nothin' back. Put it all down like it happened. 'Just like it happened,' he told me to tell you. Said a lot of people would blame him for the Library gettin' destroyed after last night, an' he wanted it put down fairly. He also said he was to blame some'at. Told me he'd rather not have any Librarian other than ye to make that record. Because ye was the fairest one he knew. An' ye was there when it all happened." He clapped Juhg on the shoulder. "Ye ask me, Juhg, I'd say the Gran'magister's givin' ye quite an honor."

Grandmagister Lamplighter's trust in Juhg brought tears to the young Librarian's eyes. He hid his emotions in the shadows that clung to the stairwell landing.

"I know," Juhg whispered. "But you don't know what he's asking. I don't think the Grandmagister knows what he's asking."

Raisho took a deep breath and let it out. He was silent for a space. "All the time that I've known ye, I've known ye to be fair an' honest. Mayhap that's all the Gran'magister is askin' for, too."

Juhg thought back over what had transpired, how evil had been set loose inside the Library. *It isn't the Grandmagister who's to blame for this. It's me.*

"Apprentice," a weak, croaking voice said.

Startled, Juhg looked over at Craugh.

The wizard had managed to find the strength to roll his head to the side and gaze at him. "Wick charged you with a duty. He doesn't give such things lightly. He finds it hard not to do things himself. He prefers to do them himself, rather than pass them along. He and I share that failing. Nor does he make a habit of asking people to do things they aren't capable of. He knows you can do this, and he trusts you to do it right. To do it accurately and fairly."

"But this," Juhg said, his voice so hard and thin it came out as a whisper, "this is my fault."

"No," Craugh said. "We are all to blame for this. And even then, the blame can only be small. The trap was well laid and even better executed by those who made certain it fell into our hands. Don't you discount the skill and canniness of those who created this vile business. That would be a disservice to your master. And to yourself."

"If I had not found the book . . ."

"Sooner or later, the book would have been found. It was put out there in the world to be found." Craugh grimaced. "When we learn the truth of everything, we'll probably come to know that there were several books treated in a similar fashion."

That possibility hadn't occurred to Juhg, and now that Craugh presented it, he felt even more vulnerable.

"The gateway spell was disguised as a riddle within a riddle," Craugh said. "Perhaps a human Grandmagister wouldn't have been quite as quick to get to the solution, but the evil ones who put this attack together knew that they were dealing with Wick. That they were dealing with a dweller." His eyes narrowed. "And they knew that they were dealing with me. They knew both of us would be here."

"How could they know that you would be here?" Juhg asked.

"Think, apprentice. I know you are not that dense." Craugh gave a small, doubting smile. "Tonight's events, after all, could not have happened were I not here."

Understanding built a warm glow inside Juhg. "You destroyed the book's illusion."

"Exactly. And were I not here tonight, one of those who had helped lay the magic on the Founding Stone, the gateway spell would have never been triggered." Sadness touched the wizard's eyes. "Only after I arrived in that room, as you recall, did the spell become active. You and Wick might have gathered the books they used to knit the spell, but my presence was the catalyst that activated the gate. Our enemies planned well."

Juhg remembered that.

"We all have a part to play in the blame for this," Craugh said. "Wick knew that you would be the best person he could go to, in order to best describe what happened."

"He could write the account," Juhg protested, "and probably do it more justice than I can."

"The Gran'magister was pretty busy the last time I saw him," Raisho volunteered.

"Someday Wick probably will write an accounting of last night as he saw it," Craugh said. "But for now he knows the risks of presenting his own material as the only explanation for the destruction of this place. Others will seek to write about it, concentrating on their own points of view, of course, but you and Wick and I were the only ones in that room." He paused and shifted, as if to relieve a pain. "I can tell you now that no man will read anything I've written as long as I live."

The simple declaration challenged Juhg. From his association with the wizard through the Grandmagister, Juhg knew that Craugh—in his own way and pursuing his own interests—was widely read. Wizards owned collections of books. The Grandmagister had even risked his life to steal some of those books upon occasion.

But to read the books that Craugh had collected over the years? Even just to see the titles of those that the wizard had claimed would be an adventure. Reading any of the journals that Craugh wrote, to follow in the wizard's footsteps across the centuries, could add to the knowledge the Library already had.

Juhg looked at the book in his hands and trembled slightly. He felt certain he couldn't lay down a straight line or write legibly.

"The people of Greydawn Moors won't read any record I write," Juhg stated. Although all of the dweller children were taught to read by Librarians in schools established for that purpose, few adults pursued an interest in reading. Every year, fewer and fewer dwellers came forward to become Librarians. There was a time, according to Library records, when applicants had been turned away. These past few years, especially when the Grandmagister's penchant for roving to the mainland became noticeable to the public, the Library had taken to accepting the best candidates from a group of substandard applicants.

"The book isn't for the town populace," Craugh said. "It's for those who come after this event."

Perplexed, Juhg looked at the wizard.

"Later Librarians," Craugh explained. He shifted slightly in an effort to make himself more comfortable. "They will have more questions than the Librarians who survived the night. Those around you, Juhg, will have already assigned guilt for who was responsible for this. Including those people in the town. Wick wants you to write the truth as best as you can for the ones who will come." He paused. "If they come."

"What do you mean?"

Craugh hesitated a little, then obviously made some internal decision. "I mean that this isn't the end of it, Juhg. The attack tonight was only the beginning. Wick's enemies, the Library's enemies, have found this place. After all these centuries, they have found the Vault of All Known Knowledge."

"Who?" Juhg asked.

"No, apprentice. That story isn't for me to tell. Taking on another to train in your life's work is an important and binding decision. I would never interfere between two people who have made that commitment. You must ask your master for the answers to those questions."

Without another word, Craugh drew a deep breath and was once more asleep.

Juhg stared at the wizard. *What secrets do you have? What do you know?*

"Don't let him rattle ye," Raisho advised in a hushed voice. "Wizards, why, they're always forecastin' doom an' gloom an' such. Bad as an old sailor on his last voyage what gets the feelin' he's never gonna see his home port that final time." He picked up another puckerpear. "Just ye do what ye does best, scribbler, an' I'll make sure these dwarves don't go to sleep while they're supposed to be guardin' ye an' the wizard."

The dwarves made disparaging remarks about Raisho's parentage, but the young sailor only grinned at them. He hadn't known his parents, so the accusations meant nothing to him.

Juhg opened the journal to the first page and stared at the impossibly white expanse that looked amber-tinted in the lantern light. He took a deep breath and inhaled the soapy scent of the paper. Whenever he started writing a new book—even his journal of his experiences aboard *Windchaser*—he always got nervous, always grew afraid that his hand and eye and mind wouldn't work together. Afraid that he would mar the book with indelible scars that other Librarians would ridicule him for, he always hesitated.

So often in his studies, he'd noted that most historians and record-keepers were remembered chiefly for the mistakes they'd made. Sometimes it was a careful turn of phrase or a choice description that lingered in the mind's eye or rolled off the tongue in a particular way. But those instances were in the minority.

And to write a book that would describe the savagery that had taken place in the Vault of All Known Knowledge? Juhg knew that his name would live on forever in infamy. But he would be there twice because of his part in those actions and because he'd written the book detailing those circumstances.

 Silently, Juhg hoped that the Grandmagister simply gave the account he was writing to yet another Librarian to do a finished record. As a resource for the real work that would be written, Juhg's own efforts would seldom be seen.

"Juhg," Raisho whispered.

"Yes." Juhg didn't dare look at his friend seated beside him.

"Begin."

"It's not that easy."

"It's a voyage, mate. Nothin' more. Just somethin' ye've got to see done. Like mendin' a fishin' net. Thinkin' about what ye've got to do sometimes makes yer fingers thick an' dumb. But ye've tied knots afore, an' ye've written books. Just start an' trust yerself."

Resolutely, drawn by the paper even more than he was pushed by Raisho's words, Juhg opened the pouch and took out quills, a small knife to sharpen them, and inkwells with different colors of inks.

Raisho picked up his lantern and set it to Juhg's right so the light played over the page. Juhg folded his knees and balanced the book there as he had so often while accompanying the Grandmagister on one of the quests along the mainland.

Almost unbidden, hypnotized by the need to explore the page to find the images and the words that he would uncover, Juhg filled the quill with black ink and began. The title, usually one of the hardest things he had to think of unless the Grandmagister had already assigned it, came to him immediately.

THE DESTRUCTION OF THE BOOKS
Or an Accounting of the Attack on the Vault
of All Known Knowledge

Drawn into the events, Juhg relived them. He began the history where it had started, in Kelloch's Harbor, with the rumor of the cooper who was fencing stolen goods. He laid out an image of the harbor and the city jammed into the cracks and crevices of the ice-blasted mountains in quick strokes, surprised at how quickly his skills warmed to the task, in spite of everything he'd been through.

"Kelloch's Harbor," Raisho commented, peering over Juhg's shoulder.

Juhg nodded. "Everything began there." Knowing he would return to the ink drawing at some future time after the lines he'd laid out had time to partially dry, he moved on to the next page, letting the first stand till the ink completely dried. He'd already laid the ink on thin enough that it wouldn't run.

Time passed as he worked, telling about *Windchaser,* then adding a brief sketch of the ship. Craugh continued to sleep and the dwarves talked in low voices. Juhg was surprised at how quickly and easily his fingers worked, despite the chill that hung in the Library.

"Am I in the book?" Raisho asked.

"Yes." Taking a moment, Juhg brought to life a rough sketch of the young sailor standing in *Windchaser*'s prow. He put a sword in Raisho's hand and a cloak billowing around behind him.

"I am handsome, ain't I?"

Somehow the incongruity of the question against the backdrop of all the horrible things that had happened brought a smile to Juhg's lips. "And so modest, too."

"Women don't like a handsome man what don't know he's beautiful,"

Raisho said. "Makes him come off all unconfident an' makes it so they can't be mad at themselves for likin' that man but bein' understandin' at the same time."

Juhg ignored the comment and kept working. In no time at all, he was back aboard the goblin ship fighting for his life against the wizard's snakes.

18

Aftermath

deep inside the Knucklebones Mountains, parts of the Vault of All Known Knowledge still burned.

Standing on Draden's Spur, a rocky outcropping that stood taller than the Library and offered a view down onto the edifice built into the mountains, Juhg surveyed the ruins of the Library in disbelief and dismay. Out beyond the cover offered by the rocks, the wind was chilly enough to make someone without outer garments uncomfortable, but where Juhg stood in the full view of the afternoon sun, he was comfortable enough in breeches and shirt.

Most of the main buildings still stood, despite the collapse the eradication of the gateway spell had caused. Sections of those buildings lay in collapsed ruin, while others disappeared through holes that led down to the caves beneath the aboveground buildings.

Behind the main building, where the Library reached its tallest point, a large chasm had opened up and swallowed a chunk of the mountains large enough to shove a ship through. Smoke boiled through that opening incessantly, reminding Juhg of the Smoldering Tar Pits described in *Nerestes and the Penance of Crystal-Tooth,* a lively romance from Hralbomm's Wing that the Grandmagister had recommended.

Juhg took a deep breath and flexed his hands. After hours of writing and sketching, his fingers felt cramped, like they would never be the same again. He knew from experience that the feeling was only momentary, requiring only a brief respite and a little loosening exercise before he could return to his task.

There are a lot of things, he told himself, *that won't be the same again.*

Craugh had woken only a short time ago and declared himself fit enough to walk. Juhg, remembering how grievous the wound had been, had felt certain the wizard was overestimating his own recuperative powers. Broken bones and torn flesh did not mend so easily or quickly. Surprisingly, Craugh had made the long, twisting journey up to the main halls of the Library and then out into the courtyard under his own power. Outside the Library and in the keen afternoon light, Juhg had insisted on examining the wound over Craugh's protests and was surprised to find only advanced scar tissue instead of bruised and recently knitted flesh.

The courtyard remained alive with activity. Librarians under the Grandmagister's direction worked in shifts above and below ground to haul books from the Library. From Juhg's perch above them, they looked like ants working at a hill.

280

Seemingly filled with inexhaustible energy, the Grandmagister ran back and forth among them. He had a plan for the recovery of the Library. Unfortunately, that plan received several setbacks as new levels of loss were uncovered.

But the Grandmagister remained driven.

Dwarves and Librarians descended into the Library, seeking out the rooms that had histories first, and brought volumes out. Librarians verified the editions, catalogued them, and cross-referenced them with previous catalogues.

Catalogues were also made of volumes that were badly damaged, needed reconstruction, or were lost completely. There were a lot of the latter, and those numbers continued to grow with heartbreaking speed against the snail's crawl of the rescued books. Perhaps the Dread Riders and Grymmlings had died under dwarven axes and elven swords and bows, or been pulled back to wherever they had come from when Craugh had broken the spell at such immense cost, but their legacy of destruction lived on. They had accomplished a large part of what Craugh had stated their agenda had called for.

And Juhg still had no idea of who had created the spell. Or of who might choose to still remain such an enemy of the Vault of All Known Knowledge so many years after the Lord Kharrion's fall and the end of the Cataclysm. Goblinkin carried hatred from those years, but they lacked the magical power to create such a spell.

Also, Juhg reminded himself, turning over the most unsettling part of the puzzle, *goblinkin don't read. Whoever laid this trap knows how to read and is well read.*

So where did someone come from who had those things? Reading ability, knowledge of books that had disappeared from sight at the time of the Cataclysm, and magical skill, any of which made for a rare individual indeed.

Juhg pushed his thought from that line of inquiry. He did not have enough information, though he felt certain the Grandmagister knew far more than he was telling. The fear that had showed on the Grandmagister's face at the time the gate opened had also held knowledge of inevitability. The attack hadn't been as unexpected to the Grandmagister as it should have.

Over the years, Juhg had learned that the Grandmagister held his own counsel and kept his own secrets from those who lived on Greydawn Moors. Juhg had even known Grandmagister Lamplighter to keep secrets from him, ones from before they had become acquainted and ones that the Grandmagister had kept concealed even during their journeys.

With dedicated commitment, Juhg turned his attention to the efforts taking place around the ruins of the Library. Whatever secrets the Grandmagister held, Juhg knew from experience that Grandmagister Lamplighter would never reveal them until he was ready.

The task before the Librarians, Juhg knew, was almost impossible. When the Vault of All Known Knowledge had first been constructed, armies and navies had shipped the books to the island. Thousands of people had been involved in the transportation.

Now that job of rescuing all that remained salvageable was left to the forty-seven Librarians who survived the attack, and the dwarves, humans, and elves who came up from the forest and from Greydawn Moors to help. Only a few dwellers had made the trip up the mountain. The Grandmagister had spoken vehemently to those he'd sent to secure help from the town, reminding them of the debt their ancestors had incurred on their behalf all those years ago. Only a few more had come, token laborers gathered from the young sons of the town's dweller merchant class.

Juhg had wanted to stay and help with the reclamation effort, but the Grandmagister had ordered him to continue working on the book. With a sigh, Juhg cut a fresh quill and turned to a fresh page in his personal journal. Working swiftly and surely, feeling only a twinge every now and again in his fingers from the constant time he'd spent at the task after once more stretching them out, he captured the image of the Library as it now stood.

He wasn't to that part in the book yet. At the rate he was working, if he could keep up the effort, he wouldn't reach the point of the afternoon's labors until the day after tomorrow.

The Grandmagister had seemed pleased with the progress he was making. After flipping through the pages for just an instant, doing no more than giving them a casual perusal, the Grandmagister had handed the book back, pronounced the effort a worthwhile endeavor, and told Juhg to continue working on the project.

The Grandmagister had freed Juhg from the salvage operations. That decision, even though it was the Grandmagister's, hadn't set well with the other Librarians. Of course, they couldn't be mad at the Grandmagister for that, but they could be mad at Juhg.

And they were. Juhg was painfully aware of that, even if the Grandmagister wasn't or simply chose for the moment to ignore that. Juhg knew his chosen departure from Greydawn Moors to ship aboard *Windchaser* had distanced him from the other Librarians. He'd willingly chosen not to be one of them. Then he'd returned and brought "the cursed book." That was what they were calling the trap-laden volume. He'd already overheard a few of them talking about the book that way.

"Cursed book. Cursed book and the cursed mainlander dweller who came in with it."

First Level Librarian Randorr Cotspin had survived the attacks. Probably by hiding beneath his bed, Juhg believed, though he didn't begrudge the other Librarian his health. However, now Randorr was the chief proponent among the Librarians who spoke beneath their breaths against Juhg and the Grandmagister's decision to have him working on the Library book project instead of helping them to salvage books.

For himself, Juhg longed to be gone from the Library, far away from the Knucklebones Mountains and away from Greydawn Moors. But he couldn't leave while the Grandmagister needed him. And he couldn't leave until he'd properly told the story of how the Library was destroyed. Left in the hands of a Librarian other than the Grandmagister, Juhg felt certain he would be named and vilified as the cause for all the deaths and loss. Despite the fact that he was willing to leave the Library, pushed by his own reasons, he didn't want to let someone else write the history of the attack and judge him harshly for his part in the unfortunate events.

At least, Juhg told himself, he couldn't leave at this moment. But later, after the book was finished and the Grandmagister accepted his efforts, Juhg planned to be gone the first chance he got.

Watching the ruins of the Library, having to capture the images in the book the Grandmagister had given him to work on, was almost too much. He didn't have many good memories of his younger years. With the Library's destruction, he felt an emptiness inside, as though they were being stripped away.

Juhg had put some thoughts and sketches into his personal journal for later reference because he'd wanted to capture those ideas and images in the moment they occurred, rather than try to reconstruct them later. The duplication of effort slowed him somewhat, but he knew from past experience that he'd be better able to write what he needed to when the time came to do that.

A tern cawed behind Juhg, drawing his attention for a moment.

There, in a crevice behind him and to his left, a nest of baby terns made up of twigs, grasses, and small pebbles sat in the shadows. Their world, Juhg thought, wouldn't change because of the damage that had been done to the Library. They would continue to live and mature and raise nestlings of their own that would one day do the same.

But that isn't necessarily true.

The realization trickled through Juhg and brought fatigue and dismay. Craugh had said that enemies would come one day, now that the attack had taken place.

Those enemies certainly numbered goblinkin among them. And once goblinkin chose to destroy a people and a place, the creatures destroyed everything. Goblins knew no other way to behave. Several towns that had held out against Lord Kharrion's forces and had cost several goblinkin lives had been put to death to the last male, female, and child.

The goblinkin had poured salt and foul corpse drudge (a jelly made from the bodies of their victims combined with toxic mushrooms and poisons) into the earth where those towns had stood before the houses and meeting halls had burned to the ground. In some of those places, even hundreds of years later, vegetation had still not returned.

If the goblinkin learned where Greydawn Moors was, if they learned that the Library was there, Juhg had no doubt they would travel there to destroy the island and all who lived there.

He looked to the west, out into the fog-shrouded expanse of the Blood-Soaked Sea. To the north, ships filled the harbor at Greydawn Moors. Pirate vessels as well as fat-bodied merchant vessels shared harbor space. Several members of those crews had journeyed up the mountain to help with the Library. Of all the peoples who knew of Greydawn Moors and the secrets held upon the island, only those who served as contacts with the mainland and stood as defenders against potential discovery showed the greatest allegiance to the Vault of All Known Knowledge.

But the presence of those sailors here leaves the harbor unprotected. And it leaves the sea unpatrolled.

The island's greatest defense had lain in the fact that no one knew it existed. That was gone. Whether or not the Dread Riders and Grymmlings knew where the island was, the powers behind them knew of its existence now. After seeing the efforts the unknown enemies had gone to, in order to destroy the Library, Juhg felt certain that they wouldn't give up trying to finish what they had started.

Unless they believe the Library is already destroyed.

Quick as that thought entered Juhg's thoughts, he pushed it right out again. Craugh's magic had shattered the spell. Whoever—or *whatever*—had crafted the spell, had opened the gateway, and had marshaled the armies of Dread Riders and Grymmlings had to know that someone had closed the gateway.

No doubt existed that another attack would take place. Only the amount of time between those attacks remained unknown.

Juhg turned his attention back to his work. The quill slid smoothly across the paper, despite the erratic jumping of his thoughts and the certain fear that vibrated within him.

The book took Juhg nine days to write, three days longer than the Grandmagister had expected. Thankfully, Grandmagister Lamplighter chose to be satisfied with the extra effort and time rather than remonstrate about it.

Juhg had slept only when he could no longer keep his eyes open. Even those times were brief because nightmares chased him awake again nearly immediately every time.

During those days and nights, Juhg occupied himself with nothing more than writing. He wrote with his right hand and his left, utilizing the seldom-seen skill of ambidexterity that he possessed.

In the goblinkin mines, he had learned to swing a pickaxe and use a shovel with either hand. Although those tasks normally required the use of both hands, he had taught himself to use either hand to guide the effort. Also, picking out gemstones from broken rock required both hands. And sometimes, one hand or the other had been injured, through work or torture. The goblinkin had relished inflicting pain, although they weren't supposed to disable the slaves. Sometimes they had killed victims too injured to work the next day and told their supervisors that the weak dwellers had died rather than be held accountable for their actions.

After handing in the book, Juhg had turned to helping with the excavation of the surviving collections. Often, he'd ended up working alone, foraging down deep into the Library's cavernous depths to bring out particular volumes the Grandmagister assigned him to find. The work was disheartening. So much had been destroyed. His best estimate at present was that the Vault of All Known Knowledge had lost nearly four books out of five, an astonishing percentage.

Even as prepared for the amount of destruction facing the Library as he'd thought he had been, Juhg felt hammered by the devastation and despair that hung over the place where he had spent the only truly good years he had known. Being ostracized by the other Librarians—and the Grandmagister's uncharacteristic ignorance of the matter—further weighed on Juhg.

If not for Raisho, who came and went while running errands for the Grandmagister, Juhg would have been totally bereft of friendship. As it was, Raisho was gone nearly as often as he was around. When Raisho did manage to visit, other Librarians always seemed to interrupt them so much so that Juhg could barely have a decent conversation with his friend. There was simply too much work to be done.

There was, Juhg reflected grimly as he sat along the western wall of the Library's outer courtyard, more friendship offered among dwellers in a goblinkin mine slave chain gang than at the Vault of All Known Knowledge. The ill treatment and pointed disdain offered by the other Librarians, headed up by Randorr Cotspin, proved almost more than Juhg could bear.

Through it all, the Grandmagister never seemed to take notice of his ill treatment at the hands of the other Librarians.

The only bright spot on the horizon was the news Raisho had brought Juhg two days ago that *Windchaser* was deemed seaworthy enough to once more venture out into the Blood-Soaked Sea. Even the Grandmagister's attentions had finally been drawn from the Library's book salvaging project to the fact that the Blood-Soaked Sea was going unpatrolled.

When *Windchaser* hoisted anchor and put out to sea, Juhg had every intention of being aboard her. At least, he'd feel more at home among the "pirates" watching the waves for any sign of an enemy fleet.

He ate sparingly of the plate he'd taken from the Library's kitchens. None of the food really had any taste, but he'd learned from his time in the goblinkin mines that meals were not to be missed. For the present, the Grandmagister had the workers on scheduled shifts.

Precious little time between those shifts was allowed for sleep. All the salvage workers neared exhaustion, but now and again a book survived—a remembered favorite of one of the Librarians, or a tome someone had been intending to read, or, most exciting of all, a book that still yet remained to be catalogued or interpreted—that set off a flurry of excitement and renewal of the rescue operation. Unfortunately, those occasions became fewer and fewer.

286

A group of Novices, their white robes now dirty and torn, sat beneath a cometberry tree that showed white flesh where limbs had been torn off during the attack on the Library. In spite of all the damage, in spite of the fog that clung to the Knucklebones Mountains, bright white and orange flowers with green centers blossomed among the dark green leaves that had survived the harsh treatment.

In a few more weeks, the flowers would produce cometberries, thumb-sized fruits all the colors of a rainbow and possessing the distinct elongated black hoods that grew nowhere else that Juhg knew of. The elven warders who first arrived to care for the Vault of All Known Knowledge and the town that later grew there had transplanted the cometberry trees.

The trees stood as physical proof of the promise the elves had made to protect the Library and the Librarians who cared for it.

Chewing his meal, not truly enjoying the food, Juhg listened to the poetry the Novices took turns reading. The volume was one of Haragis the Blind's efforts.

In his time, Haragis had lived a fierce life as a sellsword between warring nations, a human who had spent forty years combatting the foes of those he was paid to fight. He rose from the ranks to become a warrior of renown, a commander of armies, and—finally—the king of a small nation of mercenaries who had carved out a place to raise their families while they fought and died in other lands.

During his rule, Haragis had written many books. He'd learned to read while studying to become a general. His earliest efforts had been accounts of battles he had fought in, of wars he had waged. Then he had turned his attention to volumes of martial arts, of learning the strength of one's own mind and body, then of learning to lead first small groups of men, then armies. Up until the violent and confusing time of the Cataclysm, Haragis' books remained among those most studied by military leaders.

During his last years, though, a traitor had betrayed Haragis. After the death of his first wife, who had sired him a half-dozen sons, Haragis had forged a political alliance through marriage. Only a few days into the marriage, the young woman had viciously attacked Haragis while the old warrior was asleep, succeeding in blinding him in both eyes with the toxic poison of a sea toad before he slew her.

Despite the best efforts of healers, the old king remained blind. But as he recovered, he learned that the kingdom that had betrayed him with the assassin wanted the seaport the mercenary nation controlled. As a result, Haragis had declared war and brought the nation to its knees, warning anyone who might take up arms to defend the country that he would make war on them as well.

Haragis placed two of his sons on the thrones of both countries and ruled through them. Then his writing had changed as his interest turned to poetry. Haragis' passages were among the most vivid and heartrending of any epic poems ever put to paper.

In particular, his collection simply called *Travels* was one of Juhg's favorites for two reasons. Juhg had found the book among those uncatalogued in the Library shortly after his arrival. *Travels* had been his find, and he kept a copy *of it in his personal effects that the Grandmagister* had agreed to hold for him until his return from the mainland. But *Travels* also told Haragis' story when he'd been taken as a slave by the goblinkin for a time.

During the early days, when he had first learned to read and then to enjoy the stories and knowledge trapped between the covers of the books in the Vault of All Known Knowledge, Juhg had taken solace from Haragis' story of how he had fostered a slave rebellion and freed himself from the goblinkin.

Juhg ate and lost himself in Haragis' words, finding himself slightly irritated at the reading the Novices gave the work. He told himself he had no reason to fault them so. Once he had lacked as much as they did now. Time and exposure to the languages would take care of their failings.

Still, Juhg would have preferred to hear Haragis' words in the man's native language, filled with rolling *r*'s and the growling *k*'s so that a listener could hear the rasp of steel and the thunder of armor meeting armor on a battlefield. Haragis' action was real, not prettied up as so much of the fighting was in the volumes in Hralbomm's Wing. Men died in the mud, in each other's arms, and alone at the hands of brutish goblinkin and other evil creatures.

Knowing he couldn't force himself to eat another bite, Juhg pushed away his plate and sat with his back against the battlement along the wall. He peered out to the west, where the sun threatened to break through the dark gray rain clouds that had remained constant throughout the day. Thankfully, their luck had so far held and no rain had fallen. Tarps covered several stacks of books already catalogued and awaiting transfer to secure areas. Still more tarps awaited in case they were needed.

Closing his eyes, Juhg almost went to sleep. If only he could remember some pleasant event that was untainted by the carnage of the past few days, he felt certain he would have slumbered.

"Apprentice."

At first, Juhg thought his imagination was playing tricks on him. He recognized Craugh's voice, but the wizard had been scarce around the salvage operation. From what Juhg gathered, Craugh had sought out other sources for information about the attack, but even those efforts had to be circumspect. Few wizards, and all of them—*At least,* Juhg corrected himself in light of recent events, *it was believed all of those wizards who knew of the Vault of All Known Knowledge*—friends of the Library, knew about the island.

"Apprentice." Craugh's voice sounded sharper. "Are you sleeping?"

Juhg rolled over and peered down.

Craugh stood there in his robe and peaked hat. He frowned. "Are you awake?"

Not certain of what was going on, then suddenly seizing upon the idea that perhaps something had happened to the Grandmagister, Juhg swung around so that his feet dangled over the wall. He noted that Craugh's presence had drawn the attention of all those nearby.

"Has something happened to the Grandmagister?" Juhg asked.

"No."

"Oh." Juhg blinked. Then he peered toward the Library and saw that work continued as normal. If something had happened to Grandmagister Lamplighter, that would not be the case. Juhg glanced back at the wizard. "Then what do you want?"

"To talk with you," Craugh answered.

"About what?"

Craugh hissed in disapproval. "I am not of the habit of letting everyone know my business."

Those words further enticed the listeners, causing some of them to lean closer to them so that they might better hear the conversation they eavesdropped on. The wizard hadn't enjoyed much better treatment at the hands of the Librarians than Juhg had.

Craugh turned with solemn disdain toward the surrounding Librarians, dwarves, elves, and sailors. In his hand, his staff blazed bright green light. The eavesdroppers made haste to return their attentions to their own conversations, their meals, or the work they were doing.

Juhg couldn't imagine any reason the wizard would want to talk to him. He sat still and silent atop the wall.

"Well, apprentice," Craugh prompted.

"I'll come down." Juhg shifted, preparing to lever himself over the edge of the wall and clamber down the stone.

"Stay there. I'll come to you."

Juhg looked at the wizard. The wall stood fifteen feet tall. Climbing up or down, using the minuscule finger- and toeholds made possible by the placement of the stones and the gaps in the mortar between, was a challenge even for an elf. Few dwellers except for the very young or those who remained fit could make the climb. Even Juhg, with only a book for an encumbrance, found the climb challenging. He watched the wizard.

Craugh waved the staff before him. Sparkling surfaces, each measured with exactness, appeared in the air but never quite took form. They existed only as shimmering suggestions of steps. The wizard walked up the invisible staircase he'd created.

Everyone in the courtyard stared in open-mouthed astonishment or displeasure as Craugh ascended to the top of the wall.

Juhg knew the sight reminded the viewers of the tragedy that had only so recently struck them, and the display also underscored the difference between themselves and the wizard. They could never aspire to the magical arts.

Craugh stopped atop the wall only for a moment, acting as though ignorant of the stares that followed him. He waved again, and shimmering surfaces took shape on the other side of the wall, leading from the wall down to the flower gardens below.

"Walk with me, apprentice." Craugh started down the magical stairs. His boots struck small glimmering sparks from the steps. "I would talk to you in private."

19

The Dark Legacy of the Cataclysm

Unease ran through Juhg like lummin juice through a stubborn lock as he gazed after the wizard descending the magical stairs outside the Library's courtyard. Gazing at Craugh and feeling the natural fear of wizards and all things magical, Juhg wondered how he would feel living as a toad in the flower gardens outside the courtyard walls of the Library.

With no little trepidation, he pushed himself to his feet, took up his personal journal and bag of quills and inks, and reluctantly slid a foot out onto the shimmering steps he couldn't quite see. The surface felt surprisingly firm and not fragile. He put his weight on the step.

"Come along, apprentice," Craugh growled impatiently from a point halfway to the ground.

Juhg mustered all his courage. It helped that he was so fatigued that he couldn't feel the normal fear he would have when confronting the wizard.

"I'd like to know what this is all about," Juhg said, shamed by the way his voice broke when he tried to sound assertive.

"As would I." Craugh reached the ground and stepped in among flowering shrubs taller even than his pointed hat.

The flower gardens around the Library's north, east, and west sides weren't there just for show. Several of the shrubs possessed thorns and strong branches that would dissuade horses or other creatures from coming too close. The outer perimeter was impenetrable, the trees, vines, and bushes growing so closely they were as interlinked as a fence. The elven warders maintained the gardens, guiding the growths with their hands and with magical spells.

Librarians and guests to the Vault of All Known Knowledge were free to roam the inner third of the gardens, the only part of the gardens that wasn't impassable. Benches constructed of deliberately bent trees overhung with vines, fountains, and pools that flowed with natural springs and cisterns that fed down from the mountains, and statuary from a hundred different courts and cities and nations that had once existed along the mainland before the Cataclysm decorated the gardens and made walks in that area very interesting.

Juhg reached the bottom of the magical stairs. A tingle ran along the back of his neck. When he glanced back, he saw the shimmering steps disappear completely. There was no going back; he was trapped in the garden with the wizard.

"I've talked with your friend, apprentice." Craugh spoke without turning around. He put his hands behind his back as he walked. His hat swiveled as he took in the sights.

292

For just an instant, Juhg thought about objecting to the wizard's casual reference to the fact that none of the other Librarians chose to be his friend. The only friend Craugh could be referring to was Raisho. The young sailor returned to Greydawn Moors only that morning and wasn't expected back until the morrow.

"What of it?" Juhg asked.

Craugh stopped and turned around. His brows knitted together in accusation. "You have developed a most vexing nature, apprentice."

Juhg swallowed and came to a sudden stop on suddenly quaking knees. It took everything in him not to turn and scamper into the brush out of the wizard's withering gaze.

I, Juhg told himself, *am surely going to be a toad before morn.*

After a moment, Craugh sighed. "Please don't be afraid of me."

"I'm not," Juhg snapped.

"You are," Craugh insisted.

"Not half as much as I should be." Even as the words left his mouth, Juhg knew that he hadn't exactly said what he'd wanted to.

"Agreed," Craugh growled.

"That's not what I meant." Juhg drew himself up on shaking knees. He remembered all the evil and dangerous things he had faced over the years, first as a slave in the goblinkin mines, then as a Librarian at the Grandmagister's side along the mainland. *I will not be afraid. I will never again be as afraid as I was down in those mines.* It was a promise that he had made to himself several times after the Grandmagister had freed him from the chains.

Craugh shook his head. "I have neither the patience, the time, nor the understanding for peckish behavior, apprentice."

"And I don't want to talk to you and think that I might be turned into a toad at any moment."

Craugh grinned mirthlessly. "Well, I think that you *should* think that."

Without a word, before he even knew what he was about to do, Juhg turned to walk away. *No!* he told himself. *This is a mistake!* But he kept walking, surprised at his own impudence.

"Apprentice!" Craugh roared.

Juhg strode angrily.

"If you so much as take another step, I swear by the Eternal Darkness that you will hop to do it."

"Then do it," Juhg called back, not believing he'd dared to say such a thing. He kept walking, looking for the nearest bush to dodge behind before the wizard could cast such a spell. Perhaps summoning magical stairs out of thin air was child's play, but surely turning a dweller into a toad took more effort.

Of course, Craugh had spent hundreds of years perfecting the toad skill.

And unfortunately, the nearest bush big enough to hide a dweller was nearly twenty paces away. Juhg would have preferred a tree or a solid piece of statuary. He suddenly found himself wondering if a magic spell could be outrun. Without tilting his head down, he kept watch over his feet, waiting to see if they changed in any way or started turning webby.

"Apprentice," Craugh said.

Juhg cringed, certain that he was going to be blasted in the next breath.

"Please."

Please?

Please!

the destruction of the books

What magic spell included the word *please*? Especially uttered in that almost-pleading tone of voice? Wizards commanded magic; they didn't ask permission of eldritch forces.

Please? There is no please *in magic.*

"Apprentice," Craugh called.

"What?" Juhg croaked in immediate response. *Croaked!* He put a hand to his face, expecting to find a hideous visage covered in warts and rough skin. Instead, he felt his own face. At least, he thought he did. He wouldn't know for certain until he looked into a mirror. Craugh crossed the distance separating them. He stood and peered down at Juhg with his hands still behind his back. "I need to talk to you. It would . . . help . . . if you would take the time to listen."

Help, Juhg told himself, trying not to read anything harmful in the wizard's statement. *There's no chance of being turned into a toad if you're helping.*

"Listen," Juhg said.

"Yes." Craugh peered down at him. "Listen." He *hrrumphed* in obvious displeasure. "That's something you and your master share: an obvious reluctance to doing something that won't get you killed."

"Or turned into a toad," Juhg said.

Craugh waved that away.

"Or turned into a toad," Juhg pressed.

"Very well." Craugh sighed and clasped his hands behind himself again. He acted as though the concession cost him a great deal. "But I assure you, that last promise is extremely conditional on your behavior toward me."

"All right."

"I'll put up with no further disrespect."

"Nor will I." Feeling immensely lucky, but still unwilling to give in on the matter, Juhg pushed himself to his feet. He waited a beat, expecting to be blasted or turned where he stood, then—when that did not happen—brushed himself off.

"Walk with me," Craugh said. "I think better when I'm up and moving."

Juhg fell in beside the wizard and tried in vain to match the human's stride. In only three short steps, he was hurrying to keep up, taking two and sometimes three steps to every one that Craugh took. At the very least, Juhg hoped that the wizard's newly healed leg would pain him enough to go slower.

"As I said, I talked with your friend, apprentice."

"You mean Raisho."

Craugh shrugged. "Yes. I mean Raisho."

Juhg stared at the flower garden, remembering how frivolous he'd once thought the area to be. The Librarians managed gardens to the east, and there were several small lots inside the Library's inner courtyard where table vegetables were grown year-round. Even though some of the flowers were edible, none of them were particularly filling.

"Raisho told me something I found . . . unsettling," the wizard said.

Juhg waited. Actually, there were any number of things that Raisho could have told the wizard that might have been considered unsettling.

"He told me you planned to sail with *Windchaser* when she lifted anchor," Craugh said.

Juhg made no reply and actually let himself fall a step or two behind.

Craugh stopped so suddenly that Juhg almost ran into him.

Stepping back, Juhg thought quickly, wondering how it was that Raisho came to tell the wizard something that he had told Raisho in confidence. He blinked at the wizard, seeing the first streaks of lightning stirring the dark clouds. Full evening was upon the island now, and twilight gathered strength, turning from the gentle purple of amethyst to the deep ochre of bruised flesh.

"I made him tell me," Craugh said, as if guessing Juhg's unanswered question. "He had no choice. I'm not easily turned from something I want."

Juhg met the wizard's gaze and struggled not to look away.

"Is that what you're planning to do?" Craugh demanded.

"Yes," Juhg answered.

"Why would you do something like that, apprentice?"

Exasperated, Juhg asked, "Why do you insist on calling me that? I have a name. I am not your apprentice. Even when I was the Grandmagister's apprentice, he never called me that. Only you."

Craugh folded his arms before him, his staff clutched in his right fist. "Because you *are* an apprentice. You are Wick's apprentice."

"I was a Novice Librarian in the beginning," Juhg said. "But I have gone past that. I am a First Level Librarian."

"No, you're not."

Anger stirred in Juhg and he couldn't help giving vent to it. He was no longer a scared little dweller shackled to a mining chain gang.

"You abandoned that posting," Craugh said before Juhg could speak.

"I didn't abandon it."

"Yes, you did. And went charging off across the ocean just like you're preparing to do again."

"It's my business."

"You are Wick's apprentice."

"I am my own person."

Craugh bent and thrust his face into Juhg's. "What is it that you hope to find on the mainland?"

"My family."

"Lies." Craugh's eyes flashed. "You know in your heart that none of them survived the goblin mines."

"They may yet live," Juhg stated fiercely.

"Even if by some rare miracle they did live, how would you ever expect to find them?"

"I could go there."

"To the goblin mines?"

"Yes." Juhg felt tears burning his eyes. The cold winds blowing in from the south from the Blood-Soaked Sea not so very far away on the other side of the peaks of the Knucklebones Mountains coaxed them loose and he felt them dribble down his face.

"Now, there's a plan," Craugh roared.

"It is." Juhg felt embarrassed that he'd let the wizard get to him so.

"And what, exactly, did you plan on doing after you got your ankle fitted for a new slave ring?"

"That wouldn't have happened."

"That's exactly what would have happened." The wizard glared at him.

Juhg was suddenly aware that several heads adorned the top of the courtyard wall.

Without looking, Craugh gestured with the staff and called down a lightning bolt that crashed against the courtyard wall. There was sound and fury, but no stone was damaged. The heads along the wall disappeared.

"I hate eavesdroppers." Craugh frowned and resumed. "The worst thing of all is that Wick would probably have gone off after you once he heard of your capture. If I had been here at the time you'd chose to depart, I'd never had let you go."

"You couldn't have stopped me."

Craugh stared harder at him.

Bad, Juhg told himself, *bad decision to say that.* "You wouldn't have had any right. It was my choice to make. They are my family."

"You have family here, apprentice."

Juhg started to object, then immediately thought better of it.

"More than that," Craugh said, "you have a duty here. A very special duty that you were fortunate enough to be selected for."

"What duty?"

"To become the apprentice of the Grandmagister of the Vault of All Known Knowledge."

"There have been dozens of Novices during the time the Grandmagister has served here—"

"Hundreds," Craugh corrected.

"All right. Hundreds." Juhg knew that some of them had died during service to the Library, whether of old age or the occasional sickness that was brought back from the mainland, or they had chosen to leave the Vault of All Known Knowledge. Nearly all of the dwellers who came forward to serve in the Library only did so because of the long-standing requirements laid down by the Founders who had created the island.

Some of those reluctant Librarians had returned to the family farms and businesses after their ten years of servitude were up because they had never learned to love what they did. Others, who might have loved the books or their duties at the Library more than horticulture or trades or managing stores or services, lacked the necessary skills to advance beyond certain levels.

Juhg knew that the Grandmagister himself had spent more years as a Third Level Librarian than anyone in the history of the Vault of All Known Knowledge. In fact, Grandmagister Lamplighter had felt certain he was going to be asked to leave the Library.

But that was before the crew of *One-Eyed Peggie* had shanghaied him and took him off a-roving. After returning to Greydawn Moors with four books he had found in a dead wizard's tomb in the goblin city of Hanged Elf's Point, Craugh had taken an interest in the Grandmagister. As it turned out, Craugh worked to place information in the hands of the past Grandmagisters to secure books still out on the mainland. Grandmagister Frollo, the human Grandmagister before Grandmagister Lamplighter, had never shown any interest in Craugh or the tales the wizard told of books.

But Grandmagister Lamplighter had, and numerous trips to the mainland had brought back several books important to the collections at the Vault of All Known Knowledge.

"I couldn't stay here," Juhg said. "The day I realized that the reason I couldn't find my family was the Grandmagister's fault, I couldn't stay another moment."

Craugh's face hardened. "Whatever are you blathering about?"

"I said—"

Craugh lifted a hand and waved it irritably. "I heard what you said, but you need to explain yourself."

"Explain what?"

"How your inability to find your family could in any wise be Wick's responsibility."

Juhg sighed. *No one is going to understand. You're going to be a toad, and no one will even know why.* "My inability to locate my family is the Grandmagister's fault. But I won't stop there. I'll share the blame. I'll lay it at the feet of the last ten or twenty or thirty Grandmagisters if you want. I don't think that the problem lies solely with Grandmagister Lamplighter."

"How could any of this possibly be any lack on Wick's part?"

Knowing he wouldn't be able to simply walk away, especially not after he'd let the worm out of the apple, Juhg said, "Because he didn't give it back."

The pronouncement seemed to confuse Craugh even more. His features twitched and his eyes narrowed as he studied Juhg. "Whatever are you talking about?"

"The Library." Juhg felt the need to pace now, and he did so. But he confined his pacing to a back-and-forth pattern only a few feet to either side of the wizard.

"The Library," Craugh repeated.

Juhg nodded. "The Vault of All Known Knowledge. The Library."

"And Wick didn't give it back?"

"No. He didn't. He was supposed to."

"Apprentice . . ."

Juhg glared at the wizard.

"Juhg," Craugh said, obviously struggling to maintain control of himself, "I don't understand what you're getting at."

"All those years ago," Juhg said, "the Founders caused this island to rise from the ocean bed. They changed the sea around this place, brought up dangerous reefs on three sides and most of the fourth, and covered the land and the sea with perpetual fogs that scared off most seafaring races. Back then, with the large navies from the pre-Cataclysm days destroyed and others employed solely for military maneuvers along the mainland, most ships didn't venture out this way anyhow. But the Founders knew that the races, especially the humans with their wanderlust and need to conquer the seas, would journey out here again."

"And so they tried. Probably would have found this island as well. If the Founders hadn't decided to fill the waters with enough dangerous beasts to keep stories fresh."

"The pirate fleet helps keep them away as well," Juhg said.

"Yes."

"Back then," Juhg said, "the Library had to be hidden. Lord Kharrion fought and commanded the goblinkin hordes on the land and on the sea. The goblinkin hunted the books as much as they hunted everyone who dared stand against them."

"I know. You're not telling me anything that—"

"Once Lord Kharrion and the goblinkin were defeated, the books were supposed to be given back." Juhg stopped and looked at the wizard. He repeated his words, giving them weight and feeling his voice grow hoarse with the emotion tangled up in them. "The books were supposed to be given back."

Craugh frowned. "Oh. I see."

"Do you?" Juhg demanded. "Do you really?"

The wizard held up a hand. "The books will be given back."

"Will they?" Juhg let all the doubts he'd started fostering these past few years sound in his voice.

"Of course they will. That was the promise. When the time is right, they'll be returned."

"And when will that time be?"

Craugh's frown deepened. "I'm not in charge of these things."

"Then who is?"

"The Grandmagister of the Vault of All Known Knowledge."

"And when will the Grandmagister feel the time is right to return the books?"

Craugh made an irritated *tch.* "I begin to see what you're talking about."

"No," Juhg said, shaking his head. "I don't think that you do."

"Don't forget yourself, apprentice. Your boldness—"

"I'm not bold," Juhg interrupted. "If I were bold, I would have spoken of this before now. Instead, when I felt certain I could no longer curb my tongue and I started growing bitter with the Grandmagister as well as myself, I ran. I left this place and headed for the mainland and told myself it was only because I had the faintest of hopes that I would find my family alone and unaided."

"You left because you were afraid to talk to Wick about this?"

"Yes."

Craugh waved a hand. "You're just confused, apprentice. Nothing more. If you had only taken the time to talk to Wick—"

"If I had spoken of my feelings to the Grandmagister, we would have argued. Despite how I felt, I . . . I . . . did not want to argue with him." In the end, that desire had outweighed the need he'd felt to challenge the Grandmagister's continued withholding of the Library. Besides that, releasing the Library was not Juhg's choice to make.

"Still, there was no sense in losing you if that could have been prevented."

"It couldn't have been. Not without the Grandmagister's understanding that the books had to start being handed back to the people out there."

"What made you think that the time for that return was now?"

Despite the wizard's protests, Juhg knew Craugh was starting to consider what he had to say. He drew a deep breath and hoped that he might sway his audience even more. "You travel along the mainland following your own agendas, Craugh. You see the people there. There are more than just goblinkin out there. Things have changed since the Cataclysm. These people aren't just scattered pockets of civilization who were driven from their homelands during the battles and the war. They're people who have settled down and built new homes, new neighborhoods, and new cities. New lives and new histories."

"I don't see your point." ,

"The point is," Juhg said, "those people could use the knowledge that is kept here in the Library. They could make themselves stronger, they could fight better, provide more for themselves and their families. They could stop the encroachment of the goblinkin."

"I don't think—"

Juhg hurried on before wizard could finish. "Do you know how much the lives of the dwarves, elves, humans, and dwellers could be improved if they could resource books, essays, and monographs on building, on horti-culture, on medicine, even war and weapons—any one of a hundred differ-ent studies that were contained here in the Vault of All Known Knowledge?"

"I—"

"I do," Juhg stated. "I've seen them, Craugh. I've lived among them before I was a slave and after. I've traveled among them at the Grandmag-ister's side. The knowledge that is—" He stopped himself, remembering all the damage that had been done, and corrected his statement. "All the knowledge that *was* held here could have changed their lives." He paused. "If they had but known it was here."

"The goblinkin—"

"Still harbor resentment against books," Juhg said. "Yes. I know that. They always will. And do you know why?"

"Because Kharrion—"

"Because," Juhg said, raising his voice and speaking over that of the wizard, "the goblinkin, of all the races in the world, were the only ones that didn't develop a written language. Not before the Cataclysm. Not during. And not after."

Craugh eyed Juhg steadily.

"The goblinkin lived only a little better than animals before Lord Kharrion came along and recruited the creatures," Juhg said. "The clans were migratory, living in the wild and preying on each other until the leaders learned their numbers were sufficient to prey on the races that built towns. So the goblinkin moved into areas surrounding cities. When the clans grew strong enough, the goblinkin massed and invaded those cities, killing and enslaving the populace that didn't survive or escape to run away. The goblinkin lived in the houses in those cities, and those crea-tures ate from the larders that those people had stocked."

"Ancient history," Craugh snapped.

Juhg shook his head. "No. It's still going on. In fact, it's gotten worse."

"Worse? How?"

"Because Lord Kharrion gave the goblinkin a lot more than just guidance during a long war that very nearly wrecked these lands."

"Not true. Once Lord Kharrion was defeated, the goblinkin armies fell apart. The clans returned to their infighting."

"Not completely."

"Apprentice—"

"See? Even for all you know, all the magical spells you know and the arcane knowledge you possess, you don't see what's before you either. That's how I knew it was useless to talk to anyone about this."

"Apprentice," Craugh growled. "Whatever your thoughts, I would—"

"What Lord Kharrion gave the goblinkin," Juhg said, "was a common history. Something none of the clans had ever had before. He came among the goblins and brought his magic and his power and his deceit, and he won the clans over. He gave the goblins a common starting place, a point in time the clans could look back on and know had changed. In only a short time, he negotiated treaties among the clans and got the goblins to quit killing each other. For the first time ever, the goblinkin stood together."

"That was only because of the magick Lord Kharrion used," Craugh objected. "He used spells to blind the clans and bind the leaders to him."

"No. Not true. That's a misconception. The goblinkin banded because Lord Kharrion gave them a common history. He showed them that the goblins could stand together against the races the clans perceived as enemies. He made the goblinkin strong together. No matter what the clans did, the goblins could not forget the lessons of unification that Lord Kharrion taught them through that common history and an alliance against their enemies."

That statement halted Craugh just as he was about to speak. He closed his mouth again, then furrowed his brow in thought. He tapped his staff against the ground and tiny green sparks drifted up from the top end.

"A common history," Craugh repeated finally.

"Yes. All the violence that had gone on between the goblinkin before the time Lord Kharrion arrived among the clans was forgotten. Maybe the creatures still remember those darker times. Maybe the leaders even still talk of it. But none of the goblins act on the old grudges. The clans fight over new ones, but even those battles don't last as long or become as bloody. The goblinkin don't squander resources. Instead, the goblinkin band together and hate the other races. And the clans breed like locusts, growing stronger and ever more hungry. The goblins remember how Lord

Kharrion almost guided the clans to victory over the world, and the more aggressive goblin commanders look forward to the time when the clans can still achieve that."

"Everyone felt certain that the goblinkin would self-destruct as the clans always had after Lord Kharrion was slain," Craugh said.

"It hasn't happened," Juhg said. "Not in all these hundreds of years. It hasn't happened."

"No. And you believe that is because Lord Kharrion changed the goblins. Changed the clans' thinking."

"Yes."

Craugh paused. "No one—*no* one—has ever thought that before."

"What I'm saying is true," Juhg stated quietly. Even though he knew the wizard was listening to him, he felt near exhaustion from having to fight to get Craugh to hear him out. When the ideas he was talking about now first began to circle within his mind, he had resisted them. That line of thinking seemed too far-fetched, immensely above anything the goblinkin could do.

At least, Juhg corrected himself, *above anything the goblinkin had been able to do before.*

"The trap set in the book and the wizard aboard the goblinkin vessel in Kelloch's Harbor indicated that the goblinkin weren't working alone."

"I can see that." Craugh stroked his bearded chin with his free hand. "Now."

303

"When I was a slave in the mines," Juhg said, "there were always stories the goblinkin slavers told. The overseers talked about the Cataclysm and Lord Kharrion. Told each other over and over again how the whole world had very nearly fallen to the goblins to loot and pillage and enslave."

"It very nearly was."

"I know."

"If Lord Kharrion had not fallen in the end, it very well could have been."

"The potential yet remains for that to happen," Juhg said. "The goblinkin numbers still flourish."

Craugh frowned. "They breed constantly."

"Yes. And they've gotten more conscious of other places in the world. In these recent years, the goblinkin have grown strong enough to recapture and hold the South. How long will it be before the clans spread over the rest of the world?"

"That will never happen," Craugh said.

"Why not? Who will stop the goblinkin. Who is strong enough to stand against the clans? Who can unite the races and have them pull together as they did during Lord Kharrion's reign?"

Craugh hesitated, and Juhg could see that his words were having an effect on the wizard.

"The dwarves," the wizard said. "The elves and the humans. None of them will allow the goblinkin to grow that strong again."

"How long ago," Juhg asked, "were they saying that about the South? About how they would never allow the goblinkin a toehold in the nearly destroyed cities that line the mainland there? The South started falling a hundred years ago, and the goblinkin are firmly entrenched there. Nothing less than a war will get them out of those places. And no one wants another war with the goblinkin. None of the races can produce enough warriors to make that happen. They seldom band together to defend each other, choosing instead to fall back grudgingly before the goblinkin. I've seen that happening. You have, too."

"Apprentice, all of these things you're talking about—"

"Lord Kharrion died all those years ago," Juhg said. "But—*Don't you see, Craugh?*—the Cataclysm has continued. It is a specter that has continued to haunt our world, to leech the life from it. Only slowly."

"The Cataclysm ended—"

"*Lord Kharrion* ended," Juhg interrupted. "Lord Kharrion died. Not the Cataclysm. Do you know why Lord Kharrion truly tried to get rid of all the books?"

"To take away knowledge," Craugh replied. "Without knowledge, the humans, elves, and dwarves lacked the resources to stand against him and the goblinkin army."

"It was more than that." Juhg felt hesitant. All those months and years ago as he had formulated the ideas that had driven him from Greydawn Moors, he had doubted himself, doubted his thinking and his logic. Then he'd become convinced, but also convinced that neither the Grandmagister nor any of the other Librarians would listen to him. His theory was largely unsupported. And now, looking at Craugh, he was grimly aware of that again. "Lord Kharrion planned deliberately. The books died. The music died. Art—all the paintings, sculptures, and all the beauty that the races learned to create—died. Do you know what truly died for most people? Do you know what Lord Kharrion and the goblinkin truly destroyed?"

"I suppose—"

"With the destruction of those books, of those libraries and collections, the past for the dwarves, humans, and elves died," Juhg stated clearly. "Much of the history. Much of the way those races did things. The voices of those who had gone before and who had learned so many valuable truths were stilled forever. They could no longer look to each other's culture and find similarities. Without books, without a proper accounting of history, their lives became small and selfish. In fact, they were reduced to the same level as the goblinkin when Lord Kharrion went among them."

"What do you mean?"

"Lord Kharrion took their histories from them and left them only the uncertainty of today and the hatred of the hardships of all the yesterdays before. They forgot how to look forward to the future with hopes that better things might lie ahead."

"Bosh!" Craugh exploded. "They remembered enough. You talk like nearly everyone read in those days. It simply wasn't true."

Juhg kept focused. He was right and he knew it. The attack on the Library, the means with which it was done, made him even more certain. Grandmagister Lamplighter had taught him how to argue and present his thoughts in an orderly fashion. He leaned on that skill now. "What did they remember?"

A fierce look carved Craugh's face. If Juhg had been a true enemy of the wizard's, he knew he would have feared for his life in that instant.

"They remembered that Lord Kharrion was the most evil enemy the world has ever faced," Craugh stated vehemently.

"They did." Juhg nodded and locked eyes with Craugh. "In the end, that proved to be the undoing of all the races."

20

Evicted

hat are you talking about?" Craugh demanded. The dark scowl on his face clearly indicated that he didn't agree with Juhg's assessment that the defeat of Lord Kharrion had somehow made present matters for the survivors of the Cataclysm worse. "How can the human, dwarven, and elven remembrances that Lord Kharrion was their enemy be in any way debilitating?"

"Because," Juhg said, "in the end Lord Kharrion was defeated."

"Of course he was defeated," Craugh said. "I was there. I was among the army that brought his citadel down around his ears. That's what we were there for: to defeat him."

"Yes." Juhg waited a beat. Thunder cracked overhead. "But what happened then?"

"We pursued the remnants of the goblinkin armies and defeated them where we could. We couldn't destroy them all."

Juhg nodded. "And then?"

"And then nothing."

"Not true. A decision was made to keep the books—to keep the Vault of All Known Knowledge—secret."

Juhg studied the wizard. "How many knew then that so many of the books had been saved?"

"Not many. Nor did many care."

"Why?"

Craugh waved a hand. "Because most people during those times were illiterate. Reading—and books, for that matter—lay within the realm of kings, princes, nobles, wizards, healers, and merchants. A common male couldn't read, and even if he could, he couldn't afford the price of a book."

"But there were readers in those days," Juhg said. "I know that because I have encountered tales of them in the histories, as well as the romances, from Hralbomm's Wing. The Grandmagister has even written monographs and essays on the role of the reader in those societies. If a healer had a question about how to do a surgery, there were books he could resource. But if a common man had a question about animal husbandry or proper crop rotation in an area new to him, he could go to a reader at a library or to the owner of a small, private collection of books and receive information for a modest price."

"Yes."

"The books could have been used in those days following Lord Kharrion's fall," Juhg pointed out, "in an effort to get the devastated cities and outlying lands back into habitable shape more quickly." He drew in a breath. "But that isn't what happened."

"The decision was made not to do that."

"Why?"

Craugh sighed, letting Juhg know the argument had been a long one and full of emotion all those years ago.

"The chiefest reason was that most of the common folk didn't want anything to do with books again. They didn't share your certainty that possessing such things would be a boon. Most of them, if you'd care to ask, still don't. Many of those people you would attempt to give the books back to would only destroy them or throw them away."

Juhg shook his head. "I've read about those times. In the volumes penned by the Grandmagisters who set up the Library. Those people weren't given a choice."

Craugh stamped his staff irritably, sending off sparks. "*Faugh!* You don't know whereof you speak, apprentice! Old Ones, preserve me from some young know-it-all who believes he has all the answers in a handful of years that the Founders struggled over for decades!"

Juhg resisted his immediate impulse to disagree and challenge the statement.

"You are looking at those days from the perspective of today," Craugh went on. "In those days, having a book equated a death sentence to the survivors of the Cataclysm. To all the elves, dwarves, and humans. Especially those who had never had much to do with books when they were accessible. They didn't want books, or even rumors of books, existing in their settlements, towns, or cities. Books drew the vengeance of the goblinkin. Despite our best efforts, too many goblinkin yet remained in the world."

"Yes."

Triumph flashed in Craugh's eyes. "The goblinkin targeted any place where books were kept. Even during those days, the army of the unity still transported a few books now and again. The goblinkin were merciless in their destruction of books."

Juhg knew that. He'd read stories about those transportation efforts, even after Lord Kharrion had fallen. Goblinkin land forces had descended upon caravans and slain them to the last man, and goblinkin navies—something that had never before existed until the Cataclysm—had sent ships to the bottoms of a dozen seas.

"The goblinkin targeted those places then. Not now." Juhg drew in a breath.

"And they would again," the wizard said. "Those times haven't changed as much as you seem to want to think they have."

"They set a trap for us with a book, Craugh. Something has changed."

"The goblinkin didn't do that."

Juhg waited. When it became apparent the wizard was not going to go on, he asked, "Then who did?"

"You'll need to talk to your master, apprentice. As I told you, that isn't my story to tell."

Frustration chafed at Juhg. He wanted nothing more than to walk away. But he couldn't do that; not as long as a chance remained that he might learn more.

Craugh stamped his feet for a moment, obviously deep in thought. His voice was soft when he spoke. "I will tell you this: Fear of the goblinkin wasn't the only reason the books continued to be held in the Vault of All Known Knowledge."

Juhg waited, but he sensed that the wizard was going to do his best to make the situation no clearer than it had been. The friendship between the Grandmagister and Craugh ran too deep. So deep that Craugh had stepped over several boundaries by talking to Juhg in the first place, threatening him in the second, and third by continuing to attempt to reason with him. For whatever reason, the wizard saw Juhg's continued presence as beneficial to the Grandmagister and was willing to strive to make that happen.

"You have to remember," Craugh said, "all of those books were hauled pell-mell to this place. Without plans, without organization. Those salvagers operated under the threat of death. If they were caught by the goblinkin, they were put to horrible deaths. The island was lifted from the sea bottom and caverns formed, then structures built over them. Chests and boxes and bags of books were dumped into those places. Ships arrived, on occasion, several times in a single day. The work was just too immense to keep up with. There was no rhyme, no reason. Just a great evacuation of books from the mainland." He drew in a breath. "Centuries passed before we even knew all that we had managed to save. You saw some of that in your earliest tenure here."

Juhg remembered the vast caverns of books, the large rooms that awaited organized and orderly books that would be placed on carefully constructed shelves. He didn't have to imagine what the Vault of All Known Knowledge had been like in those early days. Every Grandmagister, from the first to Edgewick Lamplighter, had written of and illustrated images of the chaos that had been their lot to make tidy and known.

"We didn't have the luxury of transporting many multiple copies," Craugh said. "We only hoped that we were able to save a copy of each book. At least that." He gazed at Juhg. "And how could we allow those books back out of our possession until the Librarians knew what it was they had? Until the Grandmagister knew and could pass judgment on such an action? Knowing that we might never see its like again? Or that the goblinkin might hear of a community getting its books back, its libraries returned, only to go into that town and destroy those books—as well as those people?" He remained quiet for a moment.

Juhg returned the wizard's flat gaze with difficulty.

"What choice would you have made in those days, apprentice? Would you have given those books back? After warriors had come together from all walks of life to fight and shed blood for those books that most people never truly understood or cared for?"

Juhg made himself answer. "I don't know. Truly, I don't, Craugh. But I don't question what was done then. I only question how things are progressing now."

"Would you see a book leave this Library that we did not have a copy of? Do you know how many, how *much,* we have already lost?" The wizard glanced toward the broken back of the Knucklebones Mountains, where the ridgeline had collapsed in on itself and created the deep pit that plunged into the mountains. "Can you even fathom how much I destroyed only a few days ago?"

Shaking his head, Juhg said, "No."

"Then how dare you take umbrage with your master for the things he chooses to do, apprentice. His responsibility for the protection of this place and those books has not been easy. He's been the only Grandmagister to ever leave the safety of this island and journey along the mainland questing after books and rumors of books. As such, he's seen terrible things. Horrible things. Things that most dwellers from Greydawn Moors never see."

But I'm not from this island, Juhg thought angrily. *My whole life, until I arrived here, I was surrounded with those things. Murder and cruelty and depravations. That was my world. And that is the world the mainlanders live in.*

In that instant, Craugh seemed to recall that Juhg was an outsider as well. The wizard's fiery gaze softened, then turned away. An uncomfortable silence descended between them.

After a time, only so the wizard might finish whatever he had to say, Juhg said, "I . . . I am not proud of my dissatisfaction with the way things have been going here." He knew that he wasn't. Disagreeing with the Grandmagister was possibly the most futile, unpleasant, and disloyal thing he could envision.

Craugh replied, "Nor should you be," but his remark wasn't as cutting as it might have been.

"That's why I tried to leave. I knew that someday I would have this very same conversation with the Grandmagister. I didn't want to. I didn't want to hurt his feelings or our friendship." Juhg stared at the ruins of the Library, but his mind was on the Grandmagister. "The Grandmagister would never be able to understand why I feel the way that I do."

"I think Wick understands his station in life perfectly. He was supposed to protect all that was held dear here."

"But he held the Library *here*," Juhg pointed out in a quiet voice, "all in one place. That was a mistake. He made the collections more vulnerable than they would have been scattered around the mainland."

"You can't know that."

"I felt it," Juhg said. "Even before this, I felt it. All the goblinkin had to do was find this place and they could destroy everything that has been protected." He glanced at Craugh. "You've read Motherby's *Concordance of War*?"

Craugh hesitated, then nodded. "Of course."

"What is the first principle of protecting people or things?"

Sighing as understanding filled him, Craugh said, "Not to keep them all in one place."

" 'Separating multiple targets makes it harder for an enemy to get at them,' " Juhg said, quoting from the book. " 'Your enemy will be harried trying to find all the targets, and will be exposed during his efforts to gather information about those targets or to eliminate all of the targets.' "

"Yes. But we chose to hide everything in a place that we shaped," Craugh said. "A place that was not known to exist."

"Hidden things don't remain hidden."

"We didn't hide something the goblinkin knew about."

"You hid the books."

"In a place that had never before been part of the world. We were careful, and we were clever."

"Towwart has an axiom about such things," Juhg said. " 'Even an omission leaves a noticeable trail; a hole, a vacuum, an occlusion that marks the deliberate loss or the crafted lie.' "

"*Towwart's Forensics of the Discussions and Negotiations of Kings and Princes and Skilled Liars*," Craugh said. "I know the book."

"Even with all the precautions you and the Founders took, the goblinkin knew the books existed somewhere."

"Not *knew,* apprentice. Perhaps they suspected."

Juhg glanced pointedly at the ruins of the Library. "Someone did more than suspect."

Craugh said nothing.

"You stripped away the books from the mainland and hid them here, but you did more than that. You took away the history of the races that survived the Cataclysm." Juhg looked at the wizard. "They needed that history, Craugh. They needed it so they could go on. While Lord Kharrion existed, they could exist. They had survival as a goal, and an enemy that interferred with their lives. After he was gone—they had nothing."

"We saved them," Craugh said.

"Only partially. Only for a time. Those people on the mainland have become frozen. They don't grow and they don't develop. They exist and they die. With the encroaching goblinkin, they exist with harder and meaner lives, and they die much sooner. They need what they once had. History is like a river to a civilization. It comes from one place so the people living now will have momentum, a map of where they have been and vague ideas of where they will go next."

Full dark steeped the gardens now. Dozens of soft glows from the lanterns gathered inside the Library courtyard burned against the soft, sable blanket laid over the land.

"Stop anywhere along a river," Juhg continued, knowing he had Craugh's full attention, "and you can pick up residue—sand or flotsam— from other places the river has touched. Put something in the river there, and someone else downriver later may find it. Even when the river runs into the sea and passes out into the deeper oceans, the sun evaporates the water and clouds carry it back to the land to begin the journey all over again."

Craugh scowled. "I don't need a lesson in the life cycle of water, apprentice."

"It's not about water," Juhg said, feeling bad and frustrated that the wizard somehow couldn't see what was so plainly in front of his face. "It's about knowledge. The life cycle of water was just the best representation I could think of for what I'm trying to explain."

"Well, your explanation is hardly necessary. Despite your beliefs, I am not thickheaded."

"No," Juhg agreed. "I know you understand everything I'm talking about. What I want to call to your attention is the fact that you are so blind to what I am trying to explain."

He took a deep breath, surprised at how tense he was. But surprised, even more so, that he wasn't a toad.

Craugh pinned Juhg with a wary eye. Grumbling beneath his breath, the wizard turned and gazed over the garden. "You pose a compelling argument, apprentice."

The term of address galled Juhg. After everything he'd just said, the wizard still insisted on stripping him of rank or respect.

"It's more than an argument," Juhg said. "It's the truth."

"As you see fit to view it."

"Craugh," Juhg said, "the dwarves, elves, and humans are losing the mainland. More and more dwellers get chained as slaves every day. The goblinkin have forced the settlements of the dwarves, elves, and humans to spread out of the South, where the better farmlands are. Their lives are becoming more hardscrabble and desperate. And the goblinkin press on to the north. Soon, very soon, the clans will control all the coastal lands. Once they control the land they will control access to the sea. Do you know what will happen then?"

"We will fight them back."

"And if we can't? There is no one to raise a mighty army now. No single foe to unite all of those races."

"The human, dwarves, and elves will retreat to the center of the mainland," Craugh said. "There still remain places where they can live and prosper."

"For how long?"

"You vex me, apprentice, with your constant badgering of what may come to pass."

Normally, the wizard's protest would have given Juhg pause. But he somehow couldn't stop himself, now that he had opened the matter up. "But don't you see what will happen if the elves, dwarves, and humans retreat to the interior of the mainland?"

"They will live and grow again," Craugh said. "And they will probably band together to battle the goblinkin."

"By then it will be too late."

"Too late for what?"

Juhg opened his hands to take in the immediate area. "For this place. For the Library. For Greydawn Moors. For the island."

Craugh said nothing, but Juhg could tell the wizard was bothered.

"Greydawn Moors has come to depend on trade from the mainland," Juhg said. "The population here, although the elven warders have done everything within their powers, has grown beyond the ability of the island's farms and fishing beds to provide for. If you take away the trade with the mainland, everyone here will starve."

"Especially the dwellers." Craugh scowled then shook his head. "I mean nothing personal, apprentice."

Juhg nodded and tried very hard not to take it personally. When the Founders had first laid down the design for Greydawn Moors and the Vault of All Known Knowledge, they had made allowances for the populations inhabiting the island. Humans took to the seas and seldom stayed. Only the elves and dwarves needed to manage the defenses and the lands remained.

But the dwellers had stayed and multiplied and packed the town till it burgeoned. Dwellers had big families, big appetites, and tendencies not to think beyond the current day.

The dwellers, those folk who had been given the purpose in life of maintaining the Library, of reading and writing and caring for the books, had become the internal threat to the island.

"Yes," Juhg said. "The dwellers have become a liability."

"Yet without them, there are no Librarians."

"Few Librarians," Juhg corrected. Although humans had generally served as Grandmagisters in the past, few wanted a life spent among books. Fewer still of the dwarves and elves wanted that kind of life. Dwellers lived long, cautious lives.

"You pose a great number of problems, apprentice."

"Yes," Juhg replied, "but they are real."

Craugh paced back and forth, his staff thumping the ground and squirting green embers. "You should have told Wick."

"I tried. I brought it up in conversations. I wrote monographs on the subject. He denied the problems and he filed the monographs without reading them."

"And no one else read them?"

"No." Juhg grimaced. "As you may have noticed, I am not well liked here. That was another reason I had decided to leave."

"You are not well liked by your fellow Librarians for one reason only," Craugh said. "You are Wick's favorite. And he chose you to take over this place in the event of his death."

Craugh's pronouncement surprised Juhg. He didn't know what to say.

"Close your mouth, apprentice," Craugh growled. "You're going to draw flies."

With effort, Juhg closed his mouth. Then he opened it again and said, "The Grandmagister never mentioned anything like that to me."

"Of course not. Wick always assumed that you were smart enough to figure that out on your own."

More guilt heaped upon Juhg as he realized how much his departure aboard *Windchaser* must have hurt the Grandmagister.

"Wick gives you a lot of credit, apprentice," Craugh said. "I am not so lenient. I still think you have a lot to learn." He paused and stopped in front of Juhg. "However, I have to admit that you've given me a lot to think about here tonight."

"It's all true," Juhg said. "All of it."

"I have a feeling, a strong feeling, that you are correct." Craugh took a fresh grip on his staff. "That feeling makes me even more certain that now— or whenever *Windchaser*'s captain prepares to set sail—is *not* the time you should be leaving Wick."

 "Staying here won't do any good," Juhg protested.

"Staying here is exactly what you should do," Craugh said. "It is what you *will* do." He turned and walked away, bringing the conversation to an abrupt end.

Juhg couldn't believe the gall Craugh exhibited. Even for a wizard, Craugh had gone too far.

"You can't make me stay here," Juhg called after him.

"I can and I am." Craugh never broke stride as he headed back to the magical steps leading to the top of the Library's courtyard wall.

"If you prevent me from leaving, you're no better than the goblinkin that enslaved me." Juhg prepared to duck into the bushes. He'd strategically located himself near a sizable clump that would surely turn away most magical spells. A transformation spell required that the wizard see what he was affecting. If Craugh chose to pursue him, he felt certain he could vanish into the garden.

"You're staying, apprentice. And that is the final word I have to say on the subject." Craugh walked up the shimmering magical steps.

Before Juhg could think of anything else to say, Craugh disappeared over the top of the courtyard wall. Resolutely, Juhg screwed up his courage and walked toward the shimmering steps.

That's not all I have to say on the subject, he thought vehemently. *I'm not going to be ordered about and shoved around willy-nilly.* You *will listen to me, Craugh, and when the time comes that I want to leave, I'll—*

He had just started up the stairs when the magical step disappeared from underfoot. With his momentum going forward and his anger and frustration pushing him along at a furious, heavy-footed pace, he sprawled and went facefirst into the ground from three feet up when the spell ended. He had time for a single *yawp!* of surprise before he struck the ground with enough force to daze him.

Ruefully, realizing again why so many people of all races hated and feared the vagaries of wizards, Juhg rolled over on his back and stared up at the scudding clouds lashed by lizard-tongue-quick flashes of lightning. He made himself stay calm, but only through intense effort.

When the time came, he was going to leave. He would not be trapped. He was not going to live a life of futility. He had done that in the mines, and he'd done it again at the Library before he had realized all the truths he'd told Craugh. He didn't know what else the world might hold for him, but he was determined to find out.

"Are ye certain this here's what ye're wantin' to do, Juhg? Just sail away with yerself like this? Ye done up an' tried to leave this place oncet, only to find yerself right back here."

The leaden morning sunshine that barely broke through the heavy layer of swirling fog that lay over Greydawn Moors painted Raisho's dark features with grave concern and doubt. A chill hung in the air, coming from the south and seeming to blow down from the Knucklebones Mountains as if something had put spurs to it.

No, Juhg thought as they crossed *Windchaser*'s gently rolling deck as the sea retreated from the shore with the outgoing tide. Around them, the crew was seeing to the last of the preparations Captain Attikus had assigned. Rigging popped against the masts and the 'yards as he went belowdecks to the waist and forward to the crew's quarters. *I don't know what I want to do. What I* want *to do apparently has no bearing on the events going on.* Things *have gotten too confusing. This* place *has gotten too confusing.*

But he took a deep breath, shifted his pack from his shoulder to the sailor's chest at the end of the hammock that he'd claimed as his own—to be shared, of course, with two other sailors who worked other shifts than the one a day he did—and said, "Yes. I'm certain."

Raisho leaned against the door, filling the small area with his size. He rubbed his smooth chin with one hand while the other gripped the cutlass belted at his waist.

"Well, if'n ye were to ask me how I thought ye were feelin' about everything—"

"I'm not asking what you think. I'm capable of thinking for myself, no matter what you or Craugh or anyone else believes." Judging from the way Raisho stiffened, Juhg knew the reply came out more sharply than he'd intended. He blew out a breath of air. "I apologize, Raisho. I didn't mean to sound angry with you. I'm exhausted from all the work that I was doing at the Library, and from everything that happened there. Leaving that place . . . was not easy. Only the thought of staying makes leaving more possible. I can't stay here." He looked at his meager possessions in the chest. "I think—no, I *know*—there is nothing in this place for me. Not any more. And I believe I was fooling myself to feel otherwise at all. I was never from here. These past few days have done little else than remind me of that."

"Aye." Raisho nodded good-naturedly. "Not bein' natural born to this place meownself, I can understand that. Every dweller in town has been suspicionin' me, an' every other sailor what lives aboardship an' doesn't have a true home or family here. But I been up the Knucklebones no few times these past few days. An' I know there's a lot of work left for the doin'. One thing I've gotten to know about ye, ye ain't one to walk away from work."

"It's not *my* work."

"So ye're leavin' it all behind. Again."

"Yes. I told the Grandmagister a few days ago I would be leaving when

Windchaser was ready." Unable to bear the searching and concerned look his friend was giving him, Juhg turned his attention to the hammock. Whoever had tied the knots that bound the swinging bed to the masts hadn't been careful.

He took his time to untie the knot, rewrap the rope, and tie it off again. His knot was much better than the one that had existed there previously. He could be a good sailor. He knew he could. And he was smart in the way of trading. He'd already proven that before *Windchaser* had reached Kelloch's Harbor.

It was going to be difficult. The only solace lay in the fact that leaving a second time came a little easier.

"I can't help but mention that I'm findin' that hard to believe," Raisho said.

"It's what I believe that matters, and I believe I need to leave."

Raisho remained quiet for only a moment. "Ye was good up there, scribbler. I watched ye workin' up there sometimes. I saw the care ye took with them books an' that assignment the Gran'magister give ye. I know ye love them books as much as any person up in them mountains, probably as much as the Gran'magister, an' more than most of them what stayed."

That statement increased the guilt that Juhg felt. Over the past few days, with all the destruction growing more and more apparent and the barefaced fact that the Library had lost too much to ever be the same, some of the Librarians had returned to the town and the lives they had there.

Not even the Grandmagister had the heart to accuse them of desertion. Putting the Vault of All Known Knowledge back even into a semblance of working order was a monumental task. Dwarves and elves worked to haul buckets of ash, all that remained of a number of collections that once held whole rooms, from the Library. Despite everything they had to do, all of the Librarians had taken note of the ash dumping from every filled wagonload that was taken to the southern face of the Knucklebones and dumped over into the Blood-Soaked Sea. Histories, music, art, literature, science, and other fields of study poured down the barren stone mountainside. A flurry of fine dust had drifted back over the Library

"An' I'll lay a gold piece against a square knot that ye've got the makin's of a quill an' ink and—like as not—an empty book or two in yer pack there."

Juhg said nothing. Raisho's accusation was true. He did carry quills and ink and three empty books he'd made himself from the Library's supplies after getting the Grandmagister's approval.

"When are we getting under way?" Juhg led the way back through the waist to the stern cargo hold.

"Cap'n Attikus says soon. Have you eaten?"

"I'm not hungry." Since getting up before cock's crow that morning, Juhg had felt sick to his stomach. He'd known he was leaving that day since the last three, when Captain Attikus had sent word out for the crew that they were to tidy up their business and report back to the ship.

Things had gotten decidedly worse when Juhg learned that the Grandmagister had to travel to the town on an urgent matter that morning as well. Reluctantly, Juhg had tried to discover what business could possibly take the Grandmagister from the salvage of the Library. But he had failed because he wasn't privy to the quiet conversation the Grandmagister and Craugh passed between them. Both the wizard and the Grandmagister spoke in vague references. Juhg only knew that it was important. If anyone at the Library knew, no one was talking.

Still, accompanying the Grandmagister down the Knucklebones Mountains while driving the team hadn't been exactly the most relaxed of endeavors. He had said his goodbyes the day before, not wishing to have to endure them that morning. Instead, the Grandmagister had appeared only a short time after Juhg had loaded his belongings onto the wagon and had informed him that they would travel together.

"Ye gotta eat," Raisho said. "Got to keep yer strength up. We get out on them waters, why, it could be a long time betwixt meals an' the comforts of home." He grimaced. "With this foul chill wind a-catchin' the island broadside as it is, there might not be no warmth to be had out on that salt neither."

Juhg nodded. "Maybe a little something."

Raisho dropped a hand on Juhg's shoulder. "Good. Cook has got some fresh bread this mornin'. Not all of it his. The cap'n wanted to set a nice bill of fare afore we went out, so he traded out fer some of the fresh-baked goods the island's bakeries put out."

Together, they went belowdecks again and made their way to the galley.

Twenty-three sailors, nearly a third of the crew, sat around the tables and benches attached to the gently rocking galley floor. Almost half of those were new faces, men brought onboard to replace those who had died during the battle with the goblinkin ship. All of the sailors fell silent for a short time when they watched Juhg come among them. Then they pointedly turned away from him or left.

Maybe coming here wasn't a good idea, Juhg thought morosely. His welcome among the sailors seemed about as warm as his return to the Library. Ignoring them as best as he could, Juhg joined Raisho in a quick trip through the serving line at the galley. Raisho piled his wooden platter high with breads, fruits, and fresh cuts of meat. Juhg took only a few pieces of bread, some cheese, and an apple. He truly wasn't very hungry to begin with, and the cold reception aboard the ship whittled away even that.

When Raisho guided Juhg toward a small table in the back where two other sailors sat, the two sailors got up and left without a word. Juhg took his seat and sat quietly, not at all sure of what he should do with himself.

"It will get better," Raisho assured him in a gruff voice. "By the Old Ones, it will. Else I'll be yankin' on a few men's beards meownself to make it right."

Juhg didn't see how that was possible. The Librarians didn't want him there and *Windchaser*'s crew didn't want him here. The Grandmagister wanted him, but Juhg felt as though he was betraying his own ideals if he stayed.

Like a man half-starved, Raisho dug into the food piled atop his platter. Juhg turned his attention to his own meal, washing it down with weak tea.

"Have you heard anything?" Juhg asked quietly. "About how bad it is out there on the Blood-Soaked Sea?"

Raisho shook his head and washed down a mouthful of food. "Most ships, they've been at harbor here. Only four of 'em have come back since the Library was . . . attacked."

Juhg knew the young sailor was going to say *destroyed*. Everyone he'd overheard talking about the event in Greydawn Moors talked like the Library had been completely destroyed. Even from downtown, the Vault of All Known Knowledge could be seen, the walls and towers sticking up against the background of the Knucklebones. Of course, the day had to be a clear one, not the chill, blustery kind of day today was.

"None of those four were ships that were in at the harbor at the time of the attack," Raisho said.

Juhg knew that the captains that had sailed since the attack were under orders to find out as much information as they could before bringing their ships back to Greydawn Moors. They were also supposed to stockpile items they needed, in case they had to break off contact with the island for a time.

Grandmagister Lamplighter had sent those orders from the Library days ago before the first ship departed. The dweller merchants had taken to grumbling even more about the Grandmagister and the high-handed ways of his kind. None of the preceding Grandmagisters had enjoyed a terribly good relationship with the townspeople.

"The waters ain't filled with goblinkin," Raisho said. "That's somethin' to be thankful for."

Juhg nibbled at a pear slice. The fruit tasted fresh and clean.

"Of course," Raisho went on, "to hear Craugh talk of it, them goblinkin could fill the sea in the space of the next drawn breath."

"What do you think is going to happen?"

Rolling his shoulders, Raisho said, "Them Dread Riders an' Grymmlings came from somewhere. Course, it was magick what brung them here, but there's a chance we'll see more of them. Whoever sent them, why they've probably got as many magical spells tucked away as Craugh."

Juhg doubted that. He knew the wizard kept a large number of spells at his disposal.

A flurry of motion sounded out in the hallway. In the next moment, Herby appeared in the doorway. The young boy was as unkempt as ever, and Gust the monkey sprawled across his narrow shoulders and gripped fistfuls of his hair. Sweeping his gaze across the room, the boy locked on Juhg at once.

Crossing the floor, Herby stood by the table just out of Raisho's reach. "Juhg! Have you heard about the town meeting?"

"No," Juhg answered.

"The Town Elders called it," Herby said. "Told the Grandmagister he was gonna have to attend."

"What's it about?" Juhg asked.

"The news just got out," Herby said. "The Town Elders just told the Grandmagister that they ain't gonna support his efforts to rebuild the Vault of All Known Knowledge. Furthermore, they just ordered the Grandmagister to find some other place to keep them books what survived that attack. They said he can't keep the Library here no more!"

21

The Grandmagister's Ire

O ut of breath from running through Greydawn Moors to reach the town meeting, Juhg slipped through the massive oaken doors shaped by skilled dwarven hands. There on the doors, in bas-relief, was an abbreviated telling of how the Vault of All Known Knowledge had been built. The images fell surely, one after the other, depicting the raising of the island, the erection of the Library, and the eventual founding of the town at the foot of the Knucklebones Mountains.

Voices echoed in the outer halls. Anger and frustration rode the words, but the walls were so thick that Juhg couldn't make out what was being said. Though he knew Herby wouldn't make up the tale he'd brought to *Windchaser* with him, Juhg couldn't believe that the Town Elders would dare tell the Grandmagister that they wouldn't support the efforts necessary to rebuild the Library.

Dressed in breeches and a shirt, looking more like a sailor than a Librarian, Juhg felt intensely self-conscious as he passed through the glare of the human guardsmen outside the town hall's main chambers. When the faces of the four men outside the doors hardened and turned sharp, Juhg knew that the warriors recognized him even without his Librarian's robes. Possibly at another time they might have been inclined to say something to him, or even prevent his admission to the main hall, but Raisho was at his side and none of them dared say anything to the fierce young sailor.

The massive three-story town hall was the first permanent building built on the shores around the Yondering Docks. The structure squatted on the highest hill in the cleared lands around the harbor. Peaked roofs poked through the swirling clouds of gray-white fog. Blue-green slate shipped from half-forgotten quarries in the South covered the roofs. Constructed of white wood and white marble, the town hall would immediately grab the attention of a newcomer.

Before the town hall had been constructed, the dwellers who had gathered on the island to undertake the responsibility of the Vault of All Known Knowledge had met under the canopies of trees, under tents, and finally under temporary buildings. They had camped out in ships pulled up onto the shore, in temporary structures, and even in lean-tos the elven warders had helped fashion out in the forest that had been magically grown.

The main assembly hall was on the first floor. The room was huge and round, cavernous, and built to carry the voices of speakers. Constructed in a circular design, the center of the room provided a round stage where speakers could inform or debate before the crowd.

During Juhg's time at Greydawn Moors, the town hall remained largely unused. Dwellers gathered there upon occasion for someone's birthday or a holiday or a festival. In the past, Grandmagisters like Frollo hadn't allowed the meeting hall to be used by anyone for anything outside of Library business. Yearly addresses between the Town Elders and the Grandmagisters were the most common events.

Lanterns filled with lummin juice glowed in wall sconces and on the high ceiling. The ceiling was well lighted, providing views of great artwork that were copies of images of great art kept in the Vault of All Known Knowledge, as well as original images rendered by Librarians. The ceiling provided reflections on why the Library existed, on how it had come to be there, and who some of the Founders had been. Craugh was up there with those people, looking hardly the worse for wear, despite the passage of years.

A crowd had turned out to watch the confrontation between the Town Elders and the Grandmagister. The dweller townsfolk sat together in groups representing the merchants. Their group outnumbered the factions of dwarven warriors and craftsmen and eleven warders and human sailors by a factor of four or five. Most of the grumbling came from that group as well.

Grandmagister Lamplighter stood at the round rail that marked the center of the debate area. He looked resplendent in his robes. Craugh stood only a short distance away—probably, Juhg reflected, at the Grandmagister's insistence because the wizard's glowering expression offered immediate threat—but no one would mistake the fact that he was there with Grandmagister Lamplighter.

Craugh's own attire, clean and neat and powerful, bespoke of the severity of the issues being dealt with. Normally, the wizard dressed like he'd just come in from a long journey, which was usually the case. Green embers circled the top of his staff constantly, a grim reminder of the eldritch forces that were his to command.

Juhg knew the faces of all the Town Elders. Over his years of living in Greydawn Moors, he'd gotten the chance to meet all of them at one point or another.

Feron Dilwiddy acted as Chief Speaker for the assembly. Dilwiddy owned the hostels where the sailors stayed while they remained in Greydawn Moors. He was old and fat, even for a dweller. Time had sloughed his face down and given him thick, corpulent jowls that looked like tallow that had melted from the sides of a candle. His wide, fat lips held an unhealthy purplish hue. A ribbon bound his white hair back and matched the thick beard he wore down to his chest.

". . . don't want to be subjugated by the Vault of All Known Knowledge or its Grandmagisters any more," Dilwiddy stated. "Nor do we ever wish that so again."

"You were not subjugated," Grandmagister Lamplighter said.

" 'Not subjugated'?" Lisster Brokkle sneered. Like Dilwiddy, Brokkle was a dweller. He was only half the Chief Speaker's age, but gray flecked his gray hair and beard. Brokkle owned several warehouses around the Yondering Docks and speculated constantly—and successfully—at buying and selling along the mainland.

Brokkle had been a frequent visitor to the Library to read up on civilizations that had once flourished along the mainland and had stood Blood-Soaked Sea sailors to drinks in exchange for tales of their travels. Juhg had noticed the dweller merchant prince several times in his own research of potential markets.

"Perhaps, Grandmagister Lamplighter," Brokkle spat, "for all your vaunted knowledge of words, you don't know what the word means."

"I know full well what the word means," the Grandmagister replied in a level voice. "I say again, neither the Library nor its Grandmagisters have ever subjugated this community."

"Then you lie," Brokkle shouted.

Craugh turned then, his face a mask of frozen rage. Green embers swirled from the tip of his staff. The dwarves and elves and humans stood as well, hurling epithets and threats among the dwellers for the disrespect that they showed the Grandmagister.

The dwellers who stood so boldly along the railing suddenly drew back from the wizard. Four of them pulled back so far that they had to step back into the seats that surrounded the discussion area.

Without turning, the Grandmagister lifted a hand and said, "Please. I'll handle this."

Craugh halted, but his jerky movements showed his exasperation and the amount of restraint he had to exercise. "Better you than me, Grand-magister. I'd turn the lot of them into toads and be done with the matter." He stamped his staff irritably. "And if they don't cease their yapping, I'm like to do it anyway."

The dwarves growled agreement, and their suggestions for the fates of the dwellers was more bloody and more final. With obvious reluctance and distaste, the dwarves and elves and humans took their seats.

Juhg stared in wonderment at the chaos about to break out around him. The door at the rear of the meeting chamber opened as more people, many of them ships' captains due to get under way that morning, entered. None of them looked happy about the situation either. Of all the Grand-magisters, Grandmagister Lamplighter was one of the favorites.

"Has anything like this ever happened before?" Raisho asked.

"No," Juhg replied, watching the dweller speakers slowly move back to the railing. Some of them even took care to separate themselves from Dilwiddy and Brokkle.

"I know them town dwellers don't much care for the Library or its Gran'magisters," Raisho said.

"They never have. Since the earliest days, dwellers have turned more and more from the Vault of All Known Knowledge." Over the years, Juhg knew from his review of past Grandmagisters' journals, a certain enmity had always existed between the Grandmagisters and the dwellers who lived in town.

Dilwiddy pulled himself up to his full height at the railing and glared around the room. "We asked you here this morning, Grandmagister Lamplighter, so that we might air our grievances over the events of these past few days. We did not invite the ruffians in your employ to attend."

"Why, ye thick-necked, warty-headed mud ape," one of the dwarves exploded, rising to his feet. "If'n ye call me or me friends 'ruffians' again, why, I'll come over there and wallop ye, I will."

"Erolg," the Grandmagister said in a calm voice of reproach. "That will be enough."

"Aye," the dwarven warrior replied. " 'Twill be. Because I've already had me a craw full of it come this mornin', what with them little halfers a-frettin' over whether they're going to make their profits or keep their hollow bellies full. They're forgettin' themselves, an' I'll slap some knots on their heads if I have to, in order to get a show of proper respect."

An angry buzz whispered through the ranks of the dwellers.

"If I see Erolg in a tavern any time soon," Raisho said, "I'm gonna stand him to a drink."

"The way you're always ready to fight," Juhg observed, "you should have been born a dwarf."

"Mayhap I was," Raisho said. "Just a really tall dwarf."

Erolg stamped his feet and adjusted the harness of his battle-axe across his back. His chain-mail shirt jangled against his weapons. He pulled on his beard and sat.

"Do you see what this is coming to?" Dilwiddy demanded. "You're putting everyone who lives here at each others' throats."

"The dwellers who live here," a quiet, calm voice stated clearly for all to hear, "have never cared much for the dwarves, elves, and humans who have shared this island with them."

A thin, beautiful elf stood up from the warders gathered to the right of the dwarves. He wore green leathers and leaned in a relaxed fashion on his longbow. A longsword hung at his waist. He moved with the graceful economy of a cat, languid and at ease. His pointed ears showed at the sides of his head under hair the color of split cedar.

Brokkle's eyes narrowed contemptuously. "Do I know you?"

"No," the elf replied. "I do my best to stay out of this town. It's dirty, unkempt, and unclean. You people live nearly as badly as goblinkin."

Angry muttering filled the meeting chamber.

Juhg watched the events unfolding, hypnotized as if he were watching an avalanche take shape and slip toward the final, fatal plunge. All of the old aggressions between the races were coming to the forefront. Those prejudices and jealousies had been a constant problem since the island had risen from the sea floor.

"I would have your name," Brokkle stated.

A small smile fitted itself to the elf's beautiful lips. "I am Sayrit Threld, leader of the Brotherhood of the Falcon. My kith and kin have served the Vault of All Known Knowledge from its inception, and we will continue to do the same as long as blood yet remains to us."

"I will remember that name," Brokkle threatened.

"It would be better for you if you did," Sayrit said.

The implied threat caused Brokkle to draw back a little.

"You dwellers—" Amused at his own forgetfulness, Sayrit glanced in the Grandmagister's direction and inclined his head. "I beg your pardon, Grandmagister Lamplighter. There are exceptions to any rule."

"Sayrit," the Grandmagister said, "please don't—"

"I fear I must," Sayrit stated. "It was not easy for my kin and I to leave the forests and come here today. But once we found out what these . . . petty beings hoped to do here today, I found I could not stay away. You know me, Grandmagister. You know how much I hate even coming to this place, where these people wreck the natural habitat with their filth and want and ignorance."

"When an elf gets mad at ye," Raisho muttered, "ye'd best be listenin' as attentive as ye can. Ye get one mad enough an' ye're not listenin', that elf's apt to leave a blade or an arrow stickin' out of ye somewhere."

Juhg knew it was true. Of all the races in the world, the elves tended to be the most solitary. They considered themselves above the other races, and they disliked great gatherings, even of their own kind. An elven city usually took advantage of natural divisions in trees, along rivers and streams, to carve out individual places for themselves.

Where a dwarf or a human killed out of passion—out of anger or jealousy or fear—an elf was most likely to kill a being in cold blood. Death was a decision, not a response. In the annals of the elves, human and dwarven populations were sometimes killed to the last man or woman to open up territories or protect lands they had elected to serve as guardians. Horror stories of the vengeance of elves existed within the histories of dwarves and humans.

"When the decision was made to save the books of the world," Sayrit said, "and this place was chosen as the location of that great repository, all the races were asked to provide for the common defense and good of that effort. The dwarves agreed to stand as the Library Guardsmen and to protect Librarians, the tomes of the Library and the townsfolk in the lands surrounding the Library. The elves assigned kith and kin to manage the island's natural resources and to place the monsters in the Blood-Soaked Sea. The humans brought here agreed to serve as seafarers, to safeguard the waters of the Blood-Soaked Sea and conduct the trade and the spying necessary to keep the Library secret and safe from the rest of the world."

Quiet rolled over the meeting room.

"The only thing dwellers were asked to do was to maintain the Library," Sayrit said. "The dwellers who lived here on the bounty of this island were supposed to see to it that their children learned to read and spent some time in the service of the Vault of All Known Knowledge."

"An' eat," one of the human sailors accused.

Laughter followed the comment, but Juhg could still hear the anger and animosity in the sound.

"Over the years," Sayrit continued, "the number of dwellers who went to the Library changed. Every child was still required to learn to read, but soon only one child out of a family had to serve time as a Librarian. Then the length of that service was renegotiated so that the one-in-a-family member put in less than a third of the years that were initially required."

"We have lives," Brokkle said. "There are things here that require our attention. Our businesses. We were asked to give up too much. All that reading . . ." He shook his head. "What do you really think was gained by all that reading?"

Sayrit's voice grew sharp. "Enough!"

Brokkle leaned across the railing, having to stand on tiptoe because the railing was more a human's height than a dweller's. "What we gave up . . ."

Smoothly, in the space of an eye blink, Sayrit fitted an arrow to his bowstring and released the shot. The shaft, fletched in the blue-purple feathers of a falcon, sank into the rich oak of the railing only inches under Brokkle's nose.

Juhg's heart stopped for a moment. If the shot had been off by as much as a fraction of an inch, the shaft would have ricocheted up into the dweller merchant's face.

"No more," Sayrit ordered. "Your people gave up little. You've always gotten more than you were asked to give. Your ancestors were given the safest place in all the world while the rest of that world fought the goblinkin and died."

"We were given a pretty prison," someone among the dwellers said.

"You don't know what a prison is," Sayrit said. "Most of the members of my brotherhood have not seen any land except this place. They've not seen any animals, save those that we watch over here." He drew in a breath. "This is no prison for a dweller, but it is to an elf who was born with an unbridled wanderlust and a desire to see everything there is in the world."

"No one asked you to stay," one of the dwellers said.

"We were asked," Sayrit said. "We swore oaths that our brotherhood and the other brotherhoods would remain here to protect and watch over this island as protectors, to serve nature strong and healthy enough to provide for the constant demands put on this island's resources."

"You could leave."

"We are bound by our oath. Just as are the dwarves and the humans."

As he listened to the elven warder's words, Juhg realized how much the elves had truly given up to hold up their ends of the arrangement. Dwarves and humans gave up a lot, too, but both of those races could still enter into the service of the sea and rotate out with each other.

The elves never did.

"Those warders in my brotherhood," Sayrit said, "live their whole lives learning how to take care of this place. They don't negotiate to put in less time or shirk their duties. When the Library was attacked, my brotherhood shed its lifeblood to keep the destruction that claimed the Library from rolling down the Knucklebones. Few of you came up the mountain to defend either the Library or yourselves."

The accusation hung heavily in the sudden silence that filled the meeting chamber.

"We are not warriors," Dilwiddy said after an uncomfortable time. "We are not trained to fight."

"I know you're not warriors," Sayrit said. "I spent days burying the warriors that were in that battle in the days that followed. They wore the faces of dwarves and elves and humans."

"A few of them, though," Erolg added, "were dwellers. An' they wore the robes of the Library."

Pride touched Juhg for a moment, but it was quickly consumed by sadness and hurt. Those Librarians had earned the respect of warriors, but the cost had been so high.

"You dwellers," Sayrit said, "have cut back on the time you give the Library. Getting the books organized took longer because of that selfishness. Not as many copies were made, which is going to be even more telling in the days that come with so much lost. And with less time spent reading and dedicating yourselves to the craft that you were assigned to, even less is going to be known about what was lost."

"Our children know how to read," Dilwiddy argued.

"Perhaps," Sayrit conceded. "Perhaps they do know how to read. But many of them have no love of it. You may have taught them the mechanics of reading, but you haven't taught them the passion for doing a job well. They, like you, begrudge any time spent at that craft."

"You could teach your own children to read," Brokkle said.

"I have," Sayrit said.

A buzz of concerned voices filled the room. Juhg noticed that even the Grandmagister seemed surprised by the announcement.

"There isn't an elf on this island that doesn't know how to read," Sayrit declared.

"You presume too much," Dilwiddy said. "Reading is the purview of the dwellers."

"No," Sayrit replied. "Taking care of the Library, learning everything there is in the Library, that is the purview of the dwellers. That is your duty. And you don't live up to the expectations of those who first built this place." He paused. "That's why I started teaching all the warders here on the island to read."

"To replace us?" Brokkle demanded.

"If necessary."

A cry of outrage rose among the dwellers.

Juhg sat, feeling nearly stunned. How was it that the elves had dedicated themselves to learning to read, but no one had noticed? More than that, if the elves had been reading, had they been writing?

"The warders I train don't just learn about a plant or an animal," Sayrit said. "They learn the ecology of those things, the good properties about that plant or animal as well as the bad properties, and they hear how all of that works together. But I don't let them end their education there. I make them learn this island. They have to know where those plants grow and where those animals nest. In order to do that, they have to walk and explore every foot of this place over and over again."

"Aye," one of the human captains spoke up. "Just as I train ever' man on my ship to repair an' rebuild ever' stick on her. I've got crews what could build new ships if we've a mind to an' we end up without a ship at some time."

Erolg stood. "We train constantly, always ready for the enemy. Ever' warrior what counts is in our numbers. An' if'n it should someday come to it, our wives an' daughters have been trained to fight as well."

"Now," Sayrit said in a sarcastic tone, "here is the lot of you, daring to tell Grandmagister Lamplighter that you're done with serving the Library and have no intentions of helping him rebuild." He shook his head. "Over the last few years, your births have exceeded the allotted numbers. Your population continues to grow, despite my warnings and instructions to the contrary. Those numbers endanger the balance that the warders have worked diligently to create for years."

More grumbling tumbled into the quiet pause that the elven warder let hang.

"If you should decide—*truly* decide—not to help the Grandmagister rebuild the Vault of All Known Knowledge," Sayrit said, "then you will be left on your own. The warders won't help you. We won't tend the forests and your fields. We won't hunt predators that prey on your livestock. We won't clean the wells and streams that you all work so hard to foul." He shrugged, an eloquent expression that showed exactly the contempt he held for Brokkle and Dilwiddy. "I'd venture to guess that within two generations, you will be destitute and dying of starvation and malnutrition."

"If'n ye ain't dead afore then," Erolg said. "As fer the dwarves, we'll let ye fight yer own battles, should anyone else find ye. We'll gladly go a-rovin', looking fer the treasures most of us have had to give up on by agreein' to stay here."

"You'll also have to build and sail your own ships," the human captain said. "For I'll have no more to do with you. Going into business for myself will be a lot more profitable for me and my crew than splitting profits with the likes of you."

Stunned, Juhg looked out over the assembly hall. Dilwiddy, Brokkle, and the other dwellers who had banded together to challenge the Grand-magister could not have counted on the responses given by the elves, dwarves, and humans.

"Well, now," Raisho said, grinning, "that'll give 'em something to think about, now, won't it? Let the land become an enemy to them again. Strip them of their protection and their profits."

Dilwiddy stood with a sour expression. He glanced down at the arrow that stood out from the railing in front of Brokkle.

"Grandmagister Lamplighter," the Chief Speaker said.

"Yes."

Gazing at the Grandmagister, Juhg knew that he was as shocked by the turn of events as everyone else.

"Is that how you plan on dealing with us?" Dilwiddy demanded.

"Begging the Grandmagister's pardon," Sayrit said. "The Grandmagis-ter had no part in the planning of this. We've talked among ourselves since you first started this little rebellion."

Dilwiddy seized the railing before him in both hands. His fat face turned purple with anger. His jowls quivered. "You are trying to enslave us. You're no better than the goblinkin."

"That's not true." The elven warder stood straight and tall with one hand on his bow. "Your greed and your lack of initiative have enslaved you. Just as you've shirked your duties to the Library—which I would not have allowed to happen, nor would I have put up with the burgeoning popula-tion numbers the Grandmagister has—you've also shirked responsibilities to yourselves. You were put here on this island just as we were. Most of you have chosen to pursue selfish goals."

"Grandmagister, I have to protest. Are you going to let this . . . this . . . person continue to harangue us so unmercifully?"

Grandmagister Lamplighter started to speak, but the elven warder hurried on.

Sayrit gazed around the room and talked quickly, with more passion than before. "Many of you chose to pursue no goals at all. That's why you sold off your rights to the lands Dilwiddy and Brokkle and other dwellers now control. You were given the right to live on this island for free, to build homes, to raise your families. Instead, you squandered those rights to dwellers among you who took advantage of your own foolhardiness. Your ancestors took whatever paltry sums Dilwiddy's family gave them all those years ago, then waited while Dilwiddy's family made deals with the dwarves to build houses that were later rented to your ancestors. Houses that all of you still pay on, even now."

Juhg knew that the elven warder's assessment was true, but no one in Greydawn Moors talked about what had happened or how landowners and renters had come into being.

However, now that the elven warder had put such a fine point on the occurrence, dweller tongues were wagging. No few of the dwellers who had gathered around Dilwiddy and Brokkle in a show of support had started to distance themselves.

"You victimized yourselves," Sayrit said. "By not wanting to take responsibility for yourselves and for your actions, you've become dependent on Dilwiddy and others among you like him. Over all these years, Grandmagister Lamplighter and most other Grandmagisters before him have stood to hold the elves, dwarves, and humans together to help the dwellers, who in turn cared for the Vault of All Known Knowledge. If not for the Grandmagisters, if not for the promise of the Library, we would have left you long ago."

"You can't do that," one of the dwellers wailed. He was one of the landowners who held with Dilwiddy's circle of associates. "You took an oath. You swore to . . ."

"We," Sayrit said, "still take our oath. *We* still stand by that oath. Every child who begins his or her studies of the ecology of this island and everything that we can teach him or her about the lands that lay across the Blood-Soaked Sea takes the oath that the first of our ancestors took when they agreed to shepherd this place."

Conversations broke out all around the meeting hall. Juhg listened to the voices and heard the fear and anxiety in them. Many of the dwellers had retreated from Dilwiddy's camp now, starting to see for the first time that they wouldn't enjoy the safety they'd had if the humans, dwarves, and elves chose to leave. In fact, since few dwellers ever ventured out in anything more than small fishing boats, they realized they would be stranded on the island.

"Quiet!" Dilwiddy roared. He pounded his fist on the railing to call the meeting to order. When silence returned, filled with anticipation of what would come next, Dilwiddy glared at the Grandmagister. "So this is how it is to be, Grandmagister Lamplighter? You would blackmail us with our fears for our own safety?"

"I'm not blackmailing you," the Grandmagister replied.

"Then what do you call this?"

"I stand ready to deliver on the promise of the Vault of All Known Knowledge," the Grandmagister said. "As has every Librarian before me."

Juhg looked at Grandmagister Lamplighter, seeing how confident and unassuming the Grandmagister was. During their travels along the mainland, during their harrowing adventures, the Grandmagister had always somehow managed to stay a step ahead of the blinding fear that reached for them. Grandmagister Lamplighter was not by nature a brave person, but he had learned to be brave.

"The Library is destroyed," Dilwiddy protested. "I've heard reports that only one book in five survived the attack."

"Yes."

Dilwiddy raised his eyebrows in surprise. "That figure is accurate?"

"Yes." The Grandmagister's shoulders bowed a little at the terrible weight of accepting that toll of destruction.

Juhg reached inside his shirt and took out the journal and small cotton bag of charcoal sticks that he had put there that morning. He hated not having something to work with if an idea hit him so he was prepared this time.

"Then the Library is destroyed," Dilwiddy said.

"If it were," Sayrit said, "we would have already been gone from this place."

Many of the dwellers started frantically whispering among themselves. If the Library were destroyed, if the books were all gone, what remained to hold the elves, dwarves, and humans there? Evidently no one had thought about that in their haste to try to usurp control over the Grandmagister.

the destruction of the books

"We can rebuild it." The Grandmagister stood his ground. "We have to rebuild it."

With a sure hand, Juhg laid out lines, shaping the meeting hall and the dwellers who stood there at odds across the circular area.

"You've lost the books."

The Grandmagister nodded. "We've lost a great number of them."

"Then what good would it do to rebuild a Library only to hold empty shelves?"

"They won't always be empty."

"Why?"

The Grandmagister hesitated, then said, "Because they won't be."

Interest came to attention within Juhg. He felt the Grandmagister's answer was part of the mystery that had kept him busy in his own studies the past few days.

"What does he mean by that?" Raisho asked.

"I don't know," Juhg replied.

Dilwiddy clearly wasn't happy. "Grandmagister Lamplighter, I am aware—as are a number of others in this room—that you have journeyed to the mainland on a number of occasions and brought back books you discovered there."

The Grandmagister didn't bother to deny the statement.

"In fact," Dilwiddy said, "one of your Librarians recently brought back a book that led to the attack at the Vault of All Known Knowledge."

"That is not your concern."

"Not my concern?" Dilwiddy suddenly appeared apoplectic. "How can you stand there and say that? If those Grymmlings and Dread Riders had come down the Knucklebones—"

"An' they didn't," Erolg growled. "We seen to that, sure enough."

"No, Grandmagister, with all due respect, I think that anything you do that could potentially harm those who live here is our concern."

Exasperated, the Grandmagister fixed Dilwiddy with his gaze. "I've listened to your accusations and veiled threats long enough." His voice sounded strong, and his words silenced every whisper in the room.

Dilwiddy looked disconcerted and started to speak.

"No," the Grandmagister said, holding up a hand. "I'll not listen to another word. Craugh, if Dilwiddy or Brokkle speaks before I am finished, you may turn them into toads at your leisure."

Sparks leapt and snapped at the end of the wizard's staff. "Thank you, Grandmagister. I look forward to serving in whatever small but happy way I might."

The Grandmagister walked around the table as he spoke, breaking the unwritten rule that both sides debating across the round table would have their own spaces.

"I've listened to your complaints for a long time over the years, Dilwiddy," the Grandmagister said.

Dilwiddy started to speak, glanced at Craugh, and thought better of it.

"You've led the complaints about the Library since even before I was made Grandmagister. You've whined about the fact that the Library takes a percentage of all the profits that are made by the townsfolk. You've stated on repeated occasions that you don't like the way the Library also gets a percentage of all the goods brought to the island, knowing that the Vault of All Known Knowledge only takes goods that can be used in the pursuit of our work or by my staff."

That had always been a large complaint.

"You forget yourself," the Grandmagister said, "and I take my share of the blame for not reminding you." He turned and gazed around the room. "This place was not given to you to be your home. This island was formed by magic, raked from the bottom of the sea, and made habitable as a place of protection for the Vault of All Known Knowledge. This place was intended as the last bastion of all learning, of all the information the races have managed to accumulate."

Juhg turned the page and began sketching hurriedly, captivated by the Grandmagister's words.

"Until Lord Kharrion united the goblinkin hordes and tried to destroy us," the Grandmagister said, "our races lived apart. We had our separate lives and we had our separate histories. There were occasional cultural fairs and exchanges of information during times when sickness or a natural disaster like drought struck an area. But for the most part, all the races—and even smaller groupings of them—lived away from each other."

Dilwiddy backed up as the Grandmagister came to a halt near him. The fat dweller glanced fearfully at Craugh, who watched the Grandmagister with a mixture of pride and wariness.

"For nearly one hundred and fifty years," the Grandmagister said, "I've served the Vault of All Known Knowledge. I've labored with reports, catalogues, and repair work. I've learned old languages as well as dead ones. I've celebrated past successes and wept over the heartbreak of defeat with races who were gone long before the Cataclysm, with authors who were elves and dwarves and humans."

Pride touched Juhg as he realized he knew exactly what the Grandmagister was talking about. He'd felt the same way a number of times. A glance at Raisho revealed that the young sailor was mesmerized by the Grandmagister's words.

"I did not know," the Grandmagister said in a softer voice, "how much all of those races were alike in some ways—in the best of ways and in the worst—until I read the books about their lives and dreams." He stared at Dilwiddy.

The dweller looked away and wouldn't meet the Grandmagister's gaze.

"There were even people like you, Dilwiddy," the Grandmagister said. "Small-hearted people with narrow minds and a greedy nature. Not all of them were bad people. Just self-involved."

Dilwiddy hung his head.

The Grandmagister turned his attention back to the crowd. "I listened to Sayrit speak this morning. And Erolg and Captain Artoona as well." He paced, stepping away from Dilwiddy and Brokkle. "I heard their words and their pride in their accomplishments, in their dedication to the promises their ancestors made on their behalf." He paused. "I took pride in the knowledge that I know these individuals as friends."

Juhg turned the page and blocked out the faces of the three the Grandmagister had named. Only then did he realize that the ship's captain had indeed been Artoona of *Jeweled Dragonfly,* a pirate ship that had taken prizes on a number of occasions out in the Blood-Soaked Sea.

"I've always been loath to exercise the powers I have as Grandmagister of this place when dealing with the townsfolk here, but if I choose not to exercise those powers now, I know that I will be remiss in my duties." The Grandmagister stopped and looked around the room. "Dwarven warriors and elven warders and human sailors died up in the Knucklebones Mountains only a few days ago. They gave their lives fighting for promises made by their ancestors, without ever truly experiencing the same circumstances that propelled their ancestors to make those agreements in the first place."

No one spoke inside the meeting hall. Juhg's charcoal almost sounded loud against the journal page.

"I've seen how dwellers live along the mainland," the Grandmagister said. "Many are still in slavery. I was sold as a slave in Hanged Elf's Point when I first journeyed from Greydawn Moors. First Level Librarian Juhg lost his family and was a slave himself in the goblinkin mines. He wore shackles for years. His ankles still bear the scars."

Juhg felt Raisho's eyes on him then and realized that he'd never told the young sailor about his years spent as a slave. He focused on his work in the journal, distancing himself from the memories the Grandmagister's words dredged up.

"Dwellers live and die in poverty and pain there," the Grandmagister said. "They weren't given the opportunity to safeguard the books in the Vault of All Known Knowledge, as were your ancestors." He paused. "As were *you*." He gazed around the room and Juhg watched as all of the dwellers were too ashamed to meet his eyes. "And here you are this morning, brazen enough to tell me and these loyal friends of the Library that the Vault of All Known Knowledge is an imposition to you." He drew in a deep breath. "How dare you even think of not rebuilding."

No one said anything.

"Without the mandatory schooling required by the Library of every dweller on this island, your children would only be an ocean away from a life of servitude, pain, and disaster. And when they got too infirm to work, the only future they would have would be a goblin's stewpot."

The dwellers sat huddled, their shoulders rounded and their heads down.

"As Grandmagister of the Vault of All Known Knowledge, I hold the power over this island. I decide, after deliberation with advisors whom I see fit to name, what will be done." The Grandmagister crossed the room and stood in front of Dilwiddy. "I decide who stays here, and who goes. Not you." He took a breath. "If I choose to, I can have you put on a ship, Dilwiddy, with only the clothes on your back."

"Grandmagister," Dilwiddy pleaded.

Raisho shifted beside Juhg and whispered, "Can he do such a thing?"

"Yes," Juhg whispered back, trying to keep everything in perspective. Throughout the years of his association with Grandmagister Lamplighter, he'd never seen his mentor so firm.

The Grandmagister of the Vault of All Known Knowledge had final say over every aspect of the Library, as well as the island. But in all the history of the Library and of Greydawn Moors, no Grandmagister had ever stood in the meeting hall and threatened to deport townsfolk.

In years past, the sailing crews had been carefully chosen. It wouldn't do for a sailor to jump ship and tell stories about dwellers who could read and write and lived in a huge building with thousands of books.

The Grandmagister turned away from the dweller and faced the rest of the audience in the meeting hall. "I'll make that offer now. To all of you. Anyone who does not want to stay here at this place will be given passage to the mainland on the next ship headed that way. But you will leave *now*. This instant."

No one spoke.

Turning, the Grandmagister faced Dilwiddy and Brokkle again. "Decide," he told them. "Here or somewhere else. Where do you want to spend the rest of your lives?"

"Here, Grandmagister," Dilwiddy whispered. "Please. I want to live here."

"So do I," Brokkle added.

Letting his response hang for a time, the Grandmagister finally nodded. "Fine. Then so long as you support the Library and its mission here, you will be welcome."

"Thank you, Grandmagister," both dwellers said.

"This will be an end to the fighting," the Grandmagister declared. "Erolg."

"Aye, Grandmagister."

"See to it that we have a jail established here in town. If there is any more trouble, any more sedition from the dwellers regarding the rebuilding of the Library, I want a place to keep them till we can ship them away from here."

"Aye, Gran'magister. 'Twill be done."

"Primary Warder Threld."

"Yes, Grandmagister."

"Please take control of our resources in the town, as well as at the Library. I'll need lists on what we have, what we need, and projections on what we can do if we lose the sea lanes for a time."

"It will be done."

"Captain Artoonis."

"Aye."

"We'll need to discuss the need for patrol fleets, as well as supply ships, until we find out where we stand."

"Aye."

"And we'll need to discuss what ports we might chance recruiting more sailors to our cause."

"Aye, Grandmagister."

Listening to the Grandmagister give directions, Juhg was astounded. The Grandmagister had always had a quick and able mind, and even over the years that Juhg had known him, the Grandmagister had gotten quicker about his resolve, but he had never seen his mentor as he was now. So . . . so . . . in command.

Without thinking, hearing the decisive tone in the Grandmagister's words, Juhg had turned to a fresh page in the journal. Even as the Grandmagister had spoken to the three leaders, Juhg had taken notes about what each was supposed to do. During their travels abroad, when knowledge and planning where the only things that had kept them alive—with an inordinate amount of good luck thrown in, Juhg had often kept notes to match the Grandmagister's. That way, if they were separated or one of them lost his journal, they would still have a copy to rely on.

He has a plan, Juhg realized, watching the Grandmagister in motion. The knowledge excited him, but it also dismayed him. He'd made his choice about leaving. Hadn't he?

Feeling someone's eyes on him, Juhg glanced around and found Craugh looking at him intensely. A look of speculation was held in the wizard's green eyes, but the speculation held a mocking glint as well.

"Sounds as if the Gran'magister's up to something," Raisho whispered.

"I know," Juhg replied.

"An' the wizard's sure enough givin' ye the hairy eyeball."

Juhg nodded. Part of him wanted to go to the Grandmagister and talk to him. If there was a plan, Juhg wished very much to know what it was.

And then there was the certainty the Grandmagister had spoken of regarding the shelves at the Vault of All Known Knowledge that wouldn't remain empty. What had that been about?

"C'mon, then," Raisho said, standing. "Show's over in here, an' I'd

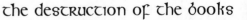

like to keep on the good side of Cap'n Attikus as long as I can afore we set out. Like as not, he'll be a-waitin' in the harbor for word of what went on in here."

With more reluctance than he wanted to feel, Juhg stood and followed Raisho out of the meeting chamber. Craugh watched him go but didn't try to get his attention or detain him.

Outside, the fog continued to fill the streets. The chill had grown stronger, leeching into Juhg's flesh and clinging like barbed fishhooks. Rigging pinged against the masts out in the harbor.

Juhg pulled his traveling cloak more tightly about him and shivered with the cold. He peered out at the harbor, wondering when the last time was that he had seen the fog so thick.

"The Gran'magister did really good in there," Raisho said. "Really gave them halfers what for, didn't he?"

Juhg just looked at his friend.

Raisho stopped grinning. "Oh. Well, what I need to mention is that I don't exactly dislike all halfers. Why, some of me best friends is halfers. One of them, anyway."

Glancing around, Juhg saw that the street was packed with travelers, despite the inclement weather. So many residents had come to the meeting hall to find out what was going to happen. *How many,* he wondered, *were shocked by the turn of events?*

He glanced up toward the Knucklebones Mountains. With the layers of fog as thick as they were, he couldn't see the Vault of All Known Knowledge. Despite that, though, he knew what it looked like: broken and jumbled.

Will it be fixed the next time I see it? Juhg wondered. *Or will I never see it again?*

And what is it the Grandmagister is keeping under his hat?

Without warning, Raisho stepped in front of Juhg and drew his blade. "Look out!" the young sailor yelled, whipping the cutlass forward.

Mind whirling as the excitement of the moment briefly spun his senses, Juhg tracked the whipping movement in front of him. Something had flown through the air only a short distance above Raisho's head. The fog swirled behind it.

Then the sound of metal against stone rasped and filled Juhg's ears just before the first screams cut loose along the street. Spinning, staying close to Raisho's sheltering bulk, Juhg glanced along the street as he saw improbable shapes drop through the fog.

Some of the shapes landed in the street, where they stood on splayed legs. Others gripped the eaves of buildings and hung upside down, tucking themselves up under to take advantage of the cover offered by the structures.

There were, Juhg noticed in immediate horror, dozens of them. An army had silently invaded Greydawn Moors and now stood poised to attack.

22

The Battle for Greydawn Moors

uards! *Guards!*" someone yelled, sounding nearly panicked.

It took Juhg a moment to recognize his own voice with all the raw emotion in it. Although he had never seen the creatures scattered around the street before him in the flesh, he knew what they were.

When the Unity armies of dwarves, humans, and elves had finally started to turn the tide against the hordes of goblinkin, Lord Kharrion had used the darkest arts of magick to call forth a new army. As the goblinkin had been forced back over battlefields where they had left their dead strewn behind them, sometimes half-eaten by those goblinkin armies, the Goblin Lord had resurrected the bodies of those dead goblins.

In most cases, those dead goblins were nothing more than skeletal remains, either through time or the bones having been scraped for meat into a goblinkin stewpot. When Lord Kharrion used those freshly killed, he'd commanded the goblins to carve the flesh from them. Using the dark eldritch energies he called to his power, he forged the remains of the goblins with the echoes of the raw pain and suffering and fear of the humans, dwarves, and elves who had died in those places as well. Although, possessing no real identity, the Boneblights were far more than mere automatons.

They stood tall and gaunt as elves, with dark gray flesh sculpted from the bloody soil of battlefields and mixed with the ash of hardwood trees and iron slivers. Deep-set ruby eyes looked as though they'd been punched with an awl into the blunt-featured face covering the squared-off head. A piggish snout thrust out above a wide mouth filled with razor-sharp teeth. Rusty mud clung to the Boneblights. Most carried scythes and axes for weapons, but every single one of them had long claws at the ends of skinny, powerful fingers and two tusks that curled up from the lower jaw almost to the eyebrow. Like a snake, Boneblights could unhinge their jaws to devour huge bites.

Without hesitation, Raisho stepped forward and struck the Boneblight facing them between the eyes with his cutlass. The blade scraped away a patch of magically hardened flesh and batted the creature's head back, but didn't even serve to knock the Boneblight from its long, narrow feet with toes splayed like a chicken's.

The Boneblight laughed, a hissing sound that came from atrophied vocal cords. "Foolssss! You sssshall be punissssshed! You sssshall die!"

Quick as a wink, the Boneblight struck with its rusty, pitted scythe, aiming at Raisho's neck and no doubt intending to cleave the young sailor's head from his shoulders. Raisho barely got the cutlass up to block the attack. He disengaged his blade and struck again and again, driving his opponent back with his blows but achieving no real success in harming it. He blocked the scythe again, then put a booted foot into the middle of the dead flesh-and-bone face and shoved the Boneblight backward into a crumpled mass on the street.

Raisho cursed as the Boneblight hauled itself to its feet again. The creature unfurled the leathery wings kept close and tight to its back. Although Boneblights couldn't fly under their own power, the creatures could glide for long distances when the wind was right.

Where did they glide from? Juhg wondered as he peered at the dozens of Boneblights that had filled the streets of Greydawn Moors. For a moment, he stopped being afraid as he considered the problem of the presence of the creatures—where they had come from and who had brought them there, but he quickly remembered the danger he was in when the Boneblight launched itself at Raisho and him.

Moving gracefully to one side, Raisho slashed the cutlass down across the Boneblight's outstretched arms. Off balance, the creature dropped to the street. Immediately, though, it pushed itself to its feet again.

"What are these things?" Raisho demanded.

"Boneblights." Juhg glanced around, spotting the public stables across the street. "They're something old. Something from the days of the Cataclysm."

Raisho backed away warily. "Mayhap not so old an' not so far away today."

"No," Juhg agreed. "Not at all."

Ahead of them, a Boneblight released its hold on the underside of an eave, spread its wings, and glided down to pounce on an unsuspecting dweller woman. She screamed and fought, but her efforts were to no avail because in the end the Boneblight snapped her neck like kindling. The creature dumped her body and immediately scouted around for more prey.

"Can they be killed, then?" Raisho asked, fending off the creature that confronted them. His cutlass blade rattled harmlessly against the Boneblight's arms. The hardened soil that served as flesh, as well as the ridge of bone that stood out against the gaunt frame, made the thing nearly impervious to even a keen blade's edge.

"Yes." Juhg hurled himself forward, racing across the cobblestone street. "You'll have a hard time killing them with blades. Follow me."

349

Raisho feinted with his cutlass, then lifted a boot into his opponent's face, driving the Boneblight back. He turned and raced after Juhg.

Senses alive, keeping track of as many things as possible, Juhg ran. A wagon rolled toward him, out of control as the horses panicked and the driver fought with the Boneblight that had landed in the bed behind him.

Catching a glimpse of a shadow slicing through the foggy air above him, Juhg reached back and caught the sleeve of Raisho's cloak. "Here!" Pulling the young sailor after him, Juhg dove under the wagon, rolling and pulling his arms and legs in, barely missing the heavy, ironbound wheels as they clattered across the cobblestones.

The wagon shuddered, though, when the Boneblight that had glided down in pursuit of them crashed against the wagon's bed. So great was the creature's speed that it shattered against the wooden surface and rained down on Juhg in splintered bones bound together by frayed clothing as the wagon kept rolling forward.

Almost immediately, another Boneblight landed in the street in front of Juhg while the out-of-control wagon thundered away.

"Get up!" Juhg told Raisho. Quicker and smaller than the Boneblight, Juhg sidestepped the thing's attack, got so close he smelled the moldy odor of death clinging to it, and stamped his right foot down on the side of the Boneblight's right knee.

Bone snapped as the vulnerable joint gave way. Still, the Boneblight distended its massive jaws wide enough to envelop his head as it lunged at him. Juhg ducked again, knowing he would only barely escape—if at all. Then Raisho stepped in, caught the Boneblight behind the neck with his empty hand, and kicked the creature's good leg out from under it.

The Boneblight crashed to the ground amid the clutter of the other attacker.

"Are ye all right?" Raisho asked with grim concern. He grabbed Juhg roughly by the hair on his head and tilted his head up so that he could better look at him.

Juhg yelped in pain at the coarse treatment. He didn't have a choice about tilting his head back. "I'm fine."

"Ye were lucky. I thought that thing done went an' carved yer face off, I did. 'Twere a near thing, I'll warrant."

The Boneblight struggled to get to its one good leg.

 Trapped by Raisho's strength, Juhg stared up at his friend's worried face, then above him to the foggy sky. For the first time, he realized that the heavy fog wasn't a natural occurrence. The fog had easily masked the Boneblights' approach.

But where have they come from? They can't have flown across the Blood-Soaked Sea.

On the night the crew of *One-Eyed Peggie* had shanghaied Grandmagister Lamplighter, three Boneblights had arrived in Greydawn Moors stalking the human warder and the package Grandmagister Frollo had sent to the Customs House. Juhg had read about the events in the Grandmagister's personal journals, and he'd heard the stories—grown much larger over the years in the telling—several times while in town or at the Yondering Docks.

If Grandmagister Lamplighter had ever learned what was in the package the human warder had carried away that night, he had never revealed it in his journals or to Juhg. The incident had remained in Juhg's mind, but the Grandmagister had a tendency to ignore questions he didn't want to answer.

Watching the cottony swirls of fog, Juhg became even more convinced that the fogbank that had rolled in across the outgoing tide to fill the town was an unnatural thing. And only a wizard could bring forth such a big change in the weather.

Fear plowed through Juhg's heart in that moment, galvanized by the shapes of the winged Boneblights soaring through the sky. The creatures plopped in the middle of the streets, on victims running for their lives, or on the tops of buildings so they could better plan their next move. They were predators hunting those who lived in Greydawn Moors, and they were merciless in their pursuit.

"Juhg," Raisho called.

Overcome by the stunned fascination that filled him, trying to accept the fact that Greydawn Moors—the most secret place in the whole world— was now a battlefield again in only a matter of weeks, Juhg couldn't answer at first.

Growling impatiently, Raisho grabbed Juhg's shoulder and pulled him away from the crippled Boneblight limping steadily toward them.

"You will be punisssshed," the thing threatened in a loud, hoarse cry. Its ruby eyes glowed like liquid fire. "I will ssssuck the marrow from your bonessss."

Raisho stood and whirled his cutlass, hacking at the thing brutally. The sword blows rocked the thing's head but only served to slow it rather than stop it.

"How do ye kill these blasted things?" Raisho snarled as he pushed Juhg into motion.

"The heads," Juhg yelped as he sprinted forward again. Another Boneblight dropped to the cobblestone street only a short distance away. "You have to smash the heads. You can break the body into pieces, but as long as the head is intact it will come after you."

"The head, then." Raisho assumed an attack position, then went at the Boneblight with all his skill and strength.

Juhg made for the stables, conscious of all the battles going on around him. Greydawn Moors was overrun with Boneblights now. The creatures raced through the streets, swooped through the air, and sat like gargoyles on rooftops while they picked out victims.

Dwarves boiled out of the meeting hall. Thankfully, quite a number of them had shown up there to stand in support of the Grandmagister as he faced the dweller committee. They broke into axe and anvil formations, taking the offensive, then going on the defensive, breaking their magical foes down. But the cost was high. Even as skilled at warfare as the dwarves were, the Boneblights were fearsome opponents.

Elven warders took up positions in the street as well. Most of them had magical weapons that had been handed down throughout families for generations, and they had limited spellcraft for defensive or offensive measures. As a general rule, the warders—elven and the few humans who had undertaken the training—fought alone. They weren't in their native forests and open lands and the town was a foreign battlefield for them, but they stood up to the Boneblights as fiercely as the dwarven warriors and human sailors.

Many of the warders had animal companions, bound together by magic and the nature of the forest that surrounded Greydawn Moors. Since the whole island had been raised by magic and possibly made from the bodies of monsters, the magic that bound the creatures of the island was rumored to be stronger than that in many other places. Over on the mainland, where Lord Kharrion's foul magicks still played havoc with the land, Juhg had heard that many animals no longer bonded with warders and that the Old Ways of the elves were fast disappearing.

Even as he reached the wide-open area of the public stables under the deep eaves where the wagons and horses were kept, Juhg saw a large brown bear rear up on its hind legs and snap its jaws over a Boneblight's head. The creature's skull went to pieces and the rest of its body shook loose and scattered across the cobblestone street. The bear roared, bleeding from three or four different wounds it had received from the Boneblight. An elf dressed in warder's leathers lay in a crumpled heap between the bear's feet.

The second Boneblight that had landed nearby waddled toward Juhg as he scampered inside the open-faced stable. Since the structure faced the south, no wall had been built on that side.

The stable smelled strongly of hay and animals and manure. Hay covered the floor. Stalls held several horses that whinnied in fear and reared up. Evidently the horses scented the Death that clung to the Boneblights.

"Sssstay," the Boneblight coaxed. Its wings dragged through the hay.

The creature came on faster than Juhg expected. It reached for him suddenly, raking the scythe it carried at his head. Juhg threw his feet out from under himself and slid across the hay-covered floor and under the nearest stall fence.

Inside the stall, the horse reared and stamped its hooves, coming dangerously close to Juhg. As big as the horse was and as small as he was, Juhg knew that if the hooves struck him he'd be dead or broken too much to defend himself against the Boneblight.

Pushing himself to his feet, Juhg ran for the opposite side of the stall, narrowly avoiding getting brained by the horse's flashing hooves. He tried to stop but skidded into the opposite stall railing, just as the Boneblight clambered atop the railing he'd just left.

Moving quickly, thinking clearly in spite of the fear that rattled through him, Juhg gained the top of the stall and leapt up for the edge of the open loft above him. Standing on top of the stall railing, he was less than two feet below the lip of the loft. He caught the loft's edge with his fingers and pulled himself up, lifting his feet and hoping that his fingers didn't slip and he didn't fall because he knew the Boneblight would be on top of him then.

With his legs lifted, the Boneblight glided just below him, missing him by inches. The creature hit the floor in the next stall and immediately came up squalling and spitting. The horse in that stall attacked the Boneblight, hammering the creature with its hooves. Quick as a wink, the Boneblight raked its scythe across the horse's neck and slashed its throat.

Sickened by the sight of the handsome animal meeting such a rough death, Juhg glanced upward and pulled himself to the loft. He clawed his way up and levered his body over as the Boneblight climbed after him.

The only weapon Juhg had was the boot knife Raisho had given him. But he knew there were other weapons inside the stable. Many of the animals belonged to the Library and were used to ferry goods and people up and down the Knucklebones Mountains. A dwarf cared for the animals and kept them shoed, as well as keeping their tack in good repair.

Pushing himself to his feet on the loft, Juhg ran across the straw. Quick as a scalded cat, the Boneblight pulled itself up almost immediately afterward and cut Juhg's lead down, despite his best efforts. As he passed between the haystacks, Juhg caught hold of one of the retainers and spilled it after him.

The hay tumbled over the Boneblight and almost knocked the creature over the side of the loft, but it retained its balance and kept up its pursuit.

Juhg felt the creature's pounding footsteps vibrate through the boards that covered the hayloft. Spotting the block and tackle hanging ahead with the rope trailing to the ground, he threw himself forward in a diving rush. The hay provided a slick surface and he shot over the loft's edge immediately.

The floor lay nearly fifteen feet below. Probably he wouldn't have broken his neck, but he knew he would have never risen after the fall without the Boneblight on top of him.

He curled his hands around the rope hanging from the block and tackle and hoped that he didn't break his fingers. If he survived, he knew he'd want to write up his experiences. Realizing that he had that desire might have irked him under other, less hurried, circumstances. No matter how hard he tried to leave the Library and his training behind, it remained constantly there.

In the next instant, the Boneblight flashed by over his head, drawing his full attention. One of the creature's rough, leathery wings slid across Juhg's cheek hard enough to scratch and start a warm trickle of blood.

"Juhg!" Raisho yelled from somewhere behind him.

Juhg didn't bother to reply. Things were happening much too quickly, and he still wasn't safe. For a moment, it felt like his arms were going to jerk from their sockets as he clung fast to the rope and took his own weight, but he held fast and swung out away from the loft and from the Boneblight momentarily stunned on the floor below.

He spotted the horseshoeing tools in the corner near a stack of saddles, bridles, and other riding gear. Swinging out again, he let go the rope and dropped to the floor, just as the Boneblight surged up again.

"Juhg!" Raisho squalled.

Knowing his friend would arrive too late to help and that his fate rested solely in his own reflexes, Juhg sprinted for the horseshoeing tools. A wooden box held an assortment of knifes, rasps, and cutters. He grabbed one of the hammers with a solid rectangular head on it, just as the Boneblight caught hold of his shoulder.

"Now, dweller," the Boneblight hissed. "Now I sssshall—"

Turning into the creature's grip, Juhg brought the horseshoeing hammer up and over his shoulder, judging the weight and feel of it automatically from all those years spent down in the goblinkin mines. He brought the hammer down even more quickly, hitting the Boneblight squarely between the eyes with everything he had.

The heavy hammerhead smashed through the creature's skull and broke out big pieces of hardened dirt flesh with a loud *thud*. The pieces exploded across Juhg, bouncing off his chest and face and arms, and the dank taste of the dust filled his mouth and noise. Realizing what the pseudo-flesh was made from on the Boneblights, Juhg gagged and nearly threw up.

For a moment, the Boneblight stood its ground, even though the ruby eyes had disappeared inside the wreckage of the creature's smashed skull. Then it unraveled, coming apart and cascading to the stable floor in a rush of falling bones.

Raisho pounded up in front of Juhg. The young sailor sucked in his breath and looked at Juhg.

"Ye killed it."

"Actually," Juhg said, "it was already dead. Or it was never alive. However you want to look at it."

"From the looks of it, it ain't gonna be gettin' back up again."

Looking down at the bile of bones and tattered cloth, Juhg nodded in agreement.

"How did ye do it?"

"Hammers." Juhg held up the one he'd used. "I knew hammers had to be in here." He gestured at the wooden box of tools. "There are plenty of them, and they'll be more useful than the cutlass you're carrying."

Sliding the cutlass back into his waist sash, Raisho stepped forward and seized two hammers from the box. Both of his choices were bigger than the one Juhg carried.

"All right, then," Raisho grimaced, "let's have a look at those blasted creatures, now that I'm more outfitted to take care of them."

Raisho insisted on taking the lead. Juhg didn't argue, though he did suggest that they might join up with the dwarves or the other sailors.

Outside, Juhg had to harden his heart against the sight that greeted him. Several dwellers and more than a few elves, humans, and dwarves lay dead or horribly wounded in the street.

Stepping into the fight, Raisho proved himself to be a ferocious fighter with the twin hammers. He used one to block, then brought the other around to smash in the skulls of the Boneblights that confronted him. His clothing hung in shreds and long, deep scratches decorated his body.

The dwarves worked in concert, leaving piles of bones in their wake. The elven warders and humans were no less successful in their own endeavors. Even Juhg, despite his lack of stature and strength, proved a formidable opponent against the Boneblights in tandem with Raisho.

"Hold the streets!" one of the dwarves roared. Blood masked one eye and his thick, bushy black beard. "Hold the streets an' protect yer flanks! Watch them beasties a-clingin' to them rooftops an' eaves!"

As he peered around, Juhg felt certain that there were fewer Boneblights than there had been earlier. The sky still remained thick with fog, and moisture filled the air now, making breathing harder and the cobblestones slippery and treacherous.

"The docks," Juhg gasped. "We've got to get to the docks."

"Why?" the dwarf leader asked as he brought his war hammer crashing down on the head of another Boneblight, turning the creature into a heap of broken and splintered bones. "All the fightin's here. Them creatures is tryin' to take over the town."

"No," Juhg said, bending down and picking up a small buckler from a fallen human that was large enough to serve him as a shield. "The attack here is a distraction. If you want to control a port city, you control the harbor." He knew that from the books on war that he had read, and what he had seen of goblinkin overtaking ports in the South.

The dwarf regarded Juhg suspiciously. "What are ye talkin' about, halfer?"

"He's not just a halfer," Raisho growled as he bashed another Boneblight. "He's a Librarian. First Level Librarian Juhg."

"Look out!" another dwarf cried, stepping forward and lifting his great shield.

Juhg glimpsed a brief spasm of frantic movement as the Boneblight that had glided from one of the nearest buildings tried to alter its glide path. Unfortunately, once the creatures had committed to a course of action, they lacked maneuverability.

The Boneblight crashed against the dwarf's massive shield with a ringing *clang*. Unable to hold against the Boneblight's weight, the dwarf staggered back. Recovering from the impact, the Boneblight tried to get to its feet, only to be met by a half-dozen dwarven war hammers that shattered it to pieces. Those pieces crunched under the dwarves' hobnailed boots as they kept moving.

"We've got to get to the docks," Juhg insisted. "That's where the next wave of the attack will come."

"What wave?" the dwarf demanded.

"This was planned," Juhg said. "The Boneblights didn't just happen here. They can't fly. They glide. They had to glide in from somewhere. They can't glide across the whole of the Blood-Soaked Sea. The only place that's possible to do that from is the—"

"The docks," the dwarven warrior said, understanding then. He rallied his men and got them moving, running pell-mell through the street.

Juhg struggled to keep up. His own exertions, the drain of the emotions he'd warred over within himself these past few days, and having to carry the buckler, which was so heavy for his size, made movement difficult.

"Look!" one of the dwarves cried as they rounded a curving street that led down from the main part of the town to the Yondering Docks. "The sun's coming through."

Juhg glanced at the round ball burning through the thick layers of fog that twisted through the air and made seeing more than fifty feet in any direction almost impossible. Then he realized the sun lay out over the harbor when it should have showed more in the direction of the mainland.

"That's not the sun," Juhg shouted. "The sun has never risen in the north." He stared at the glowing ball, realizing that in addition to glowing, the ball was also getting considerably larger.

Just a heartbeat later, Juhg saw the twisting flames fluttering across the ball's surface and knew what he was looking at.

"*Catapult!*" he yelled in warning. "*Take cov—*"

He didn't get to finish his warning because by that time Raisho had recognized what they were staring at too and was already in motion, taking time to seize Juhg and shove him toward the nearest alley.

The flaming catapult load of pitchblende and rock slammed into the pottery shop on the other side of the street and farther down the hill. The rocks smashed through the shop's shuttered windows, the door, and the canopy. Fiery pitchblende clung to the walls and roof, igniting fires that sent up thick black smoke to mix in with the skirling fog.

Even twenty feet away, Juhg felt the heat from the pitchblende. Then he heard the screams of dwellers who had been trailing the dwarves who got caught by the spatters of the catapult loads.

He pushed free of Raisho's protective stance and stared in shocked horror back at the individuals who had been caught in the attack. The stench of burning hair and flesh filled the air, so thick breathing was almost impossible and even then was the stuff that summoned nightmares in the stillness of night.

The dwarves gave anguished cries and started forward, but Juhg knew the only thing the brave warriors could have done was provide a brief release from the burning agony that befell the unfortunates who got caught in the catapult shot. He stared in open-mouthed horror, the buckler and hammer heavy in his arms.

In only a few heartbeats, the terrible event ran its course and the flaming things who had once been living flesh and blood dropped in their tracks and burned where they lay. The fog swirled over the still forms, yielding and making pockets as concession to the great heat.

Then the suspension of the moment was broken as a half-dozen other catapult loads filled the air, arcing high from out in the fog-swaddled harbor.

" 'Ware!" one of the dwarves shouted hoarsely. "There's more of 'em comin'!"

The dwarven leader called his warriors to order and led them deeper into the safety of the alley. Glancing back, Juhg saw three of the pitchblende-and-rock catapult loads smash against other homes and shops. Before he'd drawn a breath, more catapult loads arced by high overhead. He felt the impact of the catapult loads striking their targets and the ground. Black smoke curled up, twisting and threading through the fog, turning the moving mass of low-lying clouds murky.

Juhg ran, following Raisho, who followed the dwarves. They reached the end of the alley and turned again toward the harbor.

A catapult load dropped onto a wagon full of dwellers as it careened across the street. Two Boneblights savaged the group of dwellers in the wagon bed, their great tusks and claws and scythes bright with blood. Then the horrifying sight disappeared before Juhg's eyes as the pitchblende load dropped squarely onto the wagon and turned it into a fiery wreath of flames.

Pitchblende spattered across the rumps of the horses, setting their tails alight and causing them to panic. The driver tried in vain to control the rampaging animals, but he was covered in flames himself and fell from the seat.

At the end of the street, the horses tried to take the corner too fast. The wagon came up on two wheels, then twisted and fell all the way over, spilling pitchblende and rock, as well as flaming dwellers and Boneblights, across the cobblestone street.

The dwarves Juhg was following ran through the street intersection, stepping around the dying victims. Clad in flames, one of the Boneblights stood up suddenly and drew back its scythe.

The dwarven leader blocked the scythe with the long hilt of his war hammer, then swept the Boneblight's legs from beneath it. By the time the creature landed on its back, the dwarf reversed the hammer and smashed its skull to a thousand pieces. The bones spasmed, then relaxed.

Skirting the pile of splintered ivory that had once been a Boneblight, Juhg again followed the dwarves. The other flaming Boneblight snapped a hand out and caught hold of his foot. He fell, sprawled out across the buckler, and began kicking to free himself.

A shape flew from the sky, descending with the speed of a crossbow quarrel. The falcon flew straight and true, then slammed its talons into the Boneblight's face. The talons probably would not have harmed the creature, but it provided enough of a distraction that the Boneblight reeled backward and released Juhg's ankle.

Raisho reached back and helped Juhg to his feet, pausing only long enough to smash the Boneblight's skull as the falcon flew away.

Gazing across the street, Juhg noticed an elven warder carrying two small dweller children from a burning building. Juhg waved to thank him. The warder nodded and hurried along, favoring an injured leg.

Closer to the harbor now, the street turned more steep. With the light mist covering the cobblestones, the street grew slick. Juhg fell twice, nearly bringing Raisho down one of those times.

Catapult loads continued to smash against the town. Much of Greydawn Moors was already burning. Smoke warred with the fog, which was now beginning to lift, whether because the magick that had bound it no longer worked as well or because of the heat of the burning buildings and homes, Juhg wasn't certain.

Out in the harbor where the fog grew thinner, the massive bulk of ships appeared. From his position along the docks, Juhg clearly saw the goblinkin ships and the fierce warriors aboard them.

The goblinkin had come to Greydawn Moors.

The sight nearly knocked Juhg from his feet. The unthinkable had truly happened. Cold fear filled his body from head to toe.

"There!" one of the dwarves called. "They're rallying in the harbor!"

Following the dwarf's outflung arm, Juhg saw that dwarven groups had joined together to make a formidable force. Human sailors and elven warders raced to add to their numbers.

But the effort appeared to be too little, too late. The sheer numbers of the goblinkin in a short time would overrun the island's defenders after the enemy ships reached the harbor. As it was, the large mass of warriors drew fire from the catapults aboard the goblinkin ships.

Then a bolt of green energy sizzled through the sky, splitting into five forks that destroyed five pitchblende-and-rock loads in midair. Cherry-red rocks dropped into the harbor and threw up great clouds of steam.

"Craugh," Raisho yelled in triumph.

A ragged cheer broke from the dwarves as they raced along the harbor.

Bouncing on his toes, straining for height and throwing himself up to peer over the shoulders of the dwarves, Juhg spotted the wizard's pointed hat advancing rapidly to meet the goblinkin ships at the shoreline.

Frustrated with not being able to see properly, Juhg took his leave of the dwarves and raced to the nearest warehouse. Flames wreathed the top of the building and pitchblende still oozed from the eaves, where a direct strike had set the roof on fire.

Breathing rapidly, lungs burning from the smoke that eddied in the salt air, Juhg watched in disbelief as Craugh walked rapidly to the shoreline. Grandmagister Lamplighter hurried along at the tall wizard's side.

Arrows struck the boxes of cargo and the wooden docks around Craugh and the Grandmagister. But the goblinkin archers didn't fire with complete impunity. Elven archers took positions along the shore and on ships sitting at anchor. Although drastically outnumbered, the elven archers still proved steadier and truer than their goblinkin counterparts. Also, the elven longbow shot farther and more powerfully than the short bows used by the goblinkin.

Brightly fletched elven arrows sped across the harbor water and found target after target. Goblins staggered back with arrows piercing their flesh or tumbled over the ships' sides as the vessels fought the outgoing tide to reach the shore.

Timber cracked.

Juhg flung himself from the warehouse, just before the roof gave way and the structure came crashing down. Smoke and cinders billowed out, chasing him as he raced toward the Grandmagister and the wizard.

Craugh stopped at a high point between two of the main wooden docks. He spoke and gestured, and Juhg could feel the power of the spell building. Judging from the amount of the mystical force and how quickly it worked, Juhg knew the wizard wasn't so much summoning magic as he was releasing it.

A sapphire-blue nimbus suddenly rose from the ground in front of the wizard. Rock and hard-packed earth split asunder in front of the wizard and the Grandmagister, then an amethyst tower thrust forty feet into the air. The base of the tower straddled the land and the harbor water.

The Tower of Shrikra's Calling, Juhg thought, recognizing the structure of the thing. Amazement swept through him. The Tower of Shrikra's Calling was one of Greydawn Moors' defensive spells. But since the island had been summoned from the sea and inhabited, no one had ever seen it. When people talked of it, which they seldom did, it was only thought to be a legend, a myth.

But it wasn't.

Juhg glanced up the gleaming amethyst sides of the Tower to the golden horn that sat at the very top. According to the legend, the Grandmagister could use the horn to summon the monsters that lived in the Blood-Soaked Sea.

Even knowing the legends were true now, and possibly even the part about being able to summon the monsters that gave the sea its name, Juhg didn't hold out much hope. The creatures hadn't ever been seen in the harbor waters. And wherever they were, it was going to take too long to get to the island to be of much good.

Still, Craugh and the Grandmagister started running up the circular stairs.

Several of the goblinkin ships had reached shore, but they had suffered tremendous losses. Dead littered the decks, all of them jutting elven arrows that offered mute testimony to the warcraft of the warders.

The goblinkin crews swarmed from the ships, obviously eager to plunder and pillage. Many of them headed for the Tower of Shrikra's Calling but were met by the dwarves, humans, and elves who intercepted them. Blades and axes rasped against each other. Goblins and island defenders were cut down in droves. Fresh blood spilled into the harbor water, turning it a different color than normal.

Catapults fired again and again, pelting the Tower with pitchblende and rock. Flaming pools clung to the amethyst surfaces of the Tower and the circular steps.

Juhg gained the steps and hurried up them. He threw the buckler away, fearful that something would happen to the Grandmagister, despite the fact that Craugh was with him. He was rounding to the seaside again when he noticed that the goblinkin had pressed the island defenders nearly to the base of the Tower.

But the combined defensive forces of Greydawn Moors held the invaders there. Juhg kept running, feeling his breath wheeze through him now and a painful stitch start in his side.

Glancing up, he saw that the Grandmagister and Craugh were almost at the top of the Tower. A pile of flaming pitchblende nearby reflected in the gold finish of the horn. He pushed himself on, glancing at the dizzying panorama below as the harbor battle swung below him.

Movement out to sea drew his attention. At first, he thought it was the billowing sails of the ships locked in battle. Several of the goblinkin ships were now embroiled in deck-to-deck skirmishes with human and dwarven pirate crews.

But the movement belonged to a trio of dragonets. Much smaller than their massive cousins, the true dragons, the dragonets remained rare and surly creatures. Bereft of the true intelligence of the dragon race, the dragonets were driven by cruel and constant hunger.

Twenty-five feet long from snout to tail, with a thirty-five-foot wingspan, the dragonets possessed hatchet-shaped heads, long beaks filled with serrated teeth, and a whiplike prehensile tail they could use to hang from or grasp prey with. They had powerful hind legs and tiny gripping hands at the forward edges of their wings. Dulled brown and green scales covered the tops of their bodies, and light blue and white patches adorned their underside, making it more difficult to see them in the air. At least, they were more difficult to see when they were directly overhead.

Each of the dragonets carried two riders on special saddles. All six of those riders were human. The ones in front guided the beasts with a harness, and the ones in back carried bows.

As Juhg ran, the dragonets circled the Tower of Shrikra's Calling. Their leathery wings actually touched the stairs on occasion. He dodged back, narrowly avoiding an arrow one of the archers sent speeding at him.

He reached the final leg of the stairway, just as the Grandmagister ran to the horn and blew.

The force of the magic knocked Juhg from his feet, sending him sprawling back dangerously close to the railing. He hit hard enough to have the breath knocked out of him. Dazed and trembling, he forced himself to his feet, ready to go to the Grandmagister's aid.

One of the dragonets perched on the railing, holding the amethyst bars in its two cruel hind feet. The lead rider was a lean human of middle years. He wore short-cropped brown hair and a short chin beard and mustache that made him look handsome and dangerous at the same time. He wore riding leathers and a hood. A sword gleamed at his side.

The man stared at the Grandmagister with a mocking smile. "Well, Lamplighter, you see, I've found your little hiding place after all. I told you all those years ago that you couldn't keep this place from me forever." He made a point of glancing south, across Greydawn Moors and up the Knucklebones Mountains, where the Vault of All Known Knowledge stood in shambles. "If you'd only capitulated, perhaps you could have prevented the deaths of so many of your followers."

The Grandmagister stood firm, even in the face of the dragonet. "Not true. Don't go putting their blood on my hands, Aldhran Khempus."

Juhg seized the man's name and memorized it, searching through the years to see if he had ever heard of him. There was nothing, and that was surprising because he had a very good and very orderly mind for remembering things.

But the Grandmagister seemed to know the man quite well.

"This Tower is fascinating as well," Aldhran said. "I find it somehow soothing that it does exist. With all the stories I've chased down over the years trying to find this place, I didn't know if it would be."

"The Tower is real," Craugh said in his strong voice. "So is the power of the horn."

"You mean, to call up the monsters that supposedly lurk in the sea around the island to protect this place?" Aldhran grinned as if he was a boy and the wizard had told him a good joke.

"Yes," Craugh said.

Aldhran eyed the wizard in open speculation. "You are Craugh."

Craugh said nothing.

"Over the years, we have crossed paths many more times than I have crossed paths with the Grandmagister."

"Pity you weren't more forthcoming," Craugh said. "Else you'd have been dead by now and of no bother to us at this moment."

Aldhran laughed, and the sound was strange when mixed with the noise of the battle below and the wind that whistled through the Tower and made the horn echo. "You do have your confidence, don't you, old man?"

Craugh looked contemptuous. "I've ground a hundred like you beneath my boot heel over the centuries. You're not worth the breath it would take to conjure a spell to flay the flesh from your bones and drop you into a goblin's chamber pot."

Aldhran's features darkened with rage, but he forced a grin. "One day, old man. One day soon." He shrugged. "Maybe sooner than you think."

"I await your call," Craugh said, spreading his hands out from him a little. "Then again, mayhap I'll come calling myself one day."

Ignoring the veiled threat, Aldhran switched his gaze to Juhg. "Ah, the apprentice. It was you who brought the book to this place so the gate could be opened and the way could be found."

Juhg scarcely held on to the guilt that thrummed through him.

"How are you called?" Aldhran asked. "Pot? Pan?"

"Juhg," the Grandmagister said. "And he is a better Librarian now than you'll ever hope to be."

Librarian? Juhg couldn't believe it. The man sitting astride the dragonet was a Librarian? *It can't be. I've been at the Vault of All Known Knowledge for thirty years. He's a human, and barely older than those years now.*

"But a Librarian isn't want I've wanted to be," Aldhran answered. "That position was only a means to an end. Just as Craugh there has taught himself to prowl through books in search of power."

A great hurrah sounded below.

Glancing down, Aldhran said, "It appears your defenders are getting the better of my goblinkin. Man for man, that is." He looked back at the Grandmagister and grinned. "It's a good thing I have ships filled with goblinkin out in the harbor who can't wait to go ashore."

Suddenly, a cacophonous *boom* of energy sounded out in the harbor.

Despite the tension of the moment, Juhg found his attention drawn to the harbor. Huge bodies crested out in the harbor, monstrous apparitions with tentacles and long necks and jagged teeth. Any one of them was larger than the largest ship out in the harbor.

As Juhg watched, the monsters attacked the goblinkin ships. Some struck them with their bodies, while others roped tentacles around the ships and pulled them under. In heartbeats, the goblinkin navy became shattered fragments floating on the surface of the Blood-Soaked Sea or sinking in the harbor.

"It appears," Craugh said dryly, "that the horn works as well as the Tower." He smiled. "And there's less and less goblinkin all the time. I take it you never have taught the vicious creatures to swim, have you?"

Snarling a fierce oath, Aldhran turned his attention to the wizard. The younger human chanted and gestured, then he threw his hand out.

Craugh held up his staff. Virulent purple light splintered against his staff. However, whatever spell Aldhran had used threw off enough force to cause the wizard to stagger back.

Before Craugh could recover, Aldhran kicked the dragonet in the sides. The beast belched a great gulp of liquid fire at the wizard.

Craugh held up a hand and put out the flames of the dragonet venom, but he couldn't stop the arrow that leapt from the bow of the archer seated behind Aldhran from piercing his chest.

A shocked look filled Craugh's face as he gazed down at the arrow in the center of his chest. Without a word, he toppled over the railing behind him and fell.

"Craugh!" The Grandmagister ran to the railing, grabbing frantically, as if he might somehow save his old friend. But he arrived too late. The wizard was already gone by the time he got there.

Horrified, frozen in terror and disbelief, Juhg stood against the railing.

Aldhran lifted a net from the saddle, spoke a few words, and threw the net through the air. The net flew true, unfurling and wrapping around the Grandmagister, bringing him to the ground as the strands magically tightened.

Breaking away from the terror that held him, Juhg raked his boot knife free and ran for the Grandmagister. His movement startled the dragonet, though, and the great creature spread its wings instinctively in preparation to throwing itself into the air.

The wing slapped into Juhg and knocked him backward effortlessly.

Before he knew it, he was across the railing and falling. Headfirst, he plunged toward the broken rocks in the harbor below. He spotted Craugh's body already lying there.

Unable to stop himself, Juhg put his hands in front of his face and hoped that his impending death would be quick and relatively pain-free.

Then burning agony bit into his ankle and his fall was stopped short as he began gliding out to sea. Glancing up, he saw that one of the dragonets had wrapped its talons around one of his feet and was carrying him off like a fish plucked clean of the sea.

Overcome by the rapid stop and the blood pounding at his temples, Juhg could only make a token effort to try to pull himself up before he passed out.

 366

epilogue

The Book of Time

Someone threw cold seawater over Juhg and woke him to the constant pain that had been his most frequent companion in the dark hold of the ship for the last several hours. He moaned a little in the darkness, knowing from experience that whoever was delivering the water liked to know that he was in discomfort.

Earlier, he'd tried being quiet and had nearly gotten his ribs kicked in. Of course, the time before that he'd moaned and gotten kicked, which had led him to the mistaken belief that crying out that time had led him to getting kicked.

No matter what happened, whenever someone entered the small storeroom where he was being held captive, he was going to get kicked or stomped or hit or beaten by a chain. His jailer just liked doing those things and didn't derive any satisfaction from hearing his charge cry out or beg for mercy.

Under other circumstances, Juhg might have tried begging for mercy, but he had learned long ago in the goblinkin mines that begging was just a show of weakness that marked a target for further abuse.

"Sit him up."

Juhg recognized Aldhran's voice. He didn't know how to feel about that. Since Juhg had regained consciousness on the goblinkin ship after the attack on Greydawn Moors, his captor hadn't ever visited.

Dozens of questions popped through Juhg's head. Chief among those was what had happened to Grandmagister Lamplighter, if his mentor was still alive and whole and healthy? When he'd awakened on the goblinkin ship as a prisoner, Juhg had felt certain the Grandmagister had also become a prisoner.

Juhg also wanted to know more about the relationship between Aldhran and the Grandmagister. The two of them knew each other, and it had sounded like Craugh—

A sob tightened the back of Juhg's throat as he remembered the wizard lying broken on the shattered rock at the harbor. He had never spent much time with Craugh, not truly, but he had liked the wizard well enough not to wish any harm to him. And Craugh had seemed indomitable, unbreakable, a force of nature rather than a man.

Juhg forced himself to breathe out as he moved gingerly and sat upright. The shackles on his ankles were old and familiar weights, but the shackles on his wrists were new. A hood covered his head and reminded him uncomfortably of the executioner's block he'd seen in Green Troll Gap, a small town in the South that consisted of bandits and thieves. Things had gotten so bad there that they had taken their worst offenders and chopped their heads off, just to keep the others from stealing from each other or committing murder.

368

"Juhg," a quiet voice said.

Excitement flared through Juhg when he recognized the voice. "Grandmagister?"

"Yes." Grandmagister Lamplighter sounded tired and worn.

Juhg wondered if the goblinkin had been beating him too.

"Are you all right?" the Grandmagister asked.

Juhg didn't quite know how to answer that question. He still tasted blood inside his mouth.

"He's alive," Aldhran growled. "Get that hood off of him."

When the hood was removed by one of the goblinkin guards in the room, Juhg had to squint his eyes against the harsh lantern light that filled the storeroom. In addition to the Grandmagister and the mysterious Aldhran and six goblinkin guards, there were two other humans.

One of the humans was tall and gaunt, with long gray hair and beard and eyes that looked flat and dead. The other man had fiery red hair and a mustache. His freckled skin looked too warm, as if he were carrying a recent sunburn. The older man wore a long robe and the younger man wore a warrior's harness festooned with weapons and scarred from numerous battles.

"He doesn't have to remain alive," Aldhran warned. "Of course, Mikros can chop a number of pieces off of him before he actually kills him."

The redheaded man grinned. "My specialty. My da was a butcher."

The storeroom was cold with the chill of the sea. However long they had been at sail, Juhg knew they had been on the ocean. He knew that from the swells the vessel rode out. All that time, and they had gone farther and farther from Greydawn Moors.

In the darkness, Juhg had thought of the town nestled at the foothills of the Knucklebones Mountains often. None of those races living there (outside of the dwarves, who always stayed prepared for such things) had been prepared for an invading goblinkin navy. No one there had ever believed it would happen. Even after the Dread Riders and Blazebulls and Grymmlings had appeared in the Vault of All Known Knowledge, no one had thought such a thing would happen. He wondered how much of the town still stood against all the fires that had been set.

Juhg shivered and coughed, feeling weak and scared. He hated lying in the wet that covered the storeroom floor.

Grandmagister Lamplighter looked at Aldhran. "I don't want him treated harshly any more. I won't have it." His voice was strong and full of conviction.

" 'Won't have it,' he says," the redheaded man said, laughing without humor. "And what will you do about it, Grandmagister? Chastise me? Make me copy sections out of books?"

The Grandmagister didn't turn from Aldhran. "That will be our agreement, yes?"

That amused Aldhran. "Do you trust me?"

"I don't have a choice."

Aldhran lifted a speculative eyebrow. "I could lie to you. Is that what you want? A lie from me? Will that make you feel better?" The man laughed. "I'm sure any promise I make you won't help your apprentice feel better at all. Even if you believe me, I don't think that he will."

"I want you to promise."

Aldhran shook his head. "The time for fun and games is over. I want that book."

"That book doesn't exist," the Grandmagister answered.

Despite his pain and fear, Juhg couldn't help being interested in the conversation. First of all, he wanted to know what book it was they discussed. And second, and he didn't know whether to feel bad or good about this, there was a chance he knew where the book was.

Of course, there was also a good chance—*four in five,* he grimly reminded himself—that the book had been destroyed in the fires that ravaged the Library.

Aldhran cursed and paced in short quick steps, which was all the storeroom allowed. "What kind of fool do you take me for, Librarian?"

The Grandmagister made no reply.

Directing his attention to Juhg, Aldhran said, "What about you, apprentice?"

The term immediately galled Juhg and reminded him of Craugh at the same time.

"Do you say the book doesn't exist?" Aldhran asked. "Do you believe that I am a fool?"

Juhg looked from the Grandmagister to the human several times, finally ending up looking at the human. Despite his pain and the chance for making his situation even worse, he couldn't put aside his innate curiosity. "What book?"

"*The* book," Aldhran snarled. He slammed his fist into the storeroom wall. "The only book that matters. The lost book that Lord Kharrion searched for while he burned the world's Libraries."

The Goblin Lord searched for a book? Juhg blinked at that. In all the legends and stories he'd heard about the Goblin Lord, he'd never once heard that Lord Kharrion searched for a book. The idea just seemed . . . impossible.

"*The Book of Time,*" Aldhran said in exasperation. "Golden Tohras' final spell to unveil the ages woven into an illuminated manuscript. Written but lost after Golden Tohras was betrayed and murdered by his king."

Amazed, Juhg said nothing. That the enemies, whoever they were, searched for *The Book of Time* was even more astounding than learning Lord Kharrion was looking for such a book. Everyone connected with books and libraries knew the myth about the book that showed everything that happened for all times past and all time to come was nothing more than a myth. There was no way any one book could hold all that information.

Unless the world ends really soon. Sitting in the storeroom in the dank bottom of a goblinkin ship made that possibility suddenly seem very real and very near to hand.

"I've heard of that book," Juhg said cautiously. Everyone who worked with books had heard of *The Book of Time*. The story was one of the grandest myths ever, but only children paid it any real attention. Every adult knew the book wasn't real, that it couldn't be real. In fact, no one had ever proven that Golden Tohras was a real person or where the mythical kingdom had existed.

Aldhran cursed, then nodded at the goblinkin closest to Juhg. Without preamble, the goblin lifted its foot and brought it crashing down on Juhg's wounded leg. The dragonet's claws had lacerated his ankle and those lacerations had already started to become infected because of the damp conditions of the ship.

Pain exploded in Juhg's mind and he almost blacked out. The goblinkin dumped another bucket of water over him. He sputtered and kept himself from crying out as the cold saltwater burned into his freshly opened wounds.

"I grow weary of this exercise, Grandmagister," Aldhran warned. "Keep disappointing me and I'll set Mikros free with his knives. I'll let you keep the pieces of your apprentice as trophies."

Brushing through the goblinkin, the Grandmagister dropped to his knees at Juhg's side. Worry showed on his face.

"Juhg," the Grandmagister said, "I'm sorry I got you into this." He held Juhg's head. "I swear I never meant for you to be involved in this matter after all these years. Until recently, I didn't know about Lord Kharrion's true quest, nor of *The Book of Time*."

Years? Juhg looked at his mentor with surprise. How had the Grandmagister kept anything hidden from him after all these years?

"This is about Golden Tohras' book," the Grandmagister said. "It *is* real. And being real, with all the powers ever imagined to it and more, it is a most dangerous thing."

Juhg tried to digest that.

"That was what Lord Kharrion searched for when he burned all the libraries all those years ago," the Grandmagister said. "Aldhran, these people around us, they are part of the library that Lord Kharrion set up without the goblinkin knowing. They documented and researched the book, but they didn't have everything they needed. But Lord Kharrion knew that the book is real."

"You mean he *believed* it was real," Juhg said. He struggled to make sense of everything he was hearing. How could the book be real? How could Lord Kharrion have hidden his quest from the goblinkin?

How could the Grandmagister hide all of these things from him?

"No, Juhg. The Goblin Lord didn't just believe the book was real. He *knew* it was. He and that book were bound in ways that I can't go into now." The Grandmagister shook his head. "The book is real, Juhg. And whoever holds it, whoever commands its power, can command this world."

Juhg looked at his mentor. "Do you—do you know where the book is?"

"I don't know. Mayhap." The Grandmagister shrugged. "I can't be sure. I was still researching everything I'd found out. There was so much. Lies. Half-truths. I'd hoped one day to have you help me. But you were so conflicted about what you needed in your life that I couldn't add the complication of knowledge of the book." He sighed. "Just knowing the book exists . . . it's very confusing even for me."

"Grandmagister," Juhg said, not knowing what he was going to ask, not certain if he just wanted to know his mentor had discovered the greatest secret any Librarian could hope for, or if he only wanted information to help bargain for his life.

"I can't tell them, Juhg. I apologize for that. I didn't mean for you to get caught and brought into this. But there were so many things I couldn't foresee, so many chances I had to take." The Grandmagister paused, looking years older than he was and more tired than Juhg had ever seen him. "The book is in a safe place. A dangerous place. A place that mortal beings might not even be able to get to. At any rate, it's a long way from here—if it's there. And that serves us now." He held his hand so that only Juhg could see the two small glass vials cupped in his palm. "Remember Imarish?"

"The canal city?" Juhg asked, recalling the dangers he and the Grandmagister had faced there not so long ago. He was confused that the Grandmagister would bring the city up, but he was mostly confused by all the secrets that had spilled out in just a matter of moments.

Aldhran and his cohorts listened attentively, and Juhg knew they were trying to decipher everything the Grandmagister said, looking for some clue among his words and half-spoken thoughts.

"Yes," Juhg responded. "I remember Imarish. The canal city."

"Good." The Grandmagister smiled and looked pleased. "I've left something for you there."

"The book?" Aldhran demanded, stepping closer.

"You must go and get it, Juhg. You must get it and carry on in my stead if I am unable to complete my quest here."

"All right," Aldhran snarled. "That's enough of that. Now we're going to do things my way."

The Grandmagister ignored the human. Deftly, the Grandmagister opened the two small bottles in one hand, using skills a pickpocket would have envied, and mixed the two contents. One liquid was red and the other was clear. When they were mixed, however, they glowed a virulent green against the Grandmagister's palm.

The color reminded Juhg of Craugh.

"What are you doing?" Aldhran demanded. He turned to the goblinkin. "You checked him, didn't you?"

The goblinkin nodded.

"There's magic in this room," Aldhran said, "and it wasn't there a moment ago!" He stepped toward the Grandmagister, sliding a knife free from his hip.

"Drink this." The Grandmagister poured the contents of the two bottles into Juhg's mouth. "Swallow." He gripped Juhg's face and massaged his cheeks.

The liquid tasted bitter and dry, like roasted almonds. Since he'd been without drinking water for hours or possibly for days, Juhg had a hard time swallowing the liquid. But once he did, he started feeling lighter, healthier.

Cursing, Aldhran yanked the Grandmagister back and shoved the knife forward, obviously planning on sticking Juhg with it.

Unable to stop himself, Juhg backed away, knowing the wrist and ankle shackles would keep him from being able to move completely out of the way. He felt the coldness of the knife plunge into his chest.

Strangely, there was no pain.

Scared and puzzled, Juhg peered down at the knife thrust into his chest. There was also no blood. Then he noticed that Aldhran's hand had plunged into his chest as well, crowding in all the way up to the wrist.

Magic, Juhg realized, remembering the spell Craugh had used in the Library to pull him and Varrowyn's dwarven warriors through the floor to escape certain death. Even as he thought of that, the wrist shackles dropped through his arms and splashed to the wet floor.

Gaining courage, Juhg stood, moving through Aldhran and pulling free of the ankle shackles as well. A goblin swung a sword at him, passing the blade through his hands and neck as Juhg instinctively tried to defend himself.

"He gave him a potion!" Aldhran yelled.

"Go, Juhg," the Grandmagister said. "Escape. You've got to get to Imarish. I'm sorry I have to leave this to you, but Craugh can help. And there are others."

Craugh? Craugh is dead. Juhg looked at the Grandmagister and wondered if his mentor was becoming mentally unbalanced. They had both seen the wizard shot with the arrow and plunge over the side of the tower.

And what others?

Aldhran stepped over to the Grandmagister and put his knife to his throat. "If you try to escape, apprentice, I'll cut his throat."

"He won't do it, Juhg," the Grandmagister said. "He needs me. Without me he can't find the book."

Aldhran eyed Juhg fiercely. "I'll kill him! By the Eternal Darkness, I swear I'll kill him!"

"He won't," the Grandmagister said. "I gave you the potion so that you could escape. If you stay here, Juhg, they will make me talk." Sadness showed in his eyes. "I can't protect you and protect the book. I can only hope that through saving you I can save the book from them. But you must hurry. The potion will only last for a short time."

"Grandmagister—" Juhg started.

Grandmagister Lamplighter stood straighter, causing Aldhran to yelp in fury and surprise and pull the knife from his captive's throat before he cut him.

"First Level Librarian," the Grandmagister said in an imperious voice, "you have been given your assignment. Do not fail or you will fail us both." His voice lowered. "I will not be dishonored, Juhg. I won't be known as the Grandmagister who lost *The Book of Time* to those that would destroy the world. Now . . . *go.*"

Juhg felt the power of the spell waning. He was already starting to feel a little heavier, and the pain was sharpening again, becoming more than a dim echo. Tears blurring his vision, not knowing why the Grandmagister hadn't saved himself, he turned and reached for the wall behind him.

"Stop him!" Aldhran roared.

The goblinkin rushed forward and tried to grip Juhg, but their hands and their weapons passed through him.

Knowing he didn't have enough time to run through the goblinkin ship and effect his escape, Juhg took the more direct route. If he hadn't been through the floors of the Library, he knew he wouldn't have thought of escaping through the ship's hull.

But he did.

Passing through the wood, stepping from the lantern-lighted hold to the cold blackness of the sea, was disconcerting. There was a moment of greasy resistance, then he was free of the ship and floating in the ocean.

His immediate thought was of the monsters that lurked in the Blood-Soaked Sea. Images of the great and terrible beasts that had attacked the goblinkin ships out in the harbor filled his mind and he grew desperate and afraid.

Despite being underwater, he breathed naturally. He didn't even think of that till the cold grew stronger and he sipped his first taste of salty seawater. Instinctively, he knew the potion's effects had ended before he choked on the sea, and he held his breath.

Frightened but telling himself that he couldn't be more than twenty or thirty feet beneath the ocean's surface, he swam upward. Just as his lungs were about to give out, he clawed through to the air.

Night hung over the Blood-Soaked Sea. Clouds obscured the stars and fog rode the waves.

Floating there and taking in deep draughts of air, Juhg knew he had no idea where he was. Or how far it was to shore. Or even in what direction to swim.

Gazing to his left, he saw the goblinkin ship pressing forward under full sails. Evidently she had been going full tilt to get away from Greydawn Moors and the monsters that lived in the Blood-Soaked Sea.

As Juhg watched, lanterns ran up and down the deck. Evidently Aldhran had set his goblins to searching for Juhg, not realizing that the ship's speed would take it away from him. There was no possibility that the ship would be able to turn around any time soon and come back, or even find the place where Juhg had slipped through the hull.

He hoped with all his might that the Grandmagister was right and that Aldhran had not killed him. But Juhg knew the Grandmagister was right about one thing: If they'd both stayed on the goblinkin ship, one of them would have been killed.

In minutes, the ship was gone, disappeared over a rolling wave and into a fogbank.

Juhg treaded water, wondering if the Grandmagister had truly saved him or banished him to a long, lingering death in the middle of the ocean.

Cold leeched into his bones. Resolutely, knowing that if he at least swam in the direction the goblinkin ship had apparently come from that he would be getting closer to Greydawn Moors, he started swimming and tried desperately not to think of the enormity of the task before him.

His thoughts careened inside his head. *The Book of Time. Lord Kharrion's actual designs. Imarish.* All those things and more bounced like puzzle pieces in his mind and he tried to make sense of them as he swam.

Before he knew it, a ship crested a rolling wave of water and nearly ran over him. The vessel looked hard and bleak against the darkness of the sea and the moonless night. He couldn't help thinking that any ship out on a night like this, especially in the Blood-Soaked Sea, couldn't be out for any good purposes.

"Help!" Juhg yelled up. "Help!" He choked on a mouthful of seawater and worried that he might get caught in the ship's undertow and drown. He was more used to bad luck than good.

"Avast there!" a man's deep voice roared. "There's someone down there!"

Movement rolled along the ship as deck hands raced along the hurtling length of the vessel. She was passing Juhg by quickly, and he grew afraid that the same problems that had prevented the goblinkin ship from pursuing him would mark him for doom if this mysterious ship missed him now.

Just as the ship passed him, a fishing net flew from the stern. It splayed like a spider's web, barely visible in the darkness, then fell over Juhg and gathered him in tight, taking him into the brine.

For a moment, he was again afraid he would drown, then he was pulled clear of the water and hauled to the deck. Sailors gathered around him in the darkness as he fought free of the net.

"Give 'im a hand, lads," a coarse, deep voice said. "Give 'im a hand."

In short order, Juhg was freed from the net and stood on his own two feet for inspection by lantern light. Someone brought him a blanket.

The crew was dwarven, not unheard of in the Blood-Soaked Sea, but not common either.

A broad dwarf taller than most of his kind faced Juhg. The dwarf's broad shoulders made him seem almost as wide across as he was tall. A long, fierce beard hung down to his belly, and yellowed bits of bone cut into fish shapes held the beard in braids. Gold hoops dangled in his ears.

"Well, now," the dwarf said. "Ye're the strangest fish we've taken up outta these waters in a long time."

The crew laughed.

"Thank you," Juhg said, teeth chattering. "Thank you for saving my life."

"Ain't like I ain't done it afore," the dwarf said.

Recognizing the voice then, knowing he hadn't before only because he'd been so overcome and distracted with everything that was going on, Juhg peered up at the big dwarf. "Hallekk?"

"Aye, Juhg." Stepping into the lantern light so that he could be seen more clearly, the dwarven pirate frowned. "Don't go an' be tellin' me ye've already forgotten me."

"Never," Juhg said, feeling joyful. Hallekk was first mate on *One-Eyed Peggie,* the ship that had shanghaied the Grandmagister all those years ago. Juhg had met the ship's crew while traveling with the Grandmagister.

Hallekk pulled at his beard. "I know it's been a lot of years, but I ain't one most people forget."

"I didn't forget," Juhg said. "I just didn't expect you to be here."

Hallekk grinned. "Oh, now, we didn't just happen along."

Understanding dawned in Juhg. "You were following the Grandmagister."

"Aye," Hallekk agreed. "That we was."

"But how?" But even as he asked the question, Juhg knew. "Through the eyeball of the monster."

Hallekk nodded again.

Part of *One-Eyed Peggie*'s history included the tale of One-Eyed Peggie, the ship's builder and first captain. One-Eyed Peggie had run afoul of a sea creature in the Blood-Soaked Sea that had taken one of her legs. For revenge, she'd hunted the sea monster and taken one of its eyes, though she hadn't been able to claim its life.

The eyeball was kept in a jug under the bed in the captain's quarters. Every sailor who was made a member of the pirate crew had to swear an oath of fealty on the jug containing the eyeball.

Juhg had never become a pirate, despite traveling with them while accompanying the Grandmagister on occasion, but he had seen the eyeball. The orb still lived within the jar, and through it the ship's captain could find any of his men when they were separated from the ship. The bad thing was that the sea monster could also see *One-Eyed Peggie* through its missing eyeball and sometimes came to attack the ship.

"We've got to hurry," Juhg said. "They've got the Grandmagister. They're going to kill him."

Hallekk looked troubled. "Well, now, that ain't what we're supposed to do."

"What?" Juhg doubted he'd heard the dwarf correctly.

"Ol' Wick, now he's up an' got hisself a plan," Hallekk said. "He's goin' along with them people what's up an' catched him to figure out the lay of the land, so to speak. He knows some'at of the story of *The Book of Time*, but he don't know it all. That's why he up an' let himself be catched as he was."

"He let himself be caught?" Juhg asked. And just behind that was the realization that the Grandmagister had told Hallekk about the book. "The Grandmagister told you about *The Book of Time*?"

Was there anyone the Grandmagister *hadn't* told?

"Aye." Hallekk grinned. "Why, Ol' Wick is a slippery one, he is. I taught him everything he knows." He shrugged and looked sour. "Well, me an' Cobner, I guess it was, truly."

Juhg felt like he was going to fall over.

"An' ye best not be a-frettin' over Wick," Hallekk advised. "He's got himself a potion Craugh whipped up that will see him clear of that ship when he sees fit to be. The sea monster's eye will let us see that when it happens. Then we'll pick him up."

"How many potions does he have?" Juhg asked.

"One," a new voice answered.

Turning, recognizing the voice, Juhg saw Craugh standing on the stern castle. The wind billowed the wizard's cloak.

"You were dead," Juhg said hoarsely. "I saw you shot with an arrow. I saw you fall."

The wizard shook his head and looked amused. "You saw what I wanted people to see. Wizards are hard to kill. When we want to be."

Juhg focused on the problems at hand. There were so many. "How many potions?" he asked again.

"One," Craugh said. "They are very hard to make. Very time-consuming. And if it hadn't been for Wick, I wouldn't have bothered at all."

The despair over what had happened hit Juhg like a punch. "You should have made more than one."

Craugh frowned. "The first one was bother enough. Having to divide the potion into two components that weren't magical apart but were together, have you any idea of how hard that is? Near impossible, I tell you. And I—" Then understanding widened his eyes. "Wick gave you his potion. That's how you escaped."

"Yes." Juhg felt terrible.

"Then he is trapped aboard that ship with them goblinkin," Hallekk said. All the humor had drained from his voice. "We've got to—"

"Think," Craugh interrupted. "We've got to think. If we try to take Wick back by force, they may well kill him out of hand." He stroked his beard. "No, to accomplish this, we'll need to be devious and deceitful."

Hallekk nodded. "That sounds like somethin' more along your callin'."

"I don't know whether to be insulted or not," Craugh said.

The dwarves nearest Hallekk quickly moved away. A wizard's wrath generally came quickly and unmindful of whom was around.

"That there," Hallekk said quickly, his left eye ticking nervously, "now that there, why, 'twas a compliment, 'twas. An honest an' . . . an' complimentary compliment."

Juhg looked at Craugh. "The situation is worse than that. Aldhran knows *The Book of Time* is in Imarish."

"The canal city? I didn't know it was there."

"The Grandmagister told me I needed to go there as soon as I could," Juhg said. "Right before he told me to leave." He paused. "They'll try to get there as well, as soon as they put into port."

"Well, then, apprentice, it appears that you're going to have to run your master's race for him," Craugh declared. "At least for a time." He turned his face toward the ship's prow, and Juhg had no doubt that the wizard was thinking of the Grandmagister.

As Juhg stood there in the wind whipping across *One-Eyed Peggie*'s deck, shivering under the blanket in his soaked clothes, he felt the doubt and fear grow in him. He looked back at Craugh.

"I can't do it," Juhg said.

The wizard turned his steely eyes on him.

"I'll try," Juhg said, wanting to make that clear, "but I'm not as good as the Grandmagister is. I don't know everything he does." He swallowed hard. "I'm afraid, Craugh. I'm afraid that I'm going to make a mistake or not know something I should, and that I'm going to get him killed."

The wizard descended the steps and walked to Juhg. He threw an arm around his shoulders.

"Now, you listen to me, apprentice," Craugh said in a hoarse voice. "Wick is my friend. I've got precious few of those in this world. He brought me into this and I believed in him. Now, he chose to set you free instead of himself, even though everything in the world appears to be at stake."

Juhg blinked back tears.

"I'm not going to believe that my friend made a mistake," Craugh said gruffly, "or that he threw away his life for no reason. I choose to believe that he knew what he was doing and acted in all our best interests. Do you understand?"

Juhg nodded. "If I hadn't been up on that Tower—"

"But you were," Craugh said. "And maybe that was meant to be."

"I was the one who brought the book to the Vault of All Known Knowledge and got all the books destroyed."

"And forced this confrontation," Craugh agreed. "We were not ready for them, but hopefully they weren't ready for us either. We will see." He paused. "Now, compose yourself, apprentice. There is much we need to do and precious little time remaining to us to get it done."

Juhg nodded.

mel odom

"You're not alone in this, apprentice," Craugh said. "We will help you."

But with everything facing them, as unprepared as he was, Juhg wished that he were still aboard the goblinkin ship and that the Grandmagister was still free. All of them, he felt certain, would have a better chance if that were so.